CHINESE WALLS

Also by David Clive Price

FICTION

Alphabet City

NON-FICTION

The Other Italy (photos by Gotthard Schuh)

The Scent of India (translated from the Italian of Pier Paolo Pasolini)

Travels in Japan (photos by Jean-Francois Guerry)

Between Two Seas: A Journey into South Korea (photos by Jean-Francois Guerry)

The Food of Korea (photos by Masano Kawana)

Neon City: Hong Kong (photos by Keith Macgregor)

Within the Forbidden City

Buddhism: The Fabric of Life in Asia

CHINESE WALLS

David Clive Price

Published by The Olive Press 2010

First published in the United Kingdom in 2010 by The Olive Press and David Clive

Price

www.davidcliveprice.com

A CIP catalogue record for this book is available from the British Library

ISBN: 978-1-4461-3089-6

To Simon

"In a time of universal deceit - telling the truth is a revolutionary act."

George Orwell

"Because the Romans did in these instances what all prudent princes ought to do, who have to regard not only the present troubles, but also future ones, for which they must prepare with every energy, because, when foreseen, it is easy to remedy them; but if you wait until they approach, the medicine is no longer in time because the malady has become incurable; for it happens in this, as the physicians say it happens in hectic fever, that in the beginning of the malady it is easy to cure but difficult to detect, but in the course of time, not having been either detected or treated in the beginning, it becomes easy to detect but difficult to cure."

Niccolo Machiavelli, *The Prince*, written 1513-1517

About the Author

D avid Clive Price was born in London and studied history at Cambridge and in Italy, where he farmed and began to write. Among his books are the travel narratives *The Other Italy, Travels in Japan,* and *Between Two Seas: A Journey into South Korea.* He has also published a short history of the Forbidden City as well a book on Buddhism in the daily life of Asia.

David's first novel, *Alphabet City,* was set in the Lower East Side of Manhattan in the early 1980s and was described by the novelist Edmund White as delivering 'the heart of New York, alive and throbbing on the page'. David is an authority on the life and works of Pier Paolo Pasolini, whose travel narrative *The Scent of India* he has translated into English. He lives in London and Hong Kong.

Chapter 1

T his is not the moment to be checking out guys, Nicholas thought as he hurriedly averted his eyes from the young newspaper vendor at the entrance to the Bank who was looking at him with a sweetly innocent smile. Fortunately, it seemed that no one else in the lobby had noticed.

Flashing his new ID card, he made straight for the steel-and-glass interior of the elevator that would take him up to the senior executive floor of United International Bank. As the doors closed, he took in a deep lungful of air, relishing the sense of anticipation tinged with nervousness that coursed through his veins. Here he was in one of the world's largest and most famous financial organisations, with its headquarters in the City of London. The decision to move to the Far East had not been easy, but as he gazed down through the glass walls at the rapidly receding pavement, he told himself that if all went well, an even better position in London or New York would be his in the not too distant future.

'Good morning, sir,' said the brown-eyed security guard as he turned left out of the lift into the lobby.

He walked at a more measured pace now, taking in the solemn, almost monastic atmosphere of the offices to his left overlooking Victoria Harbour, the framed nineteenth century water colours of Hong Kong, the displays of Bank-issued bank notes and coins. This was a sanctuary, an almost cathedral-like space, in which to speak quietly and with reverence. As he passed the framed portraits of the Bank's founders and the long-dead Chairmen with their amply filled, old-fashioned lapel suits, he felt a pang of regret that it was not to one of those hallowed, leather-trimmed offices that he was now heading. It was down the escalator, through the central membrane of Sir Alexander Senso's post-modernist building, and on to the 32nd floor where stood an office that he had just been told that morning on the phone was not yet ready for him.

He glanced over at the open door to the Group Chairman's office but he could see nothing apart from the square glass coffee table and the harbour beyond. His boss had assured him that he would be interacting with the Chairman on a regular basis. But he had sensed a slight reluctance when Martin said it, a feeling that he wouldn't be giving away the keys until he was satisfied that Nicholas was completely 'safe'. Not for the first time Nicholas wondered if he had been wise to take on the job without having a fully defined job description; apart from his grade and salary and duties as speechwriter. Martin Heatherington had been very welcoming, sharing his own experiences of Oxford and telling him how much the world of bankers needed people like him, 'ideas men', people who brought 'a touch of the creative'. But he had also been wary.

Nicholas reached the bottom of the first flight of escalators and turned to the right. He could see men in shirtsleeves in the open-plan offices to either side, all stamped with a similar look: well-combed hair, muted tie, creased suit trousers, several with their shirts still damp from hurrying to the air-conditioned building through the hot and humid streets. Hong Kong blazed like an inferno outside but in the Senso Building the atmosphere was cool, efficient, controlled.

He paused in front of the closed door marked Group Public Affairs and wondered whether he should ring the bell. There was a keypad to the right of the door but he didn't have the code. More men in suits, accompanied by the occasional woman in grey or black skirt and jacket, were coming up the escalators from the lower floors, their faces drawn and pale in the morning light.

'Hello there.' Nicholas turned and found himself facing a stout, almost matronly woman, with cropped silver-blonde hair, frank blue eyes and lightweight silk suit. She was carrying a Friends of The Earth shopping bag.

'I'm the new boy. Nicholas Powell.'

'Eunice Sage.' She put down her bag to shake hands before keying in the number. 'We've heard all about you. My head of section's been talking about nothing else.'

He smiled and followed Eunice into the room, feeling slightly flattered. He wanted to carry on the conversation but suddenly Eunice straightened like a startled hare, mumbled 'see you soon' and hurried off towards her workplace.

The department was large, long and open plan, cut into sub-sections by grey partitions and by a series of closed-in rooms along the near wall. He could see a figure through the glass windows of each of the closed offices, a self-consciously active incumbent whether male or female, each at their phones and each looking at print-outs or correspondence on the large reading lecterns on their desks. No one was idle, no one was eating their breakfast, reading *Hello* magazine or complaining about their hangover as they did in London. A trickle of secretaries was still coming through the door. As he moved forward looking for Frank Shearer, his appointed guide for the first week, he had the impression he was looking into a series of goldfish bowls.

He came to an open door and suddenly realised that the man on the phone inside was gesturing for him to enter. Nicholas smiled politely as he entered and moved towards the seat in front of the desk. The man made no attempt to offer him the seat nor interrupt his conversation.

'Yeah, that's my view entirely,' said the man, who suddenly exploded into a roar of laughter that shook the room's walls. Nicholas noticed a pale-faced, intelligent looking young woman at a desk opposite look up from her work and frown in their direction. 'Take no prisoners,' spluttered the man in a mid-Atlantic accent. 'You always know how to handle things, Marty.'

The conversation continued with several more 'Martys' and a good deal more laughter as the man made no move to address Nicholas or to gesture him towards the seat. Nicholas estimated his age to be something like thirty-five, a couple of years younger than him, but his loud confident voice and shaven skull made him seem older. Finally, he was through on the phone.

'Welcome on board.' He turned towards him. 'You must be Nick Powell. I'm Frank Shearer, your boss.'

Nicholas leaned forward to shake his hand, wondering whether to point out that he only reported to Martin Heatherington, who in turn reported to the Group Chairman. 'I think you have a rather grand title don't you? Head of External Relations?'

Frank's smile faded. 'That includes you and my deputy, Sarah, out there.' He did not get up nor move after his initial handshake. He leaned back against his chair with his hands behind his head. Nicholas noticed that his blue eyes seemed particularly round and large, perhaps in contrast to the sharp black goatee.

'I think you'll find I report to Martin.'

Frank brought his hands together on the desktop. He attempted a further smile. 'I'm sure Martin will set you straight about that. Meanwhile, I suppose we'll have to get you a desk.'

'That would be nice,' said Nicholas, imitating his tone.

'Guess it won't be what an Oxford man is used to. We're still clearing up after the exit of your predecessor. Martin hasn't decided on your room yet but we have fixed you down the end of the row for now. Let me show you. You'll share a secretary with Sarah.'

Nicholas made room for Frank to pass and followed on, wondering how far he could stretch his politeness.

'Here we are,' said Frank, indicating a desk in a corner partition at the end of the row of glassed-in cubicles. 'The PC's a bit old, I'm afraid. Your extension number is on the phone. That big box on our desk is the speech file for the past three years. Start on that and I'll come by later.'

Nicholas tried not to show any reaction: a cubby hole in the corner of an impersonal department with just a few dusty books and filing cabinets to keep him company. He was back at school. Even his shared secretary was two partitions away and the sympathetic looking Sarah was god knows where.

Just as he reached the door, Frank turned back and looked Nicholas up and down. 'That jacket...'

Nicholas raised his eyebrows. 'Yes?'

'Too fancy. You'll have to stick to black and grey like everyone else. Matching jacket and trousers. It's very corporate here.'

Nicholas couldn't quite believe it. As a director at Oliver & Kemp, he had always worn smart casual. The light blue Armani blazer was a deliberate choice. 'I'm sorry?'

Frank leaned his arm against the partition wall. 'Look, I'll send you down a history of United International in a minute. It's full of tips on our history and culture. Belonging and teamwork are the watchwords. We don't encourage...' He stroked his goatee like a school psychiatrist faced with a difficult pupil.

Nicholas smiled. 'No doubt we have much to learn from each other. Now, if you'll excuse me, I'd better settle in.' Nicholas dropped his briefcase on the computer chair, which he would have to exchange for a proper office chair as soon as possible.

'My first days were the same. Everyone's got to learn,' continued Frank with a shake of the head. And as he walked back towards his office, he shouted 'Sarah!'

Nicholas sat down and examined the list of telephone numbers next to his phone, telling himself to stay calm. He had been hired to advise UIB on the handover of Hong Kong to

China, to develop strategy for the Bank in the post-colonial era. He hadn't been brought in to sit in a corner cubicle and read corporate history.

'I see you've met Frank. You'll be needing a coffee I don't doubt.' He looked up and saw Eunice smiling down at him. She was bearing two coffees and several sachets of sugar. 'I took the liberty of adding milk. Of human kindness if nothing else. You'll be needing it.'

'Is he always like that?'

'Oh yes, and he's not alone. They've all been tarred with the same brush, including some of the Chinese. You'll have to watch your back.'

'Thanks for the coffee. I thought I'd joined the army.'

'You have, Nicholas. They'll try to put you through the hoop. You'll get a lecture on most subjects. I'm in Publications, which is ruled over by another of them. "Madame" we call her. I shouldn't be talking to you right now. She'll have my head on a plate.'

Nicholas looked hard at her. 'Aren't you a little mature to be bullied?'

Eunice giggled and touched her neck, where a heat rash was forming. 'Only the pecking order counts here. I've thirty years' experience in editorial but I'm still Pee-on Grade A.'

He felt his stomach muscles tighten. He'd given up a good deal in London to come to this: a lucrative client list, a company flat in Bloomsbury, good prospects. The transition of Hong Kong to China had seemed like a great opportunity, but he was having second thoughts.

'Hey,' whispered Eunice, gesturing at two figures edging towards them through the No Man's Land beyond Frank's open door: the pale, short woman he had seen earlier, and a shy Chinese woman of about the same age.

'Hi, I'm Sarah, and this is our secretary Karen. We've heard a lot about you,' said Sarah, who despite her melancholy air and mousy complexion radiated a sharp intelligence at odds with the way Frank talked to her.

'It seems that everyone has, especially Frank. I've just been told how to dress properly.'

Sarah gave him a pitying look. 'He's the office bully. Watch out if he's allowed to judge your writing. He thinks he's the world's last grammarian. He can't write a memo himself, he delegates everything. But he'll cover a whole page with corrections just to show how good he is. He might have a bit of trouble with you though.'

'As far as I understood, I'm only supposed to report to Martin.'

'They probably forgot to mention Frank at the interview. I suppose you're Grade F or G,' said Eunice.

'Grade F.'

Sarah sighed and rolled her eyes. 'Frank got himself made Grade G because he was a journalist for the news wires and he knows all the journos. He's really Martin's bum boy and does exactly what Martin tells him. They're either bum boys or bullies, depending on their grade. You'll soon find out.'

'Sarah thought of forming a committee,' whispered Eunice. 'A revolutionary council.'

Nicholas wondered for a moment. 'What're you going to call it?'

'We haven't really decided yet. Have you got any ideas?'

Nicholas grinned. 'The Red Brigade?'

Sarah laughed. 'Not very PC considering who's taking over Hong Kong soon, but it has the right ring.'

'Watch out, enemy at 3 o'clock,' said Eunice, and darted into the photocopy room next door.

'Another at 6 o'clock.' Sarah hurried off.

Frank's shaven head appeared over the partition wall. Nicholas waited a moment before looking up. 'Started on those speeches yet?'

Perhaps the talk of the Red Brigade had fired him up or perhaps it was just the sight of this stuffed-up ex-journalist stroking his beard and gazing down at him from on high. Whatever it was, he had a burning desire to reach up and grab him by the neck. 'I don't need supervising Frank. I'm a professional who works to his own deadlines. I'll look through these speeches in my own time but I won't be reporting on my progress to you.'

Frank stared back at him as if he had just been slapped. 'Come to my office at noon.'

Nicholas was about to reply but Frank had already turned away and was marching down the corridor. Nicholas stood exactly where he was. He knew all about bullying from his adolescence. Flicking the speech file shut, he headed straight towards Martin Heatherington's office.

Chapter 2

N icholas looked up from the briefing notes on his lectern and gazed at the beige phone with the automatic dial-up to the Chairman, the extensive bookcases with their bound editions of *The Economist* and *The Asian Wall Street Journal*, the black leather sofa and glass coffee table, the twinkling sequins of the long Burmese tapestry he had bought in a Hollywood Road antiques shop and hung on the wall opposite his enormous desk. He loved the contrast between the Zen-like minimalism of the office's grey walls and the rich abundance of the scene the tapestry depicted: a white elephant floating in the sky above the sleeping figure of an Indian prince, while a maternal figure – possibly his mother – looked on. The old Chinese guy in the antique shop had explained that Prince Gautama's dream of a white elephant meant that the Prince would become a Buddha. It wasn't quite a reflection of his own career trajectory, but it somehow suited his advancement.

He glanced at his watch. It was almost 12.15 pm, which meant that Sarah and possibly Eunice would soon be in for a gossip before lunch. They loved the tapestry, in marked contrast to most of the other members of the department, particularly

Frank, who looked at it with scarcely concealed disapproval. Sarah reckoned it was because they didn't like anything that reminded them of a human personality, or indeed of anything apart from work. This was possibly true of Frank, who had absolutely nothing of any interest in his office, but it was hardly true of Jeanette, whose workplace was filled with all kinds of bric-a-brac – rather like her mind.

Nicholas stretched and smiled to himself, glad to take a break from the speech he was writing for the Asian Society conference in New York. He stood up, shook his legs and moved to the window that gave out onto Mercantile Bank next door. Three men in white shirts and with their ties loosened were standing out on the bank's upper terrace having a laugh and a cigarette, regardless of the drizzle. How relaxed they seemed; how unconcerned with office politics.

There was a knock on the door. Nicholas spun round and there was the petite form of Sarah, an ironic smile on her pale face, clutching a small notebook as if she were about to take dictation. 'Can I come in?'

Nicholas grinned and beckoned for her to enter and close the door behind her. This had become a daily ritual. Both of them knew that anything they said with the door open could end up in Frank's office, or possibly even in Martin's. The adjacent photocopying room had a constant flow of secretaries.

'Anything on the grapevine?' said Sarah, flopping onto the sofa and putting her feet up on the glass table.

'Not much. They're finally going to promote a local Chinese to the upper ranks,' said Nicholas, sitting down opposite her.

Sarah's pale blue eyes widened. 'Who? I'm assuming it's a man. It's hardly likely to be a woman.'

Nicholas laughed and looked over to the steel door to check if it was firmly closed. 'The other day I saw a memo to the Board, which Martin left in his notes to my speech. There was quite a lot of stuff about modernising, but the memo said something about the absence of women in the upper echelons.'

Sarah bit her lip. 'They're going through the motions. The only woman who's made it through the glass ceiling is Grace in Personal Banking, and she's not a General Manager. Anyway, who's the lucky Chinese?'

Nicholas made a my-lips-are-sealed gesture. 'I can't say, but I can tell you he's from Hong Kong and he's made it up the hard way. He's not one of these parachuted-in investment bankers.'

'Thank god for that,' said Sarah. 'Anyone who makes it up the ladder here deserves a medal, and if they're Chinese or female they deserve it even more.' She gave Nicholas a meaningful look. 'Or gay, come to that.'

Nicholas raised his eyebrows. 'Being gay is not as visible as being Chinese or female.'

'But it still meets a glass ceiling. And the only reason they're starting to promote local Chinese is that the handover is coming up and they're going to look complete arseholes to Beijing.'

Nicholas nodded, still watching the door. He was grateful for these interludes in his day, interludes when he could speak with honesty and without fear of something between his shoulder blades. Ever since he had taken on Frank, he had to be careful what he said in public. His inner circle was almost entirely female. Not only Sarah and Eunice, but also some of the Chinese secretaries came to him for support when they could no longer take the pressure. Only Sarah knew that he was gay of course. The rest of them had simply followed her lead to Nick's psychiatrist's couch. 'A bit overstated.'

'Come on, Nick, you know as well as I do that they're in a panic. They've only got a few months to change the whole culture, or at least dress it up to *look* as if they're local. I don't think Beijing cares much about women, and it probably wants all the gays lined up against the wall in Tiananmen Square, but the communists will expect to see a few Chinese faces when they invite UIB to the Great Hall of the People.'

Nicholas giggled at the image of the senior executives filing in to meet the State leaders, but he knew that Sarah had a point. Like almost every other institution in Hong Kong, UIB had failed to prepare itself fully for the impending transition to Chinese sovereignty. There was something vaguely depressing about this, but every time he had tried to draw senior management's attention to it he was greeted with polite explanations that the transition was gradual, there was no need to worry, 'one step at a time'. Nicholas had gone along with this, not least because he was managing his own transition, but he was frustrated by the lack of overall awareness of what becoming part of communist China would mean. 'It's supposed to be a meritocracy. There are no politically correct quotas.'

Sarah let her head fall back, her long mousey hair draped over the back of the chair. 'If it were a meritocracy, I'd have Frank's job and almost everyone on the top floor would lose theirs. It's a closed shop, Nick.'

Nicholas stood up and moved back towards his desk but stopped at the window. The three smokers were still out on the Mercantile terrace, their shirts now clinging to their bodies. He noticed that one of them had a particularly muscular torso. As the man's lips parted to release the smoke from his cigarette, Nicholas felt a strange desire to join him. 'I suppose so.'

Sarah came over to the window to see what was going on. 'Oh,' she said with amusement. 'So this is what you get up to when the door's closed.'

Nicholas held up his hands. 'I've never seen them before.' He continued to his desk, leaving Sarah to continue staring down on the terrace.

'One of them's really hot,' said Sarah. 'Not that I've much time for bankers.'

Nicholas gave her a long-suffering look. 'Nor have I Sarah. And even if I did, I wouldn't be able to do anything about it.'

Sarah folded her arms and leaned back on the glass, her grey trousers and slim hips reminding Nicholas of the Man Ray photo he had once seen of a Parisian *cocotte* in the 1930s: cigarette at an angle, fringe bobbed, pouting lips. 'The men are all like that here. It's lucky you're not after them Nick, because I doubt if you'd have much fun. I'm glad I've got Michael. I know he's a lawyer and lawyers are almost as dull as bankers, but at least he's dependable. And he keeps all his office problems out of the home.'

Nicholas smoothed down the briefing notes on his lectern. 'There's something about…' He tailed off.

Sarah looked up. 'About what? Banking?'

Nicholas fiddled with the lead to his multi-channel phone. 'Of course in every situation there are exceptions…'

Sarah moved quickly from the window to sit at the chair in front of Nicholas' desk. 'You're acting very funny Nick. Is there something you want to say?'

Nicholas stared hard at Sarah, clearly telling himself that he shouldn't. Finally, however, it was too much for him. 'I saw this guy in the Banking Hall the other day. It wasn't that obvious but I could tell he was gay. And he was really attractive.'

Saran narrowed her eyes. 'There must be a lot of attractive expats. That is, until you talk to them.'

'He's a Chinese Relationship Manager in the Banking Hall.'

'My god,' said Sarah with a triumphant smile. 'I'm impressed Nick.'

Nicholas shifted in his seat. 'About twenty-five.'

Sarah shrugged. 'Men are always after younger ones, aren't they? Sounds like mid-life crisis to me. What's so special about him?'

Nicholas thought for a moment. 'It was the lunch break and he happened to cross my path. He sort of looked hard at me and gave me this beautiful smile. I didn't have the guts to say anything. I just stood there as if somebody had kicked me and smiled. Later I found out his name.'

'Which is?'

'Daniel,' said Nicholas.

'Daniel,' repeated Sarah. 'Well I wouldn't recommend you introduce him to the Lions Den upstairs. They'll tear him to pieces.'

'Come on, I'm not a complete fool Sarah. It's just that there was something different about him, and now I'm having trouble getting him out of my mind.'

Sarah patted his arm. 'You gays are rather good at recognising each other aren't you? Do you have radar of some sort?'

Nicholas pointed to his head and laughed. 'Gaydar, Sarah. I think there's even a website for it. What do you think I should do?'

Sarah rolled her eyes. 'Nothing. There are far too many spies in this place. Why don't you find yourself a nice discreet expat that you can go on trips to the islands with on weekends and classical concerts and stuff like that?' she said. 'There's enough trouble here without you going to look for it.'

'I suppose you're right,' said Nick gloomily.

Chapter 3

5 May 1997 announced the neon calendar glowing in celebratory red above the list of cross-rates to the Hong Kong dollar: *Only 55 days to go*! Nicholas stared at the countdown Board, wondering why they had to be quite so melodramatic. It wasn't as if it was the Olympics or a new century, and according to both the Chinese and the British, not all that much was going to change. The territory was reverting to China and not being handed over, since it had never really been a British possession in the first place. However, Governor Patten was doing his best to complicate it by trying to weld on some measure of elected democracy at the last moment, which the communist Chinese pledged to dismantle as soon as they marched in on 1 July.

Nicholas turned back to the Banking Hall. There were not many bank staff around and it would have been quite easy for him to stroll across the black parquet floor on the third level of Sir Alexander's open atrium, take a coffee with the few customers in the Privilege Centre, and step into Daniel's cubicle unnoticed. The only thing that held him back was Sarah. Only the other day the 'Madame' of Publications, Jeanette Long, had passed him on the stairs and asked him if he had tried the Executive Dining Suite on the top floor of the building. He had been about to say yes when he remembered that his last visit there was to a riotously drunken dinner with the Red Brigade.

He continued to hover at the edge of the glass parapet, gazing down at the customers being borne up and down the escalators.

'Can I help you?' said a pale-faced usher.

'I'm fine, thank you,' he said with slight embarrassment and hurried away to the leather chairs grouped around the CNN News. Keeping his face averted, he once more surveyed the Banking Hall: no sign of anyone from upstairs, not even Jeanette Long. Finally, overcoming his inner resistance, he headed straight for Daniel's cubicle.

Daniel was sitting behind his desk in a grey jacket and purple United tie, looking every inch the Customer Relationship Manager. The front of his thick black hair rose in a gelled quiff and he wore rather serious dark-framed glasses that complemented his strong jaw line and high cheekbones. As soon as he saw Nicholas, he gave him a bright smile.

'I'd like to make a quick transaction,' gabbled Nicholas, accepting the seat that Daniel offered and extricating the cheque he had placed in his jacket pocket. 'I'm a staff member.'

Daniel seemed slightly surprised. 'What about the counters?'

Nicholas hesitated. 'There's quite a queue out there,' he said and watched Daniel's fingers follow his details on the debit card and on the cheque, comparing them with Nicholas' account numbers on the computer screen and entering them on the transaction slip. The digits of Daniel's hand were long and incredibly slender, like a cast he had once seen of Chopin's hand.

'Which department are you in?' asked Daniel.

'Group Public Affairs,' said Nicholas.

Daniel tilted his head as if puzzled and passed the slip to him for signing. 'What do you do?'

'I write the Chairman's speeches.'

Daniel raised his eyebrows, clearly impressed. 'I thought he wrote his own.'

Nicholas laughed. 'That's what he'd like us to believe.'

Daniel wondered about this for a moment, waiting for Nicholas to say something more. He then leaned forward with a practiced smile. 'Is there anything else I can do for you?'

Nicholas drummed his fingers on the desk. 'As a matter of fact, I got a flyer from Personal Banking the other day about investing in Index Tracker Funds. Any information about them?'

Daniel smiled, revealing a set of perfectly aligned white teeth. 'There's a special discount for staff members.' He began to flick through a ring-folder containing various prospectuses. Pouncing on the relevant one, he placed the prospectus on the table. 'You'd be more comfortable if you brought your chair round.'

Nicholas felt his pulse quicken. Even though he knew that he shouldn't be doing this, even though he knew that flirting with *any* member of staff was strictly off limits, he moved his chair as close as possible to Daniel's.

'See this?' Daniel indicated the tracker yield graph on the handout. 'The previous five-year's performance. Big returns as you can see.'

Nicholas noticed the smoothness of his skin: an olive tinge, suffused at the level of the cheekbones with a touch of amber. Glancing down, he checked out Daniel's waist.

'Despite market losses, the average annual return on capital over the last five years…' Daniel was pointing with his pencil to a chart on the far left of the handout. Nicholas half-rose from his chair to take a look and reached down to support himself with his left hand. However, instead of finding the armrest his fingers touched something warm, something that he had wanted to touch from the moment he had entered the room.

'Sorry,' he mumbled but didn't pull away.

Daniel continued to scan the sentences of the document. 'Not only is your initial investment protected, but as long as you hold the fund for more than one year…'

Suddenly there was a knock on the door. Both men quickly separated as a middle-aged Chinese man entered the room.

'Anything I can do?' said the visitor, peering through his glasses.

Nicholas recognised the man. In the annual Personal Banking seminar he always appeared as the God of Prosperity, complete with long white beard and red robes.

'No, no,' said Nicholas. 'Daniel's being very helpful.'

The God of Prosperity gave Daniel a slightly doubtful look. 'I'm glad to hear that,' he said and backed out. 'I'll be here if you need me,'

'Don't worry,' whispered Daniel. 'The staff here all call him *chau bak kung.*'

'Meaning?' said Nicholas.

'Nosey old – .' Daniel nodded to fill in the rest.

Nicholas laughed and moved carefully towards the door, closing it firmly before returning to his seat.

Daniel's right hand still lay on his armrest while his left was stretched out to indicate the relevant part of the handout. Nicholas imagined that amber flush in his cheeks deepening.

'Daniel?'

'Yes?' Daniel looked up with a clear, piercing stare.

'Would you like to meet up later?' I mean outside of the office. We could share a coffee or...'

The glow on Daniel's cheeks had deepened. He watched Nicholas as if studying him for a moment and then seemed to come to a decision. 'Okay,' he said. 'We could go to SoHo.'

Nicholas' cheek muscles twitched. The bars and restaurants of SoHo were lively, but they were also full of people from the financial district. They might not have taken much notice of him on his own, or even of the two of them, unless someone from UIB realised that Daniel was his junior colleague. 'Too many *gwailos*,' he said hurriedly. 'How about Causeway Bay?'

'Okay,' said Daniel.

'Tonight?'

Daniel closed the prospectus book and smoothed the cover before looking up with a tight smile. 'I've got a family dinner but I'll make up some excuse. 8 o'clock okay?'

Nicholas nodded. 'Lobby of Excelsior Hotel.' He searched in his inner jacket pocket and found his business card. 'My mobile's down at the bottom.'

Daniel reached across his desk to his cardholder and with odd formality handed his card to Nicholas. 'Mine too.'

'I'd better go now,' said Nicholas and quickly moved to the door to check that the coast was clear.

'Thank you for your visit,' said Daniel, his voice gaining in volume as he opened the door. 'I'll prepare a detailed plan for the Tracker Funds for you as soon as possible.'

Nicholas was about to reply but Daniel merely nodded and closed the door behind him. It was only as Nicholas reached the escalator that he felt relaxed enough to punch the air.

***

Nicholas played with the remains of Madras Chicken and rice on his plate, wondering if he could face dessert. It wasn't so much his waistline that he was worried about, it was what was welling up inside him. He had wanted to say it earlier while watching *Chinese Ghost Story*, but although they had kissed in the dark in the cinema, there was no further chance to talk until they reached the restaurant. Perhaps it would have been best if he just blurted it out. But that required more alcohol, and since Daniel had insisted on only one beer, he didn't want to get drunk alone.

'Want anything else?' he asked, looking at his watch beneath the tabletop. It was 10.15 pm. Dessert and coffee would take another thirty minutes, which was about time for a hard-working Customer Relationship Manager to be heading home.

Daniel dipped his sushi into the soya sauce. 'I'm not sure. What about you?'

'I'm fine,' said Nicholas, hoping the last of the wine would calm his stomach. 'Perhaps a coffee.'

Daniel giggled. His linen jacket was on his chair back and he had pulled up his cuffs to shell the prawns. His face was slightly flushed and there was a trail of perspiration on his upper lip. 'Okay,' he said and popped a rice ball into his mouth.

'Do you have a day off tomorrow?'

Nicholas looked round for the waiter. He was supposed to review the Bank of England speech. *Fuck it*, he thought.

The waiter appeared. 'Espresso,' said Nicholas and looked at Daniel.

'Mint tea. Or do you have to work?'

'No,' lied Nicholas. 'I could do with a break.'

Daniel wiped his mouth with his napkin and smiled. 'I could do with a day in bed.'

Nicholas wished he had ordered dessert, something to hide his nerves. It wasn't as if they hadn't talked about this. Even in the coffee shop before the cinema, Daniel had shown that he wasn't afraid of dating. But he also made it clear he wasn't looking for the usual quickie.

The waiter approached and placed their drinks carefully on the table.

'I'll try the mango mousse,' said Daniel. 'Back in a moment.'

Nicholas reached for the milk and sipped his espresso. It was now 10.27 pm and the buffet tables were beginning to empty. He had to make a move. Daniel wouldn't have come here if he didn't like him. That kiss in the cinema had been confirmation.

'It's quite fruity,' said Daniel as he sat back down at the table and found a second spoon. 'Here, try some.'

As Daniel put the spoon into his mouth, Nicholas felt as if he could explode inside. The far lights of the cruise yachts in the Causeway Bay Typhoon Shelter were dancing as if to some silent tango. And yet all he could really focus on was Daniel's eyes, framed in a kind of electric storm that hung over him while the rest of the room stood still.

Nicholas held Daniel's wrist with the smeared spoon still pointing at his lips. There was a kind of wild drumming going on in his chest.

'What're we going to do?' said Daniel, gently disengaging his hand.

Nicholas shook his head. 'It's up to you.'

Daniel looked at him with feigned surprise. 'Really?'

'We could go somewhere private.'

Daniel paused. 'Your place?'

Nicholas glanced at his watch and took a deep breath. UIB had given him a large executive flat on The Peak, which would have been perfect. The problem was that the 'band of brothers' who lived there were either confirmed bachelors or married men with families. They were also extremely nosey. If anyone saw him come home with a good-looking young Chinese, the story would almost certainly get around. Being 'out' in Hong Kong was possible if you were a discreet expat on your own, or a Chinese who lived in the country or on one of the islands. It could be kept well hidden out there, especially from the Chinese family circle, but for the average worker being gay was reserved for late night bars, Friday and Saturday night clubbing, and trusted friends.

'I live on Old Peak Road.'

Daniel put down his cup with a slight tinkle of the spoon. 'That place for executives?'

'I didn't realise how claustrophobic it is. It's like a monastery.'

Daniel shifted in his seat. 'Maybe we'd better leave it then, I mean for tonight. It's been a long week.'

Nicholas gestured for the bill. He had made his decision, and so had Daniel. 'We've got to go somewhere.'

Daniel smiled nervously and raised his eyebrows. Then they gathered up their belongings and headed for the escalator. Half way down, however, Daniel turned to him. 'How about the YMCA in Tsim Tsa Tsui?'

Nicholas pondered this for a moment. 'Okay,' he said, heading towards the taxi stand. 'Let's give it a go.'

Chapter 4

C elebration. It was only a glass of Beaujolais in the Mandarin Oriental but it had been the perfect end to a long day – indeed a long few days. And at least he felt fortified for what he assumed would not be an entirely warm welcome when he finally arrived at Daniel's place. He hadn't seen him since well before the People's Liberation Army began crossing the Shenzhen border at 12 am on 1 July and he wasn't sure Daniel was too happy about it.

Over the entire period of the handover it had rained, creating an outburst of doom-laden predictions in the press that the reversion of the British colony to its communist masters would bring about its downfall. By contrast, the Chinese said that heavy rain was a sign of prosperity, the inevitable accompaniment to the arrival of a wise and noble man who would shower the city with blessings. Whether this was President Jiang Zemin or the Prince of Wales depended on how you saw the departure of the British and the arrival of the Chinese communists. He knew as well as any of the world's journalists who had descended on the place that the whole thing could go up in flames if China went back on its word or suddenly stormed the Legislative Council with a few crack units of the People's Liberation Army.

His felt his heartbeat subside as he left behind the final steps to the housing blocks and headed for the nearest lobby. The wind was gusting around the slopes of Lion Rock but despite the driving rain he could see right over to Hong Kong Island, the tops of its skyscrapers half-hidden in ragged banners of cloud. An old man in pyjamas holding a young girl by the hand stared hard at him as he made his way, suit jacket over his shoulder, between the plastic mobile skips piled high with rubbish. As he looked up, he could see row upon row of windows, some of them with washing stuck out on bamboo poles in defiance of the rain.

He waited for the nearest of the three elevators, still being looked at with curiosity by a steady stream of Chinese who were moving through the lobby, entered the elevator and pressed the button for the 12th floor. As he was lifted upwards, he felt his neck muscles relax. He always seemed to breathe easier when he reached Daniel's place. It was something to do with the anonymity of the public housing estate, the sense that he had escaped. He was the only *gwailo* in a sea of Chinese, the only Caucasian to go to the herbal medicine store with his Chinese boyfriend and order those odd flu remedies of bitter bark and arrowroot when he was sick, the only non-Chinese to flick through the kung-fu comics at the newspaper stall or to wander in the aisles of the wet market. And although the local Chinese often stared at him, he never felt remotely threatened.

He stepped out of the elevator and crossed the battered concrete of the landing, the embers of Chinese paper money to the spirits still burning in a tin box, and reached the grille with its little shrine to the door gods at floor level. The sound of high-pitched Cantonese opera and scraping mahjong pieces came from next door. Nicholas pressed the bell and watched the diamond-shaped message for Good Luck and Prosperity flap in the wind.

Kicking back the tiny painted stool that held the door, Daniel appeared at the grille with a key in his hand. He was dressed in a red polo shirt and a pair of black shorts.

'At last,' said Daniel as he unlocked the grille. 'I thought you were never coming.' He ushered Nicholas in over the stool and the board placed across the lintel to keep out the draught. 'Ma,' he shouted.

As Nicholas strode into the room, a short, wiry woman came out of the kitchen with a large metal spatula and looked at him through thick, lop-sided lens. 'Hah-low Nick.'

'*Gay ho ma*,' he said in that diffident tone he knew would pass for enthusiasm in Cantonese. There was no immediate reply, neither from Ma nor from the various members of Daniel's family that were also in the room. However, a couple of Daniel's sisters did look up from the mahjong game they were playing and give him a shy smile.

The smell of cooking came from the kitchen, a slightly acrid aroma of vegetables mixed with flour, perhaps the preparations for that lumpy white turnip cake they had given him last time. But before he could go and take a look, Fifth Sister handed him a rose ceramic cup filled with tea. Satisfied she had done the honours, she left him to Daniel and returned to the kitchen.

Daniel motioned Nicholas to sit on the long wooden bench that occupied almost one wall of the narrow room. The television was on, showing endless reruns of the countdown ceremony: President Jiang Zemin and the new Chief Executive sitting on a vast podium as the red flag of China went up, an interminable speech in Mandarin, the confusion of the Chinese leader as the Prince of Wales appeared to turn his back on him, the farewell ceremony at HMS Tamar with Chinese girls dancing in sodden tutus and Gurkha bands churning their way through the mud.

'Is there anything else to watch?' asked Nicholas.

'I thought you loved it.'

'Hardly,' he said with a resigned smile.

'You should have been here yesterday. My mother cooked last night for everyone. You could have stayed over.'

'I know,' said Nicholas. 'But I needed a clear head for today's meeting with the Group Chairman.'

Daniel stopped joking with Monkey Head, a fuzzy-haired boy who was playing video games as if the world inside the small TV was about to implode, and looked hard at him. 'What was that about?'

Nicholas sat back, still sipping his tea, and looked at Daniel over his cup. 'He's going to promote me.'

Daniel placed both hands on the bench and swung his legs, his olive skin slightly flushed. 'Congratulations. To what?'

'To Martin's job,' said Nicholas. The sound of Cantopop mingled with the violent explosions of the video game, the scrape and shuffle of the mahjong pieces and the repetitive playing of the Chinese national anthem on the TV. 'You don't sound that thrilled.'

Daniel shook his head. 'Of course I am.' He paused a moment. 'But it's only three months since you started coming here. Now you'll have to rush off on the weekends or stay longer at work. We hardly have time together as it is.'

Nicholas was going to tell him what else the Group Chairman had said. However, he had learned not to rush things. It was Daniel's idea to introduce Nicholas to his family, his idea to ask him to stay over on weekends. But he had done it in his own way and at his own pace. 'I'll have some weekends free just like I do now. Even if I have to travel to London.'

Daniel made a strange face. 'You sound like Pinkerton.'

Nicholas sighed and shook his head. 'I'm just saying that we can keep things as they are.'

'My family might find out on day,' said Daniel suddenly and went over to watch the mahjong game. Nicholas turned back to the TV, wondering if he should take a lie down. No one seemed to take any notice as he rose and made his way between Monkey Head and Fat Boy to the bedroom, finally lying flat out on the bed.

He should have talked to Daniel before. It was he who had taken the lead in their personal arrangements. Rather than meeting secretly in anonymous hotels, Daniel had insisted on bringing him home so that they had somewhere to be together. It wouldn't have worked in an Anglo-Saxon family, but it had in a Chinese one.

A week after Daniel had introduced him, his Sixth Sister had to go into hospital for what turned out to be surgery. Daniel had told Nicholas about it on the phone and within a couple of hours he had joined Daniel at the hospital, thinking it the most the natural thing in the world to do. And yet he would never forget the way the elder members of the family took trouble to thank him for coming. Nor would he forget the way the kids ran about as they left the hospital in a taxi, waving and shouting 'Nick uncle, bye-bye' almost in unison, with his name before his qualifier as it would have been in Chinese.

Later, Daniel told him that Ma had said how lucky Daniel was to have a *gwailo* friend, especially a friend in the same company. With eight children already married to Chinese, she seemed completely unperturbed by the idea of a ninth being involved with a 'devil-man'. She prayed for him regularly at Wong Tai Sin temple.

'You want some white turnip cake?' said Daniel, appearing at the end of the bed. Nicholas nodded.

Ma was a typical Chinese mother. She cooked and washed up not only for Daniel and him, but also for Daniel's nephew who she had adopted until the end of primary school, and for Daniel's unmarried sister. Even though Nicholas was bigger than everyone else in there, within weeks he had become a regular fixture. The bed on which he was lying became officially 'his'. There was also a large double bed in the main room that they pulled out at night for the rest of the family. The whole place was really an assortment of surfaces. Lunch and dinner were served on a collapsible table taken from out the back. Snacks, tea and glasses were set on a low carved table next to the votive house for the gods and ancestors. The wonder was that it would all fit in. Anything that was needed appeared, but almost nothing was thrown away. His coffee tins were religiously kept too, every single one, as useful containers for anything from plastic spoons to sago beans or cinnamon sticks.

'Here you are,' said Daniel, handing him the last slice of turnip cake.

The family always vacated the bathroom if he had to go to the office in a hurry, and they slowly accepted that coffee was essential to his life. Similarly, he made sure he got well out of the way when Ma or the others lit incense sticks before breakfast and again at dusk. These they then placed in the various pots around the room: at the votive altar, at the outside doorway, and in front of the good-luck windmills from the temple at Wong Tai Sin. He also learnt not to take an apple from the pile at the altar or to touch food being prepared for the big table set out with chicken, celery, cake and rice on special lunar occasions like Buddha's Birthday. There were aspects of Daniel's family life that must have surprised him when he first arrived – the mealtime anarchy of sauces and soups, of half-filled glasses and bottles, the spitting out of bones onto the tabletop, the smell of fermented bean curd, the fried pig skin, the thousand-year preserved eggs or fish intestines. Now, however, he hardly noticed.

'Are you ready?' said Daniel, returning to the end of the bed to take his empty plate.

'Okay,' said Nicholas.

As the family piled out into the lift and headed out of the housing block, Nicholas smiled to himself. There was a family gathering of this sort almost every weekend. Five or six sisters would appear with children and, later in the day, their husbands would arrive to play mahjong while the kids swayed back and forth to their video games, watched Hong Kong movies, or sang to the karaoke machine. Little ones slept on the bed or sofa as occasion required, often next to him, while Sixth Sister baked cookies and cakes from the recipes she had learnt on a recent evening course. Such afternoons gave him a new sense of the phrase *en famille*, since everyone did their own thing but at the same time completely on top of each other.

Soon they had arrived at the Great Moon restaurant in the nearby shopping mall. They stood outside for a moment while their reservation was confirmed. Then they were led to two giant round tables laid out with pink napkins and a bewildering array of chopsticks, silver spoons on cradles, rice bowls, dishes, tea cups and glasses. Somewhere in the depths of the restaurant Nicholas could hear Chinese wedding music while on stage a children's singing competition was in progress.

'You want wine?' shouted Daniel.

'Okay,' said Nicholas. He knew that wine was a much better choice than the Coke or Sprite the restaurant usually offered.

The waitresses poured tea, wine, cognac and soft drinks into the glasses that stood before each diner. The first course arrived: cold meats and jellied octopus. Before they attacked the central dish, everyone held out their glass in front of them and shouted *yam bui!* Course followed course in a riotous haze of tastes, music, more shouts of *yam bui!* and flashing chopsticks. As each dish arrived, Daniel reached out and picked up something to place in Nicholas's bowl: fresh prawns, roast duck and chicken, scallops, bitter melon, steamed fish and ginger, all accompanied by the filling of Nicholas's wine glass. By the time the rice and noodles were served, Nicholas's head was spinning.

'I was just thinking...'

Daniel lunged at the centre wheel and brought back the fried rice Nicholas preferred. 'Yes?'

'About where to live,' said Nicholas.

Daniel stopped eating. 'There's nothing to think about. We need our own place.'

Nicholas swallowed a scoop of rice and took a deep breath. 'Actually, I don't just have to go back and forth to London. They're talking about a new position for me over there.'

One of Daniel's chopsticks clattered to the floor. 'Aren't you taking over Martin's job?'

'Yes, but they've plans for me down the road. Martin's moving to New York – and it's ...complicated. Anyway it's not worth us getting a place in Hong Kong now.'

Fine lines of fret appeared at the corner of Daniel's lips. 'You mean you're leaving town?'

Nicholas looked around to see if anyone was watching and moved his leg closer to Daniel's. 'Not without you I'm not.'

Daniel took a gulp of tea and moved his leg away. 'You'll be living in company housing in London and pretending you're straight. It'll be the same old story.'

Nicholas put down his rice bowl. 'We'll get a place together. There are plans to introduce a new partnership law in the U.K. I don't know how it'll work out. We'll have to fulfill some sort of co-habitation thing.' He caught the look in Daniel's eyes. 'But I want us to live together.'

Daniel half-turned in his chair. A few sporadic shouts of *yam bui!* echoed around the room as a dish piled high with pink lotus buns arrived. He was impressed, Nicholas could see that, but also wary. 'And when's all this going to happen?'

'Soon,' said Nicholas. 'UIB doesn't provide housing in London. That means we'll have to buy a flat.'

Daniel looked hard at him. 'I want a real relationship Nick. I don't want to be phoned by your secretary to tell me when you're available. I don't want to be standing about on the street waiting for you after work, or pretending not to know you. That's the only way I'll be going.'

Nicholas put down his napkin. 'Trust me Daniel.'

Daniel raised his eyebrows but said nothing as the waiter brought over the bill. Fifth Sister checked it over several times, took out a huge wad of dollar notes from her shoulder bag, counted them out and handed them to the waiter. Then the entire family stood, babies and umbrellas and doggy bags in hand, and headed for the door.

Chapter 5

T hey're here,' whispered Martin's secretary as the rather large bulk of Eddie Rochester entered the room, followed by Martin Heatherington, a sheaf of papers in his left hand.

'Good morning,' said the Group Chairman, dressed as usual in a light grey flannel suit, purple United tie and brown brogues. Wiping beads of sweat from his cheek, he looked down the table in a slightly conspiratorial manner and sat down. There was a pause while Martin fiddled with the air-conditioning. Nicholas used the hiatus to try and catch Eddie's eye but Jeanette got there first. Eddie gave her a fixed smile and then his blue eyes travelled over the long table, reaching and lingering on Nicholas.

'Welcome everyone. We are highly honoured today that the Chairman has come to listen to our views on the future of United International. The implications of Hong Kong's return to China cannot be underestimated. As we have seen these last few weeks, the transition to Chinese sovereignty has been an overwhelming success. The world's press came expecting a disaster. They went away largely disappointed. Our task now is to set the future course of United International, both within and beyond Hong Kong.'

Eddie looked at the signet ring on his right hand. 'Thank you Martin. To put it bluntly, the competition is now becoming so intense that we need to use all our capabilities and forward thinking to stay ahead of the race. What I want from you today is some ideas on how we're going to do that.'

For a moment there was complete silence round the table, as if everyone had left both their notes and their courage at the office. Nicholas looked hard at Eddie, trying to assess the speed and direction of his thinking. This was a man who was famous for his one-liners, a man used to striding down corridors and thundering out orders so that the entire floor and perhaps the entire building could hear. And yet he was also capable of deep silence, watching and brooding in his office high above the City of London if anything like a deal was in the air. One thing was clear: since the royal yacht Britannia had steamed away with Governor Patten and Prince Charles on board, he was in no mood for nostalgia.

'Who would like to take a shot?' prompted Martin. 'Are we going to follow our previous instincts and tackle the Chinese banks head on, or are we going for something different?'

Antonia Sylvetti, Head of Community Relations, glanced at Jeanette and tapped her jaw. 'I think we have to be careful. Our approach so far has been all about solidarity with the people of Hong Kong. How we grew up with them. How we faced adversity together. How we helped them prepare for the return to China. We cannot just drop this approach because some of us... ' She glanced at Nicholas, '...consider the time has come to move on.'

There was a murmur of agreement along the table. Nicholas looked round. He was not a great speaker at department meetings; he left that to others. He was often astonished how quickly his colleagues would hold forth in order to show not only how committed they were but also how important. How many times had he listened to Frank and Jeanette haranguing the assembled executives on their duties and responsibilities. Frank regarded himself as an authority on 'team spirit'. This was ironic since he had a habit of keeping a file of notes and memos on his staff from what he called their 'off days'. He hoarded these memos until the half-yearly appraisals and then simply wrote them up, keeping them on file in his locked drawer if anyone dared to complain. At the last Red Brigade dinner Sarah told Nicholas that she had discovered the file when working late one evening. She had gone looking for the stapler and found the key to his drawer.

'I agree with Antonia,' said Frank, glancing at Nicholas as if giving a warning shot across his bows. 'Now that we are through the political transition, I think we should promote our local loyalties more. We have to show that we can compete with the Chinese, and above all – ' He looked in Eddie's direction. 'We have to cultivate our new masters.'

Jeanette had shuffled the prompt cards in her hand. 'I absolutely agree. This company is built on heritage and tradition. By which I mean many years of loyalty and service to our customers, the people who have made us what we are – which is not a faceless global institution operating out of London.' Her grey eyes swept the table. 'I believe that's what we must emphasise: continuity with our past, a sense of discipline, and solidarity with the people of Hong Kong.'

Nicholas placed a hand over his mouth to hide a smile. The closest that Jeanette and Antonia got to the people of Hong Kong were the barmen at the Royal Yacht Club. And yet here they were insisting that United International must play to its local strengths. Suddenly Nicholas realised that Eddie had turned to him. 'And what do you think?'

Nicholas looked down the table. This was the best confirmation hearing he was going to get: the next rung on the ladder. Placing his hands fully on the table, he waited until everyone was silent.

'I'd like to express my thanks to Jeanette for an excellent analysis of where we are. Various members of Group Public Relations have spent a lot of time here and they have gained a tremendous amount of experience. United International Bank would not be where it is without the commitment of people like Jeanette, Antonia, and… Frank.' He looked over the table as if mentally isolating each person 'However, I have to disagree a little. I understand entirely where Jeanette is coming from but I believe things are changing.'

He glanced down the table. 'If we focus only on China we are going to make a mistake. We have to move forward. Being a global force in banking is exactly where I see our future. One of the things that occurs to me is that we are still perceived as a British, indeed to some extent as a colonial institution.' He paused. 'But this is not just a matter of perception. It seems to me to require a change of policy. China currently represents only a small part of our assets and an even smaller proportion of our profits. The fact that we have been in China for more than a century gives us an excellent position to expand aggressively into the Mainland. On the other hand, the political and legal situation in China is uncertain. If we maintain our global headquarters in Hong Kong, we're exposing ourselves to risk. I know we have been projecting ourselves as a corporation that identifies closely with Hong Kong, but shouldn't we look beyond Hong Kong?'

Nicholas glanced at the long glass windows, darkened by rain outside, and saw himself as he imagined an outsider might see him.

Jeanette pushed her chair back. 'Is it such a bad thing if we are perceived as British? Perhaps it's because we have something special to offer, such as prudence and integrity.'

'Exactly,' said Frank Shearer and this time looked down the table with an openly hostile expression.

The smile on Nicholas' face tightened. 'I don't think one precludes the other. I'm not talking about compromising our values. I simply believe that the handover of Hong Kong to China gives us a great opportunity to promote our global image while showing the Chinese that we are ideal partners for their growth in the region. This is an international bank with enormous resources. Let's demonstrate those resources globally. Let's seize the opportunity the handover presents to project United

International onto a world stage.' His voice had risen and he paused a moment, gauging whether he had achieved the necessary effect.

The Group Chairman fished in his suit pocket for a silver-plated lighter and lit a cigarette. Smoke rings drifted above him like the white puffs over a Papal conclave. 'What do you think Martin?' he said, turning to his Head of Group Public Affairs.

Martin looked as if he had been caught offside in one of his beloved rugby games. His eyes flicked uneasily between Eddie and the expectant faces down the table. 'I think Nicholas has a point. Of course we must move into China but we must also protect ourselves from uncertainty. Whether that means moving out global headquarters to London is a decision for the Board. But there is no doubt that we are in a unique position to expand our business in China while building on our global presence.'

Eddie's neck appeared to inflate. 'Yes, and yet China is a very small part of our profits so far. We must be very careful.' He waited a moment, then looked at his watch. 'Well I have another meeting, but I would ask you to think very carefully about what's been said here today. We need a new approach to accompany our expansion –'

'Excuse me.' Everyone at the table turned to look at the source of this interruption. 'Surely if we move our headquarters to London, it will cost us a lot of new business,' said Frank Shearer. 'The Chinese authorities, for example – '

Eddie flicked his eyes over Frank's face. 'We're not intending to do anything at the *expense* of our local operations. Shearer. As Nicholas suggests, it's the global synergies that count.'

Frank's mouth puckered. 'Of course, I didn't mean…' Martin looked hard at his lieutenant but Frank seemed determined to continue. 'The fact is the press is starting to talk about our merger with Mercantile – '

Eddie's face turned a deeper purple. 'Merger? There's to be no mention of mergers until I make an official announcement.

That includes External Media Relations,' he said and shot a warning glance in Frank's direction.

The silence that followed was deep and prolonged. Nicholas could hear the thud of pile drivers on Kowloon Peninsula, the ongoing heartbeat of a city seemingly hell-bent on its own destruction. Finally, the Group Chairman rose and gathered his papers together before leaving the room. The assembled executives followed his lead. Nicholas was just about to join them when he felt a tap on his shoulder. 'Do you have you a moment Nick?'

Nicholas turned towards Martin. 'Of course' he said and led Martin across the black parquet squares of the lobby into his office.

'Perhaps we should close the door,' suggested Martin and waved away the Chinese boy who came to offer them refreshment.

Nicholas indicated the leather armchair opposite the sofa. Flopping down in the seat Nicholas suggested, Martin extricated a packet of cigarettes and placed it on the coffee table. He then lit up and fell back.

'I told you it's a difficult job. Not only the workload, but also building up your relationship with the Nabobs. I spend most of my time managing people and my interpersonal skills are getting worn out.' Martin paused. 'Which brings me to my next point. My position in London will soon be open to you. There's no doubt Eddie thinks highly of you, and so does Sir John Williams. The two of them seem to be considering a Board advisory position for you in London in the not too distant future.' He attempted an encouraging smile. 'You're an outstanding performer, Nick. My only concern is that people aspect I mentioned just now. In our positions, we have to be careful. We cannot allow ourselves to choose the wrong friends.'

He took a long, slow breath. 'To be frank, I've heard there are some people in the company with whom you have been having too much contact. I don't want to labour the point but you will have to distance yourself from them in the future. That's if you want to go to the very top.'

Nicholas's expression remained impassive, although his brain was seething.

'I'm married and like everybody else I've had the occasional problem in my marriage. However, I've never let such problems interfere with my work. Nor have I let it be known to anyone in the Bank, except perhaps my most trusted peers, that I've had any difficulties. No one is to be trusted, Nick, least of all your colleagues.'

Nicholas allowed himself a slight smile. It was something to do with Sarah, he decided. Sarah had always been branded as a rebel. He would just have to be more careful.

'I'll take that on Board,' he said finally in as neutral a tone as possible.

Martin finished his cigarette and moved towards the drinks cabinet. 'Let's have a glass of something to celebrate. Remember, Eddie and I will be behind you one hundred per cent. You can always rely on us.'

Chapter 5

Sir John Williams tried to keep close to the walls of Leadenhall Street to avoid the drizzle. There was a time when he would have worn a trilby on winter days like these but there wasn't much hair on his head any more, and besides few people wore trilbies in the City these days or even carried umbrellas. It was all part of the City of London's global image. Bankers and stockbrokers were much more likely to drive posh foreign cars than Jaguars or Rovers, they took holidays in Long Island or Bali rather than the Isle of Wight, and instead of pin stripe suits they wore Hugo Boss and Gucci. An increasing number came from outside the country. The City was decidedly cosmopolitan and old hands like Sir John had to fall into line. He still wore a Savile Row suit on occasion, but he felt just as comfortable in a trendy Italian number.

After the long lunch with the prospective Chancellor's chief of staff his mood had lightened. He usually found Joe Burns rather arrogant, constantly name-dropping about the White House adviser he had studied under as a Harvard postgraduate, prefacing every other sentence with 'When I was at the FT', but they had got on pretty well this time. Personally, he wouldn't have chosen that bland Italian restaurant with the pinewood and plants in Aldgate East. The design was airport arrivals, the Pinot Grigio was lukewarm and the *osso buco* tasted like Styrofoam. But the news that Joe Burns passed on was more than welcome. The soon-to-be-appointed Chancellor of the Exchequer had not only shown considerable interest in Sir John's nomination, he had also wanted to arrange a meeting with Nick Powell as soon as he arrived in London.

Sir John crossed the road at Bishopsgate, feeling the cold drizzle against his skin and looking with longing at the sign for Dirty Dan's. Just as he felt more comfortable with the traditional stone buildings of the City than with those elongated space modules that were rising up everywhere, there was a part of him that could never quite give up the old days. He had forgotten who Dirty Dan was, but it was the availability of those Barnsley chops and pies and Young's beer by the draught that made him feel at home in its dark wood, dank interior.

He tried to imagine Roger Yates joining him in Dirty Dan's for a quiet drink, just as they used to do when he was at the Department of Trade and Industry. But the pattern so far had been two meetings in wine bars with Joe Burns, followed by what seemed to be the clincher. Although Sir John had tried to suggest an old-fashioned place to Roger on the phone, he had clearly been wary. Given that United International headquarters was just around the corner from Dirty Dan's, this was perhaps understandable. Nevertheless, Sir John had a feeling that there was something more to it than that.

He stopped in his tracks and looked at his watch. The effect of that one half-drunk glass of Pinto Grigio was beginning to wear off and he still had half an hour to go before meeting Eddie Rochester. He could do with a glass of beer. Retracing his steps, he entered the dark interior of the pub and ordered a pint of Young's from the upstairs barman, taking it with him to a table near the window. He then settled into the wooden chair and took a deep draught from the foam-topped glass.

It was extremely bad luck that Roger Yates had been at the Department of Trade and Industry when Sir John had landed the Royal Docks project. The new Exhibition Centre was approved, construction was going ahead and everything had seemed fine until the newspapers discovered that a government agency called Thames Vantage was promoting business sites in the same area. Sir John was on the Thames Vantage Board. In order to prevent the bad news from spreading, Sir John had to call in Nicholas Powell to help him out. A year or so later, he had encouraged him to join United International.

Sir John took another sip of his beer. One man's setback was another man's good fortune; that was the way of the world. He shouldn't be too hard on himself. The coup of obtaining the contract had seemed so exciting, the government connection so tenuous, he just assumed everyone else would think the same way. Even though people in the City and in Westminster talked of transparency and 'Chinese walls', he knew how little they could mean in practice. Transparency was something you declared to shareholders and the public; it was not something that clinched a deal.

Sir John tipped his glass horizontal and emptied it. All he had to do now was to persuade Eddie of the beauty of his little scheme and he would be there. He looked down at his left hand, which was slightly trembling. His doctor had recommended a course of ACE inhibitors for his blood pressure but he was unwilling to take them because of the possible side effects, particularly drowsiness.

With a nod to the barman, Sir John left the pub and set off at a steady pace towards New Change Street. He enjoyed walking in this part of London. Perhaps it was the solidity of its cream-stoned buildings or the names of the streets filled with their historical associations: Cheapside, Paternoster, Minories, Austin Friars. Perhaps it was just the general awareness of what had gone on within its ancient walls. Whatever it was, it gave him a feeling of confidence. Arriving at the steps of United

International, he passed through the revolving glass doors, crossed the lobby and took the elevator to the uppermost floor.

'He'll be with you in a minute,' said Eddie's secretary as he was ushered into the Group Chairman's suite. Eddie's large suit jacket hung on a wooden frame at the side of the leather sofa. Sir John could hear him talking on the phone: 'I want a full report on my desk by tomorrow. If they strike, they strike. But believe you me we'll let them go if they do.'

There was some sort of protest on the other end, which Eddie extinguished with a few well-chosen words and put down the phone. He turned his leather chair towards Sir John and reached across his enormous desk with its files in neat piles towards the silver cigarette box. 'Abrahams in New York. Once you start with the unions it's never going to end. I've told him that a thousand times.'

Sir John assumed a conciliatory smile. 'Perhaps you can get Martin to come up with a plan. You know, Abrahams meets the ringleaders and talks it over. Abrahams tells the press about his own hard way to the top, starting as an apprentice. You could always add something about UIB benefits being second to none.'

Eddie pointed his cigarette at the skyline. 'As soon as you start soft-soaping them they'll be asking for more. The only thing the unions understand is redundancy.'

Sir John felt a cold tremor pass down his back. He was forever advising clients not to take a hard line on industrial and stakeholder relations. However, despite using every tactic in the book, his success rate with Eddie was not very high.

'There's a limit to spin,' grunted Eddie, taking a deep drag of his cigarette and looking challengingly at Sir John.

Sir John smoothed his head with his left hand. 'That may well be, but we'll be needing plenty of media management for this merger with Mercantile.'

Eddie drew his eyebrows together. His left hand was lodged in his trouser waistband. 'Cigar?'

'No thank you,' said Sir John. 'I only have one in the evening.'

This wasn't quite true. He smoked cigars in chosen company, which didn't include his wife Marjory. She not only objected to it on health grounds but also because it made the armchairs smell in the drawing room of their Regents Park flat. He had tried to switch from the occasional Cuban to cheaper and lighter Dominicans, a Dom Thomas or similar, but Marjory had vetoed those too.

'Very wise,' said Eddie and raised his head to gaze for a moment at the ceiling. 'I suppose this is about Nicholas Powell.'

'Yes Chairman,' said Sir John. He was slightly nervous and the best way he could hide it was insisting on the proper mode of address.

'He's doing a decent job in Hong Kong,' said Eddie and reached for another cigarette.

Sir John sat forward, his hands between his knees. 'Yes, and he'll do an even better one over here. You're going to need someone like him to handle the London press as soon as the Mercantile merger takes off. And of course we have our other plan to consider.'

'There's always Martin,' said Eddie, raising an eyebrow. 'But you're right. The merger with Mercantile is the biggest thing we've undertaken. Of course, I could leave Powell in Hong Kong and get him over here on occasion.'

Sir John chewed his lower lip. 'His value is going to rise the more experienced he becomes. London is the centre of the company's business. If you're going to ride this merger into the future you're going to need someone like him near you. As you know, my suggestion is to appoint him as a Board adviser. That way you can have him on hand day and night.'

'Haven't I got you for that?' said Eddie.

Sir John tried to laugh. 'Of course Chairman. But I have a business to run, and committees to sit on, and many other things to do. You'll need someone to call on full time.'

Eddie returned his gaze to the ceiling. 'A public relations adviser to the Board will be a first. I don't know much about spin myself. Martin always claims you can measure the results but

I've never seen anything remotely convincing. What do you think Johnny?'

'I think you'll need him,' said Sir John, ignoring the question.

Eddie's frown deepened. 'He's dependable is he? I've heard a few rumours about him in Hong Kong. It's not good for the company you know. I joined this organisation from school and I can tell you that in those days the rules governing private life were strict. If anyone got married too early, let alone had had an unsuitable affair, they were packed off to Uzbekhistan or Bangladesh in a flash. There are standards to observe.'

'Of course,' said Sir John with a bow of the head, assuming that Eddie had heard the same rumours as he had. 'I can understand your concern Chairman but we don't know how indiscreet Nicholas has been. The rumours are very vague. Moreover, I'm not sure that we can afford to be too censorious.'

Eddie's face with its deep crevices and startling promontories darkened. 'It's got to stop Johnny. You can tell him that.'

'I'll do my best,' said Sir John. He paused a moment and cleared his throat. 'Which brings me to my lunch with Joe Burns. I must say he and Nicholas strike me as being a rather good match. They're both highly educated, ambitious, sharp on strategy.'

Eddie stared hard at Sir John, clearly fighting with the temptation to take another cigarette. 'Yes?'

'I think we touched on this the other day. Roger Yates is interested in having Nicholas on his team as communications director when he moves to Number 11. If that happens, we might try to keep him on as an adviser to the Board. I mean, in an informal capacity.'

Eddie gazed at the cigarette box, rose and moved towards the full-length windows that looked out over London. The dark grey clouds that pulsed across the horizon seemed to drag their skirts over the city, promising more rain. 'I don't know...'

Sir John looked at the hunched figure with his ruffled white hair and was reminded of those strange sculptures he had seen in the Boboli Gardens on his last visit to Florence with Marjory and the children. 'Leave it to me Chairman. Roger Yates is very keen on reforming public services but he'll need someone with experience in the private sector to explain his reforms, and how he's going to pay for them. I think Nicholas is just the man.'

Eddie turned towards him. 'Powell must manage the Mercantile business first. We've got to get that out of the way.'

Sir John took his cue and stood up. 'I couldn't agree more Eddie.'

The Chairman patted him on the back as they moved towards the door. 'We'll talk about this later. Let's deal with the Annual General Meeting, and then the informal Board thing. One step at a time.'

'Of course,' said Sir John at the door, knowing full well that Eddie could move at the speed of light if he wanted to. Due diligence only entered his vocabulary after everyone else had caught up.

***

Moving on down Shaftesbury Avenue towards St Martin's Lane, Sir John's mood considerably lightened. Despite the return of the drizzle that made his suit cling to his body, he was pleased with his decision to walk. He hated the crowds that pushed their way into the Central Line at this time of day, especially when the weather was poor. He was just turning down Charing Cross Road when a thin-faced youth in a dirty red fleece looked up at him from the pavement. 'Spare some change?'

Sir John was about to walk by just when suddenly the face of another young man came to him. A wasted face with strange blotches and fleshless curves. A face so sallow that it seemed as if the skull was peeping through. Hurriedly he took a fiver from his pocket and dropped it in the boy's tin. 'Thanks mate,' said the surprised beggar.

He crossed the road at the Arts Theatre and turned down St Martin's Lane, wondering how many of the people he passed had similar secrets to hide, secrets that lay hidden deep within them, rising to the surface at the very moment when they seemed to have them most successfully buried. In many ways he envied the life of someone like Nicholas. He appeared to have everything to look forward to and very little to regret. But as Sir John knew, even the most brilliant and focused careers could go wrong. Just one false turning, just one sideways glance, and the whole investment of time and money could come crashing to earth.

There was only a short queue at the advance reservations desk at the Albery Theatre. Handing over the tickets, the ticket manager in his primped bow tie seemed to give him a questioning look. Sir John wanted to explain that Harold Pinter's *No Man's Land* was entirely Marjory's choice. She adored the two old thespians in the lead roles. Sir John cared nothing for 'pregnant pauses' or famous actors (both of whom were renowned homosexuals), but he had to play fair with Marjory, who had so faithfully accompanied him to Gershwin musicals and Classics for Choirs at the Royal Albert Hall. At least the theatres and concert halls of London got them out of the house, which ever since 'that' had happened had taken on a depressing aspect. Even though their daughter often bought her children round to enjoy a picnic in Regent's Park, all sense of joy seemed to have fled the place.

Satisfied that Marjory would not nag him for forgetting the tickets, Sir John considered the Tube and thought better of it. The drizzle was light enough to walk home, as he often did from the City. He turned off St Martin's Lane to avoid the beggar and headed for Shaftesbury Circus. There he had a choice of continuing up Charing Cross Road or taking a short cut through Soho. Veering to the left, he found himself heading past the Italian coffee bars and the Spice of Life pub towards Old Compton Street. For some reason his pace began to slow. He saw a couple of men coming towards him with rings in their ears, one of them with a tattoo in the shape of a scorpion on his skull. Just as they came abreast of Sir John, the tattooed one screamed with laughter and pecked the other on the cheek.

The shiny interiors of the bars and pubs along Old Compton Street were already filling up. He could see red-faced men with muscular arms and leather caps, torn denim jeans, dangling chains. The aroma of cannabis wafted out onto the street. 'You got a light?' murmured a slim man in tight jeans and singlet. Sir John fingered the lighter he kept in his suit pocket and nodded. The man's thick, gelled hair touched his hand as he snapped it open and held out the flame. 'Thanks, he said and entered a shop with a rainbow flag over the door.

Sir John hesitated a moment, walked a little further forward, and then back again. Through the doorway he could see an array of goods in the shop: skull masks with angled slits for the eyes, leather shorts with the crotch cut out, knotted whips and wooden paddles. He stared at the display for a moment as another memory pierced him as sharply as the scent of cannabis wafted over from the pub opposite. It was the same face, but this time fuller and more animated, talking in the College Bar. He had spent an entire evening drinking with him and thought how well he looked, how comfortable with everything that Cambridge offered. Sir John lingered for a little while longer outside the shop, wondering if he could find out something that would help explain what went wrong, something that would provide at least part of the jigsaw. But deep down he knew it was hopeless. This was the world into which he had vanished, these were the people who had taken him away, and absolutely nothing he could do now would change that.

Eventually he moved on, trying to avoid the slightly curious glances on all sides. He knew why they were staring. It wasn't his immaculate suit and well-groomed appearance. It was the fact that he was standing there. Anyone who loitered at the fringes of this world was ripe for the taking.

Sir John kept his hands resolutely in his pockets as he continued past Raymond's Revue Bar and turned up past the strip joints. A woman with red hair and wearing a PVC black raincoat murmured something to him. He looked straight ahead and continued towards the market at Brewer Street. 'Grapes two pound a pound, lovely grapes, ' shouted a barrow boy.

'Two pounds,' said Sir John hurriedly. The least he could do was to buy Marjory some fruit. After all, she had borne the brunt of it. After the reality had sunk in, it seemed as if she would never get to the first base of acceptance. And yet as the months rolled by, it was she who had tried to rebuild what was left of their life. She still blamed him and at times her silence suggested he disgusted her. But it was she who mixed his Scotch and soda when he got home at night, she who insisted on school holidays with the grandchildren in Norfolk and Carcassonne, she who still went through the motions of marriage. 'There you go,' said the barrow boy.

Sir John continued up Brewer Street, past the record shops displaying their prized 78" vinyl stock, past the family butcher with the cleaved carcasses in the window, trying to recapture his previous buoyant mood. The damage had been done. What would regret achieve?

Chapter 6

C alm down,' Nicholas muttered to himself as he crossed at the traffic lights and looked up at the deep blue sky over Victoria Harbour. He stopped for a moment to admire the view. November in Hong Kong was often brilliant and cloudless, with unending days of dry heat providing much-needed relief after months of draining humidity. Two enormous Star Pisces cruise boats were docked at the Harbour Centre on Kowloon side, presiding over a procession of ferries and lighters jostling for position in front of the Star Ferry terminal. He loved the sheer chaos of Hong Kong: the ding-dong klaxon of the screechy trams, the yelps of the hawkers and shopkeepers along his route to work, the sudden dives of red taxis in and out of the crowded streets and markets. Hong Kong was the polar opposite of the world in which he worked, and whenever he was outside he had this strange desire to clasp it to his chest and embrace it.

It was obvious that Frank would move on after Martin left. A bully like him needed a new playground. Sure enough, Frank had applied for a position to head up corporate affairs at the United International Investment Bank. Nicholas had been only too happy to sign the transfer documents. The process had gone smoothly and all it needed was a short meeting in his office to shake hands on it.

He crossed Des Voeux Road and turned towards the left. Once through the glass doors of the Mandarin Hotel, he negotiated the guests in the lobby, nodded to the front desk manager and descended a couple of steps into the Captain's Bar. It was discreetly lit down here, with only a few customers, and he could immediately make out Sarah sitting alone at a corner table.

'Hi there.' He had spent the last few weeks putting a discreet distance between himself and Sarah, just as Martin had told him to do. She must have known the reason but she hadn't complained.

'Hello stranger,' said Sarah. Silhouetted against the red walls and with the spot on the ceiling shining down on her face, she looked nervous and vulnerable.

Nicholas sat down opposite her. 'I'm sorry, I've been so busy.'

Sarah pretended to look at the menu. 'Don't mix with the minions, that's the rule isn't it?'

Nicholas smiled at her. He had met Sarah and Eunice for dinner just after the handover, but ever since then he had kept a slight distance. 'I'm not Frank, Sarah.'

Sarah put down the menu with a sigh. 'I know you aren't Nick. What are you having?'

'Just a coffee.'

Sarah summoned the white-coated waiter and ordered a coffee for Nicholas and something from the menu for herself. Nicholas couldn't quite follow what she ordered because the conversation suddenly lurched into Mandarin, which she had studied at the London School of Oriental and African Studies. She often joked to him that she preferred the three tones of Mandarin to the nine tones of the Cantonese dialect: one mistaken inflection and she was telling someone to do something completely unspeakable to their relatives. 'So what do I owe this pleasure?'

Nicholas took a sip of his water. He had a feeling that Sarah was expecting something else from this rendezvous, something to do with the departure of Frank.

'I've just had a meeting with your boss.' He placed both his hands on the table.

Sarah gave him a pained look. 'And?'

Nicholas hesitated a moment. There was no one who knew Frank as well as Sarah and no one else he could rely on for advice. The waiter arrived with coffee and snacks. 'This is strictly between us.'

'Of course,' said Sarah.

Nicholas hesitated, knowing how friendly Sarah was with the much less discreet Eunice. 'As you know, Frank will exploit any occasion to score points. I thought we were going to have a pleasant chat about his new position and how good it would be to work together. However, before I knew it he had started on the difference in our management styles, and the next thing was he was telling me how well I got on with the Chinese. And when he said that, there was a sort of knowing look in his eyes – I mean about the Chinese.'

Sarah picked crumbs from the side of her mouth. 'Sounds like typical Frank to me. Any idea what he was getting at?'

There was a short silence. 'It was as if he had a particular Chinese in mind. I'm probably being paranoid but could he have been referring to Daniel?'

Sarah smiled knowingly. 'I don't think he's as well informed as that.'

'No? Then what on earth did he mean?'

Sarah sat back and watched him for a moment as if she were dealing with a particularly naïve relative. 'There's a rumour going round the office that you're having an affair. It's supposed to be with someone in Personal Banking, a married woman. I've heard it from various sources.'

Nicholas looked stunned. 'A married woman? Don't tell me they mean Grace Chu. We had a business lunch at the Ritz Carlton, but that's about it. It doesn't really qualify as an affair.'

Sarah looked at the expression on Nicholas's face and shook her head. 'It's just the kind of thing that gets round in this place. Talk about inaccurate.'

Nicholas ran his hand through his hair. 'I suppose I ought to be thankful. At least they think I'm heterosexual.'

Sarah laughed. 'If only they knew.'

Nicholas smiled back. 'It just goes to show how easy it is to start a rumour in this place.'

Sarah nodded. 'Don't say I didn't warn you about Daniel.'

'Thanks Sarah, I appreciate it,' said Nicholas.

Sarah stared at him a moment, obviously wanting to say something else, something more supportive, but she thought better of it. 'Actually, I thought you asked me here to talk about Frank's departure,' she said, changing the subject.

Nicholas's eyes skipped from the silver sugar bowl to the long-stemmed flower holder. He wondered if he could plead an urgent phone call or a meeting with the Chairman, but one look at Sarah's face told him he had no chance. 'I'm sorry Sarah, I've some bad news. It's nothing to do with your performance but we've found a financial journalist called George Duggan to replace Frank. He's been hosting a financial programme on CNBC for the past couple of years and the Chairman insisted on a journalist with international contacts. I hope you understand. You're extremely good at your job.'

Sarah remained silent for a moment, the signs of disappointment visible on her fine features. 'You were very lucky to find him,' she said. 'He sounds just right.'

Nicholas looked at the back of his hands. Sarah was mature enough to take the disappointment and move on, but that didn't make him feel any better. He had made the right choice, but it was difficult. 'I'm sure you'll like him. You'll certainly get on with him better than with Frank.'

Sarah gazed out towards the lobby as if searching for an excuse and suddenly looked at her watch. 'Goodness, is that the time? Frank'll be asking for me.'

She reached hurriedly for the bill but even before she could pick it up, Nicholas had slapped his credit card down on the table. 'That's the least I can do.'

***

Nicholas looked down at his shirt and cursed to himself. Even in November, the slightest increase in speed was rewarded with these rolling tributaries of sweat that trickled down his body as far as his groin. When he first arrived in Hong Kong, he had been surprised to see that the Chinese always walked at such a gentle pace, with a tendency to crab-like sideways movement as if sleepwalking or bludgeoned by the sun. The only time Nicholas saw a Chinese hurry was when the doors of the MTR train opened and the younger children of large families hurled themselves across the compartment towards the steel divans. Although he was tempted to do the same himself on occasions, he very rarely hurried.

The train reached Tsim Sha Tsui station, where he maneuvered his way out through the incoming passengers before negotiating the ticket machines. By the time he was up at street level, his shirt was sticking to his back and his hands were pooled with sweat.

'Copy watch, copy watch,' said the first of a series of touts that loitered along the main drag all the way from Nathan Road to Canton Road. Money-changers, gym recruiters, Indian tailors, what the locals called 'chicken-girls', all merged in a chorus of voices driving him into the stalled traffic, out of the way of a huge Kowloon Motor Bus, towards two red taxis jostling for access to the Hyatt hotel. The touts treated him just like any other foreigner, an attitude that he found particularly infuriating. Did he look like the kind of person who was going to buy a fake Rolex or order a cheap hand-made suit? Those were for over-padded *gwailos* from Bangkok or some other Lotus Eater paradise.

At last he reached Canton Road and could make out the stars above the neon signs for the Big Boss Club and Sammy's Kitchen. He glanced to right and left. The pedestrian subway would lead him safely to the Great Eagle Hotel or he could take his chances and jump the traffic lights.

The pedestrian crossing light was still blinking as he turned from Canton Road into Peking Road and reached the glass doors of the hotel. Grabbing the gilt-embossed handles, he entered the marble lobby and stopped for a moment to let his body absorb the air-conditioning. He readjusted his tie in the huge eagle-topped mirror, ran a hand through his tangled hair and buttoned his suit jacket so that his shirt would not be visible. Walking at a more measured pace, he ascended the marble steps into the lobby and looked round for Daniel. There was no immediate sign of him. Nicholas was about to take out his phone when he saw a hand waving at him beyond the brown velvet drapes. A waitress wearing a black crushed silk *cheong-sam*, her hair pulled back in a ponytail, ushered him towards Daniel's armchair.

Nicholas plonked himself down, ordered a glass of wine and fell back in his seat. Hotel lounges may not be to Daniel's liking but they were to his. Something about the plump Filipino pianist in his glistening suit playing Sondheim's 'Little Night Music', something about the huge chandeliers in the lobby, the pink-veined marble pillars, the sheeny sofa cushions and those Parisian brothel drapes soothed his nerves.

'Had a good day?' asked Daniel, fingering a plastic file on the low round table next to him.

'Yes,' said Nicholas as the glass of Chardonnay arrived. He was tired and all he wanted to do was chill out.

Daniel flicked some peanuts into his mouth. 'Anything interesting?'

Nicholas took a long sip of his wine. 'Not much, except a rumour's going around.' Nicholas gazed over towards the piano, where a slim elegant Filipina dressed in a red cocktail dress was just settling onto her stool. 'Apparently I'm having an affair with a married woman, Grace Chu in Personal Banking.'

'What?' Daniel stopped his glass halfway to his mouth. 'You're cheating on me with my boss? What a disgusting *gwailo* you are. What're you going to do about it?'

'Nothing,' said Nicholas, continuing to look around. 'Just let them talk. If people at work think I'm heterosexual, I'm not going to call a press conference.'

Daniel picked up the file with a slightly grim smile, fiddled with his glasses and began to flick through the papers. 'You would if it was a man.'

Nicholas smiled politely. He had been through this with Daniel many times before. He had explained that he wouldn't talk about his sexuality with anyone, especially anyone in United International – and he had only broken the rule with Sarah. 'I don't want to be forced into coming out, certainly not by rumours.'

Daniel sighed. 'The gossip will only grow, especially if you encourage it.' He groped for the file of papers on the table and handed them to Nicholas. 'I've been spending some time on the internet.'

'I can see that,' said Nicholas, wearily looking over the file that Daniel passed him. The cover page was headed *The Unmarried Persons' Concession for Non-European Partners*. He let his eyes run over the chapter headings: an endless list of legal definitions and strange titles. And yet the more he looked down it the less he could understand what any of it was about.

Daniel pushed his glasses up his nose. 'I printed it out at work without anyone seeing.'

Nicholas smiled at the idea of Daniel making secret photocopies in the office. 'Do I have to deal with it now?'

A look of irritation crossed Daniel's face. 'No, of course not. You just have to know the details. The most important thing is how to get qualified.'

Nicholas summoned the pony-tailed waitress and ordered another glass of Chardonnay. His unease over Frank's comments had transferred itself to this file in his hand. He was impressed with Daniel's research, but the transfer to London was still not fully confirmed. True, Sir John Williams had contacted him to say the Board would soon vote on Sir John's proposal, and it was almost a foregone conclusion. He had felt confident enough to go to a Mandarin Oriental property exhibition with Daniel and make an offer on a flat in London's Docklands. But he didn't intend to proceed any further until everything was settled. 'You go so fast Daniel. The law's only just been passed.'

'Daniel leaned back in his seat with his legs akimbo. 'That's all the more reason to get on with it. Maybe they'll change their mind.'

Nicholas grunted; Daniel may have a point.

'Someone's got to do it. You're always so busy,' continued Daniel non-plussed. 'We've got to prove that we've lived together. The current cohabitation rule is four years.'

Nicholas put a finger to his temple. 'So what's the hurry?'

Daniel turned another page of the document. 'It says here that the law's going to be changed. The government intends to relax the co-residence requirement to two years. We can finish the second year in London.'

Nicholas nodded as if still not quite convinced, although he admired Daniel's determination. 'What else does it say?'

Daniel turned another page. 'They're going to need testimony of friends and family.'

Nicholas knew he could rely on Sarah. Eunice would support him too, and probably most of the Red Brigade, but that meant he would have to tell them. 'I can think of at least one friend.'

Daniel's pen hovered over the document. 'What about family?'

'My mother,' said Nicholas and an image of Emily's shocked face popped into his mind.

Daniel rose in his seat. 'I haven't even met your mother. She doesn't even know I exist.'

Nicholas attempted another smile. 'That moment will come Daniel.'

Daniel picked up a page from the table and handed it to him. 'U.K. immigration wants evidence of commitment, both documentary and non-documentary.'

Nicholas surveyed the page, wondering if he should have another Chardonnay. How like the Home Office to come up with something that read like Kafka's *The Castle*. First of all it was called a 'Concession' when it was quite obviously referring to the basic right of any country's citizen to live together with his or her partner. Secondly, there was no real recognition of the concept of either gay or lesbian. The 'Concession' only referred to the 'unmarried', which by definition could mean just about anybody. 'I expect we'll have to show them that we can come at the same time.'

A malicious twinkle stirred in Daniel's eyes. 'Why don't we send our underwear through the post? That's what they do in Japan.'

The young waitress approached. Nicholas took one look at Daniel's expression and decided to ask for the bill. 'I'll look into it.'

Daniel seemed ready to explode. 'No, *they'll* look into it.'

Nicholas lay back and let Daniel's high spirits flow over him. One of the things that most attracted him about Daniel was his realism. He often thought of Daniel and his friends as pirates beneath their veneer of Western sophistication. They worked hard, they played hard, and they swore hard. Daniel called *chaw hau* ('dirty talk') the national language of Hong Kong. Sometimes Nicholas sat in the back of a cab with Daniel, astonished at the sheer profusion of Cantonese swear words coming at him from radio talk show, intercom and driver and Daniel on the phone. And yet the Cantonese appeared completely unperturbed by this flood of expletives.

'Let's not pretend you were a virgin Daniel, not when you met me. I don't think their requirements stretch that far.'

'What do you mean?' said Daniel with mock astonishment. 'At least I'm not pretending I'm straight.'

Chapter 7

Nicholas stood on the topmost floor of United International headquarters in New Change Street feeling slightly disoriented. Perhaps it was the build-up to Christmas – the gritted-teeth gaiety in the department stores, the incessant carol muzak, the chefs on TV competing to prepare the most insanely complicated and over-decorated Christmas lunch. But there was something about London that made him feel like a visitor from another planet. People did not automatically shove him out of the way at taxi queues or cut viciously in front of him to sit on the available seats in the Underground. There was competition for seats but it wasn't cut throat. It wasn't do-or-die like in Hong Kong. Perhaps he was exaggerating but the city seemed to lack that essential winner-takes-all attitude that came with living in a society caught between the extremes of sudden riches and equally sudden poverty, a society full of people who had made it from nothing and who often came from nowhere.

From his perch, he gazed down on the huddled figures moving through the rain-blackened streets in pursuit of last minute Christmas bargains. Those figures bent against the wind seemed to hold to their path without any particular will power, as if they could just as easily have turned back and gone the other way. Ever since he had arrived back in London he had noticed the same thing in the shops and the banks. The services were all in place, but somehow they lacked the urgency, the desire to sell, the fierce determination to clinch the deal. No doubt he had been in Hong Kong too long but something about his return to London made him uneasy. He imagined that this feeling would evaporate as soon as he was confirmed in his new Board position, which made it all the more imperative to meet the man who was talking to the Group Chairman just across the lobby from where he was standing.

If he turned his body just a little to one side, he could glimpse Eddie's tall bulky figure through the half-blinded window of his vault-like office. He could make out the slicked white hair, the arrow-straight parting, the vaguely military bearing of someone who had been an intelligence officer in Malaya at the time of the Communist insurgency. He wondered if Eddie went to any of the usual Christmas events, like carol concerts at the Royal Festival Hall and *Swan Lake* and pantomimes at the Old Vic with his grandchildren. Did he sit next to his wife at the Christmas tree and listen to King's College Choir on Christmas Eve? He tried to imagine this man, famous for his acerbic put-downs, leaning his head back in an armchair and closing his eyes to *Angels from the Realms of Glory*. It wasn't easy. He rather doubted that Eddie gave himself a single day off in the entire year. And if he did, it was probably to devote himself to a round of golf and whiskies with his closest business chums.

Sir John had been talking with Eddie for some time now, ever since the end of the Board Meeting, which had at least given Nicholas some time to prepare what he wanted to say. The Chairman and Directors had approved in principle his newly created position as Special Adviser to the Board. If Sir John hadn't been coming out of the room at the same moment as the Group Chairman, Nicholas would have been able to find out exactly what this meant.

He fingered his tie. He was wearing his usual Saint Laurent suit with a grey silk shirt but he felt more uncomfortable than usual. He watched Sir John's hands as he explained something to the Chairman.

'Thank you, Eddie. Yes, we'll meet again soon,' said Sir John, who was backing his way into the lobby in front of the Chairman's door.

He could make out Eddie standing with one hand on the desk and the other raised in ironic salute as he waved goodbye. Then he was lost to view as he bent towards the large console on his desk.

Sir John turned to Nicholas with an amused expression on his face. With his tall frame, carefully trimmed horseshoe of grey hair and square tinted glasses over a slightly hooked nose, he looked like an old Hollywood character actor. He was wearing a dark serge waistcoat, just as he had worn in Hong Kong when he came to the last Board meeting.

'Waiting for me?' he asked. 'The Chairman was in a good mood. Must be the results season. Says you'll be even more use to him over here than in Hong Kong, especially for this takeover business with Mercantile. Shall we talk in your office?'

Nicholas wondered about taking him to Laskey's Wine Bar but then thought better of it. The subject was likely to be confidential and it was bitterly cold outside. 'Yes, I had an earful of that this morning. We have to be careful to call it a merger, on the principle that all United growth is organic.' He smiled. 'We're just a good fit.'

Sir John looked at him over his glasses. 'It's going to be a major acquisition. The press will be fascinated. Even more so, if they sniff anything about moving our Headquarters.'

'Yes,' said Nicholas, leading the way with one hand in his jacket pocket and the other holding the minutes of the Board Meeting. 'But after 1997 I think we can handle anything.'

'That reminds me.' They were approaching Nicholas's office at the far end of the corridor. 'I have something rather interesting for you to consider.'

Entering the office, Nicholas gestured Sir John to the leather sofa against the far wall. He closed the door quietly and sat at one end while Sir John sat at the other. There was a short pause as they looked at each other.

'Some tea?'

'No, thank you,' said Sir John.

He turned directly towards Nicholas, the flesh of his chin made taut by his collar. 'I've been talking to Eddie and he seems to think you're just right to handle this merger. You're cool-headed, you've got a good reputation with the market and you know how to handle the press. He's very much on your side.'

Sir John's light-sensitive glasses seemed to grow a shade darker. 'There's just one thing – '

Nicholas looked up, a warning like a distant rustling in the undergrowth. He could never quite make out Sir John. There was something hidden beneath the Cambridge degree, the government quangos, that immaculate office in Lincoln's Inn Fields that seemed far too large for a boutique PR company. Even though they had worked together in many moments of crisis, Nicholas still felt that he didn't really know him.

'I don't want to make an issue out of it but there've been some rumours flying about. Eddie couldn't help hearing them.' Nicholas tried not to alter his expression but Sir John was watching him closely. 'Nothing very serious. He just asked me to give you a word of advice.'

Nicholas wondered which version Eddie had heard. If it was the same one as Sarah's, it would have been interesting to hear what Eddie had to say.

Sir John looked down at his trouser leg and picked away at a speck of white fluff. 'It's often a problem with people on the way up.'

Nicholas assumed a mock-serious expression. 'I'm sorry it got as far as Eddie.'

Sir John waved a ringed hand. 'Rumours always find their way to the top. As I say, Eddie is not particularly bothered as long as it's all cleared up. An occasional liaison is perfectly permissible in the right circumstances. But now that you are returning to London and a rather exalted position, you'll have to protect yourself. Gossip like this can be harmful, however ill-founded.'

Nicholas smiled, wondering if he should deny it. But that would only make things more complicated.

'You see, it's not your new position with us that worries me, it's what I have in mind for you,' continued Sir John. 'Assuming your professional record is spotless, which I'm sure it is, you may be just the person a certain member of the government is looking for.'

Nicholas felt a sudden jolt. This wasn't quite what he expected.

'As you know, a cabinet reshuffle is coming up and the outcome will almost certainly be a new Chancellor of the Exchequer. Roger Yates will be taking on board a whole new team of advisers. In particular, he's looking for a communications director with strong experience in the private sector, someone who can handle the relationship between the City and the Treasury. This adviser will also be the point person for some very delicate liaison with the press and stakeholders over the Treasury's plans for public services.'

Nicholas raised his gaze to settle on one of the fingers of Sir John's left hand. It was trembling.

'Successful performance in the role might eventually lead to an advisory position at the very highest level. Of course, if I were to recommend you to Roger, I might have to ask you for rather more in the way of discretion. Not that I'm suggesting these rumours were true. I'm just suggesting…'

Nicholas was hardly listening. The naming of the Chancellor had set his mind off on a dizzying trajectory of achievement. Roger Yates was an unashamed supporter of the state and therefore of public services, but he was also extremely keen on balancing the books. A self-styled ordinary man with a working class background, he would nevertheless need the support of city institutions like UIB to carry out his proposed reforms.

'I must thank you, Sir John. If the opportunity presents itself I'll certainly be interested,' said Nicholas.

Sir John looked at him sharply. 'The opportunity *has* presented itself Nicholas. All you have to do is to extricate yourself from whatever it is in Hong Kong that's entangled you. That's one of Eddie's conditions. As you know, when you work with Roger Yates you'll be under rather more scrutiny than you are now – .'

'Of course,' said Nicholas.

Sir John looked slightly embarrassed by his outburst. 'I'm sorry but Eddie always likes to play it safe.'

Nicholas paused for a moment, trying to decide how best to handle this. He couldn't very well say that the rumour was nonsense because nevertheless there was a very small element of truth in it. He *was* involved with someone in Hong Kong. On the other hand, if Sir John or Eddie found out whom that the person was, he would truly be asking for trouble. 'No need to worry.'

Sir John sat back and loosened two buttons on his waistcoat. 'As you know, the Mercantile merger will be announced at the upcoming Annual General Meeting. I don't imagine Roger will need to finalise your position until after that, so we have time to prepare the ground. However, I've done some preliminary work.'

Nicholas tried to imagine what this 'preliminary work' was. They had all been so keen to have him in London that it had not occurred to him to ask himself why the urgency.

Sir John seemed to be reading his thoughts. 'I'm not worrying you I hope. I know you have a lot on your hands.' He got up and moved towards the door. 'We can talk about this later. Suffice to say for now that you're in with a very good chance with Roger Yates and indeed with the Group Chairman.'

Nicholas hurried to join him, wondering if he should add anything. 'Thank you Sir John. I hope I won't disappoint.'

Sir John looked at him in that caustic, slightly condescending way that Nicholas knew well. Then they shook hands and Sir John took his leave.

Nicholas watched Sir John's broad back recede down the corridor and closed the door. Moving slowly towards his desk, he stood stock still for a moment and looked at the mountain of documents piled there. He picked up the phone and put it down. Then he walked round his desk and went over to the blinds, running his fingers up and down them so that they made an odd, clattering noise against the windowsill. Finally, he slammed the blinds still and snapped them closed. He had to get out of there; he needed somewhere to think. He turned to look at the door, took another deep breath, and headed straight for the corridor.

***

The taxi reached E14. He paid off the driver, crossed the road to the estate agents and picked up the keys to his new apartment. Arriving at the sandstone building, he took the lift up to the top floor, unlocked the newly varnished door and stepped inside. Turning on the lights, he moved rapidly through the echoing rooms towards the terrace.

Opening the door quickly with the new key, he stepped out. For a moment the chill wind took his breath away but slowly he became used to it. He could make out the small greenish dome of the Royal Observatory on the far hill, its edges indistinct against the lowering grey clouds. He turned back into the room to find the binoculars he had left there on his last visit and fiddled with the focus until he had the Observatory within his sight. He moved the binoculars slowly over the dome and half-smiled to himself.

From that far rising ball countless captains had set their quadrants to steer their ships around the globe, men of action and daring, men who charted their lives by the course of the stars. In the process they had created one of the greatest trading empires the world had ever seen. He moved his binoculars further round the low horizon. In front of the silhouetted towers of the City, he could see the silver triangular peak of One Canada Square belching out clouds of steam like some man-made Matterhorn. The contemporary versions of those 'masters of the universe' were right there, on trading floors and in open-plan offices filled with computer screens and Bloomberg monitors and telephone consoles. They probably couldn't tell one star in the firmament from another, but that didn't stop their global ambitions. They were at the heart of the City, the *imperium mercatus liberalis*, the hub of its all-conquering market makers. They were the creators of its new-fangled derivatives and credit swaps and a thousand new instruments that were being invented by the day.

And yet none of this felt foreign to him. This was the world to which he now belonged. This was where he was intended to be. He had made a compact between himself and this *crux polis*, and there was no way he was going back on it. As a matter of fact, part of what Roger Yates and his colleagues in government was offering were laws that encouraged people like him to take part in the sleight of hand: by living discreetly with their male partners, for example. All he had to do was observe his part of the pact and keep his mouth shut.

He took out his cell phone, wondering who should be the first to hear his news. Emily? Perhaps not. He would have to tell his mother about this expensive flat he had bought, which was not difficult in itself. But once that was done, she would slip into her usual enquiries as to how much it had cost, how much he had to borrow, how much it was likely to gain. Above all, he would have to come clean about who was going to share it with him. He looked for another number on the automatic speed dial.

'*Wei*?' Daniel's voice sounded as distant as it was.

'I'm standing on the terrace. Want to come over and take a look?'

There was a long pause on the line. 'Aren't you coming here for Christmas? I thought that's what you said.'

'I know it's what I said.' He *had* planned to go to Hong Kong for Christmas but that was before he had heard about Roger Yates' plans. If everything went ahead, he would have to complete on the sale as soon as possible and move his stuff in. 'A lot's been going on. I've got to be on hand here.'

Nicholas heard a sound like the fold of a wave, and then Monkey Head screeching in the background followed by Daniel's voice in Cantonese telling him to shut up. Finally, with a sigh, Daniel returned to the phone. 'Look Nicholas, we've spent months living apart. What's a few more weeks? If you can't come, we'd better leave it for now. By the way, have you talked to your mother?'

Nicholas looked at his watch. Daniel never missed an opportunity to ask about Emily. 'I'm waiting for the right moment. I just wanted to know your schedule.'

'We'll need her testimony,' said Daniel. 'And you'd better tell her before I get over there and start to answer the phone.'

Nicholas closed his eyes. 'It's under control.'

'Human Resources says I can still get my job back,' said Daniel.

Nicholas stood up straight. 'Okay, okay, I'll get it sorted in the next few days. You can come in on a tourist visa first.'

There was a sound of laughter on the other end of the phone. 'To be asked about how long I'm staying or how much money I've got?

'They're much more relaxed now,' said Nicholas, although he knew very well they weren't. A friend of Daniel had recently been held at Dover when returning from Paris on his British National Overseas passport. His boyfriend had to go to Dover in person to prove that he wasn't lying. 'I've told you Daniel, I can arrange it once you're here. If we can't apply first, you can study for a while until we can.'

'Very reassuring.'

'Look, I'll give you another call tomorrow. I've got to go.'

'Okay,' said Daniel and to Nicholas's slight irritation, he rang off before Nicholas could add anything else.

He stood there a moment, uncertain whether to call Emily. Better leave it, he decided. That monotone voice of hers would hone in on any vague statement about having a boyfriend. He would have to be ready with Daniel's age, the fact that he was Chinese, their compatibility, how long they had been going out.

Above all, he would have to explain why on earth he hadn't told her. It would be better for him to call his sister Kay in Shropshire. She always knew the best way to handle his mother.

Chapter 8

Daniel could see Matt Wong's squat, slightly portly figure next to the enormously tall and elegantly decorated Christmas tree on the air-conditioned ground floor of Pacific Place. In front of the dangling gold baubles a choir of Chinese schoolchildren in red ties, cream shirts and blue jerseys was singing *'Oh! You better watch out, You better not cry'* while crowds of shoppers looked down on them from the circular balustrades on the floors above. Daniel quickened his pace. He had been looking forward to seeing Matt ever since his friend had returned from London.

'Hi,' said Daniel.

Matt turned with a wry smile and broke into a stream of Cantonese, which Daniel interrupted. 'English. I've got to speak that most of the time.'

'Where do you want to go?'

'Shopping. I need a winter coat.'

Matt pondered for a moment as if shopping for clothes was similar to fielding customer complaints at London's Gatwick airport, where he worked as a baggage handler. Daniel watched him, thinking how grown-up he looked these days. And yet beneath the veneer of sophistication he could still make out the adolescent who had dressed them both in drag when they were fifteen and who had a string of adoring men friends. 'It's expensive round here.'

Daniel pointed to the gleaming black and gold lettering of the nearby department store. 'They've got a sale on. I've seen a long coat. Want to take a look?'

'Okay.' Matt wrinkled his eyebrows. 'I can play husband.'

Daniel laughed. 'Nicholas never has time for shopping. The only place he goes for clothes is the nearest men's shop to United, and definitely not with me.'

Matt sidestepped the make-up girls who were prowling the entrance to the store like restless zombies and gave Daniel a puzzled look. 'Why not?'

'It's supposed to be a big secret. At least I told *someone* about us at work. You remember Pauline Wong?'

'Mortgages?' said Matt. It was three years since he had left United International and moved to the U.K. His mother had married a retired divorcee in Haverfordwest and set up a fish and chip shop in the High Street. It didn't take Matt long to escape from that to a job at Gatwick Airport, nor to file an application for naturalisation.

'You told her about Nicholas or you told her you were gay?' They had reached the menswear section, where a stick-like male assistant with orange hair was critically observing their progress.

'I didn't tell her about Nicholas directly. She was always talking about her love life and I gave her some advice from my own experience. I suppose she put two and two together.'

Matt looked at the price tag on the back of the long, beige woollen coat that Daniel had put on. 'Not cheap.'

Daniel gazed at himself in the long mirror. 'But it hangs well.'

'I guess so...'

Daniel turned round and grinned at his friend. 'If you've got it flaunt it, right?'

'Unlike Nicholas,' said Matt.

'*M'goy*.' Daniel allowed the orange-haired assistant to help him off with the coat. 'What do you think, should I go with him to London or should I stay?'

Matt shrugged. 'Do you have to decide right now?'

'No, but what do you think?'

Matt took off his glasses, breathed on them and cleaned them with his handkerchief. He then put them back on and sucked in his cheeks. 'I reckon you've got two choices. Either you take the coat and you can still use it, or you don't take the coat.'

Daniel stuck his hands in his jeans and looked at his feet. 'I didn't mean that.' He nodded at the assistant. 'I'll take it.'

Once the purchase was made and the coat was in its carrier bag, Daniel led Matt out of the store and back into the crowds that thronged Pacific Place. The whole world seemed to be out Christmas shopping. At first Daniel thought about sitting down in a coffee shop, but he soon realised that was impossible. 'What about the Marriott?' he said, turning to Matt.

'Too expensive,' said Matt. 'How about 1997?'

Daniel's pulse quickened. For most of the week, Club 1997 was a straight club but on Friday nights it hosted a special gay evening from 6 pm to 9 pm. In the days before Nicholas, Daniel had visited it quite a lot and on one occasion he had met an Australian there who took him back to his room at the Marriott. Daniel could still see the red-and-gold striped cushions, the odd triangular windows, the King-size bed on which they had performed in full view of the *Queen Elizabeth II* anchored in Victoria Harbour. But once it was over, the Australian had got up and said he had to go because his wife was expecting him.

Daniel looked at his watch. 'Is that such a good idea?'

Matt broke into a smile. 'It's the Friday before Christmas and I've got no one. Your husband's in London. You're in a bad mood. What's not good about it?'

'I'm not in a bad mood,' said Daniel. 'It's just that I haven't been there for ages.'

'Neither have I,' said Matt. 'If we go now we can get a seat.'

Daniel hesitated. Part of him wanted to go and have some fun. Another part of him said that the Australian was fairly typical of the *gwailos* who went in there. He always seemed to end up with the wrong sort. 'I guess Nicholas won't know.'

'Not unless he phones,' grinned Matt mischievously. 'Then you can say you're at a straight party drinking Becks and watching football. Anyway, you're not imprisoned.'

Daniel laughed. The idea of Nicholas phoning in the middle of his workday was unlikely. Besides, he was only going to have a drink and a chat. 'Okay, *jow-la.*'

The taxi deposited them outside Club 1997 where a tall thin guy with purple-rimmed glasses gave them leaflets for the Chinese Tonghzhi '(Comrades') Association and a schedule for Sunday Hikes. They stepped through the door into the interior, all tassels and baubles like a Moroccan kasbah, and reviewed the room. A fractured silver ball spun over the dance area, where an occasional young Chinese in tight T-shirt and stone-washed jeans leaned his elbows on the wooden balustrade and swayed his hips. Several of the seats around the central bar were empty but Daniel indicated an alcove on the far side of the room. A friendly young Filipina came over and took their orders: beer for Daniel, Margarita for Matt.

'So what's the big deal?' asked Matt as they waited for their drinks to arrive.

Daniel frowned, feeling awkward. 'It's no big deal. We've been together almost a year. Everything's fine, except that we can never seem to have a normal life together. I've been trying to get him to find out the details about these new partnership laws in the U.K. He knows someone in the Home Office who can help, but whenever I ask him what he's done about it he says he's been busy.'

Matt put his hands behind his head. His slight paunch rose as he leaned back on the cushions. '*Gwailos* are like that. They're always busy. Look at those two.' He nodded towards two Caucasians with their suit jackets slung over their shoulders, propping up the bar and looking in their direction. 'I bet they come here once a week, score with the youngest guy available, and get on their business flights on Monday as if nothing has happened.'

Daniel made a faint clucking sound. 'I know what you're trying to say. They just fit us into their schedules. But I had a good job until Nick made me give it up. It's not that they've got jobs and we haven't, it's just that it's all about them.'

'Sounds like Nick is a bit into himself,' said Matt, taking the first sip of his Margarita.

Daniel looked around the bar. 'He's bought a flat, which I'm pleased about,' he said in a low voice. 'But sometimes it seems like he's too important for the practical things. It's me that's got to find out about the partnership law, me who's got to find a place to meet because he's too scared to take me to his place. I'm not expecting him to shout it from the rooftops but he hasn't even told his mother.'

'And have you told yours?' asked Matt, popping some chips into his mouth and looking in the direction of the *gwailos*.

Daniel swigged his beer straight from the bottle. 'Maybe she knows, maybe she doesn't. You know what it's like. I think my sisters know but no one says anything, even though Nick was half-living with us for a while.'

'I expect he'll get round to it,' said Matt, smiling at one of the Caucasians, who wore horn rims and a brightly coloured tie.

Daniel glanced over at the bar. 'CNBC financial news,' said Matt, his expression unchanging. 'I've seen him before.'

'Oh?' Daniel wasn't particularly interested, but when he next looked up he saw that the Caucasian was indicating him to his companion, a muscular blond man he faintly recognised.

'One of yours?' said Matt.

Daniel leaned back behind Matt's shoulders. The man had taken up a strategic position directly in their sight lines. 'Nick and I aren't just dating you know.'

Matt raised an eyebrow. 'That hasn't stopped you in the past has it?'

Daniel took another sip of beer, trying to re-gather the thread of the conversation. 'I guess Chinese are better at acceptance than talk. The trouble with *gwailos* is that they seem to like talking but they can't easily accept difference. Even though I'm going to London, Nicholas's still acting as if I'm someone he's picked up in a bar.'

Matt assumed a mock-serious expression. 'Which you couldn't possibly be.'

Daniel shook his head. 'I've done all the hiding I want to. I agreed to it for his sake. But now I just want us to be normal – '

'Can I get you a drink?' interrupted the man with horn rims and bright tie, hovering at the edge of their alcove.

'I'll have a Margarita,' said Matt.

'What about your friend?' The soft-spoken man looked straight at Daniel. 'I think my colleague knows you.' He indicated the blond muscular guy still sitting on the far side of the bar.

'I'm okay,' said Daniel.

'He'll have a Becks,' said Matt confidentially. 'He's just shy.'

'Great,' laughed the man, stretching the crow's feet at the corner of his eyes. 'I'm George.'

'Matt,' He leaned forward to shake George's hand. 'This is Daniel.'

'Nice to meet you,' said George. 'Care to join us?'

Matt glanced at Daniel and then at the far side of the bar, which was now filling up with Caucasians in shirtsleeves and Chinese guys in weekend gear of faded jeans torn at the knee, baseball caps and sneakers. 'It's getting crowded.' He looked at Daniel and then at George. 'You could come and join us. There's room for a chat, isn't there Daniel?'

Daniel nodded weakly.

'Great,' said George and headed back towards his companion.

'What are you doing?' said Daniel in a dull monotone.

Matt took another sip of his drink. 'I said for a chat. I don't know about you but I'm getting horny.'

Daniel sighed. 'I thought you only liked Latinos.'

'He'll do for tonight.' Matt giggled. 'What's wrong with you?'

'I have a partner.'

Matt's eyes flashed. He tucked up one of his legs under the other and surveyed the bar. 'Sounds like he's a ball and chain. If you ask me, you could do with some fun. Forget the partner for now.'

Daniel said nothing but watched the two men pushing their way through the dense throng around the bar. Perhaps Matt was right. Perhaps that was exactly what was wrong between them. They needed some space. After all, the simplest way to get him to pay more attention would be to show some independence.

Soon they were all sitting close together in the same alcove and Matt was deep in conversation with George. The blond guy introduced himself as 'Mike' and then for some reason sat back and simply stared at him.

'Guess what George does,' said Matt, turning to Daniel.

Daniel raised a polite eyebrow. 'I don't know.'

'I've just started at United International,' said George. Matt shot Daniel a rapid glance. 'You know somebody there?'

Daniel considered lying but then his expression hardened. 'Nicholas Powell. Do you know him?'

'He's my boss,' said George and nervously brushed some crumbs from his trousers. 'Don't tell me you're his boyfriend.'

Daniel's heart thumped against his ribs. It would have been simple to come out with it. 'I don't think Nicholas has boyfriends.'

George's skin seemed to darken, although it was difficult to tell in the light from the bar. There was a silence, broken only by George's hesitant cough. 'Matt says you used to work in United International.'

'That's right,' said Daniel, and made a big show of looking at his watch. 'Hey, I have to go. Maybe catch up later.' He got up quickly but as he rose he gave Matt a meaningful look, indicating his cell phone.

George also rose. 'Don't take what I said seriously,' he added with a weak laugh. 'I have a habit of shooting my mouth off.'

Daniel waved a careless goodbye. 'Don't worry,' he said and slipped through the side curtains and out onto the street.

Walking quickly through the crowds surrounding the heaving bars, he told himself to take a deep breath. If it had gone on any longer, the whole thing would have come out. Not that it made the slightest difference to him, but he knew that Nick hated that kind of gossip and George was apparently one of his latest appointments. 'Fuck it,' he muttered to himself. He shouldn't have to be so secretive.

He stood for a moment at the corner of Lan Kwai Fong and Pedder Street wondering what to do next. If he headed west, he could follow the steps up Wellington Street to the moving escalator that led to Mid-Levels. There was a gay sauna and steam place up there, a mixed club for Caucasians and Chinese that stood conveniently next to the main thoroughfare to the SoHo restaurants. That would be a away of marking his independence, and Nick wouldn't have to know anything about it.

But the more he thought about it, the less attractive it seemed. It was alright to go and get his rocks off, but he knew he wouldn't feel good afterwards – however anonymous it was. The past was the past, and he'd had as good a time as anyone being free of responsibility. But all he'd been really trying to do was find someone. And now he *had* found someone, there really wasn't much point in going back. His best bet was to go home and play around in the internet chat rooms. It was safe and there was quite a nice Dutch guy in Outpersonals last time, 'hothotguy1', who had talked extremely dirty and then given him a guided tour of Amsterdam and a rundown of what the Dutch ate for breakfast.

Chapter 9

They huddled together like three excited children as they watched the big red shining letters on their gold background going up over the Senso Building's lower facade. It was cool in the wind that blew straight in from the harbour, but nothing like as cold as London. Nicholas had learnt enough basic Chinese calligraphy from Daniel to pick out *Kung Hei* from the celebratory sentence, and even if he didn't remember the letters for *Fat Choy* he knew what was coming in the rest of the fringed panels. That same wish for the blessings of 'Seaweed', the symbol of wealth, was going up all over Hong Kong, accompanied by shaggy-mouthed dragons, men in black caps and red Chinese gowns, and huge Gods of Prosperity for the Year of the Dragon.

'Last year, I wanted to have a rabbit for the Year of the Rabbit. But they wouldn't allow it,' joked Nicholas to Sarah and Eunice.

Sarah turned to him. 'They probably thought a pair of floppy ears would upset Beijing.'

Nicholas laughed. He had been only too glad to accept their invitation for a Friday night drink, although he felt a bit guilty that they had to wait so long for him to finish a series of calls to London and New York, a short briefing with the CEO, and several memos concerning the rapidly approaching merger with Mercantile. Chinese New Year was not a holiday; indeed, it looked like five days in the office. A drink with friends was just what he needed.

'Glad to see you laugh. You've been looking so stressed recently,' said Eunice, taking his arm and leading him towards the traffic lights. 'Don't you think so, Sarah?'

'Yes,' said Sarah warily. Although she and Eunice were good friends, Sarah was conscious that Eunice's outbursts of solidarity were usually followed by waves of complaint about Jeanette Long or some other offending manager.

'The problem is trying to coordinate the two companies so that everyone is reading from the same script. I've got a pile of papers in here for the weekend,' Nicholas said and lifted his briefcase.

'How's it going?' said Sarah, holding him back a little as they proceeded towards the Captain's Bar. 'I mean with the transfer.'

Nicholas turned to her. 'Daniel's over in London and we've moved in to the new flat. I've asked the Home Office and we can begin the application now. The trouble is we don't know how long the whole thing will take. He won't be able to leave the U.K. until it's all sorted out.'

'But that's not for ever,' shrugged Sarah.

'No, but...'

Nicholas felt Sarah's eyes on him. He wanted to say that he could just about take being on his own in Hong Kong but sometimes he had the urge, late at night when he was alone after the office. It was a stupid urge he knew, but it was an urge nonetheless.

'You know, I had to put up with living on my own when Anthony was away. I just learned to call up friends and enjoy the freedom. At least no one tells you to take your feet off the sofa.'

Nicholas smiled as they moved through the lobby. Sarah always hit the right note. It was more than six weeks since he had returned to Hong Kong and he was feeling increasingly impatient at the 6,000 or so miles that stood between him and some form of intimacy. He missed Daniel, missed him with a fierce longing that made him sometimes stop in the street. Hong Kong was not the same without him. It was particularly ironic that the legal requirements of their being together were now likely to ensure that they were apart for the foreseeable future. The telephone and the e-mail were his main source of company.

Eunice had moved ahead into the rugby scrum of suits and cigars at the Captain's Bar, but Sarah held him back. 'You know, there are other things in life than work. I shouldn't think you could go much further in United International.'

He said nothing. He hadn't told anyone about Sir John's future plans and this was not the moment. He had never seen such a mountain of work as that involved in persuading shareholders and the press that United International's merger with Mercantile was not a hostile takeover. The publications, circulars to shareholders and press releases for the Annual General Meeting were enough to fill a lorry.

'What will it be, Nicholas?' shouted Eunice from the midst of the scrum. Men in suits with loosened ties stood three deep at the L-shaped bar, their companions crushed between them.

'A dry white wine,' he replied. He usually stuck to mineral water these days, scared that an unguarded word or two could compromise everything. Even here in the festive Mandarin Hotel, there was a chance that a journalist or a United analyst was lurking.

They found a table against the wall as Eunice pushed through the crowd with their drinks. 'You have to be Superwoman in here,' she said and placed two glasses on the table, taking the third from a red-faced gentleman in a checked suit that she had enlisted to help. 'Here's to Mercantile!'

Nicholas flinched. He left it a moment or two and then leaned over to Eunice. 'Please don't mention it in public. I'm sure you've read the memo.'

Eunice swung round, her cheeks ablaze. 'I'm sorry, Nick.'

Nicholas exchanged glances with Sarah. Both of them liked Eunice's frankness and sense of fun but they also knew she was a loose cannon. Suddenly, Nicholas caught sight of a figure at the bar that he recognised: high forehead, thinning brown hair, owlish glasses. The figure turned in their direction, waved and broke away from the small circle of drinkers that surrounded him. 'Am I interrupting?'

'We were just discussing your future,' said Nicholas and the others smiled. 'Want to join us?'

'Actually, I'm off to a Cuban Evening on The Peak. You can come if you like. I'm covering it for one of my magazines.'

Nicholas nodded non-commitally. He had allowed George to continue with his travel and food journalism when he joined up, although strictly speaking it wasn't allowed. At least it gave George an outside interest. He had no time for the high life himself but it amused him to imagine what George got up to in the evening. Whatever it was, it didn't seem to interfere with his work. He was a skilled handler of the journalists and he always looked the part of the spokesperson with his double-breasted suits and Versace ties. He had a slight lisp and a Canadian lilt to his accent, which gave him a boyish charm that worked well with outsiders, particularly women.

Sarah smiled and looked embarrassed as Eunice delved into her bag. 'I don't know Nicholas...' Eunice consulted a schedule. 'I've got a man to go home to. He'll be waiting for his dinner.'

Sarah looked relieved. 'Why don't you go?' she said, turning to Nicholas. 'You need a bit of salsa.'

Nicholas shifted in his seat.

'You could do with a good night out,' said George. 'We can take a taxi. There's plenty of wine, Cuban food, music. Get some of the weight off those shoulders – '

Sarah gazed at him. Her small, compact body seemed to stiffen. 'There's nothing to stop you, is there?'

Nicholas smiled and finished his drink. He had just been complaining to Sarah that he had no company outside the office, nothing to look forward to in the evening except for work. 'Okay,

I'll have to stop off at my flat first. I can't take my briefcase with me. I'll have to change.'

'Just sling your jacket over your shoulder. People like the after-work look,' replied George.

'You make work sound like a fashion accessory,'giggled Sarah.

'You should have seen Jeanette's pashmina this morning,' said Eunice. 'Must have come from Liberty's.'

'Let's not start on the office.' Sarah rose from the table. 'Come on, we'll put you in a taxi.'

Sarah paid the bill and soon they were making their way towards the taxi stand through lines of tasseled red lanterns that were hung round the Mandarin's entrance in preparation for Chinese New Year. Huge pots of orange trees and peach blossom hung with red money packets flanked the outer doors. Sarah stared at the display as they waited their turn in the queue. 'Did you know that if a peach tree blossoms over New Year, it means that romance is in store?'

Nicholas half-turned. 'What?'

'According to Chinese belief – '

'Damn,' he shouted and ran towards the bar.

Another party was already sitting at the table where they had been but fortunately the briefcase was still there. He apologised, grabbed the handle and hurried back towards the others.

'God that was close,' he said. 'Thank goodness I noticed.'

'What've you got in it?' asked Eunice. 'The crown jewels?'

'Not quite,' said Nicholas, following George into the taxi. 'But it's not for public consumption.'

'Don't leave it at the party,' said Sarah through the open window of the taxi.

Nicholas made an exaggerated gesture of forgetfulness. 'I haven't got Alzheimer's but thank you Sarah. We'll do this again.'

'Yes, we should,' said Sarah with a crook of the head.

The taxi swerved through the mid-evening traffic and then lurched sharply right onto a curving expressway. Nicholas could see the sleek cube-and-box skyscrapers gleaming with their colorful messages of Prosperity and Happiness, the neon lights refracted on black sheets of glass that plunged towards the crowds of shoppers and commuters. As they headed towards the canyons of Mid-Levels, the rush and swirl of the traffic made him feel somehow elated. Everything about Hong Kong announced one and the same thing: not a moment must be lost, not a traffic light stopped at for a second too long, not a gap for acceleration must be left unattended. Everyone in this town was on a wild and relentless hunt. What the hunt was for no one seemed to know. But every evening as he drove up to his United apartment on Peak Road he had the same feeling. They were engaged in some sort of life-and-death struggle. In London, he would be thankful for going from A to B on a regular and well-marked route. In Hong Kong, everyone was racing straight off the cliff.

'Let's keep the taxi. I'll stay while you dump your things,' suggested George, who then leaned forward to tell the driver. 'Peak Brasserie, near Peak tram. First to Peak Road, number 99. *Gau-gau-ho, m'goy sai.*'

Nicholas smiled at George. Both of them knew enough Cantonese to get by – just.

'*Da-la,*' said the driver and waved his hand. 'Okay.'

The red Toyota pulled up to an inclined drive with a large entrance grille, beyond which was just visible the walls of a white apartment block.

'I'll stay here,' said George.

'But where are your things?'

George smiled. 'I left them at a friend's place. I'll go back for them later. I'm afraid my salary won't stretch to a place on The Peak.'

'It's not as wonderful as it looks,' said Nicholas. 'I won't be long.'

He quickly keyed in his security number and the glass door clicked open just as the security guard came to wave him in. Nicholas frowned to himself. Every time he invited anyone here, the same guard appeared from nowhere and watched him closely.

It would never have worked with Daniel. The elevator took him up to the top floor, where he exited and walked directly to the left, unlocking his door quietly just in case his neighbour, Alex Higgins of Human Resources, came out for some United gossip. He seemed programmed to do this whenever he heard Nicholas's key in the lock. Although Nicholas had become used to Alex's florid features and irreverent manner, evidence of a long love affair with the bottle, this wasn't the moment.

Once inside the spacious split-level apartment, he hurried to dump his briefcase on his desk but then thought better of it. Habits of a lifetime caused him to unlock the case and extract the papers, placing the files in correct order on his desk and laying the most urgent set of Mercantile documents, stamped *Highly Confidential*, on his typing stand. He then set the empty case on the floor and was about to walk away when he thought better of it and for some reason, returned to place a white sheet of blank paper over the first page of the Press Release. Taking a quick look in the long mirror, he decided that the jacket could go. He wondered about the cell phone and put it in his trouser pocket. It was lunchtime in the U.K. Finally, he brushed his hair, dabbed on some aftershave and was ready for the off. Closing the door quietly, he moved to the elevator.

'That's fine,' said George as he reached the taxi. He leaned forward towards the driver. '*Jow-la*, let's go.'

'Cuba will make a change to the Chairman.'

'We should both get out more,' said George.

The taxi snaked its way up the side of The Peak, between tall sugar-cake mansion blocks, theatrical boulders that seemed to have dropped from the sky just like that, and thick clusters of tropical trees. As they neared the top, Hong Kong spread itself below them like a starlet in an old Chinese film, sensuous and glittering in a multi-coloured *cheongsam*. The city pulsed and throbbed in their sight, suffused with electricity that seemed like a frenetic discharge of the desperate energy with which its seven million or so inhabitants led their lives.

'Here we are,' said George as the taxi swung into the forecourt beside The Peak Tower. Fountains splashed to one side, while to the other lay a more traditional, colonial-style building with a low hedge. The sound of Latino music thumped out against the night. Nicholas instinctively checked his cell phone: nothing.

They joined the queue of guests at the entrance to the Brasserie. The route was lined with tables on which boxes of Cuban cigars had been placed. The blonde manager immediately recognised George and they were hustled to the front. 'A table is waiting for you. Don't worry about signing in. Is this your guest?' The woman smiled at Nicholas. 'My boss actually,' said George. 'In need of R&R.'

'You'll find plenty of that here,' laughed the woman, all teeth and projection. 'We've got Cuban food and wine, every Latino drink under the sun. You'll love the buffet. Enjoy.'

They entered a long, high-ceilinged room hung round with old photos and prints of colonial Hong Kong and the Peak Tram station. As George found him a caipirinha and put a Monte Cristo in his other hand, Nicholas suddenly realised that he had not been to a party in years. Mounds of Cuban dishes were laid out on a series of white-clothed buffet tables, along with platters of cigars and clusters of wine bottles. The Latino band made a deafening noise in the enclosed space as they played *Rueda de Casino*, with the title announced on a screen above their heads. He dropped the cigar at the nearest table and signaled to George to move out onto the terrace where the sound of the salsa was more muted. Women in tight-fitting white dresses, men in dark suits or expensive designer jackets, young people with open shirts and moist laughing mouths, all stood in groups between the perfumed casuarinas and lemon trees. A stream of different languages filled the air, counter-pointed by the rapid switching of Cantonese into English and back.

'Like it?' said George, who seemed to have attracted a group of admirers. He hooked another caipirinha from a passing waiter and replaced Nicholas's empty glass. Suddenly a round American woman in her early fifties was standing beside Nicholas. She was dressed in a kaftan far too tight for her and was wearing long silver earrings. 'I'm Amanda Beaufort, food critic. Would you like to dance?'

'Not now,' said Nicholas and turned for help to George, who was grinning broadly. Amanda looked him up and down, jerked her head at George and dragged him towards the dance floor.

Nicholas stood there for a moment sipping the caipirinha that George had given him. Gradually he felt the blood rising and then, almost imperceptibly, his body began to move in rhythm to the music. The circle of admirers that George had attracted had moved out around the dance floor, but they returned every so often to the same drinks table where George had left his tequila. The members of George's circle were mainly Chinese, apart from a silver-haired man in a white tuxedo and open pink shirt who appeared to be Amanda's husband, and some mixed couples that were flirting with each other. Most of them were in their late twenties or thirties, all of them discussing the latest tips for the Hang Seng Index or the newly listed Red Chips from China, the quickest route to make a few million dollars, the best way to pluck 'the low-lying fruit'. Fast bucks. Fast sex. Fast returns. Nicholas told himself that he had little in common with them as they watched George and Amanda and commented on their display. But deep down he wasn't so sure.

Suddenly, he became aware of someone standing slightly apart from the others and looking in his direction: a Chinese in his early twenties, a bottle of Tsingdao beer held to his lips, long black hair matted and untidy. He wore a T-shirt printed with Japanese characters alongside the garbled English phrase, *You Live Like Nice Time*. Over the T-shirt he sported a lightweight green windsurfer. As he sipped his beer, his pale features visibly reddened at the edge of the eyelids and cheek line and for some reason Nicholas began to imagine that flush extending right down to his groin.

'Funny, isn't he?' he said suddenly, indicating George.

'Sort of,' said Nicholas.

The young man pushed away from the table and approached. 'Can I get you a drink?'

Nicholas put out his empty glass and the other took it. A crescent of amusement lit his eyes. 'My name's Nicholas.' He extended a slightly damp hand.

The young Chinese put down the glass and grasped it between two large dry palms. 'Call me Ray-jai.'

Nicholas's smile remained fixed. 'I'm George's boss,' he added as if this meant something.

'Yes, he told us when you came in,' said Ray and nodded in George's direction. Nicholas could see he was still very involved with Amanda.

Ray-jai was about to take Nicholas's glass but just then a couple zigzagged away from the dance floor and crashed into them, forcing Nicholas's body right up against Ray-jai's. For a second neither of them moved. Then, little by little, Ray-jai inclined towards Nicholas until Nicholas could feel his cheekbone close to his, so close that he could almost sense the blood passing beneath its surface. Nicholas tried to pull away. But as he did so something within him, something instinctive and reckless, made him lift his hand and touch Ray-jai on the cheek.

'I'll – ,' Ray-jai stood there with the bottle in his hand. ' – just go and get this.'

'Do you want me to come?' asked Nicholas.

'Why not?' said Ray-jai with a shrug.

Nicholas followed on, thinking this was a good opportunity to get away from the dance floor. No one seemed to have noticed them or their departure. He was careful to walk a few steps behind Ray-jai as they made their way to the bar, where Ray-jai ordered the drinks.

'Do you like it here?' he asked as he passed Nicholas his caipirinha. Nicholas noticed that his torn jeans revealed the white elastic top of his underwear. He was lean and muscular but not in a gym-trained sort of way. His hands suggested that he came from the rural New Territories, and yet he also wore a delicate silver band in his right ear.

Nicholas shrugged. 'I like the music but I'm not sure I want to dance to it. Not like those two.' He indicated the distant figures of George and Amanda who were still at it on the dance floor.

'Oh those,' said Ray-jai with a big grin. 'Cool aren't they?' And suddenly, without showing the slightest emotion, he reached for Nicholas's shoulder and looked him in the eye. 'You wanna dance?'

Nicholas moved his shoulder. 'I don't know, I – '

'It's Friday night. Too crowded for disco. Do you have a place to go to?'

Nicholas took a large gulp of the caipirinha. The waiters were moving rapidly around them as the dinner traffic began to build. His only hope was that by playing it slow, common sense would intervene and turn this into a lucky escape. Such escapes had a great deal of satisfaction in them, not the least being that he could go home with a clear conscience.

'What about you?'

Ray-jai smiled. 'I live on Lamma Island. Not good for someone like you.'

Nicholas cleared his throat. 'We should get something to eat.'

They made for the buffet. As they piled their plates with mango salad and Canjun chicken, Nicholas told himself that he had plenty of time to back out. He wasn't going to make any further moves. In fact, he could claim that the hand on the cheek was a simple reaction. They ate their food in silence and by the time they had finished Nicholas had begun to feel slightly better. But just as it seemed he could get up and leave, Ray-jai slipped his leg between his under the table and began to rub it up and down.

Nicholas stared hard. 'I think – '

Ray-jai stood up. 'Do you have anyone you have to say goodbye to?'

Nicholas hesitated. 'Do you?'

Ray-jai shook his head. 'Uh-uh.'

'Not even George?' Nicholas looked rather desperately around. Behind him, he noticed a group of women with their backs to him.

Ray-jai shook his head. 'He's often in the bars. I can always see him.'

Nicholas stared again at Ray-jai, trying to evaluate this fresh piece of information. George was known to Ray-jai, known in the gay bars. George probably had a couple of fucks on the weekend and then went back to work as if nothing had happened. Perhaps that was a good thing. Perhaps that's exactly what Nicholas needed: a cool fuck. Distractedly he turned his back on the new group of women diners, poured himself a glass of white wine from the bottle on the nearby table and drank it down in one go. 'I'll just go and say goodbye,' he said eventually. 'Can you wait for me at the taxi rank?'

Ray-jai collected a small rucksack that he had stowed under the table. 'See you,' he said and sauntered off.

Nicholas moved out to the dance floor, sweat beading his neck and dampening his palms. Nothing like this had happened to him before, not in Hong Kong. But as he looked around at the partying crowds, he realised that he was not alone. Beneath the perfumed canopy of jacaranda and lemon leaves, he could make out men and women with their heads softly inclined, the murmur of intimate conversation, the laughter of people who seemed to have just met but were intent on getting to know each other much better. However, he could not see George or Amanda. He was about to turn away when suddenly he noticed that a lone woman had emerged from the group at the buffet and was sitting at a table not twenty yards away, a candy-striped pashmina drawn around her. Even though she was facing the other way, he knew exactly who it was. His mouth turned dry.

Edging his way backwards, he reached a discreet position behind the double bass player. Yes it was her, probably out with some of her pals from 'Women in Business' or one of those other feminist Hong Kong groups. She had given no sign that she had seen him, but he couldn't be sure.

Maneuvering his way round the dance floor, he headed straight for the exit, but before he could make a few yards he came upon George and Amanda. Amanda was now sitting next to her husband, who was looking distinctly bored. George was talking animatedly to a slim young Chinese dressed in black silk who had his arm affectionately draped around him.

Nicholas discreetly approached. 'I have a headache George. You'll have to excuse me…'

George sat up and half-buttoned his jacket. 'Nick, I want you to meet a special friend of mine. Alan Wong, the fashion designer.'

Nicholas went through the introductions followed by a set of polite questions, but his heart was not in it. He was thinking of Ray-jai, that reddish flush extending the length of his compact body.

'By the way, did you meet Jeanette?' asked George. 'She's just over there.'

Nicholas pretended to be surprised. 'I'll have to leave that pleasure for Monday.'

George slightly coloured. 'I hope you had some fun anyway.'

'Yes, of course,' said Nicholas. 'I enjoyed it a lot.'

George smiled as if he didn't quite believe him. 'Call me in the morning if you need me. It's my Saturday off.'

Nicholas headed back through the bar and straight for the taxi where Ray-jai was already sitting in the back seat. As it moved off, he checked that his cell phone was still safely attached to his belt. If Daniel called from London, as was only too possible, he prayed it was when he was in the bathroom or within a few feet of the balcony where he could take the call.

The taxi lurched to right and left as Nicholas struggled to remember the pick-up rules. Should he say something about Daniel, or should he even bother with conversation at all?

'Just follow me,' he said to Ray-jai as he paid the driver and they got out of the taxi in front of Number 99, Lower Peak Road. There was no one around in the forecourt. Several of the apartments were dark, which was only to be expected on a Friday night. They had a good chance of getting to his place without being seen. He opened the grille and walked quickly through to the entrance door of his block, hoping that the security guard was at last off duty. His luck was in. No one appeared when he keyed in the code. No one appeared when the door clicked open. Ray-jai seemed quite unconcerned. With his black duffel bag on his shoulder, he strolled in with the air of a sailor coming home on leave. Even if Alex Higgins appeared on the landing, he would probably have given him a friendly 'Hi there'.

Both the elevator and the landing were empty. Within minutes the two of them were safely inside his apartment.

'What would you like to drink?' said Nicholas.

Ray-jai walked around the spacious lounge and then placed his duffel bag very carefully on the table leading to the back bedroom. 'Water or juice. Can I help?'

'No, no, it's okay. I've got some juice in the fridge. Have a look at the view. I'll put some music on.'

Nicholas hurried to the kitchen and found the juice and some white wine, pouring them both with a slightly shaking hand. When he came back into the room, he found Ray-jai sitting on the edge of one of the leather armchairs and looking out on the distant view of the harbour. He had found a CD of The Three Tenors and the lush orchestral introduction of *O Sole Mio* was drifting through the room. Nicholas paused in front of him for a second before handing him the juice and drinking the wine down almost in one gulp. 'Do you like it?'

'Very nice,' said Ray-jai and smiled, his face shadowed by the light of a table lamp. 'It's very big for Hong Kong.'

'Yes,' said Nicholas.

'Your company – '

But before Nicholas could say anything more, Ray-jai had risen and his lips were hard against his mouth. He could feel his tongue darting back and forth. He could taste the sharp kick of grapefruit mixed with spiced chicken and Tsingdao beer and whatever else he had consumed back at the party. Finally, both of them drew back, took a long breath and Nicholas led him to the sofa. They smiled at each other, and then without words they kissed again, gently this time. Gradually, Nicholas leaned back and let Ray-jai raise his hands to his hair, then pull his face towards him.

Nicholas held back for a moment, trying to decide whether he should or not. 'Ray-jai, I have something to tell you.' Ray-jai's smile tightened. Nicholas studied his face, thinking how easy it would have been just to plough on. There were sharp lines of experience down from his nose to the edge of his thick, rather pouting lips. 'I have a partner in London.'

'British?' said Ray-jai, without blinking.

'No, he's from Hong Kong.'

Ray-jai continued to stare as if observing this conversation from a distance. 'So you've an open relationship?'

Nicholas shook his head. 'We're separated. I mean not separated as a couple but geographically. I have to work in Hong Kong sometimes and he lives in London.' Nicholas bowed his head, as if that was an excuse in itself.

Ray-jai was silent, his eyes fixed on Nicholas. 'So he fools around too?'

Now Nicholas felt slightly angry. 'No, he doesn't. It all happened so quickly. Look, perhaps we shouldn't – '

He moved towards the edge of the sofa as if to stand up. However, he couldn't finish his sentence because Ray-jai had placed his hand firmly on his leg and held it there. 'It's okay. I don't go out very much either. I also have a partner.'

The feeling of relief was so strong that for a minute Nicholas couldn't believe his luck. If they both had partners, they both had alibis. He put his hand on Ray-jai's hand now rising between my legs. 'So where is he now? Your partner.'

Ray-jai's fingers were on his crotch. 'In San Diego. He only comes here a couple of months a year. He's a lecturer in music. One day we may live together but we're not sure yet.'

'I see,' whispered Nicholas, letting his head fall backwards. The possibility of Ray-jai and his boyfriend living together seemed somehow more remote than Daniel and he in London, but the two of them were in a similar situation. They were finding company as best they could when their partners were not around. There was logic in this, common sense even. It sounded so much better than fooling around, and it had the added benefit that they had the same investment in keeping it secret. He put his arm round Ray-jai's shoulders, looking straight into his eyes.

'Okay, I think we've got that clear. We're going into this as adults, no?'

Ray-jai didn't answer for a moment. He just leaned towards him and kissed him, delicately tasting his mouth. Nicholas felt the room and the caipirinhas revolve in his head. It was as much as he could to do to raise Ray-jai from the sofa and lead him by the hand towards the bedroom.

As they stumbled out, Ray-jai grabbed his duffel bag from the hallway table. Nicholas only just had time to reach for his cell phone and turn it off. As he did so, a piece of blank A4 paper detached itself from the typing stand and wafted slowly down to the floor, followed by the first page of the Press Release. Nicholas looked at them for a moment, wondering if he should put them back with the rest of the papers on his desk. But Ray-jai was already loosening his jeans.

He could pick them up in the morning.

Chapter 10

It was a little before 10 am on a Monday morning and the weekend's calm weather, surprising for usually wet and stormy March, was already breaking. As he handed Jeanette the Human Resources sheet on overseas and local contracts, Nicholas could see grey masses of cloud gathering over the broad yellow sandbar that was the West Kowloon Reclamation. He had already sent the information to both her and Antonia, but he thought they should at least be given a face-to-face interview to voice what he expected to be fairly serious concerns. He studied Jeanette's face. She gave no sign that she had seen him at the Cuban Evening, neither when she entered the office nor when they went through the formalities over coffee. There was even less sign that she had noted Ray-jai.

As she continued reading, he reviewed the events of the past few nights. It had not gone quite as he hoped. Their initial fumbled passion had been accompanied by affection and even laughter. Eventually, he had fallen into a deep sleep with one arm thrown over Ray-jai's shoulder. When he next awoke, it was well into Saturday morning and Ray-jai was nowhere to be seen. His duffel bag was still in the bedroom, with a toothbrush and comb and a spare pair of Calvin Kleins placed carefully beside it. Nicholas had stumbled out into the lounge to find him in one of his toweling robes, eating packet noodles and listening to some low-volume Mike Oldfield. He had been astonished to see that the apartment had been cleaned, the used glasses taken away, books and papers put in neat piles, and the washing up stood gleaming and dry on the rack in the kitchen. Even his desk appeared to have been tidied and the two pieces of paper he had left lying on the floor the night before had been replaced, the first page of the Press Release upside down, on the reading stand.

He worked hard on the Mercantile merger on Saturday afternoon, but when Ray-jai called him later to see if he was free he accepted. They went to the beach, had a discreet supper in Causeway Bay and once more headed for his place.

Two nights should have been enough. Two nights represented fun without it becoming serious. But when he had tried to suggest it was enough to Ray-jai, he had become sulky and then aggressive. Nicholas had begun to panic. If he insisted on dumping him so quickly, things could become unpleasant. Ray-jai not only knew who he was and what his position was, but he was apparently friendly with George. A reputation for sleeping around was not exactly what Nicholas wanted right at this moment. On the other hand, if he didn't get rid of him things might get considerably worse. It was a dilemma he hadn't known how to solve, until Ray-jai phoned on Monday evening and suggested once more that they meet up.

Nicholas was in too much trouble not to agree. Besides, he thought that creating the appearance of friendship might give him the opportunity to at least terminate the sleeping together. He knew very well that he was courting danger. Daniel was on his own in London, starting a new life and making do with the distant support of someone he thought of as his, and his alone. At certain moments over the weekend when he was working on the Press Release or slumped in front of late-night TV, Nicholas told himself that it wasn't worth it. Being stressed, frustrated and alone were not reasons to continue. And yet the more he continued, the more he felt tempted to try it just a little longer, as if the more he did it the more exciting it became.

'I have say that I find it grossly unfair,' said Jeanette stoutly.

Nicholas turned to her with an excuse ready on his lips but then he saw she was referring to her benefits. 'Eddie doesn't agree. His view is that local contracts provide enough benefits as it is without us adding to them. United International is willing to continue with your pension, but I'm afraid the annual increments will have to be readjusted for the new circumstances.'

Jeanette pulled strands of her hair back into the tight chinon at the nape of her neck. 'I thought the freezing of overseas contracts was discretionary.'

Nicholas stared at her. 'That's true, but we cannot have a situation in Hong Kong where two similarly loyal executives are on different contracts. Antonia has accepted the situation.'

Jeanette smoothed down the perfect crease in her grey silk trousers and attempted a smile. 'Antonia would lie down in the road for United International. I'm not quite so accommodating.'

That was certainly true, thought Nicholas. 'One of the benefits of the new local contract is that it offers low mortgage rates. I hear you've invested in some hotels on Jersey.'

Jeanette drew her pashmina around her. 'I'm not a believer in the Hong Kong leveraged debt approach. My husband and I have sacrificed for every one of those properties. If this review goes through, we'll have to postpone our retirement.'

Nicholas wanted to ask why on earth she wanted to go into hotels, but then he thought better of it. Jeanette's parents had run a spa or something in the Channel Islands.

'I understand your position, but I'm afraid the days of comprehensive expatriate packages are gone.'

Jeanette looked at him with anger in her eyes. 'That may well be, but I reserve the right to a second opinion.'

Nicholas shifted in his seat. This was exactly what he didn't want to encourage. Jeanette would do everything in her power to get her own way and United International was made for people like her. Those who knew how to use the system could accumulate years of quid-pro-quo through a mixture of obsequiouness and ruthlessness. 'Eddie is quite clear on this point. Please don't try to force the issue.'

Jeanette fingered the silver necklace at her throat. 'I don't wish to appear difficult Nicholas, but you have to understand. We require security.'

Nicholas felt a sourness in his mouth, perhaps the residue of the Hainan chicken rice he had eaten for lunch, or perhaps the idea that Jeanette's way of working was not all that far from the one he had been adopting. 'As I say, the decision is final and applies to all employees. Your contacts with senior management are your affair.'

Jeanette folded the document in her hand and stood up. 'It seems we have to agree to disagree. I should get back to my office.'

Nicholas also stood up, determined not to let her go off thinking that she had won. 'Before you go, allow me to make a simple request. I've had very little input into Publications in the past few months.'

Jeannette put a braceleted hand on the back of her chair. 'We always send you the final drafts. I'm sure you've noticed that.'

'Yes, that's true,' said Nicholas in a conciliatory voice. 'But I think I should be a little more involved in the end product. That's all.'

'You wish to oversee my work?' said Jeanette in a hardening tone.

Nicholas shook his head. 'No, but I would like to see more of it before it comes to me to be signed off. I've no wish to interfere with how you run your department.'

Jeanette looked at him as if she were dealing with a barman at the Royal Yacht Club who had poured the wrong drinks. 'I trust you have full confidence in my abilities.'

'Of course,' said Nicholas, lowering his eyes and searching the desk for something distracting.

'After all, I hear you're a great believer in teamwork,' she said with an odd emphasis on 'teamwork' and turned away, her heels making a slight squeaking noise on the parquet floor.

As she headed for the door a cold feeling ran down Nicholas's spine. That was the kind of thing that Frank Shearer did, saying something apparently innocuous that could have meant anything. Was 'teamwork' code for something more sinister? He was about to follow her and ask what exactly she meant when he saw George striding across the black parquet towards him.

'Everything okay?' said George breezily.

'Of course, ' said Nicholas, turning back to his desk. 'Apart from the air-conditioning.'

George dropped into the nearest chair and raised a quizzical eyebrow. 'Jeanette been giving you a hard time?'

Nicholas said nothing. It was true that he felt more at ease with George but Martin had warned him not to get too close to any of his colleagues, and he was only just discovering who George was. It would have been too easy to turn their shared inclinations into a certain sort of solidarity, which might turn out just as dangerous as confronting Jeanette. 'How's the merger coming along?' he said, changing the subject.

George took some papers out of his file. 'I've prepared some crisis briefing notes – rapid response and prepared rebuttal, repeating the same line, chain of command. The usual stuff.'

Nicholas reached for the document and looked down its neat columns. They contained more or less everything they had covered in their last meeting. In a crisis a team made up of Nicholas, George and Sophie from Chinese External Relations would be in charge and would decide on the strategy before sending it on to Eddie. George had provided examples of major corporate crises that had occurred over the past twenty years, such as the Exxon Valdez oil spill, with analyses of damage-control positions and the effect on stakeholders, as well as of various merger situations, financial crises, and corruption scandals.

'Good,' said Nicholas, drawing himself up. 'Specific duties must be made clear. Sarah will be your designated backup, Sophie will speak to the Chinese press and I will be the one to approve Press Releases both here and in London. We will need a full quota of administrative staff to carry out extra tasks such as answering the trip phone, allocating interview rooms and escorting people. I think that's all here.'

'Yes,' said George with more than a hint of a smile. 'I like your idea of the trip phone, and the War Room.'

Nicholas searched around on his desk for one of his favourite bits of reading when he was alone in the office, a small book with an image of an ancient fire-throwing machine on the cover. Flicking it open, he read a sentence out aloud: 'Without constant practice, the officers will be nervous and undecided when mustering for battle. Without constant practice, the general will be wavering and irresolute when the crisis is at hand.'

George looked at the book's title. '*The Art of War*,' he said with a big grin. 'Isn't that the Businessman's Bible?'

Nicholas ignored him and flipped to another page: 'When able to attack, you must seem unable. When using your forces, you must seem inactive. When you are near, make the enemy believe you are far away. And when far away, make him believe you are near.' He paused a moment and looked meaningfully at George.

'I guess we should all have it up in our offices,' said George, realising that it was his cue. 'The thoughts of General Sun Tzu, 500 BC.'

Nicholas leaned against the headrest of his chair. He liked the cut-and-thrust of debate for its own sake, the sheer pleasure of exchanging ideas simply because they were ideas. He picked the book up again. 'I suspect that the ancient Chinese have more to tell us now than they ever had. "Many calculations lead to victory, few calculations to defeat." That's a good one.'

'Actually, there was a piece in the *Hong Kong Economic News* this morning about a link-up with Mercantile,' said George, with a hint of relish at disturbing Nicholas' train of thought.

Nicholas flicked the book shut. 'Mercantile?'

'Yes, someone I gave an interview to a few days ago. Of course I didn't mention the merger. I just said we always have options for growth, which we considered as and when opportunities arise.'

Nicholas got up and walked towards the window. The flight path towards Kai Tak had suddenly darkened and thick eruptions of grey-yellow cloud filled the far horizon. 'How the fuck did he get hold of that? Get him checked out.'

George nodded, as if expecting this. 'But it's more than a week old.'

Nicholas spun on his heel, wondering what might be hidden beneath that veneer of schoolboy charm. George wasn't an idiot. This was some sort of game, as if he were testing him. 'Check out all his sources.' He paused. 'By the way, have you noticed anything different in the last few days? I mean in the department, or in the atmosphere in investor relations?'

For the first time George looked slightly disconcerted. 'I can't really say. People are a bit jumpy about the merger and having to keep their mouths shut. And then there's Jeanette of course. She's not so happy about switching to local terms. Everyone's heard about *that*. Even Frank's been over to give her advice.'

Nicholas saw a series of flashes over the Kowloon reclamation. 'Frank? What's he been doing here?'

'He doesn't drop in on me' said George with a shrug. 'He just goes straight to Jeanette's office and they close the door.'

Nicholas glanced at the book on his desk. *Many calculations lead to victory. Few calculations lead to defeat.*

'She's been doing a spot of desk-bashing too,' added George. 'We sent her down a Press Release the other day and there were so many comments on it we couldn't read a word.'

Nicholas sighed and squeezed his eyes. This was exactly the Jeanette he feared: plotting behind his back. George seemed about to say something else, but then took a look at his face and thought better of it. 'I should get on. I know you're off to

London.' He gathered his papers together and headed for the door. 'By the way did you enjoy Friday evening?'

Nicholas forced a smile. 'Of course. I'm sorry I had to go so early.'

'Yes, I left soon after,' said George, turning at the doorway. 'Too much temptation.'

And with that, he hurried into the lobby before Nicholas could say a word.

Chapter 11

The alarm clock slipped from 7.37 to 7.38 am, the red figures shining in the gloom of a drizzly London morning. Nicholas turned over in bed and could tell from the area of warmth to his right that he was not alone. The cloudbanks of sleep lifted. He could hear the telltale thumps in the kitchen of someone opening cupboards and tins, making tea and pouring cereal into a bowl. He turned back to lay his hand across Daniel's chest and gradually let it slide down his body and lodge itself between his thighs. Daniel always wore boxer shorts to bed, a habit that he found both coy and strangely sexy. As if the one with the most attractive body was precisely the one who had to cover up the most. Daniel was not shy when making love but he was strangely shy in the lead up to it. Or perhaps he was just good at remaining attractive. Nicholas was careful to restrain his hand from exploring further. Daniel would not be pleased to be woken at this hour, even less so when Emily was pottering around in the kitchen.

A few days into Nicholas's mother's visit, which appeared to have no end, Daniel had decided to take a well-earned break. He had got on well with Emily, not least because she seemed to fulfill his desire to be accepted, but sometimes he seemed overwhelmed by her appetite for conversation and her persistent demands for fresh cups of tea, cake, newspapers or anything else that entered her head. Complaining about it may have been a claim for attention, or it could have been genuine discomfort at Emily's overpowering presence. Either way, Nicholas had to handle it. He listened for the click of the lounge door closing, which would tell him that Emily was sitting down to eat breakfast alone in front of the TV. He knew her every move. He knew the slightly disappointed way she would munch her Muesli and sip her tea with an almost audible sigh, waiting for him to appear. Even though he was exhausted after a week of the Mercantile positionings and repositionings and a deluge of paperwork, he knew that sooner or later he would have to go in and keep her company.

She had been pretty tolerant about Daniel, considering the reservations she expressed for her other children's partners. According to Emily, Nicholas's younger sister Jill had married a man she would never please, despite her giving him three more or less healthy and intelligent children. And Kay had made a mockery of Emily's disapproval of her own spouse by walking out on her husband and setting up with a married woman, of whom Emily disapproved even more. It was one thing, she said, to accept early on in life that you were gay and to make the best of that by concentrating on your career. It was quite another for a woman to bear two children to a man and then drop all that for someone she saw as a 'gold-digger', a mother of three with whom she had been carrying on in secret for a long time. It was a clear case of honesty on the one hand and dishonesty on the other.

Nicholas knew this was utterly unfair. Looked at from any other viewpoint, his relationship with Daniel might be seen as dishonest and Kay's quite the opposite. But then he didn't want the scene that would go with saying so. Besides, Daniel was the best shot at a long-term relationship he had ever had, and he desperately wanted Emily to approve.

He visualised Emily's procession to the teapot in her nightie: a second cup. One more and he would have to appear. He reached over and draped his arm across Daniel, hoping that it could somehow stay fixed there. The rest of his body was firm and contoured since he had been going to the gym, but that slight softness around his middle was exactly what Nicholas most liked.

He wasn't sure if it was Daniel's attachment to him that had earned him Emily's acceptance, or whether it was because he had presented their relationship as a *fait accompli*. In the past, Nicholas had told her as little as possible about his boyfriends – such as they were – and he knew that she might be surprised, to put it mildly, by Daniel. He hadn't wanted her approval until it was all settled. Now she had spent almost a week with him in the same flat while Nicholas had gone off to work at New Change Street.

Perhaps it was a miracle that they hadn't fought, although by the fifth day it was pretty clear that Daniel, in his withdrawal to his i-Mac, was beginning to weary. Perhaps a certain amount of upheaval was to be expected for the visit of his ageing mother but Emily had a capacity to talk at random and in such a high voice through everything that she could wear anyone down. She also had an unfortunate habit of referring to people she disapproved of as *those people*, even when talking about Kay and Josie, just as she referred to Daniel's family as *your people*. It made everyone who was not white, middle class and heterosexual sound like visitors from another planet. Of course, Nicholas covered up for her whenever he could. And yet covering up made him feel even more awkward.

The clock showed that it was 7.43 am. The lounge door remained closed. He knew he had to raise himself and tiptoe to the main bathroom to avoid disturbing Daniel. Gradually, he withdrew his hand. He washed and showered and eventually, armed with tea and biscuits, he pushed the lounge door open. CNN was blasting from the TV, with the low ripple of Greenwich Park visible on the horizon beyond. He smiled at his mother and reached over for the remote control.

'I don't know if Kay is ever going to be happy,' she said as if he had been in the room all the time. 'She's so erratic, isn't she? She's already calling this new woman the love of her life. It's Josie this and Josie that, she loves her so much she can't bear a day without her. Oh my god, if there's one thing we know about Kay it's that she'll always go *too far*. I talked to her the other evening. It must have been after six o'clock and I think she'd already been over the pub. You know how she gets, all slurred and stupid.'

'Yes,' mumbled Nicholas, submissive and skeptical at the same time. Kay had fought a long battle with his mother to break free of her obligations, including that of being Emily's driver, shopper and cook, while bringing up two boys alongside a very laid-back, if warm-hearted husband. She did all this for twenty-five years, indulging Emily's desire for 'normality' and social acceptance in the seaside town where they both lived. And then one day she simply got up and walked out. As far as Nicholas could tell, Kay found in a woman's touch and company a fulfillment that she could never have dreamt of before.

'I told her that she must never make any commitment after the last one. You just don't know about people these days. Kay's always been such a soft touch and that bitch took her for a right ride. You know she's still trying to get half of the cottage back after all she took off Kay? She even tried to take the TV aerial.'

'Yes, I did,' he said as his mother turned to look at him. Now well past seventy, Emily was heavily lined and puffy-faced, her shoulders shrunk more than ever into her body, but there was still an air of combat about her. Using the word 'bitch' had obviously cheered her up.

Nicholas mulled over what to say, staring at the renewed scenes of violence in the Middle East, Northern Ireland, Africa: a numbingly familiar dance of death and retribution. There was a timelessness about CNN's anguished reportage and Emily's disappointments that seemed somehow all part of the same thing.

'This new woman sounds terribly sensible,' he offered. 'I mean, deciding not to ask her to live together until now. Kay says it was the best way, even though she's so madly in love.'

Emily nodded. 'Madly is right. Don't forget how madly she was in love with the last one.'

'There's only been one other, Mum,' he said, trying to find the right tone. 'I don't think coming out is as easy as all that, especially if you're stuck up a valley in North Wales.'

'Yes, and what was she doing up there? She didn't have to go,' retorted Emily. 'She might have met somebody else if she'd stayed put. She could even have lived with Mike.'

Nicholas had fallen into the trap. As far as Emily was concerned, she was the one who deserved sympathy because of the way her children behaved. She was the mother not of one, but of two gay children. True, her youngest daughter Jill provided her with three grandchildren but she also hitched up with someone she considered a bully. Nicholas had only just succeeded in preventing his homosexuality from ruining his life. Now he was partnered with a younger man of whose background she didn't entirely approve. Emily had played the hard-done-by role for most of her life, particularly in regard to her children, and yet most of her emotional experiences came through them. Apart from her Church circle and one or two women friends from the past, she had no social life apart from the one she derived from her family. Nicholas didn't blame her for that. He sometimes wondered what he would be like if and when he reached her age. She was a woman of strong character, and at certain moments she showed great courage and humour. But she would never move on.

Suddenly the phone rang. Nicholas leaned over and picked it up but there was just a rustling sound, long distance perhaps, and then one word. It sounded like 'urgent'. He put the phone down. It was Saturday afternoon in Hong Kong. They wouldn't be calling him now.

'I don't know why she couldn't have lived with Mike a bit longer,' continued Emily, refocusing on Kay's marriage. 'I know he was a struggle to live with but now look at him. A lonely ageing divorcee. He looks as if someone has hit him with a hammer. Meanwhile Kay goes from one thing to the other. And as for that woman – '

Nicholas sighed. He had heard all this before. Kay's first lover was a domestic help. When she persuaded Kay to leave the South Coast and start a new life in North Wales, the split between Emily and Kay became almost unbridgeable. Even though Kay begged Emily to go with them, Emily refused point blank. The relationship between them deteriorated even further, until one day the domestic help dumped Kay for another woman several years younger.

'But she's getting on nicely with this Josie now, and I think she's stopped drinking,' he said. He suspected that Emily had started on Kay's choice of partner as a way of discussing his own.

'I should hope so. We couldn't have her carrying on like that. Drunken phone calls at all hours of day and night. I told her straight out. I said that everyone has problems and break ups, not just her. I have to deal with loneliness too. I don't drink myself into a stupor to the point that I can't do a thing for myself. Sometimes I wonder about people in your world. They dramatise so much, don't they? It's not as if you haven't got everything you want. If you watch the TV now, you'd think it's us who are in the minority. What was that film you took me to see?'

'*In and Out*,' said Nicholas. It wasn't the first film with a gay theme that he had taken Emily to see, but it was the first one he had taken her to see with Daniel. He loved it.

'Yes that's right. "I'm gay too",' she said, parodying the voices of the supportive community and students in the imaginary school hall. 'Well you won't have them saying that down my church hall, I can tell you, and I don't expect in United International either. Although of course we do have Father George....'

Nicholas's smile broadened. Emily liked to tell stories about the local vicar, who despite being married had a penchant for male members of the choir and apparently went on secretive holidays with them to Mykonos. Emily's attitude to Father George was just one more example of her curious double standards: she tolerated a condition she thought of as socially deplorable, but emotionally fascinating.

She waved her finger. 'This is a great set-up you have here, Nicholas. Don't do anything that could jeopardise it. Are you sure Daniel's right for you?'

Nicholas glanced at the door. 'Yes I am.'

'Likes to have all his own way I should think. Didn't you say he was the youngest in the family?'

He nodded, feeling doubly guilty; first Kay, now Daniel. He should have a Ph.D. in betrayal. If Daniel was sometimes moody, it was probably because he had to be a polite son-in-law for days on end. He rather admired the way he stuck to it, especially when Emily questioned him every few minutes on what he was doing, what he was going to eat next, what his plans were for the day. Emily was a world-class inquisitor.

'What about a job? Wouldn't that do him some good? Surely he's not going to live on you for ever.'

Nicholas swallowed. Daniel had given up everything for him. He had moved away from his family, which was intolerable to every Chinese, and he had left a reasonably good position in United International that would be difficult to replace. He was looking around in London while waiting to apply for a work permit. Not much had turned up so far and for obvious reasons Nicholas didn't want him to go back to United.

'It's early days yet.'

'Don't let him hold you back, that's all. I expect he's been indulged. Chinese families are like that, aren't they? Big families. We used to have them in England years ago. My grandmother's family in Monmouthshire was all uncles and aunts and cousins. But it's not like that these days. You've got to go out and earn a living. He can't just cook chop suey for the rest of his life.'

'He doesn't eat chop suey, Mum. He's not an immigrant from fifty years ago,' Nicholas suddenly felt like going back to bed.

'Maybe not. But an immigrant would have had to go out and fight for a living. I'm just worried that he's going to drain you of energy just when you have all these big things coming up.'

'You don't like him?' he said.

'I didn't say that. I think we're becoming good friends and I'm sure he's keen on you. I just think that, after Kay and that woman, you should be very careful of what you're doing. You'll have to see how it goes. You don't want someone who just wants a comfortable life, now do you?'

Nicholas bit his lip. Emily had gone round in her usual circle but she had somehow hit a nerve. Daniel was far too proud to be a stay-at-home. That wasn't the problem. But he could see there were moments when Daniel wondered what he had done by following him to London. Of course he had hopes for a better life than he had in United International. But he had his pride, too. And at the moment things were out of joint.

'I don't want to chop and change all the time,' he said, knowing Emily's preference for someone more familiar, someone who could be passed of as 'Nick's friend', someone who could visit her without the neighbours gossiping.

'Maybe not,' said Emily, putting her teacup down on the low table and clearing away some crumbs. 'But just remember there's more than one fish in the sea. He's younger than you. Very nice, but a little bit spoilt I'd say. He's certainly not got your brains, so you'd better watch out. Compatibility means sharing.'

Like you and Dad? thought Nicholas. Emily had depended completely on his father and refused to snap out of it until death forced her to. Nicholas could remember him cooking the runner beans and new potatoes when he came home from running a school in the evening, simply because Emily couldn't or wouldn't do it. At least Daniel and he had learned how to share the domestic chores. And as for him being less intelligent, nothing could be further from the truth.

'And what about when you're in Hong Kong? How does he get on then?' continued Emily.

'He's fine.' Nicholas knew very well that he spent too much time at the gym because he had precious little else to do.

'What about you?'

Nicholas felt Emily's eyes drilling into him. 'I'm so busy – '

'That you don't have time for any company over there?'

He paused. 'The occasional friend.'

CNN seemed rather quiet now, babbling away in the background. He looked for the remote control.

'From work?'

Nicholas sighed; she was like a force from nature. 'Yes, from work.'

Emily looked at him sideways on, a knowing glint in her eye. 'You know Nicholas, in the past you always kept your boyfriends in the background and got on with your career. Take it from me, if you're going further up the ladder, Daniel will not be to everyone's liking.'

He stared at her anxious to tell her how wrong she was, but she clearly knew what she was talking about.

Emily placed a gold-ringed hand on his right knuckle. 'You know why I could never forgive Kay and that cleaning woman? Because they had to broadcast their relationship all round the place. They might as well have shouted it from the rooftops.'

'I know Mum,' Nicholas said soothingly while desperately thinking of a way to change the subject. 'Excuse me, I'll have to go and wake Daniel.'

He turned to open the door and hurriedly left the room. However, just as he reached the kitchen he stepped back. Daniel was standing there in the hallway, glazed-eyed in his boxers and T-shirt.

'Telephone,' he mumbled and shuffled back to the bedroom. 'Sounds important.'

Nicholas hurried into the study and picked up the phone. 'Hello?'

For a second there was no response while the voice on the other end was giving instructions. 'Nicholas?'

'Yes sir,' he said with a stab of recognition. 'Anything wrong?'

'Bad news I'm afraid. I can't say much on the phone but the merger's going to be all over the Sundays. We may have to bring the press announcement forward, the whole AGM. You'd better get over here as soon as possible.'

'Shit,' he mumbled.

'I'll be waiting for you,' said Eddie. 'I've called in Sir John.'

'Right I'll be over there a.s.a.p,' said Nicholas and put down the phone.

Immediately it rang again. He picked it up, half-expecting it to be Sir John. 'Nicholas Powell.'

'Thank god I've found you,' said George. 'Sophie tried to reach you but she couldn't get through. There's a meeting of the senior management in about an hour. Looks as if it might have come from Hong Kong. London Sundays are calling it a takeover and the coverage is hostile. Competition Commission, Takeover Panel. Latest I heard is that the London tabloids have announced big bank closures in the high streets.'

Nicholas moved towards the door and closed it, then put one hand to his temple. 'You'd better give Sophie my cell phone number. I'm just off to New Change Street. Any idea where it came from?'

'Not the foggiest. We've been so fucking tight on security. The latest briefings with the journalists were all the usual stuff, warming the buggers up. Nothing that would lead to this.'

'Okay, we'll talk later,' said Nicholas and put down the phone.

He turned to look through the window at those weird spikes they had erected for the Dome's roof. Something about their rakish angle and the crown-like form made him think of human sacrifices: the Traitor's Gate. But who was the traitor? And how had any of this started? He had to get to New Change Street as soon as possible.

Chapter 12

The sweat poured down Nicholas's face as he once more went down the list of emergency measures he had discussed with Eddie: the signing-in procedures, the double security check at the elevator, the list of approved journalists. The door to Group Public Affairs was to be firmly closed at all times and the electronic code would be changed every two days. A 'clean desk' policy was to be implemented in order to ensure that no papers were left lying around and confidential material was locked away in desk drawers at the end of working hours. All documents to the executive floors were to be placed in brown envelopes marked *Highly Confidential* and were only to be sent up by appointed courier. Phones and e-mails were to be strictly monitored.

He was about to sign off on the recommendations when a buzzing sound interrupted his thoughts. For some reason, he had forgotten to put his cell phone on Silent mode for meetings and Message Alert was clearly audible in his inner pocket. He hurried over to close the outer door to his office and returned to his desk. He paused for a second as if to be certain that no one would interrupt him, then pressed the scroll on his phone until he reached Messages: Inbox. Only two people used his text messaging service on a regular basis, and only one of them was in London. He pressed Select and immediately a short message appeared on the screen: *Hey u C. y u not tell me u leave HK? When u cum back? Or I cum 2 u? Yeah, rl...*** (lots) R.*

Nicholas swore under his breath, quickly pressed the Save button on Options, and flicked the keyboard cover closed. He then remembered that the phone was still on Message Alert and went back in to find the correct setting for Silent. It wasn't easy to find. By the time he had got it right, his index finger was shaking and he thought he could hear the voices of Eddie and Seymour Smith in the hallway.

He checked his phone again. He had already received two e-mails from Ray-jai to his official United International mailbox and he hadn't replied. He had no idea how he had got hold of the address.

He stood up and breathed in, as if movement would rid him of the vision of those Calvin Kleins rolled so neatly next to his toothbrush on the hallway dresser. 'Okay, Alice,' he said into the intercom. 'Tell Eddie's secretary I'm coming.'

Eddie and Seymour Smith were seated waiting for him like undertakers at the long table in the Board Room. As he made his way down the long table, he examined Seymour Smith's face for evidence of jet lag. Apart from a slight puffiness around his eyes, he seemed his usual self despite being summoned from Hong Kong on the next flight.

'Morning Powell.' Seymour Smith held up his coffee cup. 'I suppose we're going to get a lecture from you on how to handle journalists.'

Nicholas gave him an ambiguous smile. He had to be careful not to show his true feelings about Seymour Smith, although he suspected that the Group Chairman entirely shared them. 'I'm sure you're an expert sir.'

Seymour Smith gave Eddie a curious, sideways look, as if to say 'I told you he was an arrogant prick'.

'Quite,' said Eddie, shuffling through his notes.

Unlike most of the senior executives, Seymour Smith had not joined the company as an apprentice. He had been to Balliol College, Oxford and he had not stopped talking about it ever since. Perhaps it was this claim to academe that had persuaded Eddie to appoint him as Chairman in Hong Kong. Whatever it was, Eddie obviously regretted it. 'S.S', as he was known to his staff, was not trained as a banker, which made many of his off-the-cuff pronouncements extremely dangerous. Nicholas had given him extensive briefings with prepared answers on all kinds of financial questions that journalists might ask him, but S.S. had either ignored or forgotten them. His latest gaffe was live on Hong Kong television, when he said that United International expected any possible merger to be 'very profitable', implying that the company would be raking in billions of dollars at the expense of its customers. This was a sensitive issue in Hong Kong, since both United International and Mercantile projected themselves as global banks that were at the same time deeply committed to their local customer base. Sometimes it seemed to Nicholas that everything Group Public Affairs had done up until 1997 was being deliberately eroded.

'So what's the plan?' said Eddie, his pale blue eyes even more sharp and penetrating than usual.

'I think we should come clean,' said Nicholas with a faint smile.

'You mean tell them the whole thing?' said S.S. in a shocked voice.

Nicholas folded his arms over his chest. 'We have to get out a short message that we repeat time and time again. We must put it out on TV and radio, in print and in interviews. Most of the press coverage of the merger will be negative. Everyone in the media will paint a picture of high street closures and the loss of local branches. Our job is to restore confidence and improve our reputation.'

'It looks like panic,' said Seymour Smith.

'If we stick to one or two messages it'll work,' continued Nicholas, ignoring him. 'We have to tell our story by ourselves. And we have to tell it fast.'

Eddie looked at the ceiling as if he had seen something way up there, perhaps in the congregation of angels. '*The cost savings will enhance efficiency and bring outstanding benefits to the customer.* That's it, isn't it?'

'Exactly,' said Nicholas. 'The statement we put out on Saturday was too late to catch the Sundays but at least it reached the news desks. We have to make it clear that we're not hiding. We have to show that we're following normal procedures.'

'Normal?' observed Seymour Smith.

Eddie brought his eyes level with his second-in-command's. 'Can you not understand? Nicholas is telling us we have to restore confidence. Everyone has to read from the same script.'

'It seems to me that it's far from confident,' replied Seymour Smith with a toxic smile.

'We'll be giving Eddie a few formal and informal appearances,' Nicholas said hurriedly. 'We have to get some positive aspects into the story. I've been on to the *Financial Times*. Their next piece will mention the merger's value to The City as an international financial centre. It'll be published together with a profile of Eddie as a strategic thinker, along with a bit of stuff about the overlapping synergies of the two post-colonial banks as well as their presence in the U.K. high street.'

'And what about Hong Kong?' said Seymour Smith.

'I think we should let Eddie handle that,' said Nicholas.

'At least I know when to keep my trap shut,' added Eddie before Seymour Smith could intervene.

Nicholas looked away. For a moment an oppressive silence reigned in the room. Then, with an attempt at a smile, Nicholas took two printed pieces of paper from his file. 'I've prepared a statement for you both. We can call it the party line. I think we should take a moment to practice it. Could we start with you, Group Chairman?'

Eddie clearly knew the statement by heart. Grasping it in his left hand, he read it aloud as if he were taking an oath in court. Nicholas had nothing much to say about the delivery except that it could perhaps be a little more personal. However, as soon as Seymour Smith began, it became all too clear that he hadn't the faintest idea. Although his tone was authoritative, he sounded as if he were reciting Henry V's speech before the Battle of Agincourt.

Nicholas did his best not to look too disappointed. 'Let's try again later. Perhaps it needs a little more practice.'

Seymour Smith handed him back the statement with a reproachful stare. 'Perhaps you would allow me now to get some coffee,' he said huffily and headed for the door.

Eddie watched him disappear before turning back to Nicholas. 'Have you found out the source?'

Nicholas hesitated. He didn't want to take any speculative punts, even though they would have made him look a lot better in front of Eddie. 'All we know is that the journalists refuse to reveal their sources.'

Eddie's eyes narrowed and he seemed to struggle with his breathing for a moment. 'They would, wouldn't they? You know, it's no use their treating us as if we're a bunch of fucking white colonialists going around buying up bits of the old empire. I notice that the newspapers quoted the estimated value of the merger and also the percentages.'

Nicholas nodded as Seymour Smith came back into the room and sat down with his coffee. 'Yes, they did.'

Eddie glanced at Seymour Smith and seemed to take energy from his new obsequiousness. 'I've been taking a careful look at the newspapers. Some of them quoted our non-performing loans but there's something wrong with the figures. They don't tally with the numbers we set out in our last Interim Report.' Nicholas looked up in surprise. 'But they *did* tally with the appendices we prepared for the Hong Kong Press Release, which was much more recent.'

Nicholas felt his heartbeat quicken. This was exactly the kind of thing he should have noticed. But it was exactly the kind of thing that could get him into further trouble.

Eddie leaned forward. 'Which means that we have to find out if the Press Release was available in either of your offices. Or anywhere else come to that. Did either of you leave it out on your desks?'

Seymour Smith shook his head and gave Eddie a complacent smile. "My people always clear my desk.'

Eddie nodded and looked at Nicholas. 'What about you Nicholas?'

'We have the same policy throughout the department,' said Nicholas crisply. 'Nothing should be left out,' he said, his heart racing. *Not even in my apartment.*

***

Daniel was preparing dinner when Nicholas arrived home. As he took off his overcoat and hung it on the hallstand, he could hear Daniel chopping away on a wooden board and humming along to the Pet Shop Boys *It's a Sin*. There was an aroma of lamb and spices emanating from the oven. He dumped his briefcase in the study and moved to the kitchen doorway.

Daniel turned. 'Had a rough day?'

'Awful.'

Daniel put the chopped bell peppers and shallots of top of the mesclun in the salad bowl and poured in some honey and mustard dressing. 'Better take a shower. I can finish off here.'

Nicholas did as he was told, went into the bedroom and stripped off. Soon he was in the shower cubicle and the water was sluicing over his tired muscles. As he rubbed shower gel over his body, he again went over the scene in the Board Room. Perhaps he was imagining things but Eddie had seemed even more sardonic than usual. There was a glint in those watchful eyes that he hadn't liked, and as for Seymour Smith…He sighed to himself.

Eventually, dressed in jeans and T-shirt, he joined Daniel in the lounge. The TV was on, showing a programme about wildebeeste migrations in the Serengeti National Park. These migrations seemed to involve thousands of the animals going down to the river like pictures he had seen of Hindus gathering on the banks of the Ganges.

'You had a phone call,' said Daniel, placing the dinner plates on the table.

Nicholas raised his eyebrows and gave him a weary look.

'The caller asked me who I was, so I told him my name. He then asked me if I lived here. I asked him who he was and if he wanted to leave a message. He just repeated the same question. So then I hung up.'

Nicholas reached for the remote on the coffee table and turned the sound down. 'Sounds like a wrong number,' he said.

'Yes, he didn't mention you.'

'Plenty of nutters around I suppose,' said Nicholas and began to surf the channels with studied indifference. 'Local or long distance?'

Daniel frowned as the nature programme reappeared and then, just as quickly disappeared. 'Sounded like long distance but it could have been just round the corner. He had a bit of a Chinese accent.'

'Did you try 1471?' said Nicholas abruptly.

Daniel shook his head, obviously surprised by the tone. Nicholas continued to flick through the channels but his heart was beginning to pound against his ribs. It was 1.30 am in Hong Kong. He hadn't given Ray-jai his home number; George or Sophie would have tried his cell phone. Who the fuck could it have been?

'Just say that you're a friend if it happens again'

'A friend?' Daniel stopped laying the table and looked hard at him.

'Journalists will be snooping around while this Mercantile business goes through. We'd better change the answer phone message for the time being.'

Daniel carefully put down the serving dish he was holding. 'You want me to take my name off the answer machine?

'Yes,' said Nicholas with a slight shrug. 'The fact that we're a couple could be interesting to someone for the wrong reason.'

Daniel stood up and moved towards the answer machine. He waited a moment, pushed a button and bent down to speak into the microphone. 'Nick and Daniel can't come to the phone right now. Both of us are having sex.'

'Daniel – '

'You should be defending our rights Nicholas, not pretending I'm not here,' said Daniel, pressing the playback button. 'I had enough of that in Hong Kong.'

Nicholas gave him a pleading look as the absurd message echoed through the room. 'I had a warning that somebody might try to harm me. Not me directly, but my career. And there's a rumour going round – .'

Daniel's eyes flashed. 'I'm living here legally Nicholas. I'm your *partner*.' He turned away from the answer machine. 'Did you give this number to anyone in Hong Kong?'

For a second Nicholas was so surprised he didn't know what to say. 'Yes I did. I mean Karen has it but they always call my cell phone. I can't think of anyone else I gave it to.'

Daniel's expression darkened. 'Maybe I should've spoken in Cantonese.'

'What?' said Nicholas. 'Why in Cantonese?'

'Oh nothing,' said Daniel and headed out through the door towards the kitchen.

Nicholas stood up and half-followed Daniel's receding figure. 'I told you, it's nothing,' he said. But Daniel had closed the kitchen door.

Chapter 13

S ir John had suggested somewhere convivial to meet, such as Dirty Dan's in Bishopsgate. Although he was not exactly a fan of pubs, Nicholas had agreed. The problem was that the whole of the Embankment was closed off for a security scare, and the knock-on effect of thousand of diverted cars heading from Cannon Street for the narrow one-way roads and convoluted lanes around St. Paul's meant that the traffic was totally gridlocked.

He looked again at that week's edition of *Eye Witness*, which lay open on his knees. Someone at United International had phoned him about it the previous day and since then he had read it over several times in the privacy of his office. There was a period at college when he had enjoyed *Eye Witness*, although he couldn't quite remember how he had found those political in-jokes and scatological puns so screamingly funny. *Eye Witness* only faintly amused or interested him these days, being full of the same satirical gags and the same political scandals as it had been for the past twenty years. Nevertheless, on page four beneath the sub-heading *Mergers and Affairs* was a short paragraph that had made him pay attention:

Rumours are growing in The City that United
International has more than a merger on its hands.
A leak about the forthcoming acquisition of
Mercantile Bank has launched United
International's share price on a roller coaster ride.
Word has it that the leak comes from a private
source not too far from United International
headquarters.

Nicholas glanced at the driver, praying that he wasn't about
to slide the partition window open to launch into yet another
tirade about the price of beer and petrol in the forthcoming
Budget. The words 'private source' worried him. They suggested
evidence of some sort. And yet the journalist didn't seem to know
as much as he insinuated.

Nicholas sat back in his seat. He was exaggerating the
problem of course, just as he had exaggerated the depth of
Eddie's instincts or Daniel's suspicions. Rumours were bound to
arise in the run-up to a City deal and all that the article inferred
was that the source of the leak was somewhere outside the office
and therefore beyond his control.

The taxi shot through a gap in the traffic, throwing his body
to one side, and it took him a moment to regain his balance.
Eddie was not likely to read *Eye Witness,* and even if he did, he
was highly unlikely to connect Nicholas with the article's
contents or jump to any conclusions. Innuendo was par for the
course in the City and 'private' could mean anything. Much more
important was a sensible strategy to find out who was actually
responsible. He stuffed *Eye Witness* into his briefcase and
prepared to get out.

The interior of Dirty Dan's was gloomy, lit mainly by faux-
antique coach lamps stuffed with hollowed-out candles, and full
of red-faced men fitting awkwardly into suits that were rather too
tight for them. Nicholas spotted Sir John in a wooden seat near
the window, a half-empty bottle of Mouton Rothschild open on
the wooden table in front of him. One of the two glasses was

already filled. He set down his own glass and indicated the seat in front of him.

'There you are, Nicholas. Busy I expect.'

Nicholas sat down, accepting the glass of wine Sir John had poured. 'Sorry I'm late.' Sir John merely smiled, his spectacles almost opaque in the light reflected from the candles. Nicholas took a quick gulp of the claret. 'I had to deal with some Hong Kong business.'

'Must be like having two lives,' observed Sir John with a weak attempt at humour. 'Or even two wives.'

'I wouldn't know about that,' said Nicholas, swirling the claret around the goblet.

Sir John leaned forward to inspect the bottle's label. 'Let's cut to the chase. What are you doing about the leaks?'

Nicholas hesitated a moment, watching the wine drip down the interior of his glass. 'I've agreed on more security with Eddie. Monitoring the internet, controlling phone calls, that kind of thing. It seems that Eddie noticed clear parallels between the version of the Press Release in Hong Kong and the figures quoted in the newspapers.' He paused, wondering whether to pursue this line of reasoning. 'Of course, it's taken us all by surprise. The security arrangements in Hong Kong were much stronger than they were for the handover.'

'Yes,' said Sir John, turning the bottle in his hands and propping his spectacles up on his forehead so he could look further at the history of Baron Phillipe de Rothschild. 'I'm sure he doesn't blame you, but you know these things never look good when it come to promotion.'

Nicholas glanced up from his wine glass. There was an odd look in Sir John's eyes, but he couldn't say exactly what it meant.

'If you could find the source of the leak of course, that would greatly improve your chances,' said Sir John, leaning back.

Nicholas pondered this for a moment. It was just possible that Sir John had seen *Eye Witness* but then surely he would have come out with it. 'We're checking everyone in Public Affairs. It seems that the leak contained information that could only have come from Hong Kong.'

'Non-performing loans?' said Sir John.

Nicholas cleared his throat, impressed as always by Sir John's grasp of detail. 'We intended to reveal the numbers in the right way at the right time. However, the leak has beaten us to it.'

Sir John turned his attention to the wine list. 'Do you think there's any chance there's something personal in all this? I mean there are different motives for this kind of thing. Revenge, jealousy…'

Nicholas shifted awkwardly in his seat. 'Even if it were an outsider, someone with a personal grudge against United, they would still need a professional contact. They would have to understand what they were leaking.'

'Of course,' said Sir John, stroking his freckled skull. 'If it were an outsider. But what if it's not? I have a feeling these regular checks of yours may not be enough. Of course an employee could be doing it for money, but sometimes it's less predictable than that.' Sir John placed both his hands on the table. 'There's a certain amateurishness about it. Naturally it could just be an employee, someone in a panic. But it could also be someone not quite clever enough to cover their tracks, and yet determined to create the maximum damage.'

Nicholas wondered if he could move to the bar to order some more wine, or perhaps go to the toilet.

'Of course, I'm not saying it's anything to do with you,' pursued Sir John. 'I'm just wondering if someone might have taken offence about something.'

Nicholas stared hard at Sir John, wondering whether this was a reference to the rumours about his so-called affair. He tried to slowly read down the black-lettered adverts on the wall: *Cockburn's Port, Hobson's Ale, Barnsley Steak and Kidney.* 'Let's focus on United International. That's at least something we can be sure about.'

Sir John shrugged and looked over at the waiter as if ready to order another bottle. 'My advice would be to check out anyone with reason to harm you, especially if they have access to United International's business. A leak is like a crime, Nicholas. It has to be solved or the criminal may strike again. I don't wish to be alarming, especially with the merger announcement coming up. But I am afraid that if any of this spreads, your chances of promotion may be seriously damaged.'

Nicholas could feel the sweat prickling his palms. 'I shall certainly check on backgrounds, everyone I've worked with.'

Sir John put the bottle back on the table. 'Everyone has enemies Nicholas, especially in our line of business. If you want to succeed, you may have to do things that you might not consider quite correct. It could be someone in your own circle. It could be someone in the circle of one of your staff. It could be a disgruntled former employee. Trust no one Nicholas.'

Nicholas sat there for a moment, listening to the roar of traffic outside and feeling its echo inside his head. That was exactly what Martin had said.

Sir John's expression changed. 'As you know, the Cabinet reshuffle will be announced soon and it is only a matter of time before I can introduce you to Roger Yates. He's already arranged a little reception to which I am invited. As are you. But before we go to meet him, please promise me that you will take a good look at everyone who has crossed your path and make sure that none of them has any reason to harm you.'

Nicholas sat there unable to decide which of the several ways he should take to pursue this. Suddenly Sir John looked at his watch, glanced at the still empty bottle, and signaled to the barman.

'You're off already?' said Nicholas, surprised.

'An appointment in Oxford Street. My wife wants me to choose a new sofa,' smiled Sir John as the waiter arrived. 'Do you know much about sofas?'

'Not really,' said Nicholas, relieved to sign the payment slip and hand it back to the barman, who was looking Sir John up and down with a slightly ironic air – as if he knew him. Then, with a shrug, the barman took himself off. However, he continued to gaze at Sir John from his position behind the bar until they had exited onto the Strand.

Chapter 14

Daniel could see the River Thames bobbing in his sight through the ceiling-high windows of the Docklands gym, its grey waters slicked with milky light as the sun descended beyond the renovated warehouses on the opposite bank of the Thames. A large cream-and-red paddleboat crossed his view, a band of tourists wrapped in bright fleeces and fluttering scarves standing on its upper deck.

'Not much eye candy,' muttered Matt with a grin as they got off the treadmills. Daniel contented himself with a rub of the neck with the small towel and dropped it in the black container near the glass door that led up to the weights room. He waited until they were on the stairs. 'No, but I quite liked the beefcake in the striped shorts.'

Matt gave him a knowing look. 'Been there, done that.'

Daniel closed his eyes, imagining Matt meeting the beefcake in the steam room at the end of the day and taking him into the Disabled toilet for a 'quickie'. Since the rule was that it had to be anonymous, not to be accompanied by any hint of conversation, it was very difficult to check on the truth.

Ron was already at the weights when Matt and Daniel arrived. His body was encased in a tight black T-shirt and grey leggings that emphasised the slimness of his figure. His black head was closely shaved and his eyes were fixed on the weights he was bench-pressing. 'Hello!' he shouted. A couple of gym members, intent on their reps, frowned in their direction.

'Guess what,' said Matt, looking down on Ron and indicating Daniel. 'He's alone today.'

Ron raised himself and sat up. 'Really? Time to party my boy! There are some excellent choices here tonight.'

'Piss off,' said Daniel. 'I came here to improve my body tone.'

'I'm sure you did,' said Ron. 'And there's more than one way of doing that. Isn't there Matt?'

Matt pointed with one finger against the palm of his other hand towards a young blond who was reaching up to the handles of the lateral pull-down. 'Great pecs.'

'I'll see you later,' said Daniel quickly and moved towards the machines.

He began his circuit, beginning with leg presses and hack squats and then moving on to step ups, butterflies and abdominals. He tried hard to concentrate but it wasn't easy. All the time he exercised he could hear Matt and Ron fooling around on the other side of the room. They were so different to the usual gym crowd. Most of the men that exercised at Docklands Health Club did so with the kind of sober intensity that suggested they were attending church or registering to vote. Apart from the background music and the clink of weights, there was hardly a sound in the room. It was very rare to hear anyone say 'hello' or even 'thank you' for vacating a machine. And if Daniel dared to enforce a little gym etiquette and asked how many reps someone still had to do, the answer was usually one syllable or a grunt. In any other circumstances, he would have put this down to his being Chinese, but there were plenty of other foreigners in there.

Buoyed up by endorphins, he went over to the others and began some reps on the Smith squat. Placing his feet squarely beneath the bar, he braced his legs and thrust out his buttocks. 'What's the latest?'

'Ron's at the boyfriend stage,' said Matt, who at twenty-eight seemed to regard boyfriends as a sign of ageing. 'He was just asking about you and Nicholas.'

'Yes,' said Ron. 'I just wondered how you became so settled.'

'With difficulty,' grinned Daniel. He knew very well that Matt had just given Ron a checklist of everything that had gone wrong in his relationship with Nicholas. 'Nicholas's a workaholic,' he explained as the bar went up. 'Over-achiever.' He breathed out. 'Closet.'

Ron stopped in the middle of his pectoral flies and put down his silver weight with a sardonic smile. 'Sounds just like me.'

Daniel grinned despite the effort. Ron clearly imagined that everyone thought he was heterosexual, especially when he wore his thick black-framed glasses and put a soft trilby on his head. However, the combined impression was rather like a young, black Quentin Crisp. 'He's more closet than you.'

'Really?' said Ron so that the whole room could hear. 'No one can be more closet than me.'

Daniel could not be sure but he thought the blond on the laterals smiled. 'I've got a partner that wants to take my name off the answer machine.'

Ron placed his hands on his hips. 'Now that's what I call out of order. Whatever for?'

'So that I don't disturb him.' Daniel pushed up. 'I mean his career.' He rolled his wrists so that the silver slats could find their groove and rested the bar back in the air. He was slightly exaggerating but in his current mood he didn't care.

'They don't deserve us,' observed Matt, looking at the ceiling where the words *Relax, Unwind, Rejuvenate* were inscribed.

'Let's head for the spa,' said Daniel.

The three of them hurried down the stairs and into the basement, separating to change out of their gym gear and don towels. As they moved towards the showers Ron greeted the black attendant who cleaned the place, and introduced Daniel and Matt. The attendant, a part-time church minister, introduced himself as 'Christian'. There followed a long and cheerful conversation, during which Daniel and Matt had to move out of the way of several men using the sauna, some of whom stopped to stare at them as if they were watching some sort of cabaret.

'That was uplifting,' laughed Ron as they settled on the metal slats of the spa, the water bubbling behind their backs. He turned to Daniel, as if sensing something was wrong. 'What're you thinking?'

Daniel tried to find the words. 'If anyone had told me a month ago I'd be worrying, I'd have said they were crazy. Matt doesn't seem to understand.'

Matt pulled his hair free of the spouting water. 'I just think every couple has problems.'

Ron leaned towards them. 'Marco and I never stopped arguing. It seems that all relationships are about the same thing.'

Daniel looked at Ron's head, dark as a football above the foam line, as his white-teethed mouth shaped the letters for P.O.W.E.R. He wondered if his insistence on Nicholas's coming out was also a question of power. Perhaps he was to blame for the whole thing.

'It started with him sleeping badly,' he confided to Ron. 'I thought it was jet lag but then he began to toss and turn and get up at five o'clock. The other day I went into the lounge to see if he was okay and he was just staring at the TV, the cell phone in his hand. When I asked him what he was doing, he slipped it down the sofa.'

'Uh-uh,' said Matt.

'Not the first time. I've come in to his study on other occasions and found him messaging or answering a text. He even had an alert in the middle of the night. I haven't asked him whom he's talking to, but he shouldn't be texting people if he can just as well e-mail them. Especially if they're in the Hong Kong office.'

'Right,' said Ron firmly.

'I know he's in the middle of a big thing at United International, but for the first time since I met him I'm not sure about him.'

Matt half-turned to him with a shrug. 'We've all got eyes for other guys.'

Ron threw his head back. 'As you know, I'm totally *monogamous* but I did have fun with someone before Marco.' Daniel and Matt looked at each other and suppressed a smile: the singular 'someone' was ridiculous. 'The next time I saw him, I just said hello. So he goes all hysterical on me and tells Matt that I'm cold and that he regrets what he did and he's gonna leave London because of me. And I just want to say, "*Hello!* It was just sex".'

Daniel half-swallowed and spat out some water. 'Maybe that's what Nicholas's been doing.'

'Really?' said Ron.

Daniel shook his head. 'It's this odd feeling I get when I look in his eyes. And then there's the phone calls.'

Matt turned fully to him. 'What do you mean?'

'Someone called the house the other day. He wanted to know my name and not Nicholas's. I couldn't tell if it was long distance, so I asked Nicholas if he gave out the number.'

'And?'

'He denied it of course.'

Ron sighed. 'It's all about them, I mean it is with older men. We should really marry our own age group.'

'I shouldn't think Nicholas has any time for an affair,' said Matt.

Ron rose up the steps, the foam sluicing down his dark legs. 'You could play him at his own game.'

Daniel followed him onto the podium. 'What do you mean?'

Ron looked around the spa area as if something very suspicious was going on, something to do with the people hanging around the sauna. 'I mean you could get a few people to call you, exchange a few numbers, get some text messages.'

'Flirt,' said Matt.

Ron fluttered his hands and grabbed a towel. 'I've done it with Marco and it worked a treat.'

Daniel stood still for a moment, as if caught in two minds. He couldn't start going through those messages stored on Nicholas's phone. It wouldn't feel right and he wouldn't be really justified by the evidence he had. On the other hand, something was going on and there was only one way to find out if he was being deceived. 'He won't be happy about it.'

'He won't,' said Ron with a sisterly smile. 'But then you weren't happy about it when you found him texting, were you? And you know what they say: No smoke without fire.'

Chapter 15

N icholas looked at his watch and saw it was well into lunchtime. Eunice would be waiting for them at the restaurant on Kowloon side but he still had a few minutes alone with Sarah. They sat right at the back of the Star Ferry, with a view on the distant container ships passing through the Lamma channel. Beyond them the mountains of Lantau could be seen, and in the foreground a jumble of marine activity reminiscent of that George Chinnery watercolour he had hung in his office: a tangle of clippers' masts beneath a porcelain blue sky, the Peak looming up like a volcano above the squat arch-terraced warehouses of the early *compradores*, a lone Union Jack fluttering in the wind.

The Star Ferry's engines thudded beneath them as the Kowloon waterfront approached. An aged Chinese sailor passed wiping his hands on a rag and nodded at them, the only pair of Caucasians amidst the Hong Kong office workers and Mainland tourists.

'I'm sorry.'

Sarah pushed her jaw into the wind, her face even paler than usual. 'It's no use saying sorry Nicholas. I'm not your mother confessor. What if it gets back to Daniel?'

'It won't,' said Nicholas through compressed lips. 'Anyway Ray-jai also has a partner. He's not going to blab it all round the place.'

Sarah shook her head as if in disbelief. 'You shouldn't be carrying it on in the first place.'

Nicholas looked up and down the deck, wondering if any of those passengers could be friends of Daniel's. It was lucky that Eunice had a department meeting so that she had to come to Kowloon later. He really needed to talk with Sarah privately.

'Have you told him about Daniel?' said Sarah.

'Of course I have.'

Sarah sat back in her seat and looked up at the sky. 'Then it's obvious he's after something. Didn't you say he's living on Lamma? He's probably got no money you idiot.'

'I don't think so,' said Nicholas, knowing that Sarah was absolutely right. Lamma was full of cheap flats, cheap booze, and people on their pin ends, both expats and Chinese. Ray-jai with his torn jeans and sardonic attitude would have fitted in perfectly. 'He's got his own business, something to do with the internet.'

'My god Nicholas, after all the rules you made Daniel observe. Now you're seeing men right under United International's nose. Why don't you announce it in *The South China Morning Post*? You've got everything going for you and you seem to be trying to screw it up. I don't get it.'

Nicholas looked down the bench. Their nearest neighbours were a Chinese couple devouring dried squid from a packet and a white-shirted man playing with a medley of ring tones. 'It's difficult to explain. I got into it by mistake. Now I have to get out of it carefully.'

'No doubt,' said Sarah with a toss of her head.

Nicholas looked over at the sinuously framed roof of the Convention Centre, winged like a surf wave. It was difficult to explain because of the Press Release. If he could, he would have dropped him already but he couldn't tell her that. She would have thought him completely insane. The power rush, the thrill of the forbidden, all had been swept away by such a gathering fear of the consequences. He had to get hold of Ray-jai, preferably alone, and preferably in some place where no one else would recognise them.

'By the way Sarah,' he said, desperately trying to change tack and distract his thoughts from the morning after. 'How did you find the key to Frank's drawer that time? I mean for those appraisals.'

Sarah looked confused for a moment. 'It was on a hook in his bottom drawer, right at the back along with two others. The tag on it said "Confidential". Naturally, I assumed it was worth investigating.'

The ferry plunged on through the wake of a Star Pisces liner that blocked the Harbour City terminal and began to turn in a juddering arc of spume. 'As far as I can remember, there were two others in there marked "Confidential". They were tagged "AS" and "JL". Obviously, Antonia Sylvetti and Jeanette Long. Maybe they had similar drawers in their own offices. When I got into Frank's I found copies of reports from their sections, so it looked as if they all pooled information on the staff. A sort of central filing system,' she added.

Nicholas sat back and thought a moment. This was not at all what he expected. 'Why didn't you tell me about it?'

Sarah shrugged. 'I didn't think it would interest you. I mean you were out of Frank's section and on your own. I assumed it all must have stopped when you took over.'

Nicholas considered this; it was plausible, but on the other hand it was also very strange. 'Did you try the keys for the other desks?'

Sarah's eyes opened wide. 'You must be joking. Antonia always works late and sometimes comes back after supper or a drink at the Royal Yacht Club with her ladyship. You know what she's like. And even if Jeanette goes home early, she locks her office. I would have been in full view of anyone who came through the door.'

The Star Ferry thumped against the quayside and rocked there, the motors propelling the boat sideways. The old matelot in his blue and white baggy uniform threw the ropes towards the quay and the gangplank was lowered. At a signal from the upper deck, the metal bar was raised and the passengers began to jostle along the walkway towards the bus station, finally disgorging into the square in front of the Star Ferry Terminal. The air was thick with exhaust from cream double-decker buses as Nicholas tried to concentrate on what he had just been told. It could be totally innocent. It could be a way for Frank, Antonia and Jeanette to exchange appraisals and keep a tight hold on things. A rather unorthodox way, but a way that was within the rules. 'Do you think they're still doing it?'

Sarah looked straight at him. 'It might have stopped when Frank moved on. I can't see George being part of any KGB. He thinks appraisals are a complete waste of time.'

They had reached Harbour City and were standing on the ascending escalator that led up to the restaurant. Nicholas waited until they were at the top before turning to Sarah and saying in a low voice, 'I think we'd better keep this to ourselves. You know what Eunice is like.'

Sarah nodded knowingly as the reservations manager ushered them down the corridor into a vast circular dining space. Matronly women in pink aprons were pushing carts piled high with bamboo steamers, yellow puddings and scarlet desserts around dozens of circular tables laid out in front of a central stage decorated with gold Chinese lettering on red velvet. Nicholas and Sarah took their seats alongside Eunice, whose face was flushed from the hectic journey she had just made by subway.

'How's Jeanette?' said Nicholas, looking vaguely around the room.

Eunice stared at him with a pained expression. 'I was damned lucky to get away. She had us all in to her office. Nothing but lectures on security. You'd think she was running the whole company.'

The first cart stopped and Sarah hooked a steamer of shrimp wontons, followed by tofu stuffed with fish paste and steamed beef balls. 'Has Frank been to see her recently?' said Nicholas as Sarah put the steamers on the table

Eunice paused a moment before stabbing one of the dumplings with her chopsticks. 'Yes, he came yesterday, straight into Jeanette's office and closed the door. They're probably thinking up nasty things to say in the appraisals.'

Nicholas followed Eunice's lead and pronged a cube of steamed tofu, bringing it to his lips before swallowing it. Of course, section heads were entitled to collaborate with each other, especially if they were working in the same department. There was no company policy that said they couldn't exchange information. But then Frank was no longer a member of the department. What business brought him over to Group Public Affairs? No doubt he would say it was something to do with United's publications. But if so, why did he do it behind closed doors? 'Have you noticed anything else?'

Eunice attempted to waylay another trolley. 'Jeanette's off to London for the Annual General Meeting, which means that Antonia is running round like a headless chicken.'

Nicholas helped the woman in the pink apron find a space on the table for the shrimp wontons. 'I've noticed,' he said, encouraging her to say more.

'...Oh and Jeanette has forbidden everyone, including her secretary, to enter her office while she's away. She's going to lock the door and take the key with her. Her secretary was complaining about it this morning.'

'I see,' said Nicholas and was about to pursue the matter when he saw the warning in Sarah's eyes and decided to say nothing more.

Chapter 16

N icholas looked out on the view of Taipei from the balcony
of the rooftop swimming pool. It wasn't exactly inspiring:
a sprawl of low-rise blocks, interspersed with a few Kuomintang
Nationalist monuments in combinations of indigo and red, as far
as the eye could see. He could make out several pleasant tree-
lined avenues, hung with festoons of fairy lights and flanked by
expensive designer shops, from which a rabbit warren of side
streets with covered walkways branched out like in an old
European city. He had walked along them with Ray-jai the night
before and been surprised by the slower pace of life after Hong
Kong, a feeling of provincial calm, almost of melancholy about
the place, with its fleets of parked motorbikes and 'classical
music' bookshops and Chinese teahouses.

'Haven't you had enough?' shouted Nicholas towards the far
figure, his inflated boxer shorts protruding from the water. Ray-
jai lifted an arm to show that he had heard.

They had eaten dinner at the Ye Shanghai restaurant followed
by a trip to the spa, where Ray-jai had become increasingly
playful in the jacuzzi. Nicholas had hurried him back to the
anonymity of their room, where with the TV on and the lights

low they made perfunctory love on the soft, Shantung silk bed cover. Ray-jai fell asleep soon afterwards, his black hair splayed out on the pillow, his arms tucked up under him, and Nicholas had been about to follow when he was startled by a call on Ray-jai's cell phone. Ray-jai leaned over and answered it. Nicholas had listened intently, but it was just his lover in San Diego. They talked in low voices for a while, mumbling endearments to each other before they said good night. Ray-jai then turned off the phone and went back to sleep. Nicholas stayed up a while longer wondering if he should call Daniel.

'You coming out?' Nicholas tried again, louder this time.

Ray-jai had been quiet when they got up, happy to go to the breakfast buffet, reading his *USA Today* while Nicholas checked out the *International Herald Tribune*. There was a small piece about United International's share price but not enough to be worrying. Indeed, with so little on the horizon but the distant mountains of Taipei County and the idea of another day wandering around these back streets with their 24-hour convenience stores and markets crammed with strange smelling foods, Nicholas felt that the timing could not have been better.

'What do you want?'

'Time for a drink!'

'Okay.' Ray-jai gripped the edge of the pool and pulled himself out. Within seconds he was standing over him, water from his shorts dripping down over his thighs and calves, his cock outlined in soft profile as he lunged for his towel.

'What would you like?' asked Nicholas.

Ray-jai smacked his lips. 'Ice cream.'

'Okay, I'll have a cappuccino.' He gestured to one of the pool boys, who came over, took their order and checked the flavour Ray-jai wanted.

Nicholas waited until the boy had gone and sat down in the lounger beside Ray-jai. 'How's it all going?'

'Fine,' said Ray-jai and raised his head slightly as if wondering about Nicholas's tone. Nicholas could see the cleft of his buttocks and the tattoo of a half-naked Japanese geisha below his waistline.

'I'm afraid there's been some trouble at work,' said Nicholas, plunging in. Ray-jai frowned and flopped back into the lounger. 'A security breach at United International. We'll have to be a lot more careful about our meetings.'

The white-shorted waiter approached, placed the ice cream and drinks on the small table, and brought over the bill for Nicholas to sign. 'You'd better eat it before it melts,' he indicated, trying to read Ray-jai's expression.

Ray-jai took the ice cream into his hands, raised it in small spoonfuls to his lips and licked the spoon. A smear of chocolate was left on his nose. 'What's that to do with me?' he said in a petulant voice.

Nicholas shrugged. 'If we can't use my place, we'll have to find other things to do. Don't forget we both have our partners to consider.'

'*Your* partner,' said Ray-jai and dropped his spoon onto the plate. 'Are you saying we can't travel together?'

Nicholas forced himself to continue smiling. 'Of course not. Just as long as no one else knows.'

Ray-jai assumed a pained expression. 'Who do you think I am?'

Nicholas couldn't quite answer that, although it was a question that had been playing on his mind ever since they had started this liaison. 'I'm just saying be careful.'

Ray-jai paused. He looked Nicholas up and down as if checking him out for some hidden meaning and then with a yawn he headed for the pool, detaching the wet Lycra from his buttocks as he went. 'You coming?'

Nicholas didn't want to. In fact, he didn't want to have anything to do with Ray-jai, but he needed to get his exit right. Running straight from his recliner towards the edge of the pool, he dived in and hit Ray-jai in the mid-riff. Almost before he could surface, Ray-jai was on his back and pushing him under. Nicholas slashed wildly at the water, taking in large lungfuls of air. Within moments they had fought their way to another part of the pool and here, beneath an artificial screen of papier-maché mountains and Chinese pagodas, Ray-jai attacked again. His head disappeared beneath the water. Nicholas sensed what was coming and retreated, looking around desperately, but before he could move he could feel Ray-jai's fingers slithering between his trunks. He tried grappling, he tried kicking, but it was no use. 'I'm getting out!'

They were lucky. By the time they reached their bathrobes most people had already left the pool. Only the deck boy seemed to stare at them as they made their way towards the elevator.

It was cold back in the room, so cold that Nicholas had to adjust the air conditioning before he could take off his bathrobe. The maid had cleaned the place and made the bed. All evidence of the night before – the crumpled sheets, the box of tissues in the muslin holder, the monogrammed bath towel – had been cleared away. On the pillow was a card with gold letters stamped on purple, *In Xanadu did Kublai Khan a Stately Pleasure Dome Decree,* propped up by a small basket of heart-shaped chocolates.

Nicholas wrapped a towel around him and lay on the bed, hoping to continue their talk, but even before he could begin Ray-jai had wrapped his arms around him and was kissing him. Nicholas could feel his hands grappling with his towel. He struggled to hold it down but his efforts were undermined by the surge of blood to his penis. Pushing Ray-jai's head down in an attempt to stop him, he glimpsed his cell phone lying on the bedside table. Wrenching his left arm free, he reached over and switched it off.

'Hey,' said Ray-jai, coming up for air.

Nicholas said nothing but just laid back passively on the pillows. He could feel Ray-jai's fingers teasing his nipples, his hands caressing the inside of his thighs, and as his eyes flickered upwards he told himself that this was the very last time. He couldn't do this again – ever.

***

When he awoke he could see the dark silhouettes of the far mountains through the open blinds, the occasional patch of vertical neon flickering into life along the city's arteries. Turning to the clock, he saw that they had slept for more than four hours.

He got up, turned on the TV and found a Taiwanese basketball game before heading for the shower. When he returned, Ray-jai was sprawled silently across his side of the bed. Nicholas stopped rubbing his hair for a moment, staring at the sleeping figure. Something about Ray-jai's position, some imprint on the atmosphere, suggested that he had recently moved.

Nicholas shook him awake. 'Want to take a shower?'

Ray-jai turned and half-opened his eyes. 'Yeah,' he mumbled and covered himself with the spare towel Nicholas had laid on the bed.

Nicholas waited until he had gone before he checked the room. Nothing seemed to have changed except for the position of the phones. Perhaps they were not quite as aligned as they had been before. He picked up his Nokia and tried the keypad but it was still locked. He keyed in his PIN and went down his messages: nothing to indicate that anyone had touched it. He turned the phone off and replaced it where it had been, wondering what Ray-jai could possibly have been up to.

He was still thinking this when Ray-jai came back, turned off the TV and without removing his bathrobe crawled into his side of the bed. Within minutes he was fast asleep and Nicholas soon joined him.

When he next awoke, the room was dark and for a moment he didn't know where he was. The bedside phone was ringing. He reached over to pick up. 'Hello.'

'Nicholas? Thank god we've found you. What time is it?'

Nicholas lunged towards the water bottle on the bedside console, held it to his lips and gulped down some water. 'After midnight. Anything wrong?'

'Are you alone?'

Nicholas's heart began to pound. He could see Martin standing in front of his desk, his eyes bulging as they did when he was in a crisis, trying to find out where Nicholas was. 'Yes I am,' he said, glancing at Ray-jai.

'There's more of it.'

Nicholas winced. 'More of the leaks?'

'Yes, in most of the papers. What the hell are you doing in Taiwan?'

'Clearing my mind. I'm surprised Karen didn't give you my number.' He didn't add that she had been told not to release it except in the direst emergency.

'No one's in the office Nicholas. It's Saturday. The only number we had for you is your cell phone, which apparently was switched off, and the numbers you left in London. One of them was for your mother, who was kind enough to give us this hotel.'

Nicholas looked at the clock again: 5.17 pm in London. Daniel must have gone out, as he often did on Saturdays, and Emily was probably gardening. They could have been phoning round for hours.

'I'd better warn you. One leak might seem like an accident *but*...And then you weren't to be found.'

'I'm sorry.' He knew what Martin was trying to keep a lid on the situation. He knew very well that United International functioned on a closed circuit of power. If there was an inflection in the circuit, blame was rapidly transmitted around the company until a weak point was found. It didn't matter what *exactly* the weak point was as long as it was a weak point. That meant that something could be targeted and dealt with before normal power could resume.

'You'd better get back over to Hong Kong and investigate. Eddie is muttering about an inquiry. I've tried to put him off but this is no time to be in...Taiwan.'

'I'll be back in London on Tuesday morning,' said Nicholas as decisively as possible.

'Any idea of the source?'

'Still not clear, Martin.'

'Well, I'd better leave you to get on with it. Get some sleep.'

'Tell Eddie I'll be in London on Tuesday,' repeated Nicholas stubbornly.

'Good night, or should I say good morning?'

'Good bye,' said Nicholas and hurriedly replaced the phone.

He looked down on the bed. Ray-jai's face was turned away from him, but somehow he could tell that he was awake. Something about his body language, something about this whole trip told Nicholas that he had made a very serious mistake.

Chapter 17

S ir John looked at his watch and slowed down as he crossed in front of the Royal Exchange towards the statue of the Duke of Wellington. Eddie's phone call had sounded urgent but then his calls always sounded urgent. It was important to remain calm. He glanced up at the Duke of Wellington sitting square-backed and proud on his horse, his expression of steely determination somehow reflected in the steed's flared nostrils. Wellington was a general that knew the supreme value of patience, how to judge the enemy, how to analyse each of the possible strategies ahead of him before making a choice. That was why he had managed to outwit the great out-witter of Austerlitz, Napoleon Bonaparte. And that was why Sir John had to adopt exactly the same approach.

He stopped in front of a small cigar shop opposite the Bank of England and weighed the pleasures of a Dom Thomas against a cappuccino. He pulled his overcoat collar up against the March cold, looked up at the advancing clouds, and decided on a Dom Thomas.

Sitting on the bench in front of the War Memorial, he lit the cigar and allowed the blueish smoke to float up on the crisp morning air. The grey neo-Palladian façade of the Royal Exchange rose in front of him. Despite the thickness of the columns and the elaborate stone decorations of the frieze and the corniches, Sir John was impressed that the building didn't seem to strain for effect. It was powerful but it was also understated, almost as if it achieved its aims by some sort of trick of perspective. Perhaps there was a lesson there about power and the British, about their founding and retaining their empire. After all, wasn't it a trompe d'oeil of confederacies and local alliances that had held together millions of people by playing one off against another?

His cell phone rang. 'Eddie is ready for you,' said his secretary.

'Fifteen minutes,' said Sir John and flipped the cover shut.

All he had to do was satisfy the individual factions. He had recommended Nicholas to Roger Yates for very precise reasons and despite what had happened, his reputation was riding on him. The pieces on the chessboard had certainly moved, moved in such a startling way that he was no longer sure that he could put the main plan into action. But he had to ensure he didn't panic. If the achievement of power rested on the illusion of controlling events, even when these events moved in directions that seemed opposed to the overall strategy, he must maintain the illusion.

***

When Sir John reached the glass-fronted lobby, he was waved in by one of the security guards and headed straight for the executive floor elevator. Eddie was standing waiting for him when he entered the office, a sheaf of papers in his hand. 'Talked to Powell?' he said, waving Sir John to a seat on the leather sofa.

'Arrives tomorrow,' said Sir John and sat down. 'As far as I can make out, he's undertaken a thorough investigation in Hong Kong,

'No results,' said Eddie tersely. 'I'm beginning to think we should bring the merger announcement forward.'

'That would be most unwise,' said Sir John, his brow furrowed. 'Nicholas's strategy is to get people used to the idea. To move any quicker would make it look as if we're panicking.'

Eddie took off his glasses and gestured towards the blank TV screen. 'This leaking is making us look foolish Johhny. I've just had this Joe Burns fellow on the phone asking me if we agree with Nicholas's move to the Treasury... should it be approved. I thought of telling him that they're bloody welcome to him. And it might be a damned sight sooner than they think.'

Sir John stretched his arm along the back of the sofa. 'I'm sure Nicholas knows the seriousness of the situation. As I said, his investigations have been very thorough.'

Eddie tapped his palms on the top of the chair. 'This whole business worries me. There's something going on and I can't put my finger on it.'

Sir John swung his body forward, his hands outstretched. 'I assure you Nicholas is doing everything he can. I hardly think Roger Yates or Joe Burns would be phoning you if they had any doubts.'

Eddie gave him a long, hard look. 'The next few days are going to be crucial Johnny. I'm sure you're aware of that. I'll talk to Powell when he gets here.'

'Of course,' said Sir John. 'The fact is that Nicholas has proved himself to be very able in every other aspect of his job. We can't say that the security breach is due to him. It could happen on anyone's watch.'

Eddie gave him another sharp look. 'I'll have to take your word for that. Meanwhile, they're telling me to check through all those press releases and the merger manual. I've got no time or inclination to do so. Would you mind having a look at them yourself? I'll come back on anything you think worth marking up,' said Eddie and pushed a large dossier of documents across the table to Sir John.

'Of course, Chairman,' said Sir John. 'It'll be my pleasure.'

***

Carrying the dossier in a briefcase in his left hand, Sir John wrapped his overcoat close against the wind. A white police car with blue-and-green panda checks stopped at the traffic lights at the corner of Poultry and Princes and the driver signalled at him. Sir John hesitated, aware of the significance of what he carried, but then he saw that the officer was merely being courteous. Continuing on down Lombard Street, he turned to the left in front of the Royal Exchange and saw the pepper-pot towers of St Mary's Woolnoth church. For some reason, as he came level with its gold-painted gates, he slowed down and looked up. The soaring towers gave him an oddly sentimental feeling, an invitation to reflect, and before he knew what he was doing he had turned in through the gates.

It was gloomy inside the church and it took him a moment to adjust his eyes. Gazing around, he took in the square leaded glass, the crescent windows above the decorated pediment, the black columns of the screen behind the choir. Above his head a single gilt chandelier hung over the central aisle.

He took a seat in the chancel. The organ was playing what he took to be a Toccata and Fugue, Bach or Buxtehude, the sort of piece he vaguely remembered from his college days: endless progressions with deep swell, basso profondo and unexpected tinkling mutes. He had a sudden instinct to kneel down and pray, but then thought better of it. He had left his faith behind at Cambridge. The only time he had gone to church in recent years was in the days after 'that' had happened, and yet accompanying Marjory to Holy Communion did not provide the spiritual succour he so desperately sought. It had been the same in his childhood. All he could remember of church attendance were the cold Sunday evenings in the Gloucestershire village where he had grown up, the bedraggled choir shuffling about in the pews and the members of the congregation looking at their feet as his father's voice boomed out over the crumbling Norman vaults in yet another of his fiery sermons.

Leaning his head back, he let the deep rumble of the organ work up through his feet and for a moment his eyes rested on a plaque on the transept wall.

JOHN NEWTON
CLERK
ONCE AN INFIDEL AND LIBERTINE
A SERVANT OF SLAVES IN AFRICA
WAS
BY THE RICH MERCY
OF OUR LORD AND SAVIOUR
JESUS CHRIST
PRESERVED, RESTORED, PARDONED,
AND APPOINTED TO PREACH THE FAITH
HE HAD LONG LABOURED TO DESTROY

He stared at the plaque. The phrases seemed to pile one upon each other, just as they had at St. Clementine's when his father railed against 'the many sins of the flesh'. He shuddered with a familiar dread as the street door banged and an old lady moved down one of the centre aisles.

Cambridge was the last time he had felt the heat of his father's evangelism – at least indirectly. In his third year, he had an absurd crush on a fellow undergraduate and didn't know how to handle it. It was ridiculous, the kind of thing that happens to over-protected sons without enough experience of the world. He could still see the rooms that overlooked the Cam and the willow-fringed gardens of the Master's Lodge. He could still feel the absurd fumbling and heaving, the straining weight and dank aroma of the other body, the sense that nothing at all would fit as they grappled on the bed with its complaining springs. Afterwards he had tried to dismiss it as an accident, an experiment, but at a time when hardly anyone was 'out' and gay liberation was reserved for a few freethinkers in King's College, the subject of his undergraduate crush decided to blab it all round the place. Fearing that his father would get to hear of it, Sir John had panicked. He had chased every available girl in Girton and New Hall from then on, become a dedicated member of the rugby and football crowd, and within a few months he had proposed to Marjory. He had never looked back. He had never wanted to look back. Perhaps his father's sermons had been in his blood all along. 'Indiscretion' was a mortal sin and he had been fortunate to be preserved and restored. Perhaps one day he might even be pardoned.

His left hand quivered. He stood up and moved to the central aisle, walked slowly to a pew and sat down. For a moment he just stared at the massive wooden pulpit, the winged cherubs carved over the reredos, the commandments printed there in gold letters from the Book of Exodus and St. Matthew. Finally, he began to read down the list of sins and as he did so, one sin in particular hit him with the full fear of retribution.

IX

THOU SHALT NOT COVET THY NEIGHBOUR'S HOUSE
THOU SHALT NOT COVET THY NEIGHBOUR'S WIFE
NOR HIS SERVANT, NOR HIS MAID, NOR HIS OX,
NOR HIS ASS, NOR ANYTHING THAT IS HIS.

Chapter 18

N icholas cursed to himself as he narrowly avoided yet another squashed animal in the road. A single-lane B-road with four numerals after it was not the sort of highway for sudden swerves. The double white lines and the swinging bends, plus the tailgating Peugeot behind made his hands tingle on the steering wheel. They were approaching Hope, which according to the map lay just beyond the Long Mynd. The name alone should have encouraged him, but the endless minor road works after they reached Cheltenham, the lack of adequate signs in Tewkesbury and the detour around the business estates of Evesham had all taken their toll. He had tried to introduce the charms of the countryside to Daniel, but even though they had wandered round the open market in Ludlow and bought some fudge and Blue Shropshire cheese for their hosts, Daniel remained in that odd, lacklustre mood he had been in since he left London. He wasn't exactly bad-tempered, he had tried to help with road directions, but he seemed curiously distracted.

Nicholas glanced out of the window at the pallisade of trees on the far hill: an army of lancers frozen in time. The borders of Wales and England swept towards each other here in a wave of straggling hedgerows and emerald and ochre fields. He put his foot down on the accelerator, desperate to finish the journey.

'We're coming up to Michaelsea,' said Daniel, reading the mile signposts with a sideways glance. The AA road map was open on his legs.

'It's about two miles beforehand, turn right at a red telephone box. Was that a telephone box?'

'How should I know?' said Daniel. The town sign for Michaelsea was visible up ahead.

'I'll turn back,' said Nicholas and reversed the car at the next cul-de-sac, heading in the other direction. The hills that Kay had mentioned were now rearing to his left. At the telephone box, he saw the sign that he had missed – *Snail's Place* – and for the first time since Ludlow he exchanged a smile with Daniel as he swung the car left.

They headed up a hill between the fields and towards a church tower visible on the brow of the escarpment. But before they reached it, he stopped the car and took out his cell phone.

'Why do lesbians live in the back of beyond?' asked Daniel.

'Earth mother issues. Handling a spade better than a man,' said Nicholas as he dialed Josie's house number.

'Yes dear boy?' said a business-like voice. 'Do you want to speak to your sister. Hang on – '

'We're at Snail's Place,' said Nicholas but Josie had already gone.

A voice with a slightly toothless lisp came on the line; 'Turn to the right behind the church and down the track. Watch out for your axles.'

Nicholas snapped the phone cover back and did as he was told, trundling down a rutted, unpaved track past a row of modern bungalows until he came to junction with a turning to the right that seemed to lead straight into a field of well-nurtured cows. The figure of Kay was visible to the left, standing next to another woman of similar age. Nicholas asked Daniel to lower the window.

'Bring the car in here,' said Kay with decisive hand gestures.

Nicholas brought the Mondeo broadside on to the old Saab that shared the drive with Kay's Land Rover. Nicholas switched off the engine, jumped out of the car and gave Kay and Josie a kiss.

'This is Daniel,' he said, beaming in Daniel's direction.

Kay was dressed in a bright red fleece over a mauve T-shirt that proclaimed *I am not a lesbian. I simply like women.* She seemed to have lost some weight recently, despite all the boozing. Nicholas hoped it was Josie's influence. Of the two of them, Josie seemed more correct in her glasses and high polo neck, a cameo brooch in her cardigan. Her face was altogether longer and paler than Kay's, which gave her a more serious look, although her big green eyes radiated warmth. Kay's expression, in contrast, was rather piratical now that she had capped some of her teeth, and abnormally flushed as if she had just stormed up one of those slate mountains in the vicinity of her North Wales cottage. But the essential Kay was still there: generous, robust, confrontational. Those lesbian bashers in her hometown had picked on her car for a fight, not on her.

'God I need a drink. I didn't realize how far it is. And the traffic, even on a weekend,' said Nicholas as Kay and Josie led them round the side of the cottage into a garden full of purple delphiniums and hollyhocks and climbing sweet peas in pastel colours. Beyond them Josie pointed out the vegetable garden. 'It'll be bursting with courgettes soon.'

The fields around the cottage that led up to the old tin mines on the hill were just darkening as they entered the back door into the kitchen. The high-ceilinged room was filled with the aroma of spices. There were two PCs on the kitchen table, hitched up to long telephone and electricity cables. Something was bubbling away on the Aga stove.

'Smells fantastic,' said Daniel, going over to inspect the large pan.

'I like to try different things, don't I Josie?' said Kay as she offered Daniel a taste with a spoon.

'She's got this enormous Thai cookbook, and makes a pot of Thai curry for a week. It still seems to be there every time I come home,' said Josie. 'Overboard as usual.'

'I know what you mean,' said Nicholas. 'Like it here Daniel?'

'It's great,' said Daniel, flipping the back door shut with his foot. Something about his loose jeans and T-shirt, something about his easy intimacy as he licked the spoon clean made Nicholas feel intensely proud.

'I bet he's got you at it at home,' said Kay. 'Probably never leave the kitchen.'

Daniel laughed. 'He does the washing up.'

'That's not fair,' protested Nicholas. 'He won't let me do anything except be the menial.'

'Suppose you had to cook non-stop for Emily?' said Kay, ignoring Nicholas.

'We went out quite a lot,' said Daniel. 'Thank god.'

'Paid for by you two. Emily never puts her hand in her pocket,' said Kay and turned to look at Nicholas. 'How did it go then? Did she give you the all clear?'

'It was fine. She liked it so much it was difficult to get her to leave,' said Nicholas and caught Daniel's look. 'Let's go into the lounge. I think Josie's about to dish up.'

'That I am,' said Josie in the same tone she used on the phone.

He stopped at the fridge, where a magnet said *Dull Women Have Immaculate Houses*. He took a closer look. The one next to it said *Women Don't Grow Old, They Just Discover Themselves*. He had heard a lot about Josie from Kay but had never met her, and now that she was there in the midst of all her disorder he couldn't quite understand why he had been so scared of her. As if to underline the point, a slim grey cat and a tubby brown-and-cream companion slid beneath his feet from the flap in the back door and went to drape themselves on the furniture.

'Offa,' shouted Josie after them as they entered the lounge. 'That's the brown-and-white. Offa's not far from here actually. And Marlowe is named after the playwright.'

'Offa's Dyke,' explained Nicholas. Clearly the names meant nothing to Daniel.

'I'll help Josie,' he said. 'You chat with Kay.'

'What an adorable boy,' said Josie, rummaging around for serving dishes. 'He can come again.'

Nicholas and Kay stood for a moment at the gable windows and looked out at the broad sweep of the Shropshire valleys rising to occasional soft purple mounds in the distance; in the foreground was a row of hawthorn trees spaced along a long hedgerow and a meadow peopled with those cows they had seen, now merging with their twilight shadows.

'Seriously though, did it go all right? She can be a right you-know-what if she wants to,' said Kay indicating the shapes in the meadow and lighting a cigarette.

'That's the last one before lunch,' said Josie from the kitchen in a funny singsong. 'And only two glasses of wine. Right, Nicholas?'

Nicholas looked towards the door in amazement. No one had trodden where she had dared to tread. 'Shall I open the bottle?'

'Hang on. I'm not that desperate. Just tell us what she said.' Kay inhaled as if with her whole body and sat down on the sofa.

Nicholas cleared his throat. 'She said she liked Daniel.'

'Yes and – ?' Kay stared hard at him, letting the cigarette smoke dissipate in the draught from the log fire.

'She didn't say much about you, if that's what you mean,' said Nicholas.

Daniel appeared with two glasses full of *vinho verde*. He handed one to Kay and one to Nicholas, who attempted to look severe as Kay drank hers down in one go.

'I won't drink much tonight,' announced Nicholas, loud enough for Josie to hear. 'I have some work to do in the morning.'

'Oh yes, those wankers,' said Kay with a flick of her ash.

'I'm maybe up for a new job,' said Nicholas brightly, keeping the nature of the position vague.

'My god, what a successful brother I've got. Mind you, you were always Mum's favourite. She protected you.' Nicholas smiled and pretended to look at a book of A.E. Housman poems that shared the coffee table with Roget's Thesaurus and *Diva* magazine. 'Come on, tell me what happened. I mean, something must have happened or you wouldn't have been so keen to come over.'

'Not at all. We wanted to see you.'

'Yes, but it had to be now. What did she say?'

Kay's face was now totally focused on Nicholas's. He knew there was no way out. She and Emily had that in common. He looked towards the door but Daniel was still busy in the kitchen.

'She said Daniel seemed to be a good choice, but maybe I should take it slowly,' he said in a low voice.

Kay nodded and dragged at her cigarette. 'Making sure she remains the centre of attention. And what's wrong with Daniel, may I ask?'

'Nothing,' Nicholas shrugged and put down the poems. 'She thought he was a bit young for me, that's all. You know what she's like. First, she says I'm letting my life go by. Then she says I'm immature.'

'He looks charming to me. I should think he does you the world of good, especially after all those wankers.'

Nicholas smiled. 'I have to make a living.'

'A bloody good one too, it sounds like. Still, you'll need someone like Daniel to share it with. He looks fun. What else did she say?' Kay finished her drink and lit another cigarette.

'Oh the usual. She'd prefer me to consider my career first.'

'Yes, imagine what the neighbours might think,' grinned Kay. 'Does Daniel have any friends?'

'Yes he does,' said Nicholas with a stab of jealousy, thinking of the number of texts he had been recently receiving.

'This is all very new for him. I expect he'll be fine once he's found the right slot. You should take him along to some of those stuffy receptions you have to go to. Just to make the point.'

Nicholas felt ashamed by Kay's frankness. 'That's just what Emily reckoned I shouldn't do, especially now that I've got this job offer. It's quite high up.'

'Will Emily ever stop? Be positive, Nicholas. The next thing is you'll be having boyfriends for different occasions.'

'Actually...' he hesitated. Kay may just about have understood but this wasn't the moment.

'I'm not pretending any more,' continued Kay. 'Surely your bosses know?'

Nicholas hesitated. He didn't want a lecture on sexual discrimination just before dinner. 'There was a rumour...' He didn't finish.

Kay saw his look and gulped down the rest of her wine. Nicholas half-expected her to wipe her hand across her mouth. 'They think you're straight and you haven't told them?'

Nicholas moistened his lips. 'There's no need to. It's true that Daniel was working in United International but that's all over now.'

Kay put one hand on her knee. 'That doesn't mean you have to keep silent. It's your duty to come out.'

'Out?' said Josie, entering the room with a flushed face and bearing down on Kay's cigarette, which she took from her hand and stubbed out in the ashtray. Kay stood up and led the way to the kitchen where Daniel was laying out the plates and hunting for a serving spoon. Josie asked Nicholas to pour the wine. Daniel had already piled the plates with rice so that everyone could help themselves to the green curry and sambal. Josie passed around a plate of papadums and various fruit chutneys made from leftovers in the garden. It wasn't until they were well into the food on their plates that Josie remembered her question. 'Were you out at school?'

'I'm afraid not.'

Daniel snorted as Kay gave Nicholas a meaningful look. 'Butter wouldn't melt in his mouth,' said Kay and before Nicholas could stop her she had begun an account of how spoilt he was, which seemed to Nicholas to be based entirely on his giving the Latin speech on Speech Day. On the other hand, all she was allowed to do was to go to teacher training college and get married to the first man that came along.

'But you knew you were gay?' asked Daniel.

'Oh yes,' said Kay with a lunge towards the wine bottle. 'But I also knew I wanted children. It was the same for Josie, wasn't it darling?'

'Guilt,' said Josie and stared at them as if daring anyone to contradict her. 'I wouldn't do without my children now. I've loved having them, but we all live with guilt. That is, until we come out.'

Daniel looked straight at Nicholas. 'Did you hear that Nicholas?'

'You know how difficult it is,' said Nicholas, staring back.

Josie suppressed a laugh. 'It's difficult for all of us. We're married dykes with husbands. We've done the duty thing all our lives, including marital sex. Now we're put out to pasture we can at least have our own life.'

'Nicholas's company thinks he's straight,' said Kay in a resigned voice.

Josie turned immediately to Daniel, who was rising to help her serve the rice. 'What do you think of that?'

Daniel shrugged. 'It's up to Nicholas. He says he knows what he's doing.'

Nicholas started to explain that it wasn't up to him, but the more he explained the more the others exchanged looks. By the time the main course was finished and Daniel was complaining how long it had taken Nicholas to make an application under the new partnership laws, Nicholas felt that he could rip all the magnets off the fridge.

'What's the problem? Is it that you have to declare that you and Daniel are partners?' said Josie as they settled in the lounge and she poured the coffee.

Nicholas ran a hand through his hair. 'No, it's not. Immigration doesn't contact the employer.'

'So why don't you get on with it?' said Kay.

'I *am* getting on with it.' His cup shook.

'You'll have to take it in stages I suppose,' said Josie in a soothing voice. 'That's what we all do.'

Nicholas repressed an inner protest. If Daniel was going to start on the answer machine message, he was going to bed.

'We belong to a group of dykes called the Hells' Bitches,' said Josie as if to change the subject. 'That's what Kay calls us. We're all professional women, mainly working in health care. We live all round the country. It's a like a therapy group. Maybe you should join us Nicholas. Everyone comes to accept themselves in their own time.'

Nicholas gave her a cold smile. 'That's kind of you Josie, but I think I can manage. I'm not sure I can handle a whole group of dykes. Dykes on bikes I mean.'

'We're not *all* into leather,' said Josie. 'But I guess we are a bit overwhelming, especially in the pub. Kay loves it don't you?'

'They love my Thai curry,' said Kay with a satisfied smile.

Nicholas wanted to ask if any of them was a managing director or a solicitor or a famous sportsman but he felt too intimidated. As Kay and Josie went on about the Hell's Bitches, he let his head fall back and gaze at the row of framed photos along the mantelpiece. They were of Josie's five children by two marriages, each of them wearing a graduate gown and mortarboard: lawyers and doctors and accountants. Presumably they had no problem with Josie and Kay's lifestyle. There seemed to be no secrets in the house, no animosity. But then two women living together, two women with children, did not exactly constitute a threat to society.

Finally, he could keep his eyes open no longer. Daniel went out to the car to get their overnight bags and led him up to the bedroom to help him unpack. As soon as he returned downstairs, Nicholas flopped out on the bed and without turning off the light, fell fast asleep.

***

He awoke to a *beep-beep* coming from close by. It was dark in the room and he could feel Daniel's body next to his. He looked at the bedside clock: 11.34 pm. There were still voices downstairs, audible through the wooden floors. He could make out Kay's slightly slurred tones. Then the beeping began again and he felt hurriedly for his phone, determined to turn it off. However, the noise wasn't coming from his phone. He thought for a moment, his head fuzzy with sleep. It would be quite normal for someone to message Daniel during the day but at this time of night it was odd. Of course it was Saturday, which could have meant that Matt or one of the others were out on the town, but they should have known that Daniel was with him. Unless of course it was someone else, someone who didn't know anything about him. For a moment he wondered who this person might be and considered leaning over Daniel to pick up the phone. Then he saw it was wedged beneath Daniel's left arm.

In need of relief, he slipped off the bed and crept down the corridor. He knew the bathroom was at the left at the bottom of the stairs, but just as he reached the kitchen he stopped. He could hear Josie's voice in the lounge ahead of him.

'He'll never keep him.'

'I was also a closet once,' sniffed Kay to the sound of a cap being unscrewed. 'You'll have to give him time.'

'But he's the one with all the privileges. If you hadn't come out when you did, you would never have come out. The trouble with men is that they want it all. You heard what Daniel said about the answer machine.'

'I don't know,' sighed Kay. 'He treats Daniel very well. It's not his fault that our parents pressured me.'

Nicholas edged closer to the lounge door, guilt rising within him like damp. He knew he wasn't exactly a role model for liberation, but if the end result was a half share of a mill cottage somewhere up a Welsh valley he wondered if he could ever afford to be. He had visited Kay after the break-up and she had seemed so terribly alone, stuck in the midst of all her sky blue furniture and deserted bedrooms. Sky blue was the colour she had chosen for her first relationship with a woman and she had covered the whole house with it: kitchen kettle and place mats, bath towels and curtains, mugs and carpets. 'Blue is the colour of the imagination,' she had told him once and it all seemed so positive at the beginning, so sad at the end. He could still recall her defiance and courage despite everything. In the midst of the Gin Martinis, the Seroxat and the Temazepam, she had refused to move from the house she had shared with her lover and for a long while afterwards she had also refused to give up the love itself. Even though the woman had called her a 'fat cow' all round the tiny Welsh village where they lived and carried on with someone else behind her back, Kay had kept her photographs on the wall, her memories, even her love poetry.

'I don't think he has the guts.'

'He just needs time,' said Kay, the ice now clearly clinking in her glass.

Nicholas smiled. Outside that cottage in Snowdonia there was nothing but wet mountains and slate roofs and a stream that rushed past the lower bedroom where Nicholas had slept. It should have been depressing but somehow it wasn't. There was something about the cottage, something about the whole situation of being left alone in the middle of nowhere, which had made him wonder. Kay was out. Everyone in the village knew about her. She had lots of friends, most of whom she met in the pub at night, and the pub was the heart of the place. She had a community, a support system, a world. Would he be able to sacrifice everything one day for Daniel just as she had done? Okay, she had fallen off a cliff, and yet she had come up with a new life via the internet. He wondered where happiness resided. Was she happier because she was more liberated than he was, or simply because she was indifferent to what other people thought?

'Now you're defending him because he's your brother.'

Chapter 19

R oger Yates' square school-boyish face smiled broadly from all three TV sets in United International's monitoring room. He stood in the House of Commons giving his first major speech as Chancellor as if he had been doing it every day of his life, using his hands to chop, parcel and shift forward his sentences like some sort of mad corn thresher at high speed. The smile disappeared and was replaced by a fixed, granite look, at once heavy with meaning and redolent with irony.

Nicholas sighed to himself and scratched his head. The problem was the way he spoke. He delivered those heaped-up commonplaces – 'Build up and sustain consensus', 'The true purpose of politics is to serve our country', 'We cannot and will not tolerate inequality of wealth' – without waiting for applause or indeed for any understanding to be registered. There was no light and shade to what he was saying. It was as if a maelstrom of heaped up promises to 'halve world poverty', 'improve public services' and 'make government transparent' would somehow bend reality to his will. The imitation of the Prime Minister's urgency was perhaps understandable; less forgivable was the bombast.

Nicholas smoothed down his tie and wondered where he would begin. It wasn't that Roger didn't sound committed. It was just that his determination to recite lofty-sounding promises at all costs undermined his credibility. It may be that Joe Burns and his boss had a full dossier of policies to back up these sermons, but various government advisers had warned him about the blizzard of announcements he would be expected to make and the lack of any system to ensure that even a modicum of them would be implemented.

The new Chancellor's way of dressing didn't much help either. He usually wore a non-descript suit and a hastily knotted tie with his top shirt button undone and one collar sticking out over his lapel. His informal outfit seemed to consist of beige conservative trousers, an Arran wool sweater and a Viyella check shirt. This image had won him votes in the past, and plenty of admirers within his party, but what he needed now was a sharper look: a well-cut dark suit with white shirt and a primary colour tie for formal occasions, a polo shirt or dark T-shirt with designer jeans and perhaps a casual blazer for informal.

Nicholas flicked over the channels to see if there was anything else on the reshuffle or the merger: nothing. Not even on CNBC or Bloomberg, although the latter announced the date of United International's Annual General Meeting together with joint UIB-Mercantile logos and the headline *Bigger is Better?*

He assumed there was a story to come and quickly phoned down to the War Room to get it covered. With three days to go until the Annual General Meeting, there had been no more unwelcome leaks or comments in *Eye Witness*. The media had focused largely on the cabinet reshuffle, and for that he had to be grateful. Despite his best attempts to uncover the source of the leaks, delegating people he could scarcely spare to follow up on leads, he still had nothing to go on. Since his interview with Eddie, he had tried several times to phone Sir John and arrange a meeting in which he could further discuss the situation. However, Sir John seemed to be devoting his time exclusively to politics. Nicholas wasn't exactly sure what position Sir John had in the

Roger Yates camp, but it was he who had passed on the Chancellor's invitation to the upcoming reception in the City.

Nicholas checked his watch. He just had time to phone Emily before setting out. He moved away from the screens to the farther end of the room and keyed in her number.

'Hello. You seen the news?'

'Yes, I expect you're pleased.' Emily was not a great admirer of Roger Yates.

Nicholas caught a faint memory of his old boyhood need for approval. 'I'm going to be introduced in an hour or so. He seems very interested, although I still have my hands full with the merger.'

'Is anyone else after this job?'

'There's a short list,' said Nicholas. 'I'm the favourite.'

Emily didn't say anything for a moment. 'Nicholas, did you ever find out who was responsible for those leaks?'

Nicholas sighed. This was not a subject he wanted to discuss right now, especially not with Emily. 'I have my suspicions. I'm just going to wait until the AGM is safely over.'

'Was it someone in your company?' persisted Emily.

Nicholas looked around. The only witness seemed to be Roger Yates, still ploughing on in the House of Commons. 'Sorry, I can't talk about it at the moment. These walls may have ears.'

He could hear the sound of the phone slipping. Then a sudden clunk as Emily readjusted it. 'All I can say is you'd better watch out. Jealous people are dangerous people. Where's Daniel at the moment?'

'At home,' said Nicholas.

'You're not taking him to the reception?'

Nicholas held his breath. Both Emily and Kay, for different reasons, thought that Daniel was his constant companion.

'Why doesn't he go and see his family?' asked Emily.

'You mean in Hong Kong?'

'Yes, exactly.'

'He doesn't have a passport Mum. The Home Office took it away to process his visa. God knows when he'll get it back.'

He could hear her mumble something to herself. 'Then send him to Kay's or somewhere. Anywhere as long as he's out of the way. You've got to take this seriously. It's a big opportunity.'

Nicholas closed his eyes and drew a deep breath. 'I am taking it seriously, Mum, but the government is going to employ me, not Daniel.' He glanced at the TV screen. Roger Yates was finally ceding to the opening logo for CNN Business News. 'I've told him to be careful whom he talks to for now. That should be sufficient.'

'I see,' said Emily in that resigned voice he knew only too well. 'I'm just warning you they're after people in public life these days. Give them an inch and they'll take a mile. I know it shouldn't make any difference – .'

'I've got to go Mum. Let's talk later,' he said and with a mumbled goodbye, he rang off.

He stood there for a moment wondering if he had been too abrupt. Maybe she was right. It was true that his name would become much more prominent once he joined the Chancellor's team. But getting Daniel out of the way seemed to be out of all proportion to the possible threat. He certainly wouldn't appreciate being shoved off to the country.

His phone rang again. 'Hi, it's Kay.'

Nicholas swallowed. His family seemed to be everywhere. 'Anything wrong?'

'No, but I've just had Emily on the phone. She asked if Daniel could stay with me for a few days. Of course I agreed, but why on earth would you be sending him up here?'

Nicholas counted the number of squares on the carpet. 'I didn't suggest he comes to you.'

'So what's she on about?'

Nicholas drew himself up. 'The Chancellor needs a new communications director. I'm up for the job. She thinks that Daniel will somehow, I don't know, affect my chances. The fact of Daniel, that is.'

There was the sound of suppressed laughter. 'Plenty of people are out these days, even in politics.'

'Yes they are, but they usually wait until they're well established in the job before they put their feet in the water,' said Nicholas.

He could hear Kay coughing on the other end, whether in agreement or disagreement he couldn't quite tell. It wasn't too early in the day for one of her Gin Martinis. The Silk Cut would be out and she would be splayed in a jogging suit on her sky blue sofa. 'I don't know exactly what's going on down there but I wouldn't give a damn what anybody thinks. If you listen to Emily and the people who think like her, you're never going to get settled.'

'I wasn't – '.

'You sound just like the landlord of our pub,' persisted Kay. 'He's always on about the value of marriage and staying together for appearances until I tell him about my experience. Then he goes into reverse gear. You don't have to hide your partner away Nicholas. Just act naturally. People will judge you on your behaviour.'

A group of senior executives led by a Public Affairs guide was waiting at the entrance to the room. The guide was desperately signalling at him to leave. For a moment he didn't understand what he wanted, and then with a shudder of embarrassment he understood. Public Affairs tours for senior executives were his idea; the TV monitoring room was last on the list after the War Room.

'I'm sorry, I've got to go Kay. I'll catch up later.'

***

Adjusting the purple United logo on his lapel, Nicholas followed the steady stream of the Chancellor's guests up the slightly faded red carpet of the marble stairway. Reaching the top of the stairs, he turned right through the elaborately carved doors and entered the reception hall. A Turneresque sea battle in a huge gilt rococo frame was raging unchecked along the far wall – in the foreground the poop of a four-masted schooner was inclining dangerously towards the waves, its 'red duster' flag shot through with holes. Below the carnage, a trio of male pianist in a black turtleneck, drummer with gold necklace and saxophonist in a black beret was softly playing jazz. A white-clothed buffet table, laid out with canapés and trays of gleaming rolled sushi and bottles of Bollinger or Pol Roger champagne, stretched from where he stood almost to the end of the room. All along the table he could see men in dark suits and women in black or grey cocktail dresses topped with a demure row of pearls, perma-tanned public relations people with oily faces and fixed smiles, the occasional devil-may-care woman MP or journalist in orange or canary yellow taffeta or slashed silk exchanging business cards.

He dropped his own card onto a silver salver at the doorway, declined the offer of a sea urchin sushi but accepted a glass of Bollinger from one of the black-tailed waiters, and looked around for Sir John. All he could make out was the burly figure of Roger Yates at the centre of a group of laughing admirers that swelled, broke and reformed with every move that he made. Eventually, he caught a glimpse of Sir John to his left, the star-shaped birthmark on his temple clearly visible in the light. His proximity to the Chancellor suggested trust, even intimacy, but from where Nicholas stood he had the impression that Roger Yates was keeping him at a distance.

He moved to within a few feet of Sir John and waited his turn. Sir John saw him from the corner of his eye. 'Let me introduce you Nick.' Propelling himself forward to within just a few feet of Roger Yates, Sir John held out his left hand. 'Roger, allow me to introduce Nicholas Powell.'

'Nicholas.' Roger Yates turned immediately and shook his hand as the laughter around him quickly subsided. 'I've heard a lot about you.' Nicholas felt the intensity of his grip and was aware of an exhaustive check being made of his face, his attire, everything about him, while the others in his circle did the same.

'Good things I trust,' he said with a practiced smile. A vocaliste had joined the trio at the far end of the hall and was singing *Mama may have, Papa may have, But God bless the child that's got his own...that's got his own.'*

Roger Yates brought his jaw forward as if in appreciation of what he saw. Despite the strands of grey in his shock of black hair and a patter of crows' feet round his eyes, he exuded the air of the impudent schoolboy that Nicholas had noticed on United's TV. 'As Sir John knows, I'm not a great expert on The City. I'm sure you'll have plenty to teach me.'

'He certainly taught me a few things,' said Sir John with a fake-hearty expression.

Roger Yates turned to Sir John and smiled with a distinct coldness before turning back to Nicholas. 'I'm sure we'll have plenty to teach each other.' He glanced at Sir John. 'I've been well informed of your abilities. Give me a call next week. We'll have lunch.'

'Of course,' said Nicholas. 'I'd be delighted.'

Suddenly, Sir John caught sight of two people on the outer fringes of the crowd and signaled to them to come over. Nicholas turned to put his glass down on the table behind him and when he turned back there was Jeanette Long, a tall, grey-haired man wearing shell-rimmed glasses at her side.

'How nice to see you,' said Sir John. 'And Hugh too. Have you met Roger Yates?'

Sir John turned to the Chancellor, who had resumed that schoolboy stare with his jaw jutting out. His smile had shrunk to a thin hard line across his face. 'Jeanette works with us. Hugh is an old colleague of mine.'

Jeanette clutched at her pashmina with one hand while she stretched out the other towards the Chancellor. 'Congratulations on your appointment. Hugh and I are great fans, aren't we Hugh?'

Hugh nodded vaguely and scratched his head. His too short suit trousers revealed a pair of un-matching coloured socks. 'Hope the taxpayer doesn't have to pay for it all,' he mumbled as one or two of Roger's admirers on the edge of the circle tittered. 'I mean, for all these reformed public services.'

'Set your mind at rest,' parried Roger Yates, slipping immediately into politician mode. 'Improving public services doesn't mean that the government's going to empty the public coffers. Consumer pays will be the principle. We'll have to work hard to get that message across.' He turned to Nicholas with what appeared to be a wink.

Nicholas acknowledged the gesture, as well as the deceit, but his mind was engaged elsewhere. It occurred to him that if Jeanette and her husband were friends of Sir John, they might also know what Nicholas was doing there. He signaled to Sir John that he would like a word with him. Sir John ushered Jeanette towards Roger Yates and with a slight bow, said he would be back soon.

'We'll talk next week, Nicholas,' said the Chancellor as Jeanette glanced pointedly in Sir John's direction.

'I'm looking forward to that,' replied Nicholas, maneuvering Sir John backwards from the throng until they had reached a safe distance. 'What the hell's *she* doing here?'

Sir John raised his eyebrows. 'What do you mean?'

'Who invited her?'

'Hugh's an old friend of mine. He lectures on economics at Birkbeck College. I thought they'd like to meet the new Chancellor.'

'And what do they know about my plans, I mean with Roger Yates?'

Sir John spread his hands in a priest-like gesture. 'Nothing at all, Nicholas. Do you think I would tell anyone about something so important?'

Nicholas looked hard at him, wondering whether he should reply. There was something about Sir John tonight that puzzled him, something that didn't seem to fit his previous behaviour. 'Jeanette and I are not on the best of terms. And there's been too much gossip already.'

Sir John looked down at the floor, as if searching for the right words. 'I quite understand. We used to have the odd dinner together in Hong Kong when I came over, that's all. I think I've been to their place in Hammersmith once in all these years.'

Nicholas glanced around to make sure they were not overheard. This was the only chance he was going to have. 'I've been thinking about what you said the other day and I've come to the conclusion that very few people would have the possibility of gaining access to that leaked information. Especially in my inner circle.'

Sir John tilted his head. 'And?'

'But some of my senior managers *did* have access to it and they seem to be participating in their own rather secretive system for sharing information between each other. I don't want to go into the full details here. It may be completely harmless. However, it's clear that Frank Shearer is one of them.'

Sir John glanced around the room. 'Frank Shearer?'

Nicholas moved closer. ' Now of UIB Investment Bank.'

A deep flush spread through Sir John's cheeks. He seemed to be about to say something, hesitated a moment and then led Nicholas even further away from the Roger Yates circle. 'Listen to me Nicholas. No one with such a good position in United International would attempt a leak against you. I don't know what this circle is that you're talking about, but broadcasting accusations against one of your colleagues at the moment will not do you any good.'

Nicholas felt his hands tingle. At the very least he would have expected some sort of surprise or perhaps even shock. 'I didn't say that any of them *are* responsible Sir John. I'm just saying that it's an odd way for senior managers to behave. It could be a way for information to leak out. You will remember that it was you that suggested I look at every possibility...'

'Of course,' said Sir John. 'But the situation has become rather more delicate. By all means look at every possibility, but be very careful what you say until you have firm evidence. It doesn't pay to alienate people. You don't know who they might have in their address book.'

Nicholas glanced over to the group around the Chancellor, where Jeanette and Hugh were still hovering. He wondered whom Jeanette had in her address book. 'Excuse me Sir John. I have another meeting to attend. We'll talk again.'

'Of course,' said Sir John with what seemed relief, already turning and signaling to someone in the far crowd. By the time Sir John looked back, Nicholas was halfway across the room and walking with very elaborate intent straight past the barriers of champagne and hors d'oeuvres towards the staircase.

Chapter 20

T he refracted light of a sunny April morning filtered through the glass dome of United International's headquarters on New Change Street, filling the penthouse with the first glow of Spring. Nicholas sat at the far end of the long table facing the packed rows of shareholders, financial reporters, investment analysts and senior staff. The top tier management ranged to his left, their faces fixed and ashen as if in mourning for the billions of pounds of profits they had somehow made and for the gargantuan bonuses and share options they had since awarded themselves. The white-haired Eddie sat in the centre, tight-lipped and arms folded. In the front rows sat the non-executive Directors, including Sir John himself in a striped black suit beneath which was visible his usual serge waistcoat. Camera crews with sound booms and photographers with heavy lens bobbed up and down between the tinted glass windows and the ranks of chairs, occasionally making a wild dash down the centre aisle only to be turned back by the Group Public Affairs minders who crouched low as they padded after them.

Nicholas could see several of UIB's heads of Trading, Investment Banking and Personal Banking standing at the back of the room near the white-clothed tea tables. Jeanette Long was among them, the only woman among a sea of dark suits, purple United ties and white shirts, Frank Shearer just to her right. Everybody in the room was focused on the Group Chairman as he began to run through a long list of Corporation achievements: profits before tax, return on assets, dividend per share. Firstly, he delivered the results for the Group as a whole, and then for the individual regions: the U.K., the Americas, and finally Asia – the 'real growth story'.

Nicholas massaged his neck with one hand and waggled it gently until something clicked within the cluster of skeletal nodes. He glanced to his right. Eddie had just finished with the results of Hong Kong and was trudging his way through Australia, Malaysia, Singapore and New Zealand before heading on to the main business of the afternoon.

'Ladies and gentlemen, shareholders, members of the press, now we come to the principal announcement of the day. As you know, we are an organisation that has always functioned with a strong sense of the responsibility that we owe to our shareholders and customers. So, it is with great pleasure that we announce...'

As he came to the crucial 'M' word, a blizzard of flashes swept the room, making him squeeze his eyes before he continued to read out the finely honed sentences that Nicholas and his team had so painstakingly prepared. Finally, as he came to an end and the Question and Answer session began. Eddie smoothed down his jacket and folded his pudgy hands on the tabletop as a young woman in the front row stood up, her face flushed and her hands trembling.

'Chairman, are you concerned that leaking of the merger has affected your share price?'

Nicholas watched Eddie out of the corner of his eyes as he quietly adjusted his tie. 'No my dear, I am not. Leaks are something that occur before any major announcement. We're satisfied that in this case they weren't deliberate.'

The young woman paused and tilted her head to one side. 'I see, but do you know of other cases that *were* deliberate?'

Eddie broadened his smile and loosened his hands to make a Gallic gesture of tolerance. 'We're confident that there was no deliberate disclosure of information.'

'What was the source?' asked a male journalist, grabbing the microphone from the slightly irritated girl.

Eddie paused a moment and looked round the expectant faces in the room. 'I don't need to tell you that the marketplace in which we operate is very competitive. The demand for information for the 24-hour news cycle is burdensome but also an opportunity for those who would seek to gain advantage. As to who might or might not be responsible for such a leak, we have no evidence.'

'A competitor?' The female journalist's jaw jutted out.

Eddie's expression remained impassive. 'As I said, we don't know. After intensive investigation, we've come to the conclusion that the problem did not originate with us. As you will be aware, our standards of confidentiality and disclosure are high. We have an extremely tight and well-tested system of risk management. Our Chinese walls – by which I mean the fire-tight divisions between our wholesale, retail and investment banking arms – are impeccable. This is an important merger that has implications not only for the City of London and the U.K. but also for all those who seek better banking services throughout the world. We must ensure that our Chinese walls are extremely fire-proof.'

As if to cut off the flow of Chinese walls exposition, the nervous young woman lunged at the microphone. 'But haven't you recently complained about the reporting requirements of the Financial Services Authority?'

Eddie looked down at his signet ring with an almost apologetic air. 'We didn't complain about the FSA. We simply observed that quarterly reporting is very onerous for a large organisation such as United International. We have to comply with the regulatory demands of many different jurisdictions around the globe. We have no complaints whatever about the FSA and we work in very close partnership with our regulatory colleagues. All the details of the merger have been fully explained to the relevant authorities and we are well known for our spirit of partnership with those who regulate us.'

The young woman, who didn't seem to be listening, could hardly wait for the Group Chairman to finish. 'Excuse me sir, but the leaked information contained the *exact* number of current accounts achieved by this merger. It appears they will be more than 100 per cent greater in the new merged entity. May we ask how did that happen, given that the numbers were only made available in the Press Release that was issued today?'

For a second Eddie seemed shaken by the directness of this comment, but then his small green eyes narrowed. He smiled, a tiny knot forming at the corner of his lips. 'Could you rephrase that my dear so that I don't have to repeat myself?' He paused. 'Unlike your good self.'

The laughter that suddenly swept the room was like the effect of a match thrown into a vast pile of tinder. *Eddie was human after all!* it seemed to announce. Tension was not necessary. Indeed, not only was Eddie human, he had a sense of humour. Of course, United International had carried out due diligence on the merger. Of course, the regulatory authorities had been kept fully in the loop. After all, this was an institution that was anchored in the City of London. *Full* disclosure, rigid systems of compliance, transparent procedures and absolutely no dabbling in new-fangled instruments. Growth for United was 'organic'. It was never short-term and predatory.

Several more rounds of assurances on these matters followed, along with more informal sniping by the journalists, until at last the whole thing was over.

The senior management of the world's oldest bank began to file out in almost monastic order followed by the press with their cameras and sound booms at the ready. Then, once outside the conference room, the journalists gathered by the elevator to listen to Eddie's final utterances on the possible findings of the Competition Commission and the rumours of the relocation of the Group's Asian headquarters at some unspecified future date.

Nicholas stood to one side but close enough to Eddie in case he was needed, but the Group Chairman seemed to have no problem fielding the final questions from analysts and journalists. Once these were answered he turned to enter the elevator. However, just before the lift doors closed, he looked over the heads of the surrounding journalists and gave Nicholas a knowing glance. 'All was well' he seemed to say. It may not have been quite the perfect press conference but it was as near as damn it. Above all, it was untouched by any real protest. The minders and their masters had done well.

***

Nicholas's first thought on returning to his office on the 17th floor was to call Daniel. The whole damn thing was over, and if ever there was a moment to get a touch of warmth into his day it was now. However, even before he could reach for his cell phone, the office lines began to buzz: requests for approval, arrangements for another Press Conference, questions about 'organic growth'. There were calls from Eddie's office about High Street closures, calls from the War Room, calls from Hong Kong and New York. It wasn't until well into the afternoon that he could register that still small voice inside, that childlike request for private confirmation, which his growing sense of relief and achievement required.

The plan was to take Daniel out to dinner. He had already reserved a table for two at the Park Lane Brasserie, which was perhaps not the most adventurous choice but better than many places. He had thought of trying Capriccio or L'Oiseau Migrant or somewhere 'celebricious' like that, but then he thought a paparazzi hole frequented by world-weary TV personalities and anorexic models and 1980s pop stars would just make Daniel feel uncomfortable. The roof of the Park Lane Brasserie was pretty luxurious; they had been there for their first anniversary. Both Nicholas and Daniel liked the view of Hyde Park and Buckingham Palace. Something about that dark silhouette of ancient trees and old palaces provided a silky cocoon, a place in which to be both private and romantic.

There was no reply from the house so he tried Daniel's cell phone: still no answer. Nicholas left a message on Daniel's voice mail, assuming that he was in the gym, and then phoned Sir John to hear his reaction. His secretary said he had already gone home but she would certainly pass on his message.

Nicholas waited another hour, and then with a slight back-kick of impatience, he tried Daniel again. The automated woman's voice told him in a flat tone that the person he had called could not be reached. Nicholas put down the phone and for the first time since the Annual General Meeting he lost his cool. There had been a ringing tone the last time he called. If Daniel were in the gym, he wouldn't come out and turn the phone off.

He scrabbled in his desk drawer for his address book and picked up the phone again. There were several rings; finally someone answered.

'Matt Wong.'

Nicholas felt a huge wave of relief. 'Hi there, I was just wondering if you knew where Daniel is. I can't seem to get hold of him.'

There was a short silence as if Matt were thinking this over. 'Probably at the gym. Have you tried?'

Nicholas grimaced at himself in the gilt lobby mirror. 'Not yet, but would he go there for more than two hours?'

'Sometimes,' said Matt matter-of-factly. 'I said I'd meet him there tonight. I'm off work now.'

Nicholas tried to keep the growing sense of panic out of his voice. 'If you hear from him, tell him I'm trying to call.' Holding the phone in his left hand, he looked in his address book and dialed the number of the Docklands Health Club and Gym. The receptionist at the front desk took a little while to understand what he was asking. 'No, there's no Mr. Nig hereas far as I can see on the computer. I understand...N.G. He definitely hasn't been in here today.'

Nicholas swore to himself and rang off. Almost immediately his cell phone rang.

'You called?'

Nicholas sighed loudly. 'Where were you?'

'Shopping.' No reply from Nicholas. 'On Oxford Street with Matt. I just forgot.'

Something inside Nicholas went off like a firework. It was only five minutes since he had spoken with Matt. Daniel was now saying they were together. 'I've booked us a table at the Park Lane Brasserie.'

'What time?'

'Seven thirty.' Nicholas paused for a moment, giving Daniel plenty of opportunity to explain what had happened. 'I'll meet you in the lobby. Is seven o'clock okay?'

'See you there at seven.'

Nicholas put down the phone. The feeling of unease was beginning to spread. Daniel was incapable of lying. Surely he would turn up with a surprise, a gift that he didn't want Nicholas to know about, tickets he had bought for a Madonna concert, something that would explain what the hell he had been doing.

As he sat in the downstairs bar at Park Lane, drinking a Scotch on the rocks and gazing out at the procession of stony-faced Arabs processing through the lobby, he told himself that he was being stupid. There was a perfectly rational explanation. He was simply on edge after the Annual General Meeting. At ten minutes past seven, he turned from his stool and saw a familiar figure crossing the lobby.

'Hi.'

'Hi,' said Nicholas with an attempt at a winning smile. He didn't recognise the black velvet jacket that Daniel was wearing but he didn't comment. Without another word, they took the lift up to the top floor restaurant where the maitre d'hotel in his white tuxedo took one look at them, raised his eyebrows and decided that a discreet corner table would be best. Nicholas ordered a half bottle of Chablis and a *douzaine fine claires* oysters. He also ordered the mixed antipasti from the buffet in the centre of the room, since he knew that Daniel was an antipasti freak. The maitre d' took their orders with a smile that had now become fixed, seeming to both empathise with their situation and to commend them on their choices, especially when Daniel, who had been reading his *Evening Standard* guide, asked about the deep-fried scampi.

When the platter of oysters arrived, Daniel immediately leaned forward, took one and deftly slipped the contents into his mouth. Nicholas followed his example while attempting to fill the rather painful void in the conversation with a resume of the Annual General Meeting. Soon, however, he realised that Daniel wasn't really listening. They continued to eat their oysters in silence.

Daniel finally put aside his napkin and took a sip of Nicholas's wine. 'I had a good day. I mean, not as good as yours.' His cheeks began to redden with the alcohol. 'But a good day.'

Nicholas emptied his glass and let the waiter refill it. An ice sculpture of a Disney-like palace with impossibly high towers glowed pink in the overhead chandelier. 'Really?'

'I went to the gym, and then I bought this jacket at Hennes on Oxford Street. Matt said it cost forty-five quid. How much do you think?'

'Thirty?' said Nicholas vaguely.

'Twenty,' grinned Daniel.

The waiter placed the plate of scampi on the table in front of Daniel and the stuffed veal for Nicholas. They spent a few moments admiring each other's dishes before Nicholas said that he would give Daniel some of the veal to try. Daniel offered him a morsel of his scampi. As they both began to eat, Daniel continued to talk about what else he had seen on Oxford Street but halfway through his second forkful, Nicholas interrupted. 'You know, I called Matt earlier. I didn't know where you were.'

Daniel looked up. 'You phoned Matt?'

'Yes, I wanted to tell you something,' said Nicholas quietly.

Daniel reached forward and sipped some more of the Chablis. 'We were going to meet in the gym but he phoned to say he was near Oxford Street. So we met at Hennes. He told me you were looking for me.'

Nicholas sat back. If anything, Daniel's plausible explanation only heightened his sense of unease. 'He said he didn't know where you were.'

'Not until I called him he didn't. He was on Regent Street.'

Nicholas grabbed the bottle of Chablis and hurriedly re-filled his glass, spilling a few drops of wine on the tablecloth in the process. 'So you went to the gym before you met Matt. That's why your phone was switched off.'

'Yes,' said Daniel with a gathering frown. 'Why the questions?'

Nicholas drew a long breath. 'Nothing.' He paused. 'Sometimes I can't find you.'

Daniel looked hard at him, pitched a fork into the pistachio stuffing and held it in front of him. 'You're not the only one to have a life Nick. What's it to you if I have a few friends?'

The waiter arrived to offer Nicholas another bottle and to fill their side glasses with water.

'Well, there's the slight matter of me being your partner,' he muttered as the waiter retreated.

Daniel looked hard at him with clear olive-irised eyes. 'Only when it's convenient.'

'What's that supposed to mean?' snapped Nicholas. One or two diners glanced in their direction and hurriedly looked away again.

'When it's convenient,' repeated Daniel.

Nicholas drank his glass to the bottom. 'We may have our own lives Daniel. We also share them.'

'Exactly,' said Daniel.

Nicholas didn't know what else he could say. He couldn't prove anything and in the final analysis he didn't *want* to prove anything.

'Okay,' he said and looked around desperately for the waiter.

'That's enough,' said Daniel. 'I don't want you getting drunk.'

For the first time Nicholas felt some calm return to the bouncing ball inside. At least Daniel cared enough to stop him being stupid. 'I don't do drunk, you know that.'

Daniel finished his plate and glanced at Nicholas. 'You wouldn't have to worry if I had a job. Do you know why I haven't got a job? Because you put in that application so late. Even if I find something, they're not going to take me on unless I have a work permit. That's why I'm wandering around and don't know what to do next.'

Nicholas swallowed the last drop of his wine and felt ashamed. It was just as his inner voice had said. He was projecting his own guilt onto a situation that he himself had created. Daniel deserved his own life. Christ, did he deserve his own life.

Chapter 21

T he early morning drizzle had stopped and the sun was emerging from behind a bank of misty grey cloud as the taxi veered to the right at the Tower of London and up via Minories into the narrow streets of the City. It was something of a luxury to take a taxi to work instead of the DLR and Tube but Nicholas had a slight hangover and this was a day to celebrate. He watched the groups of City workers in their long raincoats, some of them with furled umbrellas, hurrying towards their first appointments, their breakfast meetings and early presentations, and felt proud of his achievement.

The doorman's smile as he pushed open the glass door at New Change Street confirmed his elation. The porters and ushers in the lobby seemed friendlier than usual, the receptionist's 'Good morning sir' seemed even cheerier than on the day he was appointed adviser to the Board. As he hurried down the corridor to his office, he could read respect and admiration in the looks of everyone he passed.

It was only when he reached his office that he realised that something was not quite right.

'Are you okay?' he asked on seeing his secretary's expression.

Alice stood up with a forced smile. 'You've had an urgent phone from Sir John. He wants to see you in his office right away.'

Nicholas dropped into his chair and stroked his brow, imagining the trouble ahead, Seymour Smith insulting a journalist or James Fisk, the new spokesman they'd appointed in London, making a disastrous slip on BBC Breakfast News. 'Tell him I'll be right on up.'

'Yes sir,' said Alice and closed the door softly, as if she were dealing with a worrisome patient.

He looked at the unwieldy swathe of newspapers on his desk and the already heaped-up In Tray. An endless list of tasks, but there was no need to go through all of it now. Sir John was the immediate priority.

He took the stairs to the 19th floor two at a time and soon he was being ushered into Sir John's office. His mentor was standing right in the centre of the room, a sheet of A4 paper spread out on his desk. Sir John gave him a long, appraising look. 'Sorry I couldn't get back to you yesterday.'

Nicholas shrugged. 'We had so much to do but I'm feeling more relaxed today.' He sat down on the leather sofa and crossed his legs. 'What's up?'

Sir John remained standing and approached his desk, balancing himself with two fingers on the corner. He paused a moment and then brought his upper body down to rest on his hands. 'I gather you haven't read your mail today.'

Nicholas shook his head. 'Haven't had a chance so far.'

Sir John maintained his pose. 'Well then, I'm afraid I have some rather bad news for you.'

Nicholas hesitated, weighing this up. There were many forms of bad news in United International; not all of them were necessarily damaging. Crisis often brought alarums that turned out to be fanfares. 'Really?'

Sir John reached out one hand and drew the printed page towards him. 'A rather disturbing letter has been sent to the Board and the news desks of the London papers. Would you like me to read it out?'

'I think I can still read,' said Nicholas as Sir John passed the letter to him.

Dear Eddie,

We feel it our duty to bring to your attention something, which if not addressed immediately, has the potential to harm United International's interests.

It has come to our notice that one of the senior executives had a relationship with a male employee of United International who has come from Hong Kong to live with him in London. This would be a private matter were it not for the fact that he falsified the time scale required for this person, who has since resigned from United International, to qualify for a work visa in the United Kingdom.

We also understand that he has used his position and influence with certain members of the Board to arrange a fast-track British passport for this person. We would not be bringing this matter to your attention if we did not believe that issues of this sort, if picked up in the media or elsewhere, have the potential to harm United International's interests.

On behalf of all UIB's shareholders, we ask for immediate action to be taken.

Yours Sincerely,
The Shareholder Action Group

Nicholas took off his glasses, screwed his eyes shut a moment and then stared into the middle distance. Deep below in the street he could hear the siren of a police car, a prolonged whine that was accompanied by the concerted horns of vehicles getting out of the way. It was the day of the post-mortem, an extremely sensitive day, a day when every senior executive was on edge waiting for what the papers would say. And on this very day, some joker had come up with a piece of ludicrously garbled nonsense purporting to act on behalf of the shareholders.

Sir John nodded and went to sit down in his black chair. 'That's pretty much my reaction Nicholas. No comment from Eddie yet, but one or two raised eyebrows along the corridor. It's particularly awkward in that it suggests some other Board members may be involved.'

Nicholas stared back at him, unable to speak. Sir John took off his glasses and began to clean the lens, revealing dark rings beneath his eyes. 'I know what you're thinking. But frankly anyone in your department or within United International would be a fool to embark on this. It would be far too risky. In any case... ' Sir John replaced his glasses. 'This has gone beyond United International. The press will almost certainly not believe any accusations you might make unless they are extremely well founded.'

Nicholas put a hand to his brow. He could feel a vein in his right temple throbbing. Evidence of what? There was something deeply suspect in the way the threat was framed. If the shareholders were so worried about the media's reaction to this trumped-up story, why had they sent the letter to all the newspapers? Was that the way to defend shareholders' interests? 'What do you recommend?' he said in a quiet voice.

Sir John leaned forward. Nicholas could see the sweat on his upper lip. 'Following yesterday's announcement, United International is now the second largest company in the U.K. You advise the Board and you're about to join the Chancellor's team. Even if the papers aren't that interested in the source of the leaks, they are interested in what people do behind the scenes. And I'm afraid they will now be very interested in *you*—.'

'My partner's from Hong Kong. We've applied for his visa in absolutely the normal way. It's total nonsense to suggest...'

Sir John's expression remained impassive but Nicholas could see a familiar tremor in his left hand. 'So you have a partner.'

'Yes I do,' said Nicholas pugnaciously.

'Who was employed by the company in Hong Kong?'

'Yes,' said Nicholas.

Sir John tapped his fingernail on the desk. 'Forgive me, but did you tell me about this before?'

Nicholas stared hard at him. He had said absolutely nothing about his private life to anyone, neither in United International nor privately except for Sarah. 'No, I regarded it as a private matter.'

Sir John's expression remained unchanged. 'I see. So is there anything else you should be telling me?'

Nicholas drew himself up. 'There would be no need for me to fast track a passport for my partner. We can get one perfectly easily through the normal channels. We're doing nothing illegal. In fact, we were late with our visa application.'

'Then the press won't have anything to go on, will they?' said Sir John with a tight smile.

'No.' Nicholas sat back in his seat. 'They won't.'

'It seems to me that you have only one choice Nicholas. A swift and decisive denial.'

Nicholas could feel a gathering sense of dread, similar to the unease he felt last night in the restaurant, but this time with the added fear that he had no hope of controlling events. 'You mean a statement?'

'Yes, a statement of denial. If not for the papers, then at least for the Board. I recommend a mixture of transparency, rebuttal, and a threat to sue. If the press gets their teeth into this, which is now highly likely, they'll go for the kill. I don't mean that you should lie. But as you know, it's the way that truth is *presented* that matters.'

Nicholas gazed once more into the middle distance as if the solution to all this might lay somewhere out there. This was clearly mischief on a grand scale, but he had no idea who had authored it. And it was no use going over the situation with Sir John. The damage had been done.

'Your denial must appear to be honest and give the impression that you're coming clean. Your strong points are your professional excellence and your settled relationship.' Sir John paused. 'At least I'm assuming it's settled.'

Nicholas nodded, trying to calm himself.

'Since we're living in liberal times, that should be enough to stop the rumours. You can also threaten to sue. As you know, newspapers don't like the libel law.'

'Nor will the Board,' said Nicholas.

Sir John turned his upper body towards him. 'It would seriously weaken your position if you were to mention the Board. The less said about that the better. In any case, the journalists will almost certainly concentrate on you and your private life. My recommendation would be that you get your partner out of the way for the time being. After the press get hold of this, they'll probably want to know everything about you.'

Nicholas still couldn't speak. Despite the fear inside, despite his desire to tear the letter up and scatter it all over Sir John's head, he knew he had to do what he was told. 'I appreciate your advice,' he said and rose from the sofa.

Sir John shrugged and followed him towards the door. 'I'm much better at advising than taking advice. Remember: think it and it will become true. Deny it and it will not have happened. These are the guiding principles of our profession.'

***

Nicholas sat at his desk trying to imagine what was happening on the top floor. He could see Eddie storming round his office and asking who the hell these press people were, why wasn't he given a fuller report on Powell, why Human Resources seemed to give up-and-coming executives license to do exactly what they liked. Nicholas squeezed the bridge of his nose and shook his head. There was little he could do. He could hardly go running to his colleagues and ask them to intervene on his behalf. The fact was that he had been 'outed' in the most damaging way possible and the best way to react to outing – as he had recently seen one government minister do – was to remain calm and go to work immediately to limit any further damage. At the end of the day respect was what counted, not what he did in the privacy of his own home.

He sat up, opened a Ms. Word document on his computer and began to type. For a moment the words wouldn't come, but then something moved inside him and he covered half a page.

To whom it may concern

I refute totally the accusations made in the newspapers about my private life and my professional probity. I do not have, and have never had a 'hidden' relationship with anyone while employed by United International Bank. I met my partner in Hong Kong and eventually we will apply for him to become a U.K. resident under the terms of this country's partnership laws.

Contrary to the allegations contained in the letter, the visa application for my partner to enter the U.K. has not yet been processed because the necessary co-habitation period is being completed. In no circumstances have I used my contacts with immigration officials or members of the Board to gain preferential treatment for the granting of a British passport. The suggestions of improper conduct and lack of probity are completely unfounded. If any newspaper or publication continues to print such accusations, I shall take legal action.

Nicholas Powell

He reviewed the piece again and slowly a half-smile touched the corner of his mouth. Newspaper editors thought that the only libel worth pursuing was 'good libel', which was in the public interest and therefore winnable. Everything else was clearly a waste of the newspaper's resources. This statement would make it clear what they were dealing with. He clicked the Print button, consulted his UIB Directory and went down the listings until he reached what he was looking for.

Grabbing the statement from the printer, he hurried to the elevator and pushed the button for the 14th floor. Once there, he headed up a further flight of stairs into a suite of partitioned offices crouched right under the Bank's eaves.

'Can I help you?' said the receptionist, hastily lowering a battered copy of John Grisham.

'I'm looking for the libel expert,' said Nicholas, noticing her choice of reading.

The young woman looked at him for a moment as if he had asked her to participate in a swingers' orgy. Finally, with a slight darkening of her complexion, she waved her hand towards a row of partitions. 'You'd better ask over there.'

Nicholas made a mental note of her name and moved to the nearest partition. A pimply man, thin-limbed and in his early twenties, was typing away at a computer. However, as soon as he saw Nicholas, he stood up and gestured for Nicholas to follow him through a maze of cluttered partitions and computer consoles towards a separate office that looked straight out over the roofs of New Change Street. The occupant of the room was a short, ginger-haired man with a freckled face, dressed in a brown cardigan beneath his black jacket and a shirt pinioned by a yellow-spotted bow tie. He sat in the middle of a pile of cardboard boxes and red-ribboned documents that formed irregular stepped towers all over the floor and surrounding desks.

'Hello, I'm Charles Brett,' he said as the willowy young man introduced them and hurried away. While Charles read through the statement, Nicholas kept his eyes averted from the surrounding chaos.

'Right,' said Charles, pausing a moment as if gathering his arguments for the jury. 'Don't try and be too comprehensive. The important thing is that everything you claim is absolutely verifiable.'

Nicholas nodded and inwardly groaned. This was exactly what he expected a lawyer to say. Surely one of the world's largest banks—and one of its best legal minds—had more to say on dangers ahead than that.

'As for individual elements of the story, I don't think you have to be so precise.' Charles paused and put on a pair of shell glasses to look at the document more closely. 'For example, about this co-habitation with....'

'Daniel,' said Nicholas.

'Oh, I see. Daniel,' said Charles with a covert smile. 'A United employee?'

'An ex-employee. What about the dates?'

Charles fluttered a freckled hand. 'Precision helps but you should know when to leave well alone. I suggest that you say it is your intention to fulfill all the necessary visa and passport requirements in the correct order.' He paused a moment. 'And according to the appropriate schedule. After all, I assume that the Home Office has accepted your partner's entry application.'

Nicholas glared at him, not quite certain if the pun was intended or was simply a result of him being too long around Daniel's jokes.

'Yes. They're still processing it.'

'Which must be based on the supporting documents you gave them. I imagine you didn't falsify any of those.' Charles was no longer smiling.

'Of course not,' said Nicholas and dug his fingernails into his palms.

Charles gave him a resigned smile, as if he had dealt with people like Nicholas before, people who slightly overstepped the mark, people who expected the establishment to close ranks around them. 'As for the passport application, I gather you didn't approach anyone in United International to obtain help for this.'

'No, of course not,' said Nicholas.

Charles adjusted his bow tie. 'In that case, we'll be taking all appropriate steps to defend the members of the Board against such allegations. I reassured Sir John on this point when he came up to see me this morning.'

Nicholas took a sharp step backwards. Sir John had been up to Legal Affairs, even before he had called Clive's office.

'If the newspapers come out with any of this you'll be able to mount an effective defence, but we would generally advise against any public debate,' said Charles, pushing his glasses up to rest on his forehead. 'It might make more sense for Sir John to deal with the newspapers himself.'

Nicholas felt momentarily relieved; at least Sir John would have something to do – apart from seeing if he could get in first. 'I hope you're right. I'm assuming the threat of libel will be enough to deter any further investigation or indeed any further attempts at libel.'

Charles looked at Nicholas as if weighing this up, played with his lower lip and eventually nodded. 'Yes, it could well be. On the other hand, we have to be prepared. I would recommend you threat to sue only those newspapers that clearly aim at defamation. Naturally, we'll act on your behalf in this.'

Nicholas thought for a moment. Charles' suggestions sounded logical but they also sounded like a legal minefield. He wanted to use the threat of libel to deter further articles. He did not want to end up in court himself discussing his relationship with Daniel before a jury. 'So what's the next step?' He was anxious to get back to his office as soon as possible, aware that Sir John was now several steps ahead of him.

'I suggest you leave the statement with me. I will get it back to you as soon as I can, along with my proposed amendments.'

Nicholas attempted a relaxed smile. He knew very well what 'as soon as possible' could mean with someone like Charles Brett, or indeed with any lawyer: a labyrinth of billed hours, except that they would be at the Bank's expense. 'Can you get it back to me right after lunch? I need to send it to the Chairman and the Board as soon as possible.'

Charles pulled the knot of his tie tight and gave Nicholas a reproachful look. 'I'll do my best. We'll also need a list of London newspaper editors.'

'Of course,' said Nicholas and moved towards the door, thinking that was exactly what the author of the letter must have used, lobbing this legal hand grenade into the top floor of the building. 'I'll get my secretary to send it down right away.'

'Thank you,' said Charles and gave Nicholas the kind of neutral, impassive look he must have used a thousand times in court.

***

The console of lights on his desk was still wildly blinking when Nicholas came into the room. He looked at it for a second with an impassive expression and turned towards the door. 'Alice. Tell them all I'll phone back.'

'Of course,' said Alice.

He hurried back to his desk and took out his cell phone, intending to find George's mobile number. He wanted to ask him whether anyone had seen the supposed Shareholder Letter in Hong Kong, but when he turned on the phone the first thing he saw was a Message Received notice. He pressed Select. The message opened to reveal an icon outline of a tree followed by a roll-down text. '*Hey u C, why don't u reply to me? I shall hang u from this tree if u dont. Miss u, Rxxx.*'

Nicholas stared blankly at the screen. All they had done was share a couple of nights together. His lips compressed, he turned back to the computer, pressed the connect strip for his IPS server and started Outlook Express. Opening a New Message file, he typed in Ray-jai's e-mail address and began to write. *'Hi there Ray. Thank you for your message. Sorry that I've been so busy. There've been some problems at work.'* For a moment he couldn't think of the next line and then he got it. *'I wonder how your business is doing. There's always a demand for web design these days. If you need any help just let me know...'*

Alice's voice rasped through the intercom. 'Phone call from Eddie, Mr. Powell.'

Quickly transferring the message to Save Drafts, where he could retrieve it later, he picked up the phone.

'Nicholas,' said Eddie disarmingly. 'It all went so well yesterday.'

'I think so,' said Nicholas in the most modest tone he could muster.

'So it's been a hell of a shock this morning. No doubt you've heard all about it from Sir John. I mean this Shareholder Letter thing.'

'Yes sir,' said Nicholas briskly. 'I've already talked it over with Sir John.'

Nicholas could hear Eddie swivel his chair. 'I'm sure you have Nicholas. I'm sure you have. However, on this occasion, I've decided that it will not be enough for you and Sir John to talk it over. I've ordered an inquiry, not only into the accusations in the letter but also into the leaks. I don't want to alarm you Nicholas. I'm sure it's just a formality. But your testimony will be required after two weeks' paid leave, during which time the investigating panel will have ample opportunity to examine the matter.'

There was a pause, during which Nicholas had a chance to assess what exactly this might mean. 'We're an equal opportunities company Nicholas,' added Eddie, as if careful to observe the niceties. 'I shall be treating any reports carried in the press with the greatest of skepticism,'

Nicholas wondered if he should thank him. It seemed that whatever he said would only make matters worse. 'I'm sorry...' he began but Eddie clearly wasn't listening.

'Your paid leave will commence today at 6 pm. Enjoy your time off. I'm sure you've deserved it,' said Eddie and rang off.

Nicholas sat at his desk, stunned by the rapidity of the conversation and his feeble response. But what could he have said that would not have sounded defensive? He stood and moved towards the fireplace, grasping the mantelpiece so tight that his knuckles showed bare through the skin. The Senior Management Cricket XI stared back at him from their place on the mantelpiece. It wasn't so much the attack on his reputation, although that was bad enough. It was the pre-emptive nature of the inquiry, the self-defense mechanism that came into play in UIB as soon as something like this arose, the urge to get any piece of rotten fish out of the door before it stank the whole place up.

He walked back towards his desk, trying to think of something he could do to improve his position. He couldn't go running down the corridor and shout his innocence. That would only make matters worse. He couldn't tell Eddie and Sir John the obvious: that anyone who purported to be defending the company and its shares from the media would not be releasing such ridiculous tittle-tattle to the press. The bald truth remained that he was involved in a formal inquiry and his reputation would only be restored when its full deliberations were published. In the meantime, apart from issuing a statement, he was effectively silenced.

'Hold all calls,' he snapped to Alice as he strode past her on his way down to the street. 'Tell them I'll ring them back.'

***

The taxi took forever to get down the Embankment and by the time they had reached E14 he had convinced himself that his initial reaction was exaggerated. All that had happened was that he had been asked to take some 'leave', no more than that. It was a gesture to transparency, a legal precaution, exactly the kind of thing he might have recommended himself in a similar situation. 'It's just a formality,' Eddie had said. He should be pleased that an investigation was underway because it would obviously clear him of any wrongdoing.

By the time the taxi approached his apartment block the shock of the letter was subsiding. Two weeks' paid leave was a small price to pay to recover his reputation, or at least as much of his reputation that had survived the revelation that for some reason he had been covering up the fact that he was gay. His only worry was that Daniel might have gone to the newspaper kiosk to get the *Evening Standard*.

As the taxi turned slowly into the cul-de-sac of his apartment block, Nicholas noticed a man in a beige padded jacket and a green polo neck leaning against the security box and chatting to the guard inside. He was puffing on a cigarette and while he talked his eyes ran casually over the black taxi and its occupants. They lingered on Nicholas for a moment and then seemed to dismiss him.

Nicholas's eyes reverted to the front, but something about the man made him look back. He was just in time to see the man straighten and murmur something towards a red Toyota that was parked at an angle to the driveway. Nicholas thought he saw a window being lowered and something being leveled in his direction. Obeying his instincts, he ducked beneath the window frame. When he emerged, he could see a large furniture van at the far end of the road, beyond which a small ruck of people had gathered. He stared for a moment at the men and women pouring cups of tea and coffee from their Thermoses and chatting confidently on their mobile phones, joking with each other as they perched on railings or sat on the steps to the inner garden. Then he caught sight of a couple of parked white vans, a portable spotlight, a shoulder-hefted TV camera. And before he knew what was happening, people were coming at him from all sides, someone was trying to enter the taxi, and the driver was shouting 'Fuck off!' to everyone in sight.

'Turn around,' said Nicholas, expertly pushing a journalist back through the right door and slamming it after her. 'Turn around!'

'What are you? An escaped criminal?' yelled the driver as he reversed the taxi, swinging it round amid a barrage of shouted questions:

'Is there any connection between your lifestyle and the leaks of United International business to the media Mr Powell?'

'Do you feel that you are a responsible person to be the new Chancellor's adviser?'

'Who was the Board member who recommended your case to the Home Office?'

Nicholas put his head well down in the back seat as the taxi roared off and kept it there. It all seemed so unreal, so completely out of proportion to the simple fact that he was living with his partner and had just happened not to publicize the relationship. He peered out the back of the taxi to make sure the Toyota was not in pursuit. Only as the taxi emerged from the underpass to The Highway did he feel calm enough to call the flat.

'Hi,' said Daniel. 'What's up?'

'Fucking journalists,' said Nicholas. 'They're all over the place. The porter's just phoned me. If you go out, use the car park and take the long way round.'

Daniel was silent for a moment. 'For goodness sake Nicholas.' He sounded as if he were sitting at the computer, possibly trawling for part-time jobs. 'I won't be going out anyway. Matt's coming round to set up the new modem.'

Nicholas didn't know whether to be impressed with Daniel's coolness or not. 'For fuck's sake Daniel, this is serious. They're after a story and they'll use anything they can. I'll explain later.'

'Jesus,' said Daniel. 'Calm down. You've got nothing to hide.'

'I know that and you know that, but they don't. Please do as I say,' added Nicholas and rang off.

Nicholas spent the rest of the journey seething about Daniel's response. As soon as the taxi reached New Change Street, Nicholas jumped out onto the pavement and paid the driver. Taking the elevator up to his office, he swept past the hunched form of Alice and saw that the statement was waiting for him on his desk. He hurried over, picked it up and read it through. Charles Brett had made few revisions to the original text but he had attached a note: *Please ensure that no word or phrase in this statement is technically untrue.* Muttering 'technically untrue' to himself, he spent several more minutes checking everything over. He then placed the document on his desk and smoothed out the page.

'Alice,' he shouted. 'Get me a contact list of newspaper editors in London as well as Board members. Send this out as soon as possible. You'd better start with Eddie.'

Alice came into the room, picked up the document with one of her ward sister expressions, and took it with her to the outer office.

Nicholas turned back to his computer, opened Microsoft Word and clicked on the document he had prepared. Running his eyes over the text, he frowned to himself. It still didn't convey what he wanted. He began to re-type what he had written: '*Hi Ray, I'm glad you enjoyed Taiwan. It was good to talk to you and sort out a few things. I'm sorry I had to rush back so soon to HK. As you can imagine, London has been very busy for me. However, I expect to be over there in the next few days. I'll let you know more later. In the meantime, do take care :-) Nicholas.*'

He sat back and nodded. Yes, that was it: not too involved, not too friendly. Just a smiley face. It was best to carry on like that, school-boyish as it was, until he could get over there and fully break the whole thing off. He was about to send the message when the intercom crackled into life. 'Nicholas?'

Nicholas turned his head to the speaker, at the same time typing in the e-mail address.

'I've seen the statement,' rasped Sir John. 'Eddie's got a copy too. He's been in my room. You'd better come on up.'

'I'll be there now,' said Nicholas as he finished the address, punched the Send button, and watched the narrow funnel on his screen gradually fill: *Message Sent.*

Looking straight ahead to avoid talking to anyone, Nicholas headed down the long corridor towards Sir John's office. But just as he was about to turn the final corner, he heard a door in front of him close. He stopped dead in his tracks, a sudden instinct warning him to negotiate the final corner as slowly as possible. Gingerly he approached Sir John's door, turned the handle to the right, and a tiny gap opened, through which he could see Sir John's secretary sitting at her desk. She was fluffing up her hair and re-applying her lipstick but something in the fussy way she was doing this suggested that someone had just been in the office, someone important. There was also a scent of perfume on the air.

He crept back towards the corridor and looked in both directions. The only movements were people exiting and entering the lift on the floor below. Nicholas moved towards the lift shaft at the end of the corridor and stared at the tops of their heads. He could hear subdued conversations and repressed laughter, the clink of a tea trolley. And then, just as he was thinking of turning back, he saw a figure below him: dark brown trouser suit, long grey hair, the pink-striped pashmina that Eunice had claimed came from Liberty's. She was walking down the corridor with a sheaf of documents in her hand. Nicholas continued to watch her until she passed out of his sight. There was just a chance that she had stepped out of the lift from another floor. On the other hand, she could have come directly from Sir John's office. What the hell could she have been doing there?

When Nicholas came into the room, Sir John was standing beside his desk with his hands clasped behind his back. Nicholas could see his statement at the centre of the desk next to another official document. Both papers were laid out with envelope cutters holding down their upper edges.

Sir John spoke first. 'It's the kind of thing the press will understand Nicholas. Eddie is pleased with it. Of course, you'll have to go through with the inquiry but I think your prospects are now much improved. None of us like to see our private lives in the papers. I'm afraid yours is going to seem distinctly colourful to certain members of the Board but...' He coughed and put one hand over his mouth as if to apologise for what he was about to say. 'It's highly unlikely there'll be any revelations.'

Nicholas nodded and waited. Sir John continued to look at him, his head tilted to one side. 'Eddie doesn't doubt your integrity. It's just that he has to be seen to do the right thing.'

'Of course,' said Nicholas.

Sir John took out a handkerchief and wiped his mouth. 'Proper procedure and all that. It's Eddie's way of saying take a few days off. I hear you've been to see Legal.'

Nicholas was taken off guard by the abrupt change of tack. 'Yes I have. I hear that you also made a visit'

'Yes,' said Sir John with a look of slight surprise. 'We have to consult the proper people on these occasions. The accusations took us rather by storm. By the way, do you have any plans for next week?'

'I was thinking of going over to Hong Kong,' said Nicholas on the spur of the moment and watched Sir John's face. 'I've a few things to sort out at the office. I thought it would be a good opportunity.'

Sir John made no move to offer Nicholas a seat, but walked in front of his desk to stand close to Nicholas. 'Hong Kong?' He paused a moment, as if considering his next words very closely. 'Please be careful how you handle this. I know you feel that a couple of your colleagues might have behaved oddly in recent weeks, but any unproven accusations on the back of this Shareholder Letter are going to look very off at the moment. We don't want anything to reflect badly on United International.'

'We certainly don't,' said Nicholas evenly.

'The same applies to our little business with Roger Yates. Unless the papers come up with something, you should still be in with a very good chance. I know Roger thinks extremely highly of you,' added Sir John.

'I'm glad to hear that,' said Nicholas, moving towards the door. But just before he left he turned towards Sir John. 'By the way, I hope I haven't disturbed your schedule. I expect you had to cut short your previous appointment for me.'

Sir John took a step backwards and cocked his head. 'I didn't have any previous appointment. I instructed my secretary to cancel all meetings for the day.'

Nicholas attempted a smile. 'In that case, I apologise for any inconvenience. We'll talk later,' he said and opened the door.

Chapter 22

S ir John stepped into the softly lit interior of the apartment, flicked his keys into the alabaster bowl on the hall table, and almost tripped over Marlyn in the hallway.

'Good evening Sir John,' she said, helping him off with his cashmere coat.

He grunted in reply, hoping she couldn't detect the two leisurely pints of Young's he had drunk at Dirty Dan's on his way home. She was even more of a detective than Marjory.

'Could you bring in the post?' he said, and headed out of the dimly lit hall into the drawing room. The white shutters were folded back on the long sash windows and through the elaborately cupped drapes with their gold tassels, he could see a view of pink, fluffy clouds and a chalky blue sky over Regents Park.

He settled into his favourite leather armchair near the mahogany table with its baize top and onyx penholders as Marlyn came in with a tray bearing the post. Seeing him swathed in gloom, she flicked a wall switch to turn on all the table lamps. Suddenly the long, high-ceilinged room with its two parallel flowered sofas, its double-tiered coffee table piled with new hardback art books and copies of *Tatler* and *Country Life*, flickered into life.

Marlyn placed the tray and the envelope cutter on the desk within reach of his hand. With a stoical look, she bent down to untie his shoe laces, allowing him to push the back of each shoe with his other foot and to ease it off before she placed the black leather slippers she had been carrying in her other hand in the appropriate zone.

'Thank you,' he said.

'You're welcome,' said Marlyn in that lazy, slightly ironic singsong, infused with an American twang, which always made him feel he was talking to someone from the Deep South rather than the Philippines. 'I'll tell Marjory you're here.'

Sir John wanted to say she must have heard him come in, but an envelope that Marlyn had placed to one side of the rest of the pile claimed his attention. It was without a stamp and the face of the envelope was largely empty apart from a single typed line in the centre, *To Sir John Williams*. There was also a handwritten phrase in the upper right corner where the stamp should have been: *Totally and Strictly Confidential*. He picked the envelope up and frowned.

'Did you see who delivered this?'

As Marlyn reached the doors to the hall, she turned back with his shoes in her hand and looked puzzled for a moment. But then the eyes in her dark round face shone. 'Someone pushed it under the door.'

Sir John rested the envelope on the arm of the chair. He didn't like hand-delivered messages. For one thing, he never knew how people got in to deliver them. There was a porter to negotiate downstairs, as well as an entry code and a door buzzer. It could be that someone had followed a delivery person or used a professional courier, but even then they should buzz the door and have someone sign for it. Moreover, there was something about that *Totally and Strictly Confidential* that disturbed him. The sender didn't trust the domestic situation. The sender didn't *know* the domestic situation.

'Don't worry,' he could hear Marjory say to Marlyn. 'I've always cooked rabbit with lemon and it's never come out sour before. Anyway, I hardly think my daughter's a gourmet, or the children come to that. Happy Macs are more their style.' She swung through the lounge doors towards him and laughed as if well aware that Sir John had heard her.

'What's that?' said Sir John, returning the envelope to the tray and pushing it to the bottom of the file. Marjory stopped by the drinks server and choosing one of the amber bottles, poured the whisky into a low crystal glass and added a couple of ice cubes from the container. She did this with an air of faint disapproval, carrying it towards him in boney fingers that barely held the glass aloft.

'Just domestic talk,' she said and placed the glass on his side table, bending to receive a slight brush on the cheek from Sir John. 'We have Isobel and the children for dinner. It's Charlie's birthday.'

'Oh, I'd forgotten,' said Sir John, taking his first sip of the whisky.

'We've done all the preparations,' said Marjory, turning to hover in front of him. 'There's a cake and we're having rabbit stew. Charlie said he loved rabbit when we were in Carcassonne, although I'm not sure about Kate. She's started on boys now and eats nothing.'

'Good god, she's only twelve,' said Sir John, attempting to hide his confusion. But Marjory was clearly keen to get back to the kitchen. 'When you've finished that drink, you'd better go up and change,' she said, collecting her jade necklace in one hand and letting it drop onto the collar of her blue silk blouse. 'I'm sure Charlie thinks you're some sort of High Court judge.'

Sir John wiped his left hand over his brows and eyes and squeezed his neck. 'It's been a long day. I'm not ready for birthday parties.'

Marjory crossed her arms, leaving the cardigan draped over her shoulders, and surveyed him. 'You look a bit tired. Don't do those letters now. Just finish up your drink.' And before he could stop her, she had bent over and picked up the tray, carrying it beneath her right arm towards the hall. 'We don't want a boring judge at dinner.'

'Wait a moment – .' But all he could see was the high buffon of her dyed and straightened blond hair turning towards him, a satisfied half-smile lingering in its shadows, before she disappeared towards the kitchen.

'Damn,' he muttered and with a sharp smack of his palm on the leather arm of the chair, he got up and shuffled over the deep-pile carpet to the drinks cabinet, where he poured himself a double. Taking it with him, he went out to the hallway and checked whether the letter tray had been left on the Florentine table at the centre of the hall. But apart from his theatre glasses in a silver case, the keys to the Mercedez and a seasonal guide to the Royal Opera House, there was nothing. She had taken the letters with her and would probably end up stuffing them into the rabbit if he didn't shower. He knew Marjory.

He took his drink with him back into the lounge and stood at the mantelpiece, his left hand chilled by the white marble. Beyond the framed photographs he could see his own reflection in the eagle-headed mirror. Pursed lips and a furrowed forehead looked back at him, the gentle penumbra of lamplight giving the outline of his skull a theatrical glow. He looked at the photos of his children and grandchildren: Isobel in her mortarboard and gown, her head slightly to one side and a sympathetic smile on her lips, as if trying to understand or support what he was thinking; Andrew, caught in bobble hat and ski goggles in the blinding glare of a Zermatt winter day, impatiently indicating something just out of the picture.

Sir John put the whisky glass on the mantelpiece and rubbed his lips along the glass's rim. The words *Totally and Strictly Confidential* echoed in his brain as he kept his eyes fixed on Andrew.

He was a strange child, surprisingly prone to silence as a solution to all of life's conflicts. What began as a three-year old's non-discussion of problems somehow continued into late adolescence and the way he handled more urgent issues. But there was no way that he and Marjory could have known what those issues were. It was as if Andrew's going up to Cambridge had given him privacy for the first time in his life. With Isobel it was different. She had invited them into her Girton circle, had gone out for drinks and dinner with them, had taken them to college plays and concerts, and of course introduced them to her boyfriend. With Andrew, it was different.

The problem wasn't his intelligence. He sailed through his second-year exams and appeared to be thoroughly absorbed in whatever special subject it was: the political philosophy of the English Romantic Poets, the Elizabethan House of Commons. Nor did it seem to be a social problem. He was in with a regular bar-and-football crowd. He accepted the Oxbridge class system and had even joined a Wine Club full of young toffs from Trinity College. He was never a great sportsman but he played a bit of cricket for the College Second XI, took part in Ben Jonson's *Volpone*, attended May Balls and on one occasion fooled half the College by pretending to be dead drunk on the lawns at midnight so that the Fellows had to carry him to bed.

And yet loneliness seemed to gather round him the longer he was at Cambridge. At first they thought it was difficulties in adjusting to postgraduate life. Sir John hadn't particularly approved of Andrew studying for a Ph.D. He had his own plans for him in London. But after he had achieved his First Class Honours, Sir John could hardly insist that he give up the academic life and do what his father wanted. Just after he was accepted for his postgraduate course he went to Paris with a college friend and then on to Switzerland. When he came back something about him had changed. He was more sophisticated, more ready to show off his languages, more distant too. They had assumed his studies prevented him from having a girlfriend, and although they had met some of his roommates they never had the feeling he was particularly close to anyone. Except perhaps Duff-Parker, in whose tiny family flat he had stayed in the Marais. They had distantly glimpsed Duff-Parker at a matriculation dinner they went to in the Fellows Dining Room. He had a shock of thinning, ginger hair, owl-glasses and a laugh that pierced the room, but when they had asked to be introduced to his best friend Andrew had warned them off, saying they should meet him on some other occasion.

That occasion never arose. Sir John knew the kind of people you could meet in Cambridge, or indeed in any hothouse gathering of young men, and he knew that not all of them were the sort he wanted his son to befriend. But he had to trust to Andrew's intelligence. Isobel had turned out well. Andrew, although enigmatic, appeared to have enough of Sir John's common sense to handle the world. In any case, Duff-Parker dropped out of the picture when Andrew moved out of Cambridge to stay at Madingley Hall.

'You'd better get up to the shower,' shouted Marjory.

'I'm just going,' said Sir John, still bent over the two photos.

Marjory had found the evidence in his room. Or rather, she found some pieces of evidence. The well-thumbed novels of James Baldwin and Jean Genet might have been coincidental, but in combination with the copies of *Beach Bums*, they suggested something else. They also found Xanax and Halcion in his toilet bag, anti-depressants prescribed by god knows who, and two black rubber rings in his bedside drawer, pushed right to the back along with a small bottle of something that smelled like old socks. Sir John later found out that this was amyl nitrate.

Marjory insisted they shouldn't panic. Despite it being her idea to search his room, she was adamant that Sir John shouldn't go off the deep end. She said Andrew would grow out of it and suggested that they should treat him, as far as possible, as normal. Sir John also continued to hope; he had too much invested in Andrew not to hope. But as the days turned into weeks and it became clear that Andrew was not coming to London to see them, Sir John felt compelled to phone. It was a disaster. The anti-depressants, the novels and magazines tumbled out of his mouth one after another, and what started out as an offer of help became just what Marjory most feared: a signal that his parents were deeply shocked. One week later, Sir John drove up to Madingley Hall to talk it over. When he arrived, the Warden told him that Andrew had requested a year's leave of absence and had given up his room.

They tried everywhere to get information: the local pub, the college authorities, the graduate society. They even tried the police. But the only lead they could get was from Duff-Parker, who told them that Andrew had a new friend in London who might have encouraged him to leave Cambridge. He didn't really know the friend because he wasn't acquainted with Andrew's circle. However, Duff-Parker's expression as he said this showed that he knew *everything* and that he wasn't going to say.

'Excuse me sir,' said Marlyn, startling him from his thoughts. 'Dinner's almost ready.'

Sir John turned and meekly handed her his glass, as if he had been caught red-handed. Heading up the broad staircase, he looked through the dining room doors at the lights Marlyn had rigged up on the walls from the Christmas store, and he felt lucky he had an appointment on Saturday. The children's party at Isobel's in Hammersmith would take place without him.

When he came back down the stairs, refreshed and wearing a pair of black velvet slacks and a bright Ralph Lauren polo shirt, he could hear Charlie shrieking with laughter in the kitchen. He was about to push open the swing door when he noticed that the tray of letters had been replaced on the Florentine hall table. He glanced towards the kitchen. He knew that Marlyn would come out to open the wine bottles soon before she began serving, a process that normally took a minute or two.

He lifted the small pile of letters and extracted *Totally and Strictly Confidential*. Pausing for a moment to make sure the kitchen doors remained closed, he moved quietly across the hall towards the drawing room and gently pushed the doors to. He then hurried to his desk and seized the silver envelope cutter, extracting a single page of foolscap. His eyes rapidly scanned the two sentences it contained:

Dear Sir John,

If you want to know more about Andrew, meet me
at the basement bar 23 William IV Street WC2, 9
pm Friday. Don't worry, I know what you look
like.

Sir John held the paper so long that it buckled in his hand. It
was over a year since he had put that advert in the magazines for
information, and he had heard nothing. A reply at this stage
seemed like an attempt to twist the knife, a voice from the dead.
He looked again at the foolscap paper. That last sentence was
almost like a threat. As he stared at it, he realised that was exactly
the reason why he had to go.

'What're you doing?' said Marjory, standing wide-eyed at the
doorway as Isobel and Marlyn carried plates and a large bowl of
glazed terrine topped with lemon slices across the hall.

'Just coming,' he said and slipped the note into his upper desk
drawer.

Chapter 23

The white vans had disappeared from the road in front of the building, along with the ladders and the sound booms and the red Toyota, but Nicholas could still make out one or two figures in padded jackets hanging around the steps with their telephoto lenses. The revolving door at the entrance to the nearby newspaper offices was spewing out a steady stream of workers hurrying to get home. He mingled with them for a moment as if testing to see if he would be recognised, but no one took the slightest notice of him. He then cut straight across the forecourt towards the underground car park. The huddled figures on the far side of the steps did not turn.

He pointed his key at the car park grille, which rose with a warning clatter, and within seconds he was in amongst the parked vehicles and making his way to the lift door. He unlocked it and punched the button to the elevator, stepped in and allowed it to waft him up.

As he closed the flat door behind him his first thought was how quiet it was inside, almost dark despite the approach of nightfall. Only one lamp was on in the lounge and there was no sound of the pop music to which Daniel normally worked.

'Hello,' he said. 'Anyone at home?'

No reply. He frowned, dropped his leather file on the sofa in his study and went to look in the lounge. The television was still on with the sound turned down but the place somehow looked different. He returned the way he had come, first to the kitchen and then to the bedroom where he found Daniel sitting with his back silhouetted against the lit screen of his i-Mac, apparently staring at the monitor.

'Hi,' said Nicholas and moved towards him, but Daniel didn't turn. Nicholas stood still for a moment, not wanting to interrupt. 'Sorry about that call. Someone sent a letter to the newspapers about me getting you a passport. It's ridiculous. I had to put out a statement – .'

Daniel turned. 'Who's Ray-jai?'

Nicholas looked over at the screen. An open e-mail was clearly visible there. For a moment his mind froze. 'What do you mean?'

'Who's Ray-jai?' repeated Daniel.

Nicholas went to the corner of the desk and closed his eyes. A red tide seemed to be rising within, pressing against his eyelids. 'Just someone who wants advice.'

Daniel glanced at the screen. 'In Taiwan?'

Nicholas looked around the room as if a change of subject might be lurking there. 'I went to check on operations in Taipei last time I was in Hong Kong. That's where Ray-jai works. I must have sent it to you by mistake. Sorry for the cock-up. It's been a bad day.'

Daniel shifted slowly in his seat, a pool of sweat visible at the base of his neck. 'So how come he's got his own business?'

For a moment Nicholas was unable to answer. Everything was happening at a speed that made credible stories impossible to conjure. 'Web design, outside the office...I mean, he does web design.'

Daniel kicked back from the desk and sat with his arms folded. There was something in his expression, something in the set of his jaw that frightened Nicholas. 'You approved of that?'

Nicholas nodded.

Daniel ran the tip of his tongue along his lips. 'We only add *jai* to people's names if they're younger or perhaps a close friend. It's not a form used between boss and employee.'

Nicholas wondered if he should take off his jacket. It felt as if the heating had been on all day. 'Ray-jai's just a nickname. Don't take it so seriously. They all call him that at the office.'

Daniel lowed his head onto his chest as if waiting to pounce. 'So you don't disapprove of what he does?'

'No.' Nicholas fiddled with his watch and glanced at the time. 'Every design department does it.'

Daniel continued to look down at his feet. 'So he knows when you'll arrive in Hong Kong. You've told him.'

'Yes', mumbled Nicholas. 'I just wanted to let the Taiwan office know my schedule.'

Daniel raised his face. His expression had changed, ironic observation deepening into a look of hostility. 'Does that mean he's coming over from Taipei to meet you?'

Nicholas tried one final expression of puzzlement, but the dread that filled him now was rising too fast for him to pretend. 'I'm sorry Daniel. I was going to tell you before. It just sort of happened – '

Daniel stared at Nicholas, the fury in his eyes intensified by his glasses, as if he was seeing him for the very first time. 'You brought him over to Hong Kong and you fucked him,' he said, spitting the words out.

Nicholas remained silent, thinking of some way that would make it all sound better. 'It wasn't like that. I went with him to Taiwan to sort things out.' The sentences exploded in his head like rockets. 'It was just a one-off...'

Daniel stood up with his face turned away from him but Nicholas could sense the disgust stiffening every muscle in his body. 'Go over there and fuck him a hundred times! There's a word for you Nicholas, or maybe two.' He turned back. 'You're not the person I first met.'

Nicholas stood still for a moment as if he had been punched in the stomach. 'I'm...'

Daniel took off his glasses and held them in his trembling hands, staring down at the floor. There was a moment of complete silence and then he walked straight out of the room.

Nicholas followed him to the lounge, but even as he stood there he could think of nothing to do, nowhere to hide. He had destroyed someone's dream of commitment, someone who loved and trusted him, someone who had changed his whole life to be with him. And all he could come up with was a pathetic excuse about it sort of happening.

'I love you,' said Nicholas in a final desperate attempt.

Daniel just stared at the coffee table as if the magnitude of Nicholas's betrayal was clearly visible there. Suddenly, the phone rang. Neither of them moved. Eventually, the noise stopped but then it started again. Nicholas moved over to the side table and picked up the receiver.

'Mr. Powell?' said a voice on the other end.

'Yes,' Nicholas answered briskly.

'*The Morning Herald.* Just a few questions...'

'Fuck you!' said Daniel, seizing the phone from Nicholas and pulling it from its socket. 'Fuck all you journalists and your whole stupid world!' And then, with the receiver in one hand and a stricken handset in the other, he fell back against the sofa. This time Nicholas could see tears in his eyes but before he could move towards him, Daniel held out an arm.

'Please,' said Nicholas.

Daniel turned towards the distant skyline visible through the blinds. 'It would be better if you went.'

'What?'

'I think we shouldn't see each other for a while.'

They sat facing each other, two virtual strangers in a room silhouetted against the dimmed lights of the nearby offices. Nicholas knew he had to say something. 'How about staying with Kay for a while? I can call her in the morning,' he said.

Daniel gave him a look that made Nicholas flinch.

'I've got to go to Hong Kong to sort things out. I've reserved a flight for tomorrow. It will give us a moment to calm down. I've been a fool, but please, please I only love you Daniel. Forgive me.'

Daniel looked at him for a long moment with reddened eyes and then stood up and headed towards the door. As he reached the archway he turned back. 'Do what you want Nicholas. I'll do what I want.'

Nicholas moved towards him, but Daniel had already left the room. He stood at the lounge window for a few stunned moments and then followed him to the bedroom where he stood helplessly, unable to intervene, as Daniel opened and closed drawers, taking out underwear and socks, T-shirts and jeans. The room was silent except for the thump of drawers and wardrobes and the occasional grunt from Daniel. Nicholas wanted to say something else, something about his stupidity, but he knew it would get him nowhere. Finally, he began to pack himself but even when he had finished, Daniel was still fitting everything he could into the suitcase: books, videos, DVDs. Nicholas wasn't sure that Kay had a DVD player but he stood to one side. This wasn't the end, he told himself.

After a few more minutes of hoping he gave up and went to the kitchen to see if he could prepare something to eat. He knew that neither of them was in the mood for food but he put together some salad and chicken anyway, hoping that they could at least share a glass of wine, some semblance of normality.

Ten minutes later, Daniel came in to the kitchen, took one look at the food and flipped the contents of his plate into the rubbish bin.

'Not hungry.'

'But you've got to eat something,' pleaded Nicholas, watching the lid of the rubbish bin swing.

Daniel didn't reply but returned to the bedroom, where Nicholas could hear him unzipping his jeans. By the time that he had finished cleaning up, Daniel's reading light was off and he was lying still and rock-like in the dark. Nicholas lay down beside him but he couldn't sleep. Many times he tried to wrap his arms around him, only to find himself shut out. Occasionally he thought he could hear Daniel mumbling to himself as he shifted position but when he tried to reach out to touch him he was once more rebuffed. Nicholas tried entreaties, he tried rubbing his head against Daniel's arm, he tried repeating what a fool he had been. Nothing worked. Eventually, just before dawn, he slipped into an exhausted sleep and when he next awoke he could hear Daniel making tea in the kitchen. He looked at his watch.

'Christ,' he jumped up. It was time to call a taxi and alert Kay. He also had to give Daniel instructions on the right train and the connections for Shrewsbury, as well as to call Sir John before he caught the afternoon flight. Daniel would be safe with Kay and Josie. He would go, he knew that. He could call Kay from Heathrow and explain what he had done. She wouldn't approve but she at least would try to understand. As Nicholas stared at his reflection in the bathroom mirror, he told himself that it would all be alright.

'Are you ready? We can share a taxi,' he shouted.

'No need,' said Daniel, in a surprisingly firm voice. 'I'll go later.'

Nicholas walked down the hallway.

But Daniel had moved out of earshot and was standing on the terrace, his eyes fixed on some distant point on the horizon.

Chapter 24

As the Airbus-A340 flattened its trajectory of descent into Hong Kong airport, Nicholas ran his eyes over the newspapers piled on the empty seat next to him. The story had broken. Peter Weiss' feature on the new Chancellor's prospective team in *The Monitor* included a small side-box on 'L'affaire des affaires publiques', mentioning Nicholas's present position and the difficulties he would have in dealing with unproven accusations in an anonymous shareholders' complaint. Most of the other broadsheets followed *The Monitor's* lead by avoiding any direct reference to the complaints themselves. No editors published the letter or put themselves in a position to be sued, merely declaring that 'non-attributable' or 'informed sources' had told the paper what the accusations were and that they were by no means proven. The only subject the journalists really focused on was the unexplained leaking that had preceded the letter.

If that was all, Nicholas might have been able to sit back and comfort himself. But as he worked through the rest of the newspapers, it became apparent that not every editor was so kindly disposed. The *Daily News* had a long piece full of innuendo about the possibility of insider trading. It speculated about a link between the leak of the Press Release, the movement in share prices and employees' ownership of shares. Nicholas was not mentioned by name but a senior executive was alluded to in a sidebar entitled *Passport Scandal in UIB's Top Management.* Similar gossip appeared in several other tabloids. None of it amounted to a full-scale attack but the implications were serious.

The plane's engines throttled back, forcing Nicholas to concentrate on what lay ahead. Ray-jai didn't know when he was arriving, which meant that Nicholas had time to approach George first and discuss with him the best way to handle Ray-jai.

The A340 came in over a forest of washing on bamboo poles and thick clusters of TV aerials towards Kai Tak airport, landing with a muffled thump on the water-encircled runway. As the built-up hillsides of East Kowloon wheeled on by the window, he smelled again the familiar reek of sewage in the choked water nullah, and he felt oddly at home.

It didn't take him long to disembark and to move through Immigration into the baggage hall. The overcrowded airport with its repainted walls and air of improvisation reminded him how easily he had fallen under the spell of the city: a hedonist world of glittering surfaces and seedy survival where anything went as long as appearances were preserved, a place in which the quick accumulation of money and status was far more important than where you came from. He could see it in the faces of the airport staff and the immigration officers, the shining uniforms of the service personnel, the readiness of the taxi ushers to ensure that everybody's trip got off to a rapid start.

As the taxi sped him closer to Central, he contemplated the tight clusters of high-rises, the sweep of Victoria Harbour with its turreted cruise ships and 1950s-style yachts, and concluded that his decision was right. George was experienced in what went on in Hong Kong. He would know how to silence Ray-jai.

The taxi slowed almost to a halt in the morning traffic of Central. Every artery to the upper reaches of Mid-Levels seemed to be seething with double decker buses, taxis and mini-buses, all cutting across each other with breathtaking insouciance. Some of the near misses made the hair on the back of his neck stand up. Finally, he arrived in the forecourt of Dreamlands and he could fetch his suitcase from the boot. Slamming it shut, he turned to see Alex Higgins crossing the forecourt.

'Hi there!' he shouted.

Alex's face seemed to turn a deeper shade of red as he turned to hail a taxi. 'Hi, had a good time?'

'Not exactly. How about you?'

A red Toyota roared up alongside Alex and its rear right door opened. 'Got to go now. Talk later – '

Nicholas was about to say something else, but the taxi door had closed. He stood there with his luggage, staring in the direction of Alex's departure and thinking how strange it was for Alex to miss an opportunity for gossip. With a shrug, he headed for the elevator lobby, where the Chinese guard helped him in with his luggage.

His old apartment smelt musty and uncared for, heavy with the memory of someone who hadn't lived there regularly even when he was in town. His shirt was soaked with sweat but he didn't want to turn on the air-conditioning. He opened some windows and looked around the room. His Filipina maid had been in and placed his private mail in piles on his desk. She had made another pile for faxes, some of which were already fading in the sunlight. Nicholas ignored both piles and headed for the shower.

About an hour later he was sitting on the sofa with the air conditioning on and the windows closed, sipping a glass of wine and looking hurriedly through Saturday's *South China Morning Post*. There was no mention of him or of the Shareholder Letter in any of its columns. The only comment on United International was a brief reference to its share price, which had predictably gained on the news of the Mercantile merger and now stood almost 12 per cent higher.

He sat up, took his cell phone off the side table and contemplated it for a moment. It was possible that George would be at the office now, although not very likely. People went in to the office on alternate Saturday mornings, but they usually wandered about pretending to 'research' (quick chat in Economics or Securities) or read the newspaper in the coffee bar.

He reached George's voice-mail and left a short message asking him to call back as soon as possible. He then tried his office phone. It rang and rang but no one answered, not even a secretary. He looked at his watch. It was just past 11 am. He finished off the wine and with his head slowly spinning, headed for the bedroom, forgetting to take his cell phone with him.

***

When he next awoke, it was dark outside and he had no idea where he was. He turned on the lights and saw from his watch that it was 7.07 pm. Angry with himself for sleeping too long, he fetched his cell phone to see if anyone had called. George had phoned back and left a voice message at 2.28 pm. He dialed *988 and listened to the message: 'Hi Nicholas. Glad you're back. Listen, I'm busy cooking for a family friend. But I could meet you at Slow Rice, Lan Kwai Fong, at about 10 o'clock or somewhere else if you prefer. Call me later. George.'

Nicholas listened to the message again. He certainly didn't want to meet him at Slow Rice. There was a distinct chance that he would bump into Ray-jai in Lan Kwai Fong, or perhaps a journalist who would recognise him and immediately invite him for a drink. He had to call George back and change the venue.

Nicholas tried his cell phone several times but each time he reached a recorded message. He imagined him cooking away in his garden flat in Discovery Bay, rather bored with the family guest and wanting to get to Lan Kwai Fong as soon as possible. Nicholas went to his desk and looked through his address book to see if he had a number for George's home. 'Damn,' he muttered. It was probably on the wall in his office. He phoned Directory Inquiries but they had no number listed for 13, Greenmount Drive. He tried George's cell phone but again no reply. Finally, in a fit of desperation, he left a message that he was on his way to Discovery Bay and would call George as soon as he reached the ferry terminal on Lantau Island. He suggested they either meet there or have coffee at George's place; he had something urgent to discuss.

Nicholas began to change. He would get the 8.30 pm ferry, which would mean he would probably be there towards dessert. George was an excellent cook, something he had picked up from his food journalism. His Canadian relatives were always going over to Discovery Bay for *Cassoulet a la Provencale* or *Boeuf Bourgignone*.

Just after eight o'clock, Nicholas emerged from the taxi at the far end of the Star Ferry terminal and quickly found the ticket booth for the ferry. It was only a half-hour journey to Discovery Bay, where George had told him he had found a nice garden flat on Greenmount Drive. As he huddled in a seat right at the back of the boat and the ferry veered out into Victoria Harbour, Nicholas felt a sudden tightening in his stomach. Rolling with the swell, he went out onto the rear deck. He could see the spangled arc of the Tsing Yi Bridge over to his right and the dark waters that stretched between the skyscrapers of Hong Kong Island and the speeding ferry.

An occasional small boat bobbed in its wake as if to remind him of the housing estates and the Hakka fishing folk, of the sampans and village clans and temples to the Goddess of the Sea over there in the darkness. But beyond the boats he could also see the Peak looming up like a bright-studded volcano and he recalled that Cuba evening when to the rhythms of the samba everything – money, sex, power – had seemed so readily available. All he had to do, it seemed, was reach out and touch it.

The apartment blocks of Discovery Bay reared up on the port bow. He hurried to join the other passengers as the boat docked, slowly moving down the gangplank towards the Plaza of shops and restaurants that fanned out from the jetty. A straggle of beach stretched out to the right, marked by the lights of houses and the tall pine trees that fringed its edges. George lived somewhere above the beach in a secluded house with a walled garden. Clutching the address, Nicholas negotiated the last of the passengers, sat down on a bench in the middle of the Plaza and took out his cell phone. He looked at his watch: 8.57 pm. He tried the number but there was no reply.

Just then he spotted a signboard to his right and he hurried over to take a look. According to the map, Greenmount Drive ran parallel to the beach walkway before curving away towards the International School. He peered at the darkened path that led from the Residents Club to the back of the beach where shadowy figures were sitting under the pine trees. He could hear a single guitar strumming, scurries of laughter, a suppressed phrase of *Like a Virgin*.

He shuddered in the breeze and looked again at his watch. It was just past 9 pm. He phoned: still no answer.

Holding the address in his hand, he stood up and shook his legs. He couldn't wait any longer. Heading straight up the road past the swimming pool, he turned immediately right down Greenmount Drive. The sand-coloured beach villas with their rooftop balconies curved up the slight camber of the hill. Nicholas could see from the house numbers that Number 13 was right at the end. Slightly out of breath, he came to a sudden halt at the last house. The lights on the upper floor were dimmed, the cream blinds half-closed and there was no light downstairs. The only indication of life was a faint glow in the back garden just visible between clumps of a tall flaming hydrangea at the side of the house. He stood still and listened. He could just make out distant voices, the clink of glasses, an occasional burst of laughter.

Pushing his way through the bushes, he came to a cluster of bamboo bushes that flanked the back garden. He was about to step through these when a sudden instinct told him to stop. From inside the house there was hardly a sound. He put his hand between the bamboos and gently pushed them apart. The entire garden was visible, screened on all sides by foliage through which a few slivers of moonlight penetrated. He heard another snatch of conversation. He strained his ears but try as he might, he couldn't tell its source. He moved forward, peering towards the blinds at the back of the house. A dim light came from behind the glass, perhaps the light of a bedside lamp, but he couldn't see the rest of the room. He stepped onto the back lawn. Now he could hear music and smell something wafting from an open window: incense perhaps. Keeping close to the wall, he reached the long terrace windows and looked in.

All he could see at first was a futon laid out on the wooden floor, a Japanese shoji lamp next to it. Beyond it was a white expanse, the broad bare back of someone, a thinning head of hair. The back belonged to a man who seemed to be kneeling upright while in front of him a slimmer figure bent forward on all fours. Nicholas edged closer and caught his breath. The slimmer figure was pleasing the other in a manner pictured in erotic art ever since the vases of the Greeks and the tombs of the Egyptians. A thatch of matted, black hair hid his face, but as he came up for air, as the face of a Japanese geisha bobbed into his sight, he knew exactly whom it was.

For a moment he just stood there. Then he took a giant step backwards and hurled himself down the side of the house, running along the road as fast as his legs could take him. Reaching the Piazza, he braked to a halt and tried to gulp in air. Several people turned round to stare at him. He took one look at their faces and ran to the ferry.

As the engine began to churn the waves, he made his way to the very back of the lower deck and tried to focus on what he had just seen. One thing was clear: Ray-jai did it with anyone he could. He probably thought it fun to seduce one United executive and then another. He probably thought of Nicholas as one of his easier conquests. But apart from his vanity, the crucial point was how long Ray-jai and George had known each other.

No sooner had the ferry docked on Hong Kong side than Nicholas ran over the gangplank to the quayside, where he was promptly sick in front of a newspaper stand. 'Shit,' he groaned as a couple of pedestrians passed, nervously sidestepping the mess he had left on the pavement.

The newspaper vendor gave him a packet of tissues and he was cleaning himself up as best as he could when his cell phone rang. He took one look at the number and turned it off. There was no way he could see George now. With shaking legs, he made his way to the taxi stand.

Arriving back at his apartment, he locked the door and went in search of the whisky bottle. Throwing himself down on the sofa, he took a huge gulp and almost gagged. He was being absurd. George couldn't possibly have foreseen a situation in which Ray-jai might be useful. Ray-jai had seen the Press Release but he couldn't have known how important it was. The idea that the two of them had somehow conspired against him was ridiculous. But then what on earth were they doing together?

He gulped down some more whisky, hoping that it would somehow clarify his thoughts. But the more he drank the more confused he became.

He stood up, shuffled over to the window and threw it open. The lights of Hong Kong spread out below, humming in the dark like the strange stelae of some distant world. He breathed in the humid night air, hoping that it would somehow refresh him, but all he felt was a re-gathering wave of nausea.

Taking his whisky glass back to the bottle on the table, he stared at it for a moment. And then with a cry of fury, he flung it onto the wooden floor where it shattered into a hundred fragments.

'Fuck,' he said, stumbling towards the bedroom.

Chapter 25

D aniel moved to the hi-fi and took one of his last remaining CDs out of the tower stand. He opened the pink-covered box, extricated a silver disc called *Greatest Remix Hits 1998*, and soon Kylie Minogue's rich ironic voice was spreading its sexy tones around the lounge and out onto the terrace. Moving his body in time to its rhythms, he sat down on the sofa and looked again at the contents of the letter from Steve. There wasn't much to go on in the spidery scrawl, although Matt and Ron had helped him analyse it for clues, just as they had helped him analyse the other two adverts that he had responded to in *Gay Times*. At first he had treated it as a kind of game, just as Matt and Ron had suggested, a way of storing ammunition. But now it had turned serious.

He couldn't build a very full picture of Steve from a few lines on pale grey paper with a letterhead that said *Credibullideas*. But he was attracted to what he said about liking Jackie Chan and early Bruce Lee movies, and the postscript about his first trip to the Far East, which had included Hong Kong and Bangkok. He was a manager in an events company, which sounded interesting. The accompanying photograph was promising too. It showed

Steve in his East London flat, sitting on the sofa with a fist balanced on his head and an Apple monitor and a pile of books behind him. He was wearing a tracksuit top with a Nike logo on it.

Overall, Steve's advert was a great improvement on the general run of ads for orientals in *Gay Times*, which seemed to be mainly placed by middle-aged men requiring houseboys. '*Orienteering Course*: Attractive, easygoing English M in east London, 35, seeks Chinese M 18-45 for fun and friendship, maybe more.' It was also more attractive than the other two he had answered ('*I'm the Boss of Me*: Educated, handsome, self-employed M, 37, seeks younger, intelligent M Chinese for company++', and '*Feel the Spirit!* Gay M, 32, enjoys yoga, spiritualism, countryside WLTM Oriental M for fun and maybe relationship.'). Ron had dismissed the Boss as being too condescending, and Matt had warned that the Spiritualist was probably hooked on skunk, but what had really decided Daniel for Steve was the fact that he was so straightforward.

He didn't claim to be handsome and he pointed out that he was relaxed. 'Fun and friendship' meant sex and friendship, which was fair enough, but there was also a tentative allusion to the possibility of something longer and deeper. And yet the rider was not as demanding as '++' or 'maybe relationship' (meaning for god's sake I *must* have a relationship). There was maturity too in that age range ('18-45') that gave Daniel the oddly reassuring sense that he had a good chance of making it on the market for a long time to come.

He ran his hands over his hair, careful not to disturb it now that it was gelled. Whatever happened, Steve was probably not looking for anything heavy and Daniel had plenty of time to get out of it. Deep down, all he wanted was reassurance: to burn off the bitterness of Nicholas's betrayal in the warmth of someone else's embrace. That one awkward phone call they had shared, Steve's voice hesitant and amused by turns, had been enough to convince him.

Standing up as Kylie repeated 'I should be so lucky', he hitched up his hipster jeans and went again to the hall mirror to check on his Chicago Bulls jersey. He looked at his watch: time to go.

Crossing the road at the upper end of Millwall Basin, he felt glad he had put on a T-shirt under the jersey. It may not have picked out his pecs to their best advantage, but at least it made him look bulky. Steve seemed well built from his photograph, even stocky, and there was an air of the rugby player about him. Not for the first time Daniel wondered about his signature: 'English M'. It was unusual for advertisers to point out their nationality. Daniel wondered whether it was this that had attracted him: someone confident about his background and identity. So far he had followed Daniel's suggestions in everything, agreeing to stick to text messages and e-mails, respecting his privacy apart from that one late-night message, and waiting patiently for a first date.

The basement bar on West India Quay was much less crowded than Daniel expected, even though a band was warming up at the far end of the room, and for a moment he wondered if he'd come to the right place. But a sign above the bar for *Gay & Lesbian Night, Happy Hour 7-9 pm* was pretty conclusive He looked at his watch. It was only just past eight o'clock, which was probably too early for the regulars, and for the hundredth time he wondered if he should have fixed the meeting for later. Steve might have felt more comfortable in a large crowd. Or perhaps he would have preferred dinner, which would have made the sex thing less obvious. But then Matt had said one hour was good enough to get an angle on him, and he would turn up with Ron at around 9 o'clock.

Daniel once more surveyed the bar. What if he didn't turn up? What if he was nothing like his photo? What if he was hopelessly overweight or a heroin addict or twenty years older than his profile said? That thing about *Credibullideas* suggested he was intelligent, although it could also be a sign of arrogance. And then just as he was setting off on another set of 'what-ifs', Daniel felt a slight tap on his shoulder.

He turned and found himself looking at a shaven-headed guy in a dark brown suit with some kind of shiny stripe in it, a purple open-necked shirt, and sporting a day's growth of beard. 'Hi there,' he said, holding out his hand. 'Looking for English M.'

'Yeah,' said Daniel with a nervous laugh, surprised and pleased that Steve had opened with that. The prickly stubble was another surprise, so was the casual elegant. He had seemed much more homely in his photos. 'Where were you hiding?'

Steve seemed to absorb Daniel's initial analysis and to be just completing his own. 'I was sitting over there behind the door, to watch you come in. I didn't have time to change after the office.'

Daniel nodded, not quite sure whether to question these statements. He wondered if Steve had chosen a place to see him come in just in case he decided to leave, which made him feel both vulnerable and guilty about Matt and Ron. On the other hand, the threaded suit and funky colours didn't seem quite right for the office. It occurred to him that Steve might have been doing exactly what Daniel had been doing at home. 'What do you want to drink?'

'Let me get these,' said Steve and gently pressed Daniel's upper arm. 'We can sit over there. It's a bit too private behind the door,' he grinned. 'What are you having?'

Daniel was about to say ginger beer, which was what he drank with Nicholas, but suddenly he changed his mind. 'Vodka and cranberry juice.'

'Rightie-ho,' said Steve and headed for the bar.

Daniel went over to the heavy oaken table Steve had indicated, and sat down in one of its high-backed chairs. He wondered what kind of effect vodka would have on him. Worse than wine perhaps; even more incandescent. He looked over at the bright figure now leaning with his elbow on the bar, apparently at ease with the barman and the rest of the crowd. His eyes played on his flexing back and the gentle rise of his buttocks beneath the jacket, the sharp point of his sideburns, the suggestion of strength in the broad sinews of his neck and the shaved head that gleamed beneath the arc lights. For a moment his mind struggled to match the reality of Steve with the floating image of 'English M', and he wondered which one fitted better his urge to seduce. And then, as Steve collected the drinks in two broad hands and moved towards him, his purple shirt open two buttons to reveal the shadows of a slightly hairy chest, he saw how sexy he was, how casually obtainable. He accepted his vodka with a slightly shaking hand.

'Cheers,' they both said and Steve took a draught of his pint while Daniel attempted to stifle a cough as the alcohol hit the back of his throat.

'You look different from your photo,' said Steve. He was staring frankly at Daniel as if he had a right to, as if that was exactly what they were doing there, and any attempt to pretend otherwise would be futile. 'I guess everyone does.' He took another sip of beer and added, again with a smile that softened his slightly provocative expression, 'It's a definite improvement.'

Daniel felt as if he was blushing but he couldn't be sure, it could be the vodka. 'At least I look like my pic. So do you, except for the suit and the beard. Some of the people I've exchanged with sent me the weirdest ones, usually much too young for what they said or sounded like on the voice mail.'

Steve's smile slightly faded, as if he was considering this. 'The voice mail. Does that mean..?'

'No,' protested Daniel and put down his drink. 'No, no, you're the first.' This sounded too naive and also begged the question of Nicholas and why he had started to date right now, which he certainly wasn't going into. 'I mean you're the first date I've had from the Personals. As I said, either the photos put me off or what they wrote in their letters.'

Steve's smile returned. He rubbed the stubble on his chin, making an ironic pout with his lips. 'There should be a Trades Descriptions Act for Personals. I've either had lusting OAPs – they reply to anything – or guys whose photo is incredibly tasteful, only for them to turn up looking completely different.

I'm not a body fascist, and I'm not just looking for superficial good looks, but the deliberate misrepresentation gets on my nerves. That's if they include their photo. And as for what some of them say…well – they don't leave much to the imagination.'

Daniel grinned and he took a sip of his vodka. The reference to what they said troubled him. It suddenly seemed to him that, apart from a few fine-tunings to accommodate Nicholas's betrayal, Steve's description could easily have fitted him. 'Right. I've had the same problem. It's even worse on the internet. People tell you any kind of lie, especially in the chat rooms, and you can never tell even from exchanging e-mails what the person is really like.'

'So what are you like?' said Steve, obviously wanting to leave all this negative stuff behind. 'Your letter was nice and you look even better than the photos. I hope you don't mind me saying so.'

'Thanks,' said Daniel, 'You look good too.' And then realising how banal that sounded, he added, 'We almost seem to know each other.'

'Yeah, we do don't we?' said Steve and leaned back, letting the jacket fall open across his chest. 'I haven't really been out with a Chinese. I've got a couple of friends in Hong Kong. They send me kung fu movies and that kind of stuff…' He paused, as if aware that this didn't amount to a reason for intimacy, or even a promise of it. 'But one thing I didn't get was what's been up with you. I mean, why we couldn't meet earlier…'

Daniel shrugged. This was exactly what he expected to be asked and it was exactly what he wasn't ready to discuss. 'Just a few personal problems,' he sighed. 'I don't really want to talk about it now. Things have got clearer.'

Steve nodded slowly and looked down at his drink. 'So…that's why we're meeting. Things have got clearer.'

Daniel bit his lip. 'Exactly.' He looked around for some change of topic and noticed Steve's almost empty pint glass. 'Do you want another drink?' he said and stood up.

Steve seemed ready to follow his lead. 'Okay, a pint of Guinness. I'll stop asking so many questions.'

'That's okay,' said Daniel and picked up Steve's glass.

The room with its blood red walls and polished pine floor seemed so much brighter than he had imagined. There were more people coming in now, male couples in weekend clothes from The Gap or Next, singles clutching their drinks and cigarettes as if defending themselves from something, the occasional spiky-haired lesbian with looks of friendly disparagement for her male 'cousins'. The whole thing was different to what Daniel had visualised; and so too was Steve. There were more questions to come, he could see that as he ordered the Guinness and a double vodka to hide within the cranberry juice. A date wasn't like a trip to the sauna in Hong Kong, or even like the anonymous couplings of Ron and Matt in the nearby gym. This was a person with a face, not just a cock, a person with a story and an expectation, however laid back he was. Of course, Daniel was free to do whatever he liked. They could sleep together. They could start to date each other and not sleep together. They could move in together. He had no idea how far they would go. But as he looked over and saw Steve lounging on the chair with his hand across the back of it, the outline of his cock visible beneath the table, his left hand flung casually across it as if sensing the angle and force with which he would like to use it later, he knew what he wanted.

Taking a long sip of the double vodka, he picked up the Guinness and headed towards the corner table. Outside, in the well of the stairs to West India Quay, a slice of blue sky was just darkening to blackness studded with stars. Daniel could see a plane up there, the pulse of its navigation lights like a distant warning, and for some reason he thought of Nicholas.

He shuddered and sat down.

'Are you okay?' said Steve, once more touching him on the arm, but this time sending a lightning jolt of expectation through his body. Daniel rubbed his bare skin with its lingering goose bumps and hugged himself. 'Just a bit cold. I should've worn a jacket.'

Steve looked down on him as if he was about to offer his own, and then decided against. He moved his chair closer. 'You never know what the hell the weather's going to do. Anyway, I like the Bulls jersey. How far did you have to come?'

Daniel took another sip of the vodka. 'Just across the quayside. There's a strong wind tonight.'

'So you've got your own place,' said Steve and then seemed to realise his mistake. 'Sorry, more questions.' This time he patted Daniel on the hand.

'It's okay,' said Daniel knowing that there were many such questions to come and deciding straight away that he wouldn't answer all of them. He wouldn't be taking him home, however much he might want to betray Nicholas. A shared apartment owned by an absent lover would hang over their first intimacy like a bat from hell. Anyway, Steve had his own place. 'How about you?'

'Just beyond Narrow Street,' said Steve, withdrawing his hand.

'Convenient,' said Daniel. 'I mean…if you work over here.'

'I work in Camden,' said Steve. 'That's where the office is, but Narrow Street – '

'Right,' said Daniel, cutting him off. The evening was still young and he didn't want to come across as too inquisitive.

'There you are!' said a voice from the direction of the door. Daniel turned and saw Ron approaching, an artist's beret pulled down over one eye. He was followed by the more solid figure of Matt, ambling along in the background. 'I told you this was the place to come on Friday nights. Who's your friend?' asked Ron, sitting down at the spare chair and cocking his head.

Daniel began on the introductions, encouraging as much confusion as possible. Nevertheless, he was annoyed with himself. He sneaked a sly look at Steve to his right, now crouched over the table, but from the way he was talking to Ron and accepting another Guinness from Matt he could see he didn't need to worry. 'English M' may have guessed the plan, but he was happy to go along with it.

Chapter 26

W hen Nicholas awoke the sun was piercing the blinds with diagonal bars of light. He raised himself slowly and put a hand over his eyes. This time he knew only too well where he was. He was alone in Hong Kong with a throbbing head, a tongue like shredded cardboard, and a consuming sense of guilt. He sat there for a while wondering how he ever dealt with hangovers when he was a student. Everything in that stale-smelling room, everything from the smashed whisky glass to the rumpled sheets and the half-unpacked luggage indicated that he was in trouble. He staggered from the bed and made his way to the bathroom where he retched several times, brushed his teeth, and swilled his face.

Next stop was the kitchen where he found a mop to clear away the worst of the debris and then a whole roast chicken that his maid had left in the fridge. He gnawed at a leg, washing it down with some Perrier water before shuffling over to the long window that looked down over the terrace to Victoria Harbour. The glitter on the waters only intensified his headache. Overhead, volcanic clouds formed a pulsing backdrop to the white cruise ships and the Star Ferries tracking between Kowloon and Hong

Kong Island. He stared at them a moment. They seemed like snails leaving behind their silken ooze in the glassy waters. For a moment he felt strangely at one with them.

He bent over the pile of letters and faxes and wondered whether to start on them right there and then. But he didn't trust his state of mind. He showered, brushed himself up and had two Alka Seltzers. Finally, having deposited the shards of glass in the rubbish bin, he gathered his mail together and headed for Peak Road.

As he emerged from the taxi and crossed into the windy Piazza in front of the Senso Building, he could see the usual blue-shirted guards in each of the elevator lobbies, their caps slightly tilted. There was no one else around except for one person exiting from the building. A crowd of Filipina maids had taken up most of the space on the Piazza with their picnics and Christian songs and prayer meetings, just as they did every Sunday, and it was difficult for him to step between them towards the lobby. Their birdlike voices raised in laughter and gossip seemed to follow him as he entered through the glass swing doors. He signed the registration book, added his United ID number and had just begun walking towards the elevator when he noticed the nearest security guard glance at the book and begin speaking into his walkie-talkie.

'Just a moment.' Almost before he had said this, three other guards appeared from nowhere.

Nicholas took another look at the registration book. He could see several scrawled signatures with arrival times indicating that morning. There was nothing unusual in that. United executives often went to their offices for brief periods on weekends. He couldn't tell whether anyone had gone up since noon because the guard was now approaching him. 'I'm sorry sir. No entry.'

He tried to smile his way out of this. 'Do you know who I am?'

'Sorry sir,' replied the guard as if repeating a drill. Nicholas looked at the pocket holster at his hips. He was unlikely to reach for it but Nicholas wasn't going to take the risk. He took a deep breath and headed back through the door. Either Seymour Smith had received the wrong instructions or he had taken some absurd precautions of his own. Nicholas had no choice.

Still smarting from the shock, he reached one of the enormous sculptures of Horus, which reared up on either side of the Senso Building. He stood still for a moment, watching two Filipinas crouched at the foot of the falcon-headed images eating their perfumed *adobo* pork and rice. He was about to turn away when he noticed the suited form of Alex Higgins enter one of the elevator lobbies. He took a few steps forward, reached the edge of the Piazza and waited for him to exit.

Alex did not reappear. Nicholas wiped the sweat from the back of his neck. What the fuck? It was just possible that Alex had permission to go upstairs when no one else was allowed, but that would suggest some sort of special meeting. Who on earth would hold a special meeting on a Sunday morning?

Making room for himself among the maids, he took out his cell phone and punched in a number. The song 'The Lord Believes in You' wafted over from a group of guitar players near Exchange Square.

'Sarah?' He moved away from the noise towards the harbour front.

'Yes.' Sarah sounded relaxed, probably reading the Sunday papers in front of the TV. 'Welcome back.'

'Thanks,' said Nicholas. 'Listen, do you know anything about a new rule preventing staff entering the Senso Building on the weekend?'

There was another voice on the line, Sarah explaining who it was to her husband. 'No...I don't think so. Anyway, that's the last place I'd want to go on the weekend.'

Nicholas ignored the irony. 'That's not quite the point. I'd like to know if security has been beefed up recently.'

He could sense her puzzlement. 'You should know, you set some of it up. Is anything wrong?'

'Have you read the London weekend papers?'

'It's a bit early for those Nick. It's only Sunday.'

Nicholas paused. If neither the press reports nor the Shareholders Letter were common knowledge in Hong Kong, he still had a chance. 'I need to talk Sarah. Do you have time for a coffee? I'm so sorry to spring this on you.'

He could hear Sarah asking her husband and then a decision being reached. She came back on the line. 'Okay, where?'

'Club 1997.' He knew he shouldn't be calling her but he was running out of ideas.

'Okay,' said Sarah. 'I'll put his master's lunch in the oven.'

As Nicholas embarked on the long walk from the harbour front to Lan Kwai Fong, he went over what he was going to say to her. By the time he had settled himself upstairs at Club 1997 and was sipping a cappuccino, he had more or less thought everything through. He tried to distract himself by flicking through the bar and restaurant reviews in *Hong Kong Magazine* but he couldn't concentrate. Finally, he heard a familiar voice.

Sarah approached in grey slacks and a matching top. 'I took a taxi. It's much quicker.'

Nicholas looked at his friend's open, sensible face and half-ironic expression and he felt an enormous sense of relief flooding through him. 'What can I offer you?'

'I'll have the same as you.'

He called over the waitress and ordered the coffee, turning back to Sarah with a frown. 'Sorry to call you out but there've been some developments.'

Sarah cocked her head. 'Developments?'

Nicholas took a deep breath. 'I flew back yesterday and for various reasons I urgently needed to see George. I'd called him earlier but his cell phone wasn't on. Later he left a message to say he had someone to dinner in Discovery Bay and would I meet him in Central. I didn't like the bar he chose so I tried to call him back, without any success. I then decided to go over to Discovery Bay myself. But when I got over there and found his place, the lights were off in the front room. Instead of calling it off, I went round the back to see if anyone was in.'

The waitress put Sarah's cappuccino on the table and retreated. Sarah raised a pencil-sharp eyebrow. 'Yes?'

'Someone was there with him.'

Sarah dropped her eyes and shuffled the sugar packets as if trying to decide what interested her more. 'Someone?'

'Ray-jai,' said Nicholas, blurting out the name as if it had stuck in his throat. 'The guy I met on the Peak, the one I told you about, the one I fucked Sarah. It seems he not only knows George well, he knows him *very* well.'

This time something registered deep within Sarah. She picked up one of the sugar packets and tore it over her cappuccino, stirred her coffee and looked hard at Nicholas. 'Is that what this is all about?'

Nicholas flinched at her I-told-you-so expression. 'I haven't told you before but when Ray-jai came round to my flat that first night we met I had a copy of the Mercantile Press Release on my desk. The next morning he cleaned up my apartment and replaced the first page of the Press Release on my reading stand. Now, I go over to George's place and find them humping each other.'

Sarah picked up her coffee. 'You mean, you suspect George and this stupid...whatever he is...are responsible for those leaks?' She took a deep breath, the colour rising to her cheeks. 'Look Nick, even if they did know each other, George wouldn't talk business to someone he picked up in a bar. I doubt he even knows Ray-jai's been dating you. People who are promiscuous don't go around talking about it.'

For a moment Nicholas felt ashamed by Sarah's cool assessment, but then he remembered there was more to it than just that. Taking a deep breath, he began to tell her the whole story.

Sarah sat there absorbing it all without any perceptible surprise until he came to the end. Then the enormity of the situation seemed to dawn on her. 'So that means they could sack you?'

Nicholas nodded. 'If any of the allegations are proved to be true. But of course you and I know they couldn't possibly be. In which case, why would the person who did this go to such enormous lengths to pull me down?'

Sarah plaited a strand of hair between her fingers and thought for a moment, a deep crease in her brow. 'Do you know anyone on the Board, I mean know them well apart from the Chairman and the CEO?'

'I know Sir John Williams, although you could hardly say I knew him well. I don't think *anyone* knows him really well.'

The pinch in Sarah's brow deepened. 'That's the man that Jeanette Long boasts about knowing through her husband or something?'

'Yes.'

'Can he be relied on?'

'I think so. I once helped him out in a similar situation before I got the job at United. He's the one who's been managing the fall-out for me in London.'

Sarah's grey eyes narrowed. 'You mean he's supposed to be managing the story?

Nicholas's fingers trembled as he played with the sugar. 'Yes, he has a vested interest in my career. You could call him a kind of mentor. He's the one who warned me about my colleagues and not trusting anyone too much.'

Sarah put down her cup and leaned forward, letting her long mousey hair cover her cheeks. 'How could anyone have known those details in the letter about Daniel and his visa?' She paused. 'It must have been someone who had access to the dates you met, application forms, things like that.'

Nicholas put down his coffee cup and stared at her. Why the fuck hadn't he seen that before? The only other source for the information in the Shareholder Letter was his office computer. No one could have access to that without his secretary's knowledge. And how would they get past the lobby guard in the first place? 'Can I borrow your United card?'

Sarah looked startled for a moment. She was about to say something but then, as if she sensed that Nicholas wanted action and not more speculation, she dived into her purse and put a square piece of plastic on the table. 'Be careful what you're doing.'

Nicholas picked up the card and placed it carefully in his wallet. 'What elevator lobby do you use?'

'Level 1 to 16,' said Sarah.

***

The taxi tore a strip up the road to Mid-Levels as Nicholas took out his cell phone and keyed in the number for Daniel's phone. When there was no reply, he tried Kay. Again, no success. Finally, he left a message on Daniel's voice mail, 'Arrived safely in Hong Kong. Call you soon,' before hanging up. It was all he could do not to ask the driver to head straight to the airport.

Paying off the driver, he hurried to the elevator before anyone could see him. Fortunately, Alex Higgins was not around. He rummaged in his pocket for the apartment key, slotted it into the door, and burst into the room. Without taking off jacket or shoes, he flung his briefcase on the sofa and headed straight for the Johnny Walker on the kitchen counter. Seizing it in both hands, he poured the remains of the whisky down the sink. 'Get real,' he muttered to himself.

He returned to the sofa and began sorting through the mail, throwing the letters and bills aside as he searched for anything, anything at all from United International. Finally, he turned his attention to the pile of faxes and went through them one by one until he came to a two-page document. The text was poorly printed but he could still make out the United International logo on the cover page and the time and place stamp: London, Friday, 18.07 pm.

My dear Nicholas,

I tried to call you today but there was no reply. I don't want you to take this too hard but it is my duty to warn you that my efforts on your behalf are encountering stiff resistance. I don't mean from the press. The problem is nearer to home.

There was an emergency Board Meeting this afternoon, and although I spoke up for you, it seems that Eddie and many of his colleagues are actively considering asking for your resignation. The Board is still considering the matter but for the moment it holds that even if the inquiry clears you of immediate responsibility, the damage done to United International's reputation may be too great to maintain you in your post.

I am doing all I can on your behalf and I am sure that your position will recover in the near future. In the meantime, I remain yours etc.

Sir John Williams.

Nicholas stared hard at the page for a long time. Then slowly, with the minimum of force, he screwed the page up and dropped it into the waste paper basket.

Taking out Sarah's card, he carried it with him to the bedroom and laid it out carefully on the dresser. He then turned towards the wardrobe and began to sort through his clothes.

Chapter 27

He stood in the forecourt just opposite the Senso Building and checked his appearance in the glass of the bus shelter. Pulling his scarf a little further up towards his chin, he raised his raincoat collar, opened his leather file, checked all the keys were there and closed it again. According to his watch, it was 8.16 pm. The last Sunday worker should be leaving the building. The traffic lights at the zebra crossing changed to red. He hurriedly joined the pedestrians crossing the road in the drizzling rain and then cut across the Piazza towards Elevator Lobby 1-16. He passed through the swing door and approached the lobby guard, took out Sarah's card and bent over fully to sign the visitors' book. He wrote down her surname, filled in the floor level he was visiting and added her code. He then put her ID card upside down on the top of the desk. As soon as the guard pushed it back, he replaced the pen and made for the elevator. For safety's sake, he punched the button for Level 16 but when he reached the level he moved quickly to the next elevator and pressed the Up button. Fortunately, all elevators were working. He could hear someone's keys jangling and faint crackle of a radio on a level below.

'Come on,' he whispered as the floor indicator showed 35, 32, 28, 24 and then 16. The doors opened with a clanging sound. He stepped in and put his shoe between the doors to break the sound of their closing. He then pressed the button for Level 28 and the lift set off with a slight shudder.

The lobby on the 28th floor was brightly lit and carried the faint aroma of cooked food. However, the nearby dining area was now shrouded in gloom. He made his way across the hall, his steps lit only by the lights of a giant Star Cruise liner in Victoria Harbour, and approached the diagonal escalator to the upstairs floors. As he passed the sensor it hummed into life. He turned at the first landing and went through exactly the same procedure, allowing himself to be borne upwards like one of the Hungry Ghosts of Chinese lore.

He reached Level 30, looked to left and right and then over the door at the ceiling lights inside. There was no sign of anyone in the offices. He approached the door and typed in the code. As soon as the door opened, he put one foot inside, checking for further noises along the corridors. Not a sound, not even from the air conditioning. Once inside, he ignored the light switch and used the illumination from the towers of Central to guide his way. He headed towards a glass door that closed off a large office on the right wall. Reaching the door, he rummaged in his case and found the thick set of keys that he always kept at home in case of a fire alarm or some other emergency. He tried each in turn. On the second attempt the door opened. He was alone in George's office.

Sarah had said that she was looking for a stapler that day when she found her appraisal. Nicholas began with the desktop and the utility tray. All he could find was a huge padlock. He tried the top right drawer: unlocked and full of junk. He tried the second drawer: nothing but United publications. He tried the third drawer: also locked. 'Damn,' he muttered. If she had been looking for a stapler how the fuck had she stumbled on a key?

Suddenly, the phone on the desk buzzed. A long drawn out signal, followed by several more. Nicholas stared at the phone, watching the light on the top flashing, and then the buzzing and flashing stopped just as they had begun. The voice mail must have kicked in. He held his breath and listened. All he could hear was the low hum of the fax machine next door. Where would George hide his keys? He could phone Sarah and ask her but Frank's hiding place wouldn't be the same as George's. In his anxiety to disguise himself he had forgotten to bring along his cell phone. If he used the desk phone, Security might well pick it up.

Nicholas sat down at the desk and tried the drawers on the left. They were all unlocked but stuffed with files. There was no sign of a key. He leaned back and examined the desk from top to bottom. Up near the top, he could see a thin sliding drawer for pins and staples. He pulled the lip towards him. A key marked 'Confidential' lay right in the middle of the Post-It stickers. Nicholas grabbed the key and tried it in the lower right keyhole. The drawer slid out easily. He could see a pile of United appraisal forms. To the right of these, on the wall of the drawer, there were two sets of keys. He took them out and examined them. Each one was marked with a tag: 'JL' and 'AS'. It seemed little had changed since the days of Frank Shearer. But as he leafed through the appraisals in his drawer, it became apparent that he was wrong. George's collection of appraisals contained nothing from the other departments.

Taking the three sets of keys with him, he locked the drawer, hurried to the door, and crept down the corridor towards Antonia's office. He stopped for a moment. Some instinct told him to go straight on to Jeanette's office at the far end of the department. Her door faced almost straight onto Central and in the faint glow of the harbour he could make out wooden carvings, a tapestry, and some painted masks. He opened the door with one of the two keys marked 'JL' and bent to try the other key in the lower left drawer.

'Shit,' he muttered. He tried the lower right drawer. It opened as if it had been waiting for him. There were several documents inside. He took them out and placed them in order on the desk.

He then looked back into the drawer. Despite the gloom, he could make out a square white envelope, half A4 size. He reached down and fingered the corner of the envelope; it was filled with something. He took the envelope out and extracted a black computer diskette.

He reviewed his prizes on the desk, feeling the thump of blood within his veins. The light from the office blocks was not enough. He looked over at the coded door: no sign of a guard. He listened again. He could perhaps hear the dring-dring of a distant phone but nothing else. He turned on the desk lamp.

The ink on the appraisal reports seemed wet in the arc of the electric light, although from their dates it was clear that they were written the previous year. He leafed through the names so familiar to him from countless daily tasks. Eunice's report was among them. He was about to put everything back when he noticed a few reports from Antonia's section, and then he came upon a name that made him sit up straight: *Ng Chi Kong, Daniel*. He stared hard. There was no mistake. Jeanette had a copy of Daniel's appraisal in her drawer.

He leafed through it just to make sure and was trying to put it back in the envelope when he heard a sound along the corridor, followed by the flickering of a torch on the ceiling. He clicked off the desk lamp, stuffed the document into his briefcase and closed the desk drawer. He could hear the door code being patched and was about to slip into the photocopying room next door when a slight clattering sound told him that he had pushed the diskette off the desk and onto the floor. The electronic bleeps came to an end. He heard the far door open and close, the shuffle of footsteps. A light shone up and down the department. Bending double, he closed the office door with one hand. He then scrambled back across the floor and hid behind Jeanette's desk.

The footsteps approached and reached the corner of the section. Nicholas ducked as the flashlight swept around the office, illuminating the grotesque faces of the masks, the silent laugher of a fat Chinese Buddha, Jeanette standing next to her husband at some university gathering. He waited for the door handle to turn. After a long pause, the footsteps began to recede. He watched the light on the ceiling grow dimmer. Finally, as the door closed, it disappeared. He remained still until he heard the escalator hum into life before creeping out from behind the desk.

Feeling around on the floor, his hand brushed against the diskette. He put it on the desk and turned on Jeanette's computer. The hard disk made a whirring sound as it booted up. A Microsoft Windows logo appeared, followed by a blue screen with a password and user request. The user name was filled in but the password space was blank. He forced myself to concentrate. Jeanette chose flowery names for things. What had she had chosen for her house on the Isle of Wight? Something from a film, something red and romantic. He tried 'Rosebush'; nothing happened. He tried 'Rose Garden', 'Rosegarden', 'Rosehip'. and then, with a final flash of inspiration, 'Rosebud'.

The screen changed, the hard disk whirred into action, and Jeanette's files were all lined up on the desktop. He reviewed them for a moment, their identities hidden, and then he had an idea. It was a long shot, but everything was a long shot. He began looking for the Shareholders Letter, first under My Documents and then under Briefcase, Office Folder, United International. He typed 'SAG Letter' into Search For, and then 'Shareholders' Letter' and 'Shareholders' Action Group'. Finally, he added '.doc' to each of them. Nothing. He looked over at the corridor. He didn't have any time left and in any case it was unlikely that she would keep such a document on a hard disk.

Seizing the diskette, he slipped it into the tower slot and waited for the icon to come up. He then double-clicked on the icon, chose Miscellaneous from the files and a series of folders and documents appeared on the screen. He quickly ran down the choices and double-clicked on the first file that looked promising: Benefits. A letter unfurled on the screen. He skimmed through in exasperation and then read it sentence by sentence. It was addressed 'To the Group Chairman, United International Bank' and contained a complete outline of all the documents Jeanette had submitted, together with dates, to support her claim to a continuation of her expatriate benefits.

Nicholas sighed and shook his head, closing the file and checking through the other documents. He could find nothing that seemed very exceptional except for one headed 'Cryptic'. He opened it. The screen filled with an odd assortment of codes followed by a series of numbers, credit card or account numbers, the sort of list that people kept of their PINs. The sheer accessibility of the codes made him feel like a criminal. But just as he was about to close the folder he saw one entry that looked rather different to the others: 'JW', followed by a two-part code 'sjw_86347' and 'van1995'. Nicholas stared at the file. It wasn't hard to identify who 'JW' was. He had seen her come out of his office in London and he had introduced her at Roger Yates' reception. He was the one member of the Board she always referred to. He sat back in his seat and breathed in the musty air tinged with carbon copier and the faint aroma of perfume. Why would she have a reference to him on a hidden diskette?

With a slightly trembling hand, he wrote down the codes and put them in his pocket. He then moved the contents of the diskette onto Jeanette's hard disk, found another diskette and copied the new material. He was just erasing all the files on the hard disk and ejecting the diskette when he heard the sound of the escalator moving.

Turning off the lamp and the computer, he slipped his prizes into his briefcase and put the original diskette at the back of the lower drawer along with the appraisals. Finally, his muscles tense with the effort, he closed the drawer and crept out of the office.

Chapter 28

Daniel woke to the slow rumble of a train, a viaduct just visible through the gap in the blue-and-cream drapes, and frowned to himself. The sun laid a diagonal of light across a series of lime-green trees on a large canvas over the bed. Turning gently, he could see the top of a shaven head, like a pinkish egg above the duvet, and the sharp taper of a sideburn. He wondered if he could take a leak without waking Steve, or whether he could hold it back a while longer. It wasn't so much that he didn't want to talk, but that he didn't want to talk about last night. The contemporary art on the walls and the stylish Shaker kitchen on the middle floor, the Moet & Chandon in the fridge and the array of Moulton Brown moisturizers in the bathroom, told him that Steve was sophisticated. He would expect to talk about the sex, even if only a little. He would expect to talk about the future.

He slipped one leg from the duvet and touched the floor, raising himself slowly and then sliding out of the bed towards the bathroom. He glanced towards the bed but there was no movement and the regular sound of Steve's breathing continued. Reaching the bathroom, Daniel gingerly turned on the secondary light over the mirror and took a pee. He looked at the yellowish water in the bowl, as if it would somehow disappear by itself, then with a restrained movement pulled the handle. The flush was gentle, and by straining his hearing over the last gurgles he could hear no other sound in the bedroom.

He looked at himself in the mirror. It was stupid to think that he could somehow just slip away. Men were supposed to be inured to the guilt of promiscuity, and indeed if it had been just a pick-up in a bar he might have felt differently. In that situation, the rules of the game were clear. But the Steve he had met was someone he liked, they had built up expectations of dating in those text messages. The sex had been passionate.

He stepped into the walk-in shower and wondered what time it was. He would have to get back over to E14 and bring his stuff over to Ron's. He couldn't possibly bring it to Steve's, even less so after what had happened. Ron had been very understanding and a mini-cab wouldn't cost much to get over to Greenwich. Turning on the steel taps, he held his hand briefly under the water and adjusted the temperature, trying to imagine Nicholas's expression when he returned to an empty flat. For a moment as he stood under the jets, he felt strangely light-headed. But by the time he reached for the towel that Steve had laid out, euphoria had disappeared, replaced by a feeling of deep sadness.

'Daniel?' said Steve, knocking on the door.

'Hi,' said Daniel, attempting to sound relaxed. 'Just taking a shower.'

'Go ahead, I'll use the one downstairs and get us some breakfast. Cereal okay?'

'Yes,' said Daniel. 'Fine.'

'Great,' said Steve.

As Steve's footsteps receded down the wooden stairs, Daniel shook his head and towelled his hair. He never ate cereal for breakfast, and Nicholas would never have said that he would get breakfast for the two of them. It wasn't part of their daily ritual. And if he had said it, Daniel would have told him not to bother, he could do it for himself.

With the towel firmly wrapped around his waist, Daniel retired to the bedroom. Steve had pulled the drapes back on the railway viaduct, over which the silver-clad Canada Square rose with gleaming indifference. Daniel half-opened the balcony doors to let in some fresh air.

Turning back, he saw that the bed had been remade with the quilt pulled down over the end of the mattress and his clothes had been laid out singly, item by item, on the side of the bed facing him. His white underwear was smoothed out in a perfect W shape next to his Chicago Bulls jersey. Even his socks were laid over his Nike trainers. He smiled to himself. He had noticed the same fastidiousness when Steve put out the breakfast dishes and cutlery, the coffee and tea canisters, the cereal packets and sugar bowls, before they went upstairs the night before. Nicholas was anything but neat, especially when he was running late.

Checking whether he could be seen from the street, he slipped on his T-shirt and roughly hauled on his slip and jeans. He could hear music coming from the kitchen and he prepared himself.

'Coffee?' he heard from the stairway. 'Or tea?'

'Tea. Just coming.'

Steve was standing in the middle of the kitchen when he arrived, a steaming kettle of hot water in one hand. He smiled nervously when Daniel appeared and poured the water into a teapot that stood in the middle of the dining table. Another Docklands train rumbled past on the viaduct, making the wind chime at the open window tinkle. 'Sit where you like,' said Steve, indicating the chair opposite him.

Daniel sat down and felt the cold of the metal rising up through his buttocks. He looked at the array of cereal packets, chose one and poured the contents into the bowl that stood ready. Steve passed him the milk jug with a flourish and remained standing. 'Do you like eggs? I can easily go out and get some. And sausages. There's a shop just down the street.'

'It's okay,' said Daniel. 'I don't eat much for breakfast, and this looks fine. What're you going to have?'

Steve still looked worried, as if he hadn't been hospitable enough. 'What about toast? I can do that.'

'Okay,' said Daniel. 'Let's have toast. If you're going to.'

'Yes, I'm going to,' laughed Steve, as if they had just signed the Treaty of Versailles. 'I've got some jam too, or do you prefer peanut butter.'

Daniel started to shove cereal into his mouth. He had the feeling that if he didn't start eating soon, Steve would conclude that something was wrong and an investigation would begin. Whatever time it was, it was never too early for an inquest.

Steve found some sliced brown bread in a cupboard and fed two slices into the toaster. He then poured the tea into the two waiting beige mugs, indicated the milk and sugar to Daniel, and turned back to the toaster. As he replaced the toasted slices with fresh ones from the packet, Daniel noticed how precise his movements were. He could see the hair on Steve's torso, just visible through the collar of his bathrobe, and imagine the T-shaped scar to the right of his belly button, the reddish hollow below his ear lobes that made him squirm when licked. He wondered if he could get used to being intimate with him, a younger man than Nicholas, a fastidious layer out of clothes and maker of toast. If anything, as Steve prepared the toast and searched for jams on his kitchen shelves, he seemed like a total stranger of whose real life and character Daniel was completely ignorant.

'Hey, you dreaming?' said Steve and ruffled his hair before setting down the toast rack and joining him at the table.

Daniel smiled. 'Just sleepy. Busy day yesterday.'

'You mean at work?' said Steve, pouring out Special K into his bowl.

'At home,' said Daniel and then regretted it. It had been a hell of a job to get his stuff packed up and ready to go. He resented Nicholas for putting him through all this, resented him with all his being. And yet amid all the bitterness and desire for revenge, there was a fierce regret. He wondered where Nicholas was now, whether he was meeting Ray-jai again in some bar in Lan Kwai

Fong, whether it had really been the short fling he claimed or something much more serious.

'You mean you had the day off to do something,' said Steve, spreading his toast and looking at him

'A lot of chores,' said Daniel, and wondered if he would have to explain about Ron and the change of address. He didn't feel like talking about it, and the looming question that was coming was also something he couldn't decide on. It was as if dependence on Nicholas and getting free of Nicholas were now tangled up inside him, and his mind refused to move beyond these two threads.

'So I suppose you're going to rest today,' said Steve, his eyes now fixed on Daniel.

Daniel nodded. The attraction in Steve's expression scared him. He was flattered, but the flattery stood in the way of what he truly felt. 'I expect so,' he said and wondered if he should say he was unemployed. But then he thought better of it. 'I'll give you a call later.'

The cheekbone on the right side of Steve's face tremored, but otherwise his expression remained impassive. 'My company does events for quite a few places round town, you know stores and restaurants, that kind of thing. So there's always some place interesting to meet.'

'Okay,' said Daniel, and watched as Steve took out a cigarette from a pack on the table and lit it, blowing blue-tinted rings into the air. As his head came down level with Daniel's, he smiled at him with a contented, knowing expression, and suddenly Daniel knew that this was only an intermittent stage on his journey to re-discovery. He needed a job. He needed a life. Steve might just possibly figure in it, Steve with his sexiness and his clothes obsessions, but that possibility seemed far off. For the moment it was what Steve represented that he needed: the idea of being desired by someone else.

As he gazed at the smoke still rising from Steve's cigarette, he wondered if this need would last longer than Steve himself, longer even than his love for Nicholas. And he felt a great emptiness inside.

Chapter 29

Nicholas took the lift to the top floor of his apartment block, dumped his suitcase in the bedroom, called out to see if anyone was home, and headed straight for the front room.

Perched on the edge of the sofa, he listened to his messages. There were several callers who simply rang off when no one answered, and then Roger Yates' secretary's high, nasal voice leaving an urgent invitation for him to have lunch with the Chancellor. This was followed by two rather odd messages from Emily, her tone fragile and distant, another from a journalist who left his name and number, and finally a short message from Kay. He was hoping to have some word from Daniel, but he told himself he was back rather earlier than expected and Daniel would be expecting him to call the house in Snail's Place.

He listened to Kay's message for a second time: 'Hi Nicholas, hope you have a good flight. When did you say Daniel was supposed to arrive? Don't worry we'll look after him.' He tried to check the time and date of the message but something was wrong with the machine. It kept repeating 'Message received Friday...' He assumed Daniel was on the train to Shrewsbury when she called.

He sat back a moment, his ears still numbed by the 747, and wondered which issue he should tackle first. The sun was just beginning to rise through the mist, picking out the Cutty Sark's masts just visible down the railway track beyond the terrace. He tried to imagine it was just an ordinary day, Daniel would come sleepily into the room in his T-shirt, turn on the TV and they would have breakfast together before Nicholas put on his suit. But as his eyes wandered around the lounge, he noticed that something was wrong. Several videotapes were missing from the TV stand, the CD tower had large gaps in it and the Hong Kong magazines with their lurid covers had disappeared from the coffee table. He hurried to the bedroom. Wrenching open the drawers and wardrobe, he saw that huge swathes of Daniel's clothes had gone too. Every single item that belonged to him in the bathroom cabinet was missing.

For a moment Nicholas stood stock still, trying to recall what Daniel had packed that night. He ran to the guest bathroom and looked into the store cupboard for the large suitcases. Both of them were missing. He moved to his desk and opened each drawer: passport, cheque book, credit cards, everything that Daniel owned or needed had gone. All that remained of him was his i-Mac sitting silently on his desk. Nicholas stumbled to the study, found his cell phone and called his number. No one picked up.

'Jesus.' Numb with fear, he took the cordless phone and dialed Kay's number. As he waited for her to pick up, he remembered Daniel's last words after his confession: 'You do what you want Nicholas. I'll do what I want.'

'Kay?' he blurted out as soon as he heard her pick up. 'Is Daniel with you?'

Kay seemed taken aback. 'I thought he was with you. I haven't heard from him since you last called. How did it go?'

Nicholas tried to control his panic. 'Daniel isn't here, Kay.'

'Did you try his cell phone?'

Nicholas bit off the reply, choosing his words with deliberate care. 'He's not here. His phone is turned off. We had an agreement that he would come up to you. It looks like he's taken everything...' Nicholas was about to continue but some instinct told him not to.

'We were going to call you, Nick,' said Kay in a changed tone. 'But then you left a message to say you were coming back and we decided to wait.' There was a long silence. 'Mum's in hospital.'

The circuits in Nicholas's mind seemed to stop. 'Hospital?'

'She went in yesterday. Stomach blockage, vomiting all over the place. They've left her in A & E while they try to find out the cause. Jill's been down but she'll have to go back soon because of the children. I'm going there tomorrow.'

Nicholas lowered himself onto the sofa. 'How serious?'

'The doctors say she's stable.'

'Did she know I was away?'

Kay sighed, as if Nicholas thinking about himself was exactly what she would have expected: the twelve-year-old wondering if his sisters had told on him. 'I said you were clearing up some business and would be with us soon. Jill's there at the moment.'

Nicholas stared at the wall and closed his eyes. It was just beginning to dawn on him that apart from his sisters, he was completely alone. 'What do you want me to do?'

'I'm going to take over from Jill tonight but I'll have to go back in the morning. She's at the Royal Free Hospital. Take the train. You'll be too tired to drive. Call me when you get there and I'll come and pick you up.'

'You sure she's stable?'

Nicholas could hear Josie whispering in the background. 'I can't stay much longer,' said Kay. 'I have to call work and then pick up Josie's car from Shrewsbury.'

'Okay,' said Nicholas.

'Don't worry. This is just Daniel's way of getting back at you. He'll turn up.' And with that she put down the phone.

For a while Nicholas just sat there and stared at the table. It was much worse than he expected. Daniel had completely disappeared, together with most of his belongings, and his mother was in an emergency ward.

***

Just before dawn, wrapped in his favourite dressing gown, Nicholas wandered out of the bedroom and sat in the lounge. Gradually the pale neutral light of morning crept through the blinds, picking out the curved steel supports of the reclining chair and the aluminum ceiling lamps, the David Hockney print over the mantelpiece, the silver place mats with the Chinese calligraphy still set for two on the dining table. He could hear the faintest warble of birdsong from a nearby roof and the answering squawk of a couple of sea gulls as they swooped low over the terrace.

He stood up and moved towards the door. Turning the key, he slipped out into the morning chill. The slim-limbed olive plants in their terracotta pots trembled in the breeze. Beyond them he could see the horse chestnuts in the forecourt beginning to take on shape and contour, their leaves redolent with new growth. And for some reason he was reminded of those early weeks with Daniel in London, his fascination with the first sight of snow, the day he had come back to the flat from Chinatown laden with ginger, jujube and sweet potatoes to make a 'winter soup'. Each scene that unfolded on his inner eye had some meaning, an emotional weight that was more than simple memory. And to this he added Emily's bright chatter about the neighbours' squirrels or the spitefulness of her laugh when speculating on the future of her hairdresser, a young man who had fought with his boyfriend in Newcastle and who had become increasingly neurotic.

For some reason these snapshots hit him with the full force of life. They were nothing in comparison to the realities of the office, the things with which he dealt every day and for which he had sacrificed everything. They had no intellectual or social significance and they were unlikely to attract the attention of someone like Sir John Williams. And yet, these snapshots were his real life and everything else was simply emptiness. He couldn't tell this to any of his colleagues. He couldn't call up Roger Yates and tell him there were far more important things to life than landing his communications job. But that was the truth of it.

The sun appeared above the tops of the trees and he stared at it for a while as if entranced by the simple fact of nature. He had no one to blame but himself. He had reaped what he had sown. The problem was that he had very little time left to un-reap whatever he could.

Chapter 30

Emily was lying half-propped by the pillows almost in the center of the Casualty Ward. Nicholas could see her thin arms and silver-white hair, now disheveled by sleep, even before the friendly Filipina nurse told him where to look. She was facing up towards the ceiling, as if praying to the Lord she occasionally went to honour on a Sunday morning. And her face bore that long-suffering look he knew from his childhood accidents and from her many illnesses, her mouth half-open to reveal a not quite full set of dentures, her chin held firm as if defying the urge to cry.

She saw him almost before he had moved from the ward sister's desk, and her eyes flickered. Kay had given him a full report of what to expect and what the doctors had said but she had not prepared him for the frail silhouette of his once larger-than-life mother reduced to this trembling miniature. She looked so different, so fragile, hooked up to bottles and drips like some sort of terrifying human experiment. Ignoring the machinery at her bedside, and the eyes of the rest of the ward, he bent down to kiss her pallid cheek.

'So glad you came,' she managed to say, despite the tube that went up her nose. 'I was worried.'

'Don't be silly.' He schooled himself to ignore the brownish sediment in the liquid that passed through the plastic tubes, the faint aroma of decay that surrounded her. He sat back in a seat that he rescued from an adjoining bedside. Someone, probably Kay, had tried to comb her hair, with the result that her haggard face was topped by a flat wave of thick white hair around which a spray of greasy strands stuck out in all directions. He had never seen her look so old, or so wild, and yet he had never seen her look so tender either. Her shocking vulnerability, stuck there in the middle of the ward, pained him so much that he could hardly breathe.

'I'm sorry I couldn't come down any earlier. I knew Jill and Kay were here. But don't worry, I'll take care of you now.'

Emily looked down her long nose. She didn't need her glasses. 'The doctors...' She waved an arm vaguely in the direction of the door. He saw a bruise on her underarm, a bright red weal where the syringe of the drip had been inserted. She followed his eyes. '...put it in the wrong vein. Student nurse she was.'

Nicholas winced as if it had been inserted into him. 'Did you complain?'

Emily's eyes turned back. She moved her head slowly from side to side. 'No use to complain. Complaining makes trouble. You see her over there?' Her index finger indicated a tall woman with a large mane of black hair, seated on a mountain of pillows.

He turned back and nodded discreetly. 'Yes.'

'Told the night nurse that she was to be moved to a private room. I have to be moved *pronto*, she said. Nurse told her that if she didn't behave she wouldn't get the bed pan.'

He smiled for the first time that day. Something in his mother's tone, something in her continuing, irrepressible malice told him that she was still up for it. Despite those needles jammed into her, despite the threat of the surgeon's knife, her mind was as strong as ever. He moved his chair closer and held one of her hands. It was cold and damp to the touch. 'Kay said the doctors aren't sure what to do.'

Emily squeezed his hand. 'They're trying to move the blockage without an operation, but I had to sign a document.' She paused, controlled her under lip, and squeezed his hand again. 'A next of kin document. I might not make it through an operation. I've had so many. And if I do, I may have to carry one of those bags for the rest of my life – '

This time he steeled himself for the smell as he leaned forward to take another tissue from the box beside her bed and give it her. Her eyes were reddening. 'They say they may be able to clear it away. It just takes time,' he murmured, repeating everything Kay and Jill had told him. The repetition helped to ward off the one thing that no one wanted to think of.

'I can't eat or drink. I dreamt of fruit juice last night. If I ever get out of here, I will fill my garage with juice.' Emily smiled, blowing bubbles through her water system.

'We can buy shares in Del Monte.' Nicholas was about to continue when a noise made him look round. There was a fracas at the desk: some sort of argument about a young man being admitted when he was under the influence. He could see the desperately thin, rakish figure of a youngster no more than twenty, his forehead coated in blood, slumped sideways on a mobile bed. A woman, possibly his mother, was arguing with a group of nurses and a police officer that shouted instructions into a walkie-talkie.

Emily patted his hand. 'They can't move me, they say. Not until they know if I am to be admitted. Not enough beds.'

Nicholas could see what she meant. It was like a war zone in there. New entries kept crashing through the door while untended patients were wheeled out of the way or stood in small circles at the windows or took turns to wander forlornly in the corridors like wounded refugees. In the next bed a very old man lay coughing, while on the other side an enormously overweight woman discussed her heart problems with an attentive group of relatives. 'Perhaps we can get you to a side room.'

Suddenly Emily gripped his arm, so firmly that he was scared her syringe would pop out. 'Don't move me. This bed's in the open. The nurses come by all the time.'

'Okay, I understand.'

Nicholas looked at her, the wildness of her hair now reflected in her eyes. He saw the same fear of being abandoned, the same fear of loneliness that now filled his own life. How incredibly self-important he had become, allowing the people most important to him to drift out of his life, playing endgame with his relationships. He had not brought on Emily's sickness but had he done anything to prevent it? Had he asked her how she was? Had he taken time out to go down and give her any attention? No, he had been too busy. They had all been too busy. They had neglected her while getting on with their own so much more sophisticated lives. They had assumed that she was selfish, but they were even more so. And now Emily and he were joined as they had been joined at birth: by the cord of a common pain and vulnerability.

'What are you thinking?'

He roused himself. 'I was just worried by the noise. Can you sleep at night?'

'I sleep all the time, doesn't matter when. Sometimes I just want to sleep it all away.' Nicholas smiled. Emily's turns of phrase were often weirdly poetic, with a sharp emotional precision.

He stayed a while longer and then went down to the lobby to find Kay. She was sitting outside the hospital kiosk, close enough to the door to escape for a cigarette. Her face was blotched and her jaw was clenched at an odd angle.

'Did she tell you about the colostomy bag?

Nicholas sat down beside her. 'Sort of, and the next of kin.'

Kay looked hard at him. 'Well, you know who she trusts more than anyone else.'

He didn't respond. He didn't want to start on Emily's relationship with Kay. He didn't want to hear who it was that his mother loved most. He was the male, the one with the career. He was the one who was supposed to be strong. 'How bad?'

'Hard to tell. She may pull through, she may not. She's been in hospital many times,' said Kay.

'She's tough.'

Kay sighed. 'Are you?'

He looked down at the scabbed green linoleum, feeling slightly sick. 'It doesn't matter whether I'm tough or not. She's relying on us.'

'Yes, but what about Daniel?' Kay shook herself, like an animal that's been disturbed. 'You don't have to come down tomorrow if you don't want to. Jill's coming again and I might stay. You can take over on Friday night. The doctors say it may pass by itself but you can never tell with doctors. The night nurse reckoned she has a reasonable chance.'

Nicholas tried hard to smile. 'I can't think beyond the next minute.'

Kay frowned. 'Why did you get mixed up with those people in the first place? I warned you.'

He stared at the floor.

'I need a smoke,' she said.

He followed her out.

'It's not like you're a criminal,' she glowered.

'My statement was completely up-front. I told them Daniel was my partner and we applied for his entry visa in the usual way.'

'If you want my advice, you'll have to do more than that. You'll have to take the fight to them. Look at Josie and I. Our social work gives us enough money to live on.'

'I am facing them. I'm certainly not going to resign.'

Kay breathed in and finally exhaled. She stood up and pulled her T-shirt free. 'Daniel's the loyal type. I'll give you tomorrow off and you can take it from there,' she said as she moved towards the stairs, balancing herself with the rail as she ascended.

Nicholas looked up at her as she negotiated the final bend in the stairs. 'What about Mum?'

'If we need you I'll call. She's okay at the moment. You'd better get going.'

Nicholas stood there for a moment, unsure whether to call after her or not. He felt like a small boy again, as scared and helpless as when the adults disappeared. Not only because of Emily and what might happen to her, but because being with Kay and Emily allayed the pain of returning to that empty Docklands apartment: the missing CDs, the gaps where the videos should have been, the sleek line of the VCR that he wasn't sure he could set by himself. He felt loved in the hospital, loved and understood.

He took a taxi to the station and passed the time before the next London train having a couple of Scotches in the station bar. The alcohol helped. He began to feel more and more like a good son instead of a cheating gay man with a wrecked career, a broken relationship and an empty flat in east London. But once he was on the train and settled in his seat, the fear of failure returned. He headed for the toilet, locked the door and turned towards the mirror. His eyes were yellowish and bloodshot, the lines profiling his mouth deeper than usual. He was about to ask himself how it had come to this when suddenly someone knocked on the door and he hurriedly pressed the flush.

Chapter 31

He woke early, showered as if on automatic pilot and considered calling Roger Yates's secretary. However, he was scared that the Chancellor would ask him about the results of the inquiry, and he didn't have an answer. He looked instead for Matt's telephone number. But when he searched the flat for some sign of it, all he could find was Ron's name scribbled on the back of an old notepad with the address *Markham Street, Greenwich*.

Nicholas toured the apartment with the notepad in his hand. He knew that Daniel had gone to Greenwich a number of times after his first trip with Nicholas. He had revisited the covered market on Stockwell Street, where they had browsed the stalls together, and discovered a Chinese noodle shop down by the Cutty Sark. There was something else too. Lunch in a pub: the Worcester Arms. Nicholas had been too busy to ask him why he chose to eat at a gay pub, but perhaps he was just curious.

'Fuck,' he muttered. He didn't know Ron's surname and Markham Street in Greenwich wasn't going to get him very far. He looked Markham Street up in the London A-Z and by angling the book and deciphering the grid he found it was close to Greenwich Park: one of four parallel streets on its western edge.

It was a cold, piercingly clear day with a slight frost spangling the roofs along the DLR railway line towards Greenwich. For some reason he was reminded of the first time he had been with Daniel up on Crooms' Hill. They had asked a tourist to take a photo of them on either side of the Greenwich meridian, and then with one foot in both East and West, before changing over and standing in the opposite hemisphere. At the time, it had seemed an optimistic comment on their relationship. He got off at Greenwich and headed towards the park.

Markham Street turned out to be a fairly long road of Victorian terrace houses, many of them divided into individual flats, with straggling gardens full of tool sheds and childrens' swings while out the front family-sized Lagunas and Corsas were crammed into every available parking space. Most of the three-windowed lounges on the first floor had curtains or wooden blinds that protected the occupants from the stares of passer-by. At first Nicholas thought that he would wander slowly down the street with his collar turned up in the hope of glimpsing Ron. But then he realised how absurd that was.

He passed flats painted in primary colours, flats with shabby printed wallpaper, flats left empty for rent. He could see pine bookcases that reached right up to the ceiling, smug cats in bow windows, the occasional occupant caught in a moment of bored domesticity. But try as he might, he couldn't see any sign of Ron. Even when he walked back in the other direction and on the other side of the street, he couldn't see him. He stood for a moment telling himself not to be downhearted. This wasn't the kind of street for a young American who wore shiny hipster jeans and sharp leather brogues from Charles Tyrwhitt. Surely he would be living in a new Docklands flat with steel fittings and marble surfaces, a place with a river view, a marble jacuzzi and a swimming pool. Anyway, if he did live in Markham Street, he was unlikely to be at home in the middle of the day. Perhaps, thought Nicholas, the note meant that he had taken Daniel to a friend's place in Markham Street or perhaps to some sort of party.

Nicholas hurried across the road towards the Worcester Arms, but when he looked inside all he could see was a couple of old ladies at the far end of the bar sipping Guinness. He smiled at them and hurriedly retreated, heading towards Greenwich Market.

Negotiating his way between stalls selling chunks of fresh fudge and oven-baked wholemeal, art deco lamps and vases, Turkish carpets and stuffed Greek olives, he tried to imagine what Daniel had found so fascinating about the place. The food was expensive, the bric-a-brac was the kind of thing that people put in the hallway, and the antiques could have been found at Camden Lock or Islington High Street for a much better price.

He stopped in front of a stall selling multi-coloured Indian saris and gently hit the side of his head. The point was not whether Daniel would have liked it. The point was whether the person *he was with* had liked it. Somehow this person was taking shape in his mind: a guy about his own age, with a passion for funky interiors and objets d'art and Provencale cooking. They were probably living together with a fag-hag who took them shopping in markets just like this. Indeed, there was a couple ahead of him that almost fitted the bill: a man in his mid-twenties with unkempt hair and drainpipe jeans; a woman about the same age wearing a strawberry-coloured crepe dress and jangley silver earrings.

Nicholas looked at himself in the stall mirror. Daniel thought that he was obsessed with himself and his career. In that case, wouldn't he seek out someone different? He formed a mental image of a studenty Greenwich household with people dropping in and out all the time, bring-a-bottle parties, IKEA pine furniture, meeting down the pub.

A nearby clock struck twelve. He turned north and crossed the road that led back to the Worcester Arms. It didn't take him long to negotiate the occasional coach party of tourists disgorging onto the street in front of the Royal Naval College. He pushed open the door, went straight to the bar, ordered a Black Label on the rocks and took it to one of the wooden seats at the large bay window. He sipped at it for several minutes while watching the trippers going in and out of the park gates. Twenty minutes passed. Half an hour passed.

He was just wondering if he should have another drink when he saw a narrow dark head among the crowd of men clustered at the far end of the bar. The veins at his temples began to throb. He stood up to get a better view. The dark head was nodding in conversation with a middle-aged white man in blue overalls. As he edged down the bar he caught the eye of the man in overalls and they exchanged the most cursory of glances. It was nothing but Nicholas had the strange feeling he registered familiarity, an almost conspiratorial nod. He was just about to cross the final space between them when he realised that the person he was targeting was wearing a cheap PVC jacket and sporting a two-day beard. Abandoning his glass, Nicholas headed for the door.

Back at Greenwich station, he took the DLR to Bank and changed onto the Central Line, thinking that Covent Garden was his best bet. He knew that Daniel liked to go window-shopping around Seven Dials. He tried the food shops in Neal Street first and then the bookshops and pubs around the Royal Opera House, before mingling with the audience watching the mime artists in front of St Paul's Church. But try as he might, there was no sign of Daniel.

He moved on down the sweep of Long Acre towards Leicester Square tube. Daniel often went to buy discount CDs at a shop on Brewer Street and afterwards he would visit the Panther gay bookshop to pick up free copies of the *Pink Paper* and *Boyz*. Nicholas usually waited outside on these occasions, feeling faintly above it all and slightly embarrassed, but this time he plunged in, wandering among the shelves of magazines and gay novels, the rails of expensive gym clothes and Aussie Bum swimwear, the poppers and sex toys and pornography. Finally, unable to take it any longer, he left the shop and turned towards Chinatown.

The faces in the crowd seemed to look straight through him as he gazed at windows hung with glazed Peking ducks and *char siu bau*, tripping over small children in supermarkets perfumed with spices, bulging Chinese vegetables and the lingering aroma of soy sauce, chili and dried fish. The streets glistened with water and spilled produce just as they did in Hong Kong, and suddenly he remembered the wet market at Choi Wan where he and Daniel had often gone to shop when they lived with his mother: the bleeding slabs of tuna and garoupa, the odd cuts of beef or pork hung up like Christmas garlands, the piles of gleaming vegetables weighed by hand-held catties.

On De Lisle Street, Nicholas stopped at the entrance to a small courtyard just off the road where a sign announced *Mr Ho's Kitchen: Soup and Rice £4.50*, accompanied by a series of painted arrows pointing towards the interior. Suddenly Nicholas realised how hungry he was. He plunged past a steaming front counter piled high with dumplings, down the winding stairs and into a cheerful basement filled with large round tables and stacks of Nissin instant noodles. An assortment of special offers was stuck on the walls in brightly coloured Chinese calligraphy. Seeing him staring at them, the waiter brought him a menu in English and asked him if he wanted some tea. He ordered 'Bo Lay' tea along with chicken rice and soup.

'Nicholas?'

He looked up. A stocky figure at the cash till was moving towards him. 'You must like Chinese food.'

Nicholas roused himself. 'Actually, I'm waiting for Daniel. He's got an interview today.'

'An interview?' Matt didn't look quite convinced. 'That's interesting. I haven't heard from him recently.'

'For a bank,' pursued Nicholas.

There was a slight pause. Matt looked round at the other diners as if waiting for Nicholas to say what he was really doing there. 'I guess that's better than sitting at home.'

Nicholas attempted a casual laugh. 'He gets a bit lonely when I'm not around. You two should go out together more. I mean, when I'm not in London.'

Matt returned his smile. 'We meet up at the gym twice a week.'

Nicholas looked down at his hands on the table. He would have given anything to explain what had happened. He would have done anything to come clean, but somehow he couldn't get the first words into his mouth. If Matt knew something, now was surely the time. 'In the evening?'

'Yes, Tuesdays and Fridays. I have off-peak membership.'

'I suppose that means that Daniel can go any time?'

Matt seemed to ponder this, stroking his chin. 'I usually meet him there after eight o'clock.'

Nicholas continued to stare hard at Matt. 'That would still give you time to go out afterwards,' he said, as if deducing some sort of theory.

'If we're not too tired,' said Matt with another smile. 'Actually, we went to a bar the other day. It's called Bolero, on West India Quay. It has a gay night on Fridays, not far from the gym.'

Nicholas felt the back of his head bristle. 'Just the two of you?'

'No, with Ron,' said Matt. 'We dance a bit and watch the men. We don't stay very late.'

Nicholas broadened his smile, encouraging Matt to continue. This was crucial. But before he could ask anything more, Matt looked at his watch. 'Sorry, I've got to go Nicholas. See you soon.'

'You have to?' said Nicholas, rising from the table and almost knocking his chopsticks onto the floor. 'Can you give me your number?'

Matt looked surprised. 'But Daniel has it.'

'I know,' said Nicholas, almost clutching at Matt's sleeve. 'But he's always losing things. He'll want to tell you about the interview.'

Matt gave a slightly disconcerted smile and headed towards the stairs. 'I'll call him soon,' he said and disappeared.

Nicholas sat motionless for a minute, still staring in the direction of Matt's exit. He seemed to know more about Daniel than he was letting on. As for Friday night, the outing to West India Quay must have been exactly when Daniel was supposed to be going to Kay in Shropshire.

Nicholas left the Chinese restaurant without any clear idea of what to do next. One part of him wanted to head straight towards the Docklands and check out Bolero. Another voice said that if Daniel had gone to a gay bar on West India Quay, he could just as well have gone to one in Soho. In fact, he could be there right now.

Retracing his steps back to the Admiral Nelson, Nicholas pushed his way in through the drinkers at the door towards the dimly lit interior. It was almost impossible to reach the bar, let alone get served. Finally, however, he had his Scotch and water in hand and was able to retreat towards the back room. Jamming himself against a wall, he watched the evening crowd coming in and out. There was a group of what sounded like Dutch people ahead of him, all flashing smiles whenever a new customer appeared, along with a man in a suit he recognised from United International. For some reason the presence of this man intrigued him. Before he knew what he was doing he was attempting eye contact. There was a moment's pause as his colleague's eyes locked with his and then, without the slightest flicker of emotion, the man picked up his drink and walked away. Nicholas looked down into his whisky. It was like trying to be cool in a party that had started hours earlier. In desperation, he turned to the man in leather trousers standing next to him.

'Do you know any bars for Orientals?' he asked.

The man's steel-blue eyes softened. 'There's the Ying Yang club just off Trafalgar Square, but it's only open on Sundays. Or you could try The Lemongrass at the end of St Martin's Lane. That's popular with the rice crowd.' He looked down at his glass and ran his finger round its rim. 'I used to go to The Lemongrass myself. Popped over from the ENO when I fancied a bit of mixed, if you see what I mean.'

'Mixed?' Nicholas felt confused.

The man smiled, revealing a gold-capped front tooth. 'White, brown, yellow...' But before he had finished, Nicholas was heading for the doorway.

The drizzle was turning to a light rain as Nicholas made his way through the early evening crowds emerging from Leicester Square tube. The alcohol had taken hold now, coursing along his veins, making his outer limbs feel large and clunky. He walked round Charing Cross Post Office, and then once more, until he saw a pink illuminated sign.

Crossing the road, he entered the open doorway of The Lemongrass. Groups of white and black men was standing at the curved bar, apparently indifferent to the Orientals who sat around the edge of the room in their own groups. For some reason, Nicholas was reminded of the dances he had endured as a schoolboy in South London. He ordered his usual Scotch on the rocks and moved away from the terrace towards the door, where he could get some fresh air. He stood there for a moment watching the people walking up and down a small staircase. He could hear the sound of Techno or Trance thumping up from below and he hesitated a moment before moving towards the source of the noise. Halfway down the stairs, he saw a crowd of drinkers standing at a smaller bar. He was about to descend further when a laser light from the dance floor rippled across their faces. 'Christ!' He moved back up a few steps, infuriating a couple of brightly attired Bengalis who were coming down behind him.

Peering out from behind the Bengalis, he stared at the man at the bar. Sir John, dressed as usual in a pin-striped suit, was talking to a younger man with a flushed face and tight ginger curls.

Nicholas retreated back into the shadows. The ginger head was telling Sir John a story that seemed to require emphatic gestures and long pauses. Suddenly, he gave out some sort of ultimatum and Sir John took a half step backwards. Ginger head seemed to repeat what he had said but still Sir John shook his head. Slowly, however, Sir John's right hand moved towards a briefcase perched on the bar stool next to him. He took out what looked like a cheque book and with barely a glance at the rest of the bar, wrote out a cheque. Tearing it off, he slipped it across the counter to ginger head, who gazed at it for a long time and then, with a look of complete indifference, put it in his pocket.

The barman asked Sir John if he wanted another one but Sir John shook his head. The younger man took a long draught of his beer and passed Sir John a piece of paper he took from his inner jacket pocket. Sir John read it with a fixed expression on his face, and placed it in his briefcase. Clicking it closed, he took a final drag of his cigar, stubbed it out on an ashtray and prepared to leave.

Nicholas looked round for escape. He couldn't be caught there on the stairs. He couldn't be caught there at all. If would confirm everything that Sir John thought about him. Hurrying down the last two steps, he headed to the toilets while Sir John shook the younger man's hand.

When he came back a minute or two later, there was no sign of Sir John or of ginger head. Cursing to himself for having missed the opportunity, Nicholas headed back up the stairs and ran onto the street. At least he could have bought ginger head a drink. But all he could see were two guys embracing at the corner of the Post Office.

Chapter 32

The Mondeo's headlights swung along the white road chevrons warning him that the A23 was narrowing. He just had enough time to get past the grey Mercedes-Benz ahead of him without either of them losing speed. He signalled and eased to the left, which didn't stop the Mercedes flashing him as it fell back.

The drive down from East London at speeds of almost a hundred miles per hour in places was liberating. He didn't speed in a deliberate way; he simply adjusted his foot on the accelerator to the amount of traffic and the road conditions. At this time of day not that many cars were continuing on to the coast and the open road beckoned. Emily's condition was still stable, thank god. The doctors were waiting to see what happened next.

He slowed down as he approached the roundabout. This time the woman in the Chancellor's office had been helpful. She was sure Roger Yates would understand if he postponed lunch to care for his mother. Nicholas dropped into second gear. Emily's condition had given him the tiniest breathing space.

Entering the Royal Free Hospital, he sensed at once that something was wrong. The place still had the same National

Health Service atmosphere. One of the scuffed and battered lifts still didn't work. The wooden staircase was still hung with old memorial plaques to visits by Princess Margaret and the Lords Lieutenant of Sussex. But when he reached the third floor ward Emily was nowhere to be seen. For a moment he just stood there petrified. Kay had said Emily was relatively stable, although weak, and had explained to him at length that the situation showed some signs of improvement. The ward sister and Kay had his telephone number. No one had called or left a message on his way down.

Seeing his stricken face, the young Filipina nurse who had first helped him took him by the arm. 'Don't worry,' she said. 'She's had to be moved. They've not decided.'

'Decided?' asked Nicholas.

'Whether they're going to operate. I'll take you over if you like. The other members of your family are there.'

The nurse led him up a couple more flights of battered stairs and down a long corridor until he reached a double door over which a sign said *Intensive Care*. To his right, the nurse indicated a small lounge with a payphone on wheels, some faded easy chairs, and an old-fashioned TV in front of which Kay and Josie were slumped. As soon as they saw him, they stood up.

'I tried to phone you but there was no coverage. I guessed you were on your way down. Josie said it's better for you to get here first.' Kay's usually flushed face was pale and there were dark rings under her eyes.

'What's going on?'

'The doctors have been and showed us the results. I couldn't follow it all.' Kay looked at Josie.

'That old operation she had for the hiatus hernia was botched,' said Josie. 'Something from the stomach is damaging her oesophagus,'

'She ate the wrong stuff,' said Kay. 'Too much stringy fruit. That's why she started to vomit. They're hoping to clear her system with the saline. But they may have to do a colostomy.'

'Which means a bag,' said Nicholas, borrowing Josie's realist tone. Emily would rather die than move around with a bag full of her own waste on her arm.

'I don't know,' said Kay, raising her hands towards her face. 'They said the operation might be reversible.'

Nicholas wondered if Kay had eaten or drunk anything. She was pale but he couldn't detect alcohol. 'What does that mean?'

'Kay's trying to say that your mother may not need a bag. They may be able to create a sort of pouch for the stool. There's a tube in it so that it can be emptied once a day,' said Josie, moving to put an arm around Kay's waist.

'Either that or it's the whole colon being cut,' said Kay. 'Half her intestines are already on a sling down there. They're not telling us everything.'

'God help us,' muttered Nicholas.

Josie blinked. 'I'd better get you a drink.'

Kay pulled Nicholas down to the sofa, putting her head close to his as she talked, but somehow Nicholas could only half-grasp what she said. Apparently, Jill was halfway way up the M1 but she would return if things worsened. Emily couldn't eat until they saw any signs of the blockage easing, and although there was some intimation of that, it was dangerous for her to ingest anything for the time being. 'I've signed,' said Kay as Josie came back with two teas, a half bottle of Martell brandy and some Cadbury's chocolate.

'Signed?' Nicholas's mind had now shrunk to the parameters of the room. The TV was relaying an interminable police drama featuring two cookie cops from somewhere in California.

'Next of kin form,' said Kay and grabbed the Martell from Josie, who was pouring it into the tea.

Nicholas felt a familiar wave of nausea. 'Excuse me.'

He only just made it to the toilet. Afterwards, standing at the basin and swilling his face, he looked at himself in the mirror and tried to rally himself by thinking of the car journey: the South Downs rising ahead like a long windbreak, the hope that billowed off those chalk fields.

'Are you okay?' said Kay as he returned.

'Fine,' said Nicholas. He pulled at the collar of his polo neck. 'You and Josie can go out for a while. If there's any news, I'll call you.'

Kay and Josie exchanged looks. 'We'll eat. Then you. Unless you want us to bring you something.'

'No,' said Nicholas and attempted a smile. 'I'll go and get mine. You've been here long enough.'

When they had gone he turned back to the TV, watching without commenting the unfolding California drama. After a while, a sister came to tell him that it was okay to use the sofa but it would be much better if they all found a proper place to sleep. They might have to come on several nights.

When Kay and Josie came back, Nicholas told them what the sister had said and went to eat his own barely digestible dinner of Spaghetti Bolognese and salad in an Italian place round the corner. He then drove to the Travelodge he had found on the internet, surrounded by motorway slip roads, and was offered a choice of rooms. Both were next to the car park: one Disabled and one a 'Premier' double. Nicholas took the Disabled one, thinking it would be bigger. The large bathroom with the raised floor and wall handles looked exactly like the one in the hospital. After a brief shower, he got into bed and fell into a fitful sleep. Around two in the morning he awoke, dressed and drove back to the hospital.

The scuffed wall and stained carpet in the waiting room were still there. The reek of Dettol was still there. He rubbed at the stiffness in his neck and looked around at the glazed double doors that led to *Intensive Care*. All was silence except for the occasional movement of a tired-looking nurse or a doctor who came in and out with hardly a glance in his direction. Every time the door buzzer sounded, Nicholas jumped up from his prone position and waited for someone to approach him. It was like being a refugee waiting in a train that would never leave the station. The idea of his mother dying there beyond those doors filled him with grief. And yet love was there too. She had loved them to the best of her ability. She had wanted them to enjoy the lives she had given them. The sudden starkness of choice told him that he had been a fool to be so scared of his own life, scared of what others might say. He had been given every chance of happiness, every chance to make the most of what he had, and he had thrown it away.

***

When he awoke in the Travelodge, he saw from the bedside clock that it was almost midday. He sat up straight, his stomach grumbling. Hurriedly dressing, he stumbled to the reception area and pushed and pulled until he obtained a cardboard Cheddar and Tomato sandwich from the dispensing machine. Cursing the place for not having better facilities, he realised he had left his mobile in the room. He called Kay from the coin phone in the hallway.

'She's awake and she's eating,' said Kay, her voice strangely bullish.

'Eating?' said Nicholas, putting down the sandwich.

'No further sign of bleeding and the blockage is gone,' confirmed Kay. 'They're not going to operate.'

'Jesus Christ.' Nicholas swallowed, abandoned the rest of the sandwich to the waste bin and ran to his room to grab the car keys. In no time at all he had covered the 10-mile journey into the city and was turning into the car park. Reaching the hospital doors in a few strides, he ran towards reception and followed the nurse down the corridor and over a pedestrian bridge to a more spacious building in another wing. Finally, he found himself in a small side room looking out over the seafront rooftops and a colony of cawing, black-eyed gulls.

'Doesn't she look better?' said the familiar Filipina nurse, indicating Emily sitting up in bed with her hair combed.

'Thanks to you, dear,' said Emily and motioned him to sit down.

Nicholas stared hard at his mother. She was eating some kind of porridge with a plastic spoon and the residue was dripping down the side of her mouth and into a small tray that they had hung round her neck. Her arm was still fixed to a drip but they had taken away the tube from her nose and although her hand shook, making the flesh on her arms wobble alarmingly, she somehow succeeded in getting the spoonful into her mouth. 'Do you want any help?'

'Mm, mm,' said Emily, turning her head from side to side.

'I've asked,' said the overweight woman wearing a flowered red nightdress in the bed opposite who Nicholas had seen previously in the A & E ward. 'I can get out of bed. But she won't have it. Stubborn old lady, your Mum.'

'The doctors came last night and said the blockage was going,' continued Emily. 'I can eat something as long as it's soft. They're going to put me on a normal diet soon.'

For a moment Nicholas wanted to shout out 'No operation?'

'No, but I'm still very weak,' said Emily.

Nicholas held out his hand and touched hers. She folded her slender fingers over his. 'When can you go home?'

Emily held up the arm with the red weal and attachment as if signaling for the traffic to slow down. 'I don't know yet.' She fought hard to control her breathing. 'The registrar came this morning and talked about convalescence. They have a home round the corner where I can stay, so you wouldn't have to come all the time. They can cook.'

'I'll come.' He noticed the overweight woman studying him closely. 'Any time.'

'But what about the children?' said Emily. This fiction was delivered so incisively and perfectly that for a moment the fat woman looked away and began to flick through her *Womans Own*.

Nicholas stared hard at her, remembering how many times he had played this game with her in the past. 'They'll manage.'

'We'll see,' said Emily, signalling that the room's only other occupant was about to leave.

Putting down her magazine, the fat woman rolled her huge body towards the edge of the bed and her feet searched platypus-like for a pair of slippers. 'Time for a walk. There's a real hunk on the ward tonight.'

Nicholas watched her figure in its outsized floral nightie disappear and then turned back to Emily. He waited a moment to collect his thoughts. Now that the immediate threat had gone, now that Emily had reached the first step of recovery, he realised that he had already become used to her illness. He had expected to feel revulsion, some sort of shock at her reduction to the most basic forms of eating and drinking and defecating. He had expected to run away from the hospital each night celebrating his escape. But now he felt inspired by her struggle to live. Her battle with decay, won as it was for the time being, had been entirely natural. And for the first time in his life, death seemed less terrifying.

'I talked to Kay before this happened,' said Emily, putting down her bowl. 'She told me one or two things.'

'Not worrying you I hope,' said Nicholas and attempted to push the blanket further up her shrunken body.

'She told me I shouldn't interfere,' said Emily, her voice slotting into that firm contralto he knew so well. 'But there's one thing I do know. You've been down before and you always pick yourself up. Daniel will be back.'

Nicholas was so surprised that for a moment he didn't know what to say. He knew he deserved what he had got. He knew better than Emily how much he wanted to change. But that wouldn't bring Daniel back.

Emily pinched the pillow with funny, bird-like movements. 'Everyone has to make decisions. The papers have had their fun. Now I hope you can enjoy some of the important things in life, like the happiness your father and I enjoyed. I know there were bad moments but there was also a great deal of joy.'

He sat there, still speechless. This was the very first day that Emily could sit up and she was already back to being Mum. 'Thanks,' he said. 'But you shouldn't worry. Not about me.'

Emily raised a dismissive hand. 'The more I think about what happened, the more angry I get. They set people up and they pull them down. I'm not announcing it to the whole Church but if someone asks me, I'll be proud to tell them. I always said that the difference between you and Kay was that you didn't stuff your problems down people's throats.'

Nicholas tried not to reply. Kay had lived a much more honest life than he had. That may have been one of the reasons he was in this mess. She didn't try to separate her life into compartments as he had done, hoping that the one would not impact the other. She didn't take part in the lottery of public life. She didn't cheat on her lover.

'So what are you going to do about Daniel?' said Emily and glanced at the door.

Nicholas sighed, unwilling to burden her further. 'I'm checking all the places he might go. It sounds stupid but I have to do something. Kay and Josie think he'll turn up, although I'm not so sure.'

Emily tilted her head to one side. 'You'll have a happy life, Nicholas. Don't worry.' And with that she made a zipping motion as the fat woman re-entered the room.

Chapter 33

S ir John stood in the draft of the dripping alley and stamped
his feet as if the impatient motion would somehow take
away the sight of those half-open black bin bags that were
dumped at indifferent angles, half on top of each other, against
both side walls. He looked at his watch for what seemed to be the
hundredth time. It was getting on for 7 pm, time for someone to
be getting home from work to number 32 around the corner. He
peered once more from his observation place and saw the rain
needling down in sharp diagonals beneath the street lamps,
skittering on his bare head and padded Burberry. It wasn't much
of a place for hanging around. Although there was a terrace of
spacious Georgian houses on the opposite side of the road,
bending away to the junction with the printing works, they were
all divided into shabby apartments, with a security alarm box
placed on each floor. The rest of the road was made up of
Victorian villas, also divided into bed-sits, and then came the
back doors and windows of the flats over the restaurants that
fronted Stockwell Road. Steam poured from air extractors in the
rear kitchens, spreading the aroma of burnt chicken and sour
salsa over the motorbikes and parked cars, some of them

abandoned at rakish angles to the pavement, while a shadowy procession of bearded men in loose-fitting clothes and women with their heads covered or faces veiled entered through the peeling gateway of a nearby blue-and-white mosque.

He put his hands in his Burberry pockets and sighed. He would never have believed that Andrew could live in a place like this. Even now it seemed like the residue of some bad dream. Of course there was no way of checking on his source. 'Brian' hadn't given him any personal details, only telling him what he claimed to have witnessed, as well as the place where it happened. All Sir John's attempts to find the phone number of number 32 or any previous registration of Andrew under the council tax or credit agencies had come to nothing. Even if Andrew had been staying here as the boyfriend of this other man, he must have had to pay him some rent or share in the expenses in some way. Brian said he had been going there for a while, and even though it was more than a year since Andrew disappeared there must be some record of him, some imprint of his presence on the surrounding community. But although Sir John had visited the Caribbean hairdressers at the shop on the corner and then the Portuguese bars in Stockwell Road, no one seemed to have heard of him. He was too ashamed to ask whether anyone had seen a 'gay couple' living in number 32. All he could do was describe Andrew.

A sleek red Aston Martin with its sun roof half-open despite the rain roared down the road, braked suddenly outside the mosque and idled for a moment, the throb of its engine drowned out by the sound of confident, braying rappers declaiming some indecipherable language to the heavens. Sir John could hear something like 'Fucking no! We just want fucking *ganga* man!' on the air, followed by a loud shout of laughter like a gunshot and the smash of something on a front door. An upper window opened to the side of the mosque gates and a flood of what sounded like a Middle Eastern language was directed at the car, threatening and strangely benevolent by turns. Then just as abruptly the car drove off, its deafening bass rhythms fading like the paddles of a steamer down a distant river.

Sir John re-emerged from the shadows and stared again at number 32. It was an odd-shaped building. Someone had decided to renovate the flat by ignoring the fact it looked to the back of the terrace, placing a walled patio on the second floor over a stairway that led to what was now the front door. There was a black garbage bag beside the door, which suggested that someone lived there, although the windows were unlit. The outside plastering had been painted off-white in a vain attempt to make the place look presentable, but there was something in that modernising and twisted shape that gave Sir John a bad feeling. The *ganga* in the street and the indecipherable languages didn't help. It seemed that Andrew had come to live in a ghetto. No doubt he would have called it 'multicultural' or a 'microcosm of the New Britain', the kind of language he used when they argued about politics. But this was not an attempt at idealism; it was an attempt at drowning. He had almost willed himself to be dragged under.

A fat coloured woman with frizzed hair and a blank expression approached the front door of Number 32 and Sir John was about to dart forward with an 'Excuse me!' when he saw that the woman was only placing a printed flier in the door from a pile she carried in a Tesco's plastic bag at her side. Sir John retreated towards the rubbish bags and forced himself to continue waiting.

His mind focused on the bar in King William IV Street: Brian's acned face and ginger curls, the provocative tone and his way of talking as if Sir John should have known exactly what had happened, as if it was somehow all his fault. And then suddenly Brian's story and his own memory combined to come up with a crystal-clear image of Andrew.

It was May Week in Andrew's last term at Cambridge. Both he and Marjory thought it was glandular fever because of the swollen lymphs and night sweats, which Andrew said was the diagnosis of the college doctor. Perhaps they should have thought about it a little more. But in the days and weeks after Marjory searched Andrew's bedroom they were too involved with themselves to wonder about a passing illness. According to Brian, Andrew was completely inexperienced when he met up with Brian's friend, a talented musician a few years older than Andrew. They met at a party held by a Cambridge music don in his terrace house on Parker's Piece. The relationship progressed from nights in college to weekends in Stockwell and Andrew's first tentative steps on the London gay scene. Brian reckoned that Andrew was good at drinking, and although he didn't mention drugs, it was pretty clear that Andrew had experimented with these too. The crisis followed its own inexorable logic: hospital visits and tests, his boyfriend's claims that he hadn't known he was infected when they first slept together, the fear of his family finding out, all somehow combined to push him gradually over the edge. They found him just to the east of London Bridge, his body jammed onto a piling at St Katherine's Dock. He had slipped himself off the back of a commuter ferry in the dark. The coroner reported death by misadventure but the post-mortem revealed that he was HIV positive. He had no identification apart from an old library ticket. It took the police two days to trace his family. Even then, Sir John managed to keep it out of the newspapers. By the time the police made enquiries at the clubs, the boyfriend had completely disappeared and his friends had closed ranks.

The red Aston Martin came screeching down the road and stopped once more outside the Middle Eastern house. This time the front door opened and a fat young man in a long grey *jellaba* came out and dropped something into the driver's side. 'That's *cool* man,' said an ironic voice in the driver's seat and the car lurched forward.

Sir John roused himself. A crop-haired young woman in a grey skirt and white blouse with a plain blue jacket over it was opening the door to number 32 and shaking out her umbrella.

Sir John walked quickly towards her. 'I'm sorry to disturb,' he said even before he reached her.

The woman took one look at him and hurried inside, preparing to close the door. 'Who are you?'

'I'm looking for someone who lives here. Brian sent me.'

The young woman placed a chain on the door and opened it a little wider. 'Brian?

'That's what he said his name was. He met me in a bar in town and gave me this address. A ginger-haired man with freckles.'

'Oh,' said the young woman and her expression relaxed. 'You mean Brendan. Does that mean you're his...'

'No,' said Sir John. 'It doesn't. But I am looking for a friend of Brendan's, who he said lived here with my son about a year ago. My son had an accident...' The young woman slipped the chain off the door. Half-illuminated in the bright glare of the street lamps, her face looked both intrigued and scared. She reached out a hand to turn on the hall lamp.

'You're Andrew's father?' There was a firmness to her jaw that suggested she knew the story.

'That's right,' said Sir John, trying to peer beyond her into the stairwell.

'I'm sorry,' she said as if apologising for something other than Andrew's death, something that had turned the world from a place of innocence to one where fathers of dead sons came to haunt her doorstep. 'He's not here.'

Sir John moved the weight of his body. 'Not here?'

'Andrew's friend,' she replied firmly. 'He moved away a long time ago. I live here now with Sasha, my girlfriend.'

'Oh,' said Sir John. The mention of a girlfriend unsettled him. 'I suppose you knew Andrew quite well?'

The young woman shook her head, and for some reason her pale, rather Eastern European face gained colour. 'I knew them only a little. I really took over the lease after...' She paused, struggling to find the right words. '...after Andrew had his accident. It was a few weeks later when Brendan told me about this place.'

'I see,' said Sir John and swallowed. 'This friend of Brendan's, have you any idea where he went?' He finally dragged his eyes away from the interior of the house to look at the young woman, realising he didn't know her name.

'I don't know,' she said with a finality that suggested she didn't want to know. 'Brendan's always playing games, especially when he needs money. Did he tell you he dated Andrew, I mean before he met the other one?'

Sir John's face clouded. 'Surely Andrew met this friend of Brendan's at a party in Cambridge.'

The young woman pulled down the edge of her mouth, like a policeman waiting for a confession. 'I told you Brendan's odd. He met Andrew in a pub restaurant where we both work and then went up with him to Cambridge a couple of times. Your son dumped him for a musician in some rock band he met at a party. Brendan's just a barman,' she added with a shrug.

Sir John stared at the woman. There was a new resentment in her manner, as if his confusion and reluctance to accept the truth counted for nothing in a world where anything was possible, most people were up to something, and everyone was sure to be found out.

He leaned towards the woman's badge. 'Thank you,' he said stiffly, hoping she would ask him inside.

She gave him a tight smile and quickly raised her eyebrows. 'I'm sorry I can't be more helpful. The other guy moved and I only know Brendan from work.'

'Which is where?' Sir John again craned forward. He could make out a little man striding forward in top hat and red tails, beneath it two repeating letters in red enamel.

'I have to go,' said Jessica with a fixed smile and picked up her bag ready to close the door. 'Sarah's back soon.'

Sir John was tempted to put one of his feet in the door, but he knew he couldn't. 'Goodbye,' he said and moved back into the rain-smeared street as the door slowly closed. A limping dog came towards him from the mosque gates, took one look at him and wandered off.

He moved towards a burned-out old Vauxhall with one of its deflated front tires up on the pavement and kicked at its half-detached hubcap. 'Fuck,' he said aloud. It was as clear as day, as clear as the piece of doggerel on the ceiling at Dirty Dan's, as clear as the words behind the altar at St. Mary's Woolnoth. The person to blame for Andrew's disappearance was not out there in the shadowy homosexual underworld. It was him. Several times he had taken Andrew together with Marjory for lunch at Dirty Dan's without noticing who was behind the bar. But Andrew obviously had…

He crossed the road towards the Tube station, the slanting rain now spattering his raincoat. A container truck was pulling down Landor Road and he had to hurry onto the pavement before the spray hit him.

Not only had he invited Marjory and Andrew for lunch at Dirty Dan's. He had taken someone else there, not caring who it was that brought them those Barnsley chops and Young's Ale. He stared up at the shaking green geometry of a rustling plane tree above him, trying to imagine the raw excitement of Andrew's first adventures in London, the thrill of being let off the hook, the initiation into forbidden intimacy away from his family. And then the horrifying downward lurch of all his hopes and dreams of fulfillment as one after another of his 'friends' deserted him.

And with a shudder, he realised how familiar that story seemed.

Chapter 34

There was a special delivery waiting for Nicholas in the porter's office when he reached E14. He frowned as he looked at the padded envelope, hoping that it might be some sort of message from Daniel, a clue to his whereabouts, but when he turned it over he could see the United International logo on the back flap. He stared at it for a moment, fear stirring inside. But then he told himself it was alright, he had nothing to hide.

Taking the package upstairs, he laid it out carefully on the dining table and listened to his messages. There was an urgent one from Roger Yates's secretary asking him to call her back as soon as possible. He made a note of her number and sat down on the sofa, still staring at the package. He thought of calling Roger Yates' office and even approached the phone, but then he hesitated, moving instead towards the table. Taking a deep breath, he tore the package open.

The envelope contained a report about six pages long with neatly headed paragraphs, beginning with an Executive Summary and ending with a Conclusion. Hurriedly reading down the neat columns of the Executive Summary, it was easy enough to catch the drift. The members of the enquiry had decided they were now in possession of all the facts. On the basis of these, they had come to the conclusion that there was no evidence to support the accusation in the Shareholder Letter that Nicholas had used his position to obtain a fast-track passport for his partner.

A lengthy list of qualifications to the Summary followed, the primary one being that the senior executive in question should have been more aware of the conflict of interest implied by his silence over his office relationship. The relationship was of a 'special nature', which required discretion rather than outright secrecy. It was unsuitable for someone in his position. Indeed, the relationship might have combined with perceptions of personal interest to place his professional decision-making in question. 'We recommend that any confusion of this kind should strictly be avoided in the future,' concluded the report.

Nicholas sat staring at the page for a while, shock giving away to barely subdued anger. And yet the angrier he felt, the more difficult it was to understand exactly what had happened. There was no mention of any other possible sources for the leaks, no discussion of the underground communications network that had been established within Group Public Affairs. There was not even a mention of Sir John's warnings about personal motives for the leaks. In fact, no one had come under the slightest suspicion *apart from himself.* The enquiry had focused entirely on the Shareholder Letter without even bothering to summon him for questioning.

He leaned back in his seat. It was a set-up, exactly the kind of thing he should have expected from the 18th Floor, which would do anything to keep United's name out of the papers.

He sat there breathing hard and wondering what to do. Then he noticed a small white envelope tucked into the lining of the package. He picked it up and opened it, extracting a square of beige notepaper:

Dear Nicholas,

This will come as a shock to you, but I'm afraid there is nothing I can do about it. It seems that the Board has decided that it would be better for you and United International to part company. I tried hard to convince them otherwise, and so did Sir John, but I am afraid that in this case circumstances have proved beyond our control. The best I can offer is a generous severance package, of which you will be informed in due course. I know you will take this hard but I am sure that in the long run it will not set your career back. United International will present your departure as an amicable arrangement.

Please be informed that the termination of your employment will take effect as of Monday 20th April at 6 pm.

Yours Sincerely,
Eddie Rochester

For a moment Nicholas's mind refused to engage. It was as if all this was happening to someone else, someone completely different, someone who was capable of acting with a complete lack of professionalism. The room revolved as if on its own axis. He was a failure, a proven liar; that's what they were trying to stick on him. And yet something was nagging away in his mind, something that he had recently discovered and that the enquiry couldn't possibly have known. He stood up and moved to the phone.

Roger Yates' secretary was evasive. 'I'm sorry sir, I can't really say when Mr. Yates will be available, but I'll let you know as soon as possible.'

Nicholas put down the handset and turned to face the room. Hadn't Roger Yates insisted he call him? Picking up the phone again, he called Sir John's secretary and asked for her boss. 'He's already left the office at around three o'clock. He'll be back on Monday.' Nicholas thanked the secretary and replaced the handset.

So that was the game: a conspiracy of the righteous. He looked down the hallway towards the study. Ever since he returned from Hong Kong he had a feeling that something was waiting for him there, something urgent. He moved purposefully through the lounge into the study, sat down at his desk and rebooted his computer. There was a whirring noise as the folders unfurled. His eyes searched for the icon of Jeanette Long's diskette. As soon as it appeared, he opened it and clicked on Miscellaneous, running down each file in turn: Appraisals, Letters, Press Releases, Memos. 'Come on,' he muttered. He opened a few of the letters and memos, cursing when he couldn't find what he was looking for, and then his gaze slipped to the strip at the bottom of the screen.

A Yahoo icon was visible there: a bright and startling face, wildly happy. He clicked on the *Y!* and a sign-in page came up. Entering 'sjw_86347' for the user name and 'van1995' for the password, he clocked the login button. His heart thumped against his ribs as he craned forward waiting for the contents of the Yahoo Mail page to come up. A folder marked 'JW' appeared on the desktop. With a curious reticence, he clicked the file open.

***

West India Quay was crowded with drinkers on a Friday night. The cold evening air rang with riotous laughter as Nicholas tried to concentrate on where exactly he was going. Two of the buildings along West India Quay had basement bars but neither of them was called Bolero, and from the outside you couldn't have told whether they were gay or not. He turned his attention towards the Bar Toledo right in the middle of the terrace. As he reached the bottom of the stairs he saw with a stab of relief that he was right. A sign on the door said *Bolero Gay & Lesbian Night: Raffle and Live Band.*

The barman smiled at Nicholas as he took his order and put a Scotch on the counter. A shaven-headed man in an expensive blue blazer and mauve silk shirt turned in his direction. 'Cheers.'

Nicholas nodded and took a first sip of his drink, determined not to repeat his performance at the Admiral Nelson. He was surrounded by groups of smartly dressed men in suits and ties, bankers and lawyers and accountants, most of whom seemed to know each other or be keen to know each other. Their bright engaging attitude and precise gestures, the sound of their raised voices echoing around the room with its sharp red décor and purple strobe lighting told him that it was a place where Daniel might have felt at home. 'Pretty full tonight.'

The man stared at him, as if slightly surprised. 'Do I know you?'

'No,' said Nicholas. 'You here for the raffle?'

The man snorted, as if Nicholas was a bit of a joker. 'I'm here most Fridays. The band was pretty good last week.'

Nicholas rummaged in his inside pocket and found a photo of Daniel. 'I wonder if you've seen my friend here. He's Chinese, medium height, black hair.'

The man stared at the photo, looked him over and finished his drink. 'Meet him on the internet did you? Lost his address?'

Nicholas shook his head, annoyed by the man's slightly knowing smile. 'It's a bit more complicated that that. Another?'

'Don't mind if I do,' said the man and leaned towards him, releasing a whiff of expensive cologne. 'You know, there was someone in here like him last Friday. He was with a black guy in his early twenties, shaven head, poncey glasses. Another Chinese man was hanging around the two of them. Ring any bells?'

The sound of the band warming up made Nicholas raise his voice. 'What were they doing?'

The man shrugged. 'Just drinking.' He nodded in the direction of the chairs and then put a hand to his forehead. 'There was another one too. A white guy in a brown suit, pretty much into your friend there. I didn't see them when the band finished.'

Nicholas swallowed his Scotch. 'White guy?'

'Yes, advertising type. They had a kind of party at the bar. Of course, I could have been wrong. It might have been someone else altogether. Boyfriend?'

Nicholas looked down at his feet. 'Yes.'

'Don't worry. He won't stay with him long. Want another?'

Nicholas looked at his glass. He had already drunk two large Scotches and the memory of Thursday evening was still fresh. Yet the silk-shirted man was already talking to the barman.

More people were cramming into the basement now, mainly men but also the occasional group of women. They descended in noisy groups, pretending not to scan the room while those that had already arrived watched them with the intensity of animals sensing possible prey. Their shouts of laughter rose above the roar of the music to create an intense clamour, as if they had all known each other a long time and were about to witness something uniquely interesting. Nicholas used the Black Label to loosen his tongue and soon he was taking part in conversations on all sides. But even though he mentioned Daniel and tried to pass around his photo, nobody seemed to be in the least interested. By the time the band launched into *La Vida Loca* the room was beginning to sway, faces and names were clashing in his brain, and he could no longer get his sentences out clearly.

Eventually, he found himself up squashed against a sallow man at the bar wearing pointed leather boots with delicate sewn traceries. The man turned to him. 'I'm from Sao Paolo.' Nicholas took several sips of his drink, imagining the Brazilian was a trader of some sort. 'Want to see my office?' said the trader.

Nicholas felt a cold shiver down him. 'Excuse me,' he said, lowering his shoulders queasily and heading towards the door.

He stood at the bottom of the stairs for a moment trying to avoid the incoming crowd and wondering if he could stand it any longer. He felt increasingly drunk, a bit sick, and there was absolutely no sign of Daniel. Forcing his way up the stairs, he emerged onto West India Quay and took in several deep breaths. Eventually, feeling slightly better, he made for the footbridge on the other side of Cabot Square, stopping every so often to stare at the strangely disembodied figure of himself in the dark waters. Finally, he reached his apartment block, punched the elevator button and allowed himself to be wafted up.

'Anyone at home?' he said, kicking the door shut. 'Anyone here?'

He hurried to the bathroom, where he turned on the light and hovered for a moment over the toilet. Nothing came. He headed to the kitchen, found some bread and Cheddar cheese, and ate it in raw hunks as he stood there blinking in the light from the fridge. He began to feel slightly better. He was just about to fill his glass with some Evian and head into the lounge when his hand stopped. He thought he heard a noise at the back of the apartment.

Shuffling towards the first bedroom, he looked in: a guest bed, an empty wardrobe, a suitcase with a Cathay Pacific sticker. Kicking off his shoes, he moved into the back bedroom. He peered at the heaped-up duvet on the futon before throwing himself across it to the far side. He was just searching for the bedside lamp when a hand lightly touched his arm.

'Nicholas,' whispered the voice.

A tremor ran down his spine. The muffled figure came closer. He could sense that musk aroma, the soft contours of a familiar body. Daniel's expression was wreathed in shadow but as he pulled back the duvet Nicholas could feel the glow of that well-known smile. Nicholas reached over to touch him, running his hand up and down the graceful curve of his back.

'Wait,' said Daniel, sniffing the air. 'I'll turn on the light.'

Nicholas fell back on the bed as Daniel turned towards him. 'Just as I thought, you're drunk. I'll go get some coffee while you take a shower.'

'Coffee?' Nicholas laughed. 'I don't want coffee – ' But before he could say anything more, Daniel had stepped forward to raise him and pulled him towards the bathroom, where he peeled off his clothes and threw them in a heap onto the tiles.

He was about to turn when he felt Daniel right up against him, one sturdy leg pressed against his. He turned and put a hand on Daniel's hair and pulled his head towards his own. Their lips touched for a moment as if relishing the forgiveness in what they were doing. Then they kissed again, their bared teeth almost scraping, before Daniel pulled away. 'Take a shower.'

Ten minutes later, Nicholas was back in the room, his hair scaly and wet, and headed straight towards the bed. He just had time to run his hand against Daniel's cheek before Daniel took his own turn in the bathroom. Nicholas could hear him humming as he showered, and then the sound of the electric toothbrush.

Nicholas lay beneath the duvet as Daniel returned to the room. For a moment Nicholas held back, looking instead at the body of Daniel who was there kneeling in front of him. He had imagined this moment so many times over in the past few days, he felt almost too scared to do anything. The desire that had built up inside him held him back, as if he were about to interrupt a wonderful piece of theatre. But as he held out his hand and touched Daniel's neck, he realised that he was not interrupting. He was playing his role in this scene, one that had been written for them and for them alone.

He could feel the sweat on Daniel's neck. He could run his hand down over his trained chest, encircle the nipples and feel them rise. Nicholas pushed back the bathrobe from Daniel's shoulders.

He embraced him, holding back his arms as his unshaven chin ran softly up the dip in his stomach towards his neck. Then he kissed him, savouring the sour taste of sweat and citrus, poring over his body as if over a difficult passage in a book. And he could feel a great excitement rising, stirring him into action.

The sounds of pleasure that Daniel soon began to make, the hands that held but did not push away his head, the feeling that he was somehow possessing Daniel as he lay there entwined with his bathrobe, pushed him on. There was no stopping the rush of tenderness. He stormed his target again and again, urging himself on even as he tasted and inhaled the aroma of another. Daniel's legs splayed, his breathing quickened along with Nicholas's rapid movements and then suddenly, pulling Nicholas's head away, they both came in a great shout of pleasure.

Afterwards they lay against each other, exhausted. Daniel softly ran a finger from Nicholas's neck down to his groin, then he pulled away and found them towels, drying Nicholas down. As Nicholas lay stretched out on the sheets, Daniel went to the kitchen and returned with coffee. Nicholas thought that it tasted horrible but it didn't matter. The throbbing in his head began to subside and he could sense a great calm taking its place.

Daniel turned to him. 'What happened with United?'

Nicholas looked at the clock on the bedside table and wondered how long it would take to explain, how much he needed to elaborate or leave out, but he couldn't bring himself to begin. After all, he didn't know where Daniel had been. He didn't know what had made him change his mind, or indeed if he had changed his mind. And he didn't want to know. All that mattered was that he was there close to him, which was in itself a kind of forgiveness, a gesture to the life they had shared together. 'So we're okay then?'

Daniel's face assumed a distant look. He was about to say something, but even as his lips formed a sentence he let it go. Without a further word, Nicholas pulled the striped duvet over them and folded his arms round Daniel, holding him so close that he could feel his heart beat mingle with Daniel's soft, regular breathing on his cheek. And then, still holding each other tight, they drifted off to sleep.

Chapter 35

Nicholas sat under the spreading horse chestnut tree and thanked god for London gardens. It wasn't just the beauty of the spot that pleased him, although he was surrounded by squashed catkins of white blossoms that gleamed like snowflakes in the sun splashes of an April morning. It was the beauty of last night's idea. The green painted wooden seat gave him an uninterrupted view, apart from the spiked railings, of the doorway to Sir John's mansion block, shiny and black and anonymous between its protecting Corinthian columns. Nicholas could imagine the checkered square tiles of the hallway behind that door, and the elegant gilt-painted railings of the circular staircase leading up to his apartment door on the first floor. Earlier, he had thought he glimpsed figures in animated conversation between the bowed drapes of the long windows to the left of the doorway pediment, pacing up and down what seemed like a drawing room that stretched to the bay window overlooking Regent's Park. But they might just have been figments of his overworked imagination, a reflection of the pumped-up clouds that straddled the sun with increasing frequency.

It had been easy to get past the guard in his white security box simply by looking as if he lived here and walking with assurance. He had been ready with the number of the house and Sir John William's name but in the event they weren't necessary. The same assurance had got him into the gardens when an elderly woman in a beige cashmere coat had come through the gate with her Jack Russell on a lead and let him through without question. It was too early for him to go straight up to Sir John's. He had to choose his time slot with extreme precision. According to the e-mail cache in Yahoo!, the usual London rendezvous took place on a Saturday morning about an hour and a half after Marjory had been picked up by her daughter to go to her home in Hammersmith, or wherever it was she was going to spend the day with her and her grandchildren. The ritual was almost inscribed in stone: breakfast together with Sir John, daughter arriving for coffee at 9 am, car departing at around 9.30 am. Nicholas knew it by heart because he had read Sir John's repeated and rather tedious assurances about it so many times. So he had hardly been surprised when the pale blue Renault Laguna arrived outside the door at 9.05 am, a capable looking woman in her early thirties got out and she departed with someone who looked like her mother, same aquiline nose and features, around half an hour later.

He might have gone up then, but he knew Sir John wouldn't be expecting anyone till later, until a very precise time in fact, and he knew that the maid had to leave after washing up the breakfast things. There was also a possibility that someone else might be in the house. He drew his coat closer about him and waited. Ten minutes passed, twenty minutes, thirty minutes. He was just beginning to wonder if he was right when the black door opened and a short, round-faced woman with darkish skin came out carrying a green rubbish bag that she took down some steps at the front of the house. She then retraced her route and checked that the door was fully closed before heading off towards Marleybone Road, her head moving from side to side as if she were humming a tune. Nicholas stood up and shook his legs to restore the circulation. He was eager to get into the house, and nervous too, but with the controlled nervousness of an actor confident he is going to give a good performance.

He walked up and down a moment, careful to keep to the shade of the beech and chestnut trees even though the earth was bare of grass and the mud dirtied his shoes. Those figures he thought he spied at the first floor windows might well stop and look out onto the gardens, where he was the only visitor apart from an attendant with a barrow on the far side of the circular lawn. He was just wondering if the attendant, who had stopped by his barrow and was leaning on a long-armed brush having a smoke, had noticed him lurking when he became aware of the sound of a door closing and men's voices on the otherwise silent air in the close.

He turned and with a slight shudder saw Sir John in brown corduroy trousers, beige roll-neck and sleeveless nylon jacket talking to a broad, white-haired figure in sagging cavalry twills and a cap. He immediately moved back further into the cover afforded by the bushes. He could see their voices creating little wisps of moisture on the air, cheerful and familiar but shot through with an undercurrent of complaint that seemed to follow them as they passed by two cars on the far side of the road and then crossed towards him, their tones growing louder and more comprehensible with each step.

Nicholas sat down on the wooden bench and looked in the other direction, his coat collar turned up. But they didn't seem to be coming into the gardens. Instead, they halted near a parked car that in one swift turn of the head Nicholas identified as Eddie's pale blue Jaguar S-type. Nicholas turned his head back, wondering why on earth he hadn't noticed it earlier. There was a clink of a car key, and then the electronic whoop of the doors being disarmed and the safety latches clicking up.

'Thank you for breakfast,' Nicholas could hear quite clearly a few feet beyond the railings. 'I think we sorted one or two things out.'

Sir John made a hard grunting sound, as if of pained approval. 'We certainly did. I'm grateful for you coming over.'

Nicholas remained looking straight ahead. It wasn't the first time he had overheard conversations like these in his role as special adviser. He had become used to looking straight ahead when members of the Board and senior management got together. It was an acknowledgement of his role as a power broker that he could stand there and look through space when in fact he was listening hard.

'The trouble with people like Powell is that they're too clever for their own good,' said Eddie. 'They've got the brains, and then they've got this other thing. I've got nothing against them for being as they are. That's up to them. But they're so busy putting on a show for the rest of us that they think life is one big show.'

Sir John cleared his throat. 'I couldn't agree more Eddie. In fact, I would say they are all potential deceivers. You've done the right thing. I mean there are limits to one's tolerance for this kind of thing. What would happen if he carried on like that when he was in Number 11?'

Nicholas's pulse began to race as he waited for Eddie to put his dismissal in some sort of proportion. After all, he had said earlier that he had complete faith in him and had fought for him against the Board. His only crime has been to get his name in the papers on a charge that was completely unfounded.

'You shouldn't be asking *me* that Johnny,' said Eddie with a sour chuckle. '*You* were the one who recommended him to us. I can't think what you had in mind, bringing someone like that into the place. As I said, it's not their sexuality I object to, but the tricks they get up to. He knew he was in the wrong carrying on with a member of staff.' Eddie's voice seemed to grow louder as he said this, amplifying his gravelly tones into a dull boom that reached well beyond Nicholas's hiding place. Nicholas sat there, his fists clenched in anger, but with a new and strangely thrilling feeling of combat rising inside him.

'I'm sorry,' said Sir John in a clipped, offhand voice that betrayed his sense of guilt. 'An error of judgment. It's really not like me at all. He showed no signs of it when we worked together. I just assumed he was married to his work and had the odd girlfriend on the side. It was very untypical of me not to check...'

'Your assumption cost us pretty dearly,' said Eddie with a kind of grim satisfaction, as if he would be calling in the debt at some time as yet unspecified. 'United International's been plastered all over the press for possible corruption, insider dealing and I don't know what else. And now we have no one on the Chancellor's team.'

Sir John made a sort of weary noise, more like a groan of resignation. 'But we can always have another go. I have one or two people in mind.'

Nicholas could hear the car door open and a grunt as Eddie arranged himself in the driver's seat. His next words were less authoritative, as if muffled by the Jaguar's leather trim. 'I should have known it was coming by his attitude. So blasted clever. Half the time he sat there without saying a word. I know the type. They're counting up all the mistakes and criticisms so they can present them to you later. I always thought there was something odd about him.'

'Indeed, Eddie,' said Sir John with a hint of impatience, as if he had something more pressing on his mind. 'First it was me, then you and the Chancellor. I saw how he got his hooks into Roger Yates straight away. I could have been invisible when I introduced them. It's typical of their kind that they use all their charms to get what they want. Then they ditch the people that have helped them up. No loyalty you see.'

Nicholas sat there in a strange confusion of feelings: fury at Sir John's refusal to defend him and bitter amusement at the lengths Eddie would go to revise his opinions in the light of expediency. What angered him the most was the attempt to brand him as a manipulator and liar because of his homosexuality when both these men's careers were built on naked ambition and double-dealing. Sir John, in particular, was an arch exponent of manipulation. To be accused by him of disloyalty after what he had found out about him was almost a tribute to his integrity.

'Aye, well…' said Eddie and Nicholas heard the door slam shut, then the window roll down. 'They don't have any family like you and me. Nothing to worry about apart from themselves.' He started the car. 'Thanks again for breakfast. Johnny. Make sure the Chancellor is fully informed of the enquiry's findings.'

Nicholas heard Sir John mumble something but it was lost in the sound of the car engine as the Jaguar pulled away towards the gatehouse, and then there was nothing but the click of footsteps returning to the other side of the street followed by a door closing. Nicholas sat there, stiff with shock, wondering if he still had enough time to stop the wheels that had been set in motion. It was one thing to be bad-mouthed by Sir John. He had been expecting that. After all, he must have been the instigator of much of what went on behind closed doors after the Shareholder Letter. But to see them both in their casual weekend clothes, or what passed for 'casual' mixed with a touch of the military, suggested that Eddie had been ready with a strategy as soon as the news came in. There was a plan that swung into immediate action at moments like these, and because their offices at United International were too public for the kind of conversation he had just overheard they had to meet in private on a Saturday morning. Whoever had been the leader in the beginning, they were now in it together. And the strange thing was that although he was impressed, he was also shocked by how dreary and petty-minded they were. He felt detached from their stupidity, and more determined than ever to exploit it.

He looked at his watch, rose and made a very slow and surreptitious circuit of the gardens, and then another two circuits, watched occasionally by the gardener as he stood to admire a clematis bush or a bed of rhododendrons. Finally, he could stand it no longer. There were still more than thirty minutes before the allotted time but he was pretty sure Sir John would let him in. The extra minutes would give him breathing space.

He pressed the buzzer at the intercom and waited for a reply. 'You're early,' he heard eventually. He didn't reply but pushed the door open, walked across the checkered marble floor and up the mauve-carpeted stairs until he reached the landing for 52. Here too the door opened for him as soon as he gave it a gentle push.

He closed it quietly behind him and stood in a spacious lobby with a heavy round oaken table in the centre set with a square Chinese ceramic vase full of tall white and red irises. Below it was a swirl-pattern beige alabaster bowl containing clumps of keys and bric-a-brac. He could see a staircase bending away from the lobby to the upper floors, fringed with landscapes and portraits in ornate gold frames, two half-open louvered doors to the right of him that seemed to lead to a dining room, a short corridor beneath the stairs that might lead to the kitchen, and another set of half-open and delicately carved doors ahead. He thought he heard a sound from behind them and walked forward, his shoes making the wooden 'sunbeam' floor creak.

'Come in,' he heard Sir John say and he entered what he had guessed from below in the gardens was a long drawing room. 'I'm just finishing something,' he added and for a moment remained bent over his desk with his back to him, signing a document with a fountain pen, until Nicholas coughed slightly. Sir John swung round, his tall figure silhouetted by the light from the bay windows. 'Good god,' he said. 'Nicholas.' And it seemed as if the colour had drained from his cheeks. He held the fountain pen in one hand as if unable to decide what to do with it. 'What are you doing here?'

Nicholas gave him a reassuring smile. 'I was just in the area and thought I might drop by. You were very difficult to trace these last few days, and as you know, Monday is my last day in the office.'

Sir John stared at he fountain pen, waggled it in his hand, and put it firmly on the desk behind him. His puckered lips and brow gave Nicholas the impression he was thinking of several things at the same time. He glanced nervously at the ormolu clock on the mantelpiece. 'I see, well....Do come in.'

'Thank you,' said Nicholas, moving towards the offered perch on the sofa. He took off his raincoat, which Sir John made an awkward attempt to lift from him and carry towards the hallway. When he returned, he carefully and somewhat inexplicably closed the doors.

Nicholas was sitting on the sofa with his legs crossed. 'I hope this isn't a difficult time,' he said, looking at the photos of young people he took to be Sir John's son and daughter on the mantelpiece. The room seemed to hum with the discussions that had just taken place there. Nicholas could almost smell the aroma of one of Eddie's forbidden Benson & Hedges, mixed with the sharp tang of a cigarillo. The top was off the sherry decanter and a thimbleful of dark liquid could be spied to the corner of Sir John's desk.

Sir John made a curious grunting sound that seemed to express a variety of emotions ranging from 'of course not' to 'what the hell are you doing here?' and looked at Nicholas over his glasses. 'How can I be of help?'

Nicholas leaned back in his seat as if stretching, and then clasped his hands over his stomach. 'I don't really know how to begin Sir John. As you know, I'm on my way out on Monday.'

'Yes, sorry about that. I tried as hard as I could with Eddie and the rest of them, but they were adamant. Of course, the enquiry could have been a bit more positive in the way they acquitted you. I think that must have played a significant part,' he said as if he had been nothing but a bit player in the drama and everything else had happened in some adjoining room.

'Mmm,' said Nicholas and gave Sir John another soothing smile. 'You may well be right. What puzzles me, however, is how the enquiry came to be so negative in the first place. I imagine you had some input didn't you?'

Sir John nodded slightly, and he put one hand on the desk as if to support himself or perhaps to match Nicholas's casualness. 'I did, but it seems they didn't want to listen to me. It was the press you see. That really frightened them. And then of course they have to come up with something to justify all the fuss. It was an unfortunate combination of circumstances. I'm sure it won't have any effect on your plans with Roger Yates.'

Nicholas made an exaggerated shudder of surprise. 'Really?' He eyes scanned the room. He could almost see an indent in the leather chair where Eddie had sat, a sign of the urgent discussions that had taken place. 'After the enquiry more or less found me guilty of conflict of interest? I don't think it's quite as easy as that Sir John.'

Sir John sighed and looked again at the clock on the mantelpiece. 'Look, I think we should discuss this in the office on Monday. I'd be quite happy to give you some advice on Roger. It's just that I have an appointment and I have to...'

'Prepare yourself,' finished Nicholas but made no move to stand up.

'Yes, prepare myself. That's right,' said Sir John and made towards the closed doors as if to lead him in their direction, talking with elaborate sympathy as he went. 'Of course, I think the whole thing is appalling. There was no need to push you off like that, especially after you handled the Mercantile business so brilliantly. It really was a knee-jerk reaction.' He stood at the door waiting for Nicholas to rise from his seat.

Nicholas looked over at him. Sir John had that hanging jowl expression he wore when he was tying to express solemnity or solidarity. But beneath it he sensed panic, a growing puzzlement as to what exactly he was doing there. 'I wonder if the knee jerk was entirely on United International's side,' said Nicholas.

Sir John looked as if he hadn't quite understood. His tall body leaned forward. 'I beg your pardon. I didn't quite catch that.'

'The knee jerk,' repeated Nicholas, and leaned to the right to make sure he was heard. 'I don't think surprise at my being a homosexual was confined to United International. In fact, I don't think it even began in United International.'

Sir John slowly removed his hand from the doorknob and slotted his left arm into his armpit, bringing the thumb and index finger of his other hand up to his lower lip as if in thought. 'No, you may be right there Nicholas,' he said with a wrinkled brow. 'It's an unfortunate but sad fact that the times are not always as liberal as they appear to be. Or rather, some people are not. I'm afraid you've suffered unfairly from what may well be still a hard core of intolerance in society. But of course that shouldn't make any difference – '

'I'm not talking about society,' interrupted Nicholas.

Sir John frowned, as if annoyed that he had been stopped in mid-flight. 'Then what *are* you talking about? I don't think I'm with you.' With a sigh he gave up policing the doors and came to sit in a comfortable chair near the fireplace, placing both his hands out straight on the armrests in a manner that suggested he was ready to lever himself up at the earliest opportunity.

Nicholas pushed his hair back and cocked one leg over the other, leaning his clasped hands on his kneecap. His contempt for Sir John had coalesced into a thin white line of anger, only held in check by that picture up on the mantelpiece of a young man in a snowy landscape. 'Can you recall when we first worked together?'

Sir John raised his eyebrows in weary resignation. 'I think so. You came recommended to me at A & B from Oliver & Kemp. You helped me out a good deal in the Royal Docks project. We learned to work together, and I recommended you to Eddie.'

'Exactly,' said Nicholas with a cold smile. 'And was there any time during this …honeymoon period let's call it, when you became aware of my homosexuality?'

Sir John seemed to slightly redden, a flush of scarlet around the gills. He clearly didn't like the word 'homosexuality'. 'I don't think so. It was never an issue. Our relationship was entirely professional,' he said, almost off-handedly as if the thought had never crossed his mind.

'I see,' said Nicholas and bit his lip. 'Then why did you take against it, or rather me, so dramatically when you did become aware that I was… homosexual?'

Sir John burst into a nervous laugh. 'Took against you? Don't be ridiculous. I supported you through and through for the job with Roger Yates. I really don't know where you're going with these – '

'You and Eddie devised a strategy to get me into Number 11 so that you would have one of your own men in place, but the whole thing came off the rails when you realised I was gay.' Nicholas stared hard at Sir John, who was alternately shaking and stroking his head. 'You thought it might look bad for you. You distrust gays don't you?'

'I don't know what you are talking about,' said Sir John, all attempt at sardonic dismissal now abandoned. 'I've never distrusted gays, as you put it. I've never had any reason to, nor for distrusting you.'

'Except for your son,' said Nicholas tersely and looked straight up at the mantelpiece. Sir John's expression froze for a second, as if he was gazing into some very private world, and then with a look of astonishment he followed Nicholas's eyes to the framed photo of Andrew.

'What do you mean?' he asked.

'I know.' Nicholas uncrossed his legs and leaned forward, like a priest at a confessional. 'I know about Cambridge. I know about him coming down to London and what followed. I know you blamed yourself, but above all you blamed the homosexual world for ruining his career, and all the potential you saw in him. I know and I'm sorry.'

Sir John fell back in his seat and said nothing for a while. He looked crushed, all the stuffing knocked out of him. Gradually, however, the granite set of his features flickered with a new sign of life, a question that had to be answered. 'How do you know?'

Nicholas took a deep breath. He could hear the ticking of the clock above him as his mind reached back to the scene in the gardens, the worldly assurance of two powerful men in their corduroys and cavalry twills putting their plans ruthlessly into effect, and he knew he had no choice. 'I've read your letters to Jeanette.'

The shock in Sir John's eyes turned to fear. Beads of perspiration stood out on his forehead. 'My letters?'

'I'm not going to tell you how I managed to access them,' said Nicholas hurrying on in order to prevent Sir John from interrupting. 'But I have to admit it was a good idea to store them on the internet, an anonymous place safe from her husband and United International, and it took me quite a while to go through them. I suppose love really does blind us, Sir John, especially if it means following a woman bent on revenge. I knew she didn't like me. I knew she was jealous of me. But I didn't know how far she would stoop. I don't think even *you* knew that did you Sir John? To arrange leaks against me was one thing, but to organise a smear campaign was quite another. Of course she had you to do the letter writing and the press manipulation and all the rest – that is, as soon as she could convince you that I was dangerous, and above all that I was vulnerable and could be got rid of. I suppose you just thought I was another of those about to be destroyed by their homosexuality, by their fatal flaw, and you weren't going to have it again.'

Nicholas paused, his leg slightly trembling. Sir John was looking at him with total disbelief.

'Well I have news for you. I am not going to be destroyed, neither by you nor by Jeanette nor indeed, by my fatal flaw. I have everything I need on you Sir John. The whole cache of letters has been copied and sent to my lawyers. It seems to have been going quite a while, either here or in Hong Kong,' said Nicholas with a final barb, as if the more specific he could be the more likely Sir John was to succumb.

Sir John sat there for a long time, his finger propped against his forehead while the beads of perspiration began to detach themselves one by one and slip down his cheek. Finally, with a forceful clearing of his throat that seemed to imply both embarrassment and a refusal to concede, he stood up and walked slowly over to the great bay windows. He stood and looked out on Marleybone Street for a while, at the Saturday morning traffic bunched up before the Great Portland Street traffic lights, as if he could find some comfort out there in the general busyness and steady thrum of London. 'You've done very well haven't you, Nicholas?' he said, without turning.

Nicholas wondered if any courtesy required him to reply. He turned in his seat and shrugged. 'I had no choice.'

'Yes,' drawled Sir John. 'I can see that. Tell me, when did you start doing well?'

Nicholas stood up and glanced at the clock. Again he wasn't sure that he was required to answer. 'I would have to say when I joined United International.'

'And how did you get to be there?' asked Sir John, still without turning.

Nicholas's lips tightened. This wasn't a line of questioning he had anticipated. 'I was recommended by you, although I think I made a pretty good impression on my own account.'

'Quite,' said Sir John. 'You always made a pretty good impression, even when you were at Oliver & Kemp. And I think you will agree that I was one of the first people to see your talent and appreciate it. I introduced you to some very interesting clients and to some powerful and remarkable people reaching right to the top of the tree...'

'Yes you did,' said Nicholas and took a deep breath. 'That is why I'm so astonished about what happened, especially together with Jeanette. It really didn't make sense until I read those letters.'

Sir John slightly turned at this with a look of distaste, as if this was exactly what he would have expected from someone like Nicholas. 'But didn't it occur to you when you read them that Jeanette may have had a case. I don't wish to go into my private relations, but can't you see that she was worried how your closet homosexuality would play out for my plans for United International and the Chancellor, and more importantly for the institutions themselves? I know I over-reacted and you have found me out. But I would never have wanted to get rid of you, and I would never have listened to her, if you had been honest with me. Goodness Nicholas,' he said and rolled his eyes towards the ceiling. 'All I wanted from you was *loyalty*. What you gave me was deceit.'

Nicholas fought with an overwhelming desire to go and push the pompous, lying ass through the window. The extraordinary thing to him, which was also the most revealing, was that at no time did Sir John say what was so terribly wrong with him being a closet homosexual, or a partnered one, or any other sort, except that perhaps the very idea of him being relaxed with a stable gay relationship was anathema to him. At no point did he suggest, either now or in the letters, that Nicholas had done something basically wrong. It was just his assumption, and Jeanette's, that someone that kept quiet about their private life had a secret. That itself was a fault, and a challenge to the usual rules, and a reason to get rid of him. With people like this it was almost not worth fighting, but Nicholas allowed himself one final salvo. 'I gave you plenty of loyalty Sir John, much more than you gave to me. And don't you think it's a bit much to be talking about loyalty when you're fucking another woman behind her husband's back?'

The very directness of the attack, clearly undreamt of from the direction of Nicholas, pushed Sir John back towards the window. 'You stupid little shit,' he said, his face contorted. 'You think you can put your emotional life on the same level as mine? It's people of your kind that tore Marjory and me apart, that ruined our marriage. It's people of your kind with their promiscuity and indifference that took my son from me. And now you stand there and tell me that you and I are in the same boat. Who do you think you are, Nicholas Powell? How do you think you got to where you are?'

Nicholas stood up and drew himself to his full height, although his legs felt unsteady. 'At least I didn't get there by willfully misusing my position and spreading malicious lies. You and Jeanette seem to have been experts in that. Calling me names won't make much difference. I am now in a position to ruin you. Both of you.'

The effort of unleashing his anger seemed to take a dramatically physical toll on Sir John. His eyes were half-shut. He gazed at him from a backwardly inclined head, his left hand closing and unclosing in a tight, nervous grasp. He looked confused for a moment, as if he had no idea what had taken hold of him or where he was. And then, a convulsive tremor seemed to pass through his whole body. 'What do you want?'

Nicholas raised his eyebrows towards the phone. 'You call Roget Yates and tell him the enquiry has cleared me completely of any wrongdoing. You continue to recommend me highly. You explain that as soon as my position in the Treasury is confirmed, I will be resigning from United International.'

Sir John's shoulders slumped. He put a hand to his eyes. 'Is that all?'

Nicholas shook his head. 'No. I shall be keeping a very close eye on you Sir John, and any other attempt to undermine me will see the entire collection of letters end up on Eddie's desk, as well as on the desks of various newspaper editors.'

Sir John gave him a smile that was more crooked than sardonic. 'We've learnt the ropes well haven't we?' He came over to his desk, leaning on it with both hands as if he were about to give a lecture. But as quickly as the idea came to him, it seemed to disappear, leaving the impression of a man suddenly exhausted, a balding headmaster in crumpled trousers struggling with the breakdown of his authority. He stared at the phone, and then at Nicholas. 'I wonder if you would mind going outside?' he said. 'I can't do it with you here.'

Nicholas considered this for a moment. 'How can I know what you're saying?'

Sir John stood up and closed his eyes for a moment, as if counting to himself. 'Look, you've got me by the balls Nicholas. Just give me some space and I'll do as you require. You can hear everything if you just stand in the hallway and keep the door ajar.' He looked with slightly panicked eyes at the ormolu clock and checked it with his watch.

Nicholas shrugged and moving towards the doors, opened them carefully, passed through and stood in the hallway. 'Fire away Sir John,' he said and continued to stare at the elaborate carving of a pink rose on the left door's central panel.

Sir John dialed the number of wherever Roger was to be found on a Saturday morning; eventually someone on the other end picked up. The conversation started promisingly enough, with Sir John explaining about the results of the enquiry and Nicholas's intention to resign from United International once his new position was confirmed. Nicholas heard Sir John mention something about him 'deserving it' and the 'time being ripe'. There were several ironic jokes and Nicholas was just assuming from the congratulatory tone that his position was secure when Sir John stopped in mid-sentence. 'I see…'

Nicholas couldn't follow exactly what the Chancellor could see, but there was a long period when Sir John said absolutely nothing and the dignitary on the other end talked. Every now and then, Sir John made a half-hearted attempt at protest, as if it were a painful duty, before once again falling silent. Finally, with elaborate promises that he would inform Nicholas, he put down the phone. Nicholas pushed against the rose, the petals of which were surprisingly sharp to the touch, and re-entered the room.

Sir John was standing by his desk with a glass of something in his hand: not the thimbleful of sherry he had on standby earlier. His face seemed refreshed in the light from the windows, and there was a flicker of a smile around his lips. 'It's done.'

Nicholas sensed immediately that something was wrong. 'You mean it's confirmed?'

Sir John put his head to one side. 'In a manner of speaking. Roger has just told me that he's very happy that the enquiry exonerated you, and he's very happy with your record.' Sir John held up a hand as if to prevent Nicholas from interrupting. 'But a further concern has arisen.'

Nicholas went pale. 'What do you mean?'

Sir John shrugged. 'I told him exactly what you wanted me to. In fact, I pleaded your case. But there's been a problem with clearance. It seems that your name has been linked to a young Chinese man, not it seems your partner, whom the Hong Kong police are investigating for participation in a racket targeting expatriates. I'm afraid your credit card was found in the young man's apartment. Apparently he also kept a diary, which lists in detail a number of meetings with people of your taste whom he had his friends were targeting for various forms of extortion.' Sir John bit his lip, as if trying to swallow the mixture of embarrassment and triumph he felt. 'In the circumstances, Roger has withdrawn his offer for the time being.'

Nicholas took one step forward and then stopped. Any further and he would be tempted to use his hands. 'The circumstances?'

'Roger's view is that having a man of your persuasion on board will not make the slightest difference,' continued Sir John. 'Unless, of course, they've been involved in something as damaging as this.'

'You mean, it's my fault,' said Nicholas, furious at himself for not guessing the reason for Ray-jai's secrecy. He hadn't even had time to check his credit cards. All the maneuverings and risk-taking, everything he had pursued in public life was ending up tainted by involvement with a ridiculous Hong Kong criminal. He cleared his throat. 'I suppose you think this exonerates you. I'll be dropped as too dangerous, and you presumably continue just as before, indispensable to all.' He summoned a grim smile. 'I don't think so Sir John.'

Sir John looked at him over the rim of his glass as if momentarily chastened, but then his eyes flashed. Abandoning his drink, he moved towards Nicholas. 'You know...' He came round the front of his desk with an insinuating smile on his face. 'I might still be able to help you Nicholas. It's not necessary that any of this go too far, neither for you nor me. We can consider it as a quid pro quo. After all, those letters rather exaggerate the situation. I very rarely see Jeanette these days and it would destroy her husband if he knew, quite apart from Marjory. It will be difficult to explain – '

Sir John was moving towards him as if in a trance. Nicholas thought he might have to sidestep but just then the doorbell rang: three times in swift succession. Sir John stopped dead in his tracks, his long nose raised like a fox sniffing the wind.

'Aren't you going to answer the door?' said Nicholas, enjoying the irony of the moment.

'I expect it's my maid,' said Sir John in a strange, husky voice and moved slowly to a buzzer on the wall beneath a framed still life of apples, figs and grapes. But even before he had reached the buzzer, Nicholas heard a key in the apartment door and a timid shout. 'Hi there. I remembered the keys.'

Sir John hurried forward to step in front of Nicholas and close the doors on him as he had done earlier, but it was too late. A shadowy figure was already standing in the hallway, unraveling a long swathe of grey fabric from around her shoulders. Nicholas stepped out into the hallway just as the figure turned.

'Nicholas?' she said and looked in disbelief between Nicholas and the tall, stooping figure of Sir John behind him.

'Yes,' he said, with an attempt at jauntiness. 'Don't worry, I was just leaving.'

Chapter 36

Nicholas thumped his hands on the steering wheel. The idea of Ray-jai joining together with some cheap rent boys infuriated while at the same time it humiliated him. Ray-jai had not asked for money. Probably those other victims they met at receptions like the Cuban Evening or in bars like Club 1997 had not been asked for money either. They became friends, Friday night pals, out-of-office liaisons. Perhaps, after one or two months, the executives started noticing that increasingly large amounts were coming off their credit cards or out of their accounts. But they couldn't say a thing. Not in a town where homosexuality was not publicly mentioned.

What a fool he had been. He had made so many accommodations without realising that people like Sir John and Eddie could take it all from him, whenever they wanted. Yes, he had found Sir John out and he would be dealing with him, but his own reputation was now in ruins. He took one hand from the steering wheel and massaged his forehead with the tips of his fingers. He could hear again that debate in the Conference Room when he had secured Martin's job, and he saw as if on some inner screen the precipitous nature of his fall: worse than anything he had imagined.

He stepped out of the car and locked it, took the elevator and arrived back in the apartment. He was about to call out to see if Daniel was home, but as he took off his coat and glanced into his study, he saw something else that made him pause: a pale green, square envelope propped up on his laptop monitor. It hardly needed a second glance to identify the handwriting. With a feeling of dread, he sat down at his desk chair and extricated the folded page.

> Dear Nicholas,
>
> I didn't tell you these last couple of days but I've already booked an air ticket to Hong Kong. I'm going to see my family. They haven't seen me for a while and maybe this is a good moment. I know you have a lot to sort out and we both need some space to think. I'm on the CX 250 at 18.20 pm. I'll phone you from Hong Kong. We can talk from there.
>
> Love you, Daniel.

Nicholas lowered the page, still holding it, but somehow it slipped from his hand to the floor and he didn't have the energy to pick it up. He just stared at it as it laid there, its written side turned away.

It wasn't a letter of rejection. Daniel wasn't the type to pretend, and he would have the decency to tell him if he was walking out. That 'Love you' at the end was supposed to be reassuring. Even if Daniel already had a ticket, their renewed intimacy should have come as a relief, a reason to interrupt his plans rather than to put them into action. But even as Nicholas rehearsed these possibilities, he could hear a dark opposing voice. Daniel always discussed his travel plans with him. He could have got up this morning and told him he was going before he went out, not pretended to be asleep. He could have called him or left a message on Nicholas's phone. And then there was that sentence about him having 'a lot to sort out', and needing 'space to think'. It implied that there was a great deal left to resolve. It suggested that even before that time apart and that thinking, Daniel was considering leaving him.

He looked at his watch. It was almost 3 pm. He tried Daniel's mobile but the phone seemed to be turned off. Hurrying around the apartment, he grabbed an overnight bag and threw enough in it to get him through. Picking up his passport and wallet and car keys, he left a message for Daniel on the answer phone, locked the flat door behind him and headed for the underground car park.

Driving the Mondeo with barely controlled impatience through the afternoon traffic, he headed past the sharp new, beige-brick developments of Limehouse Marina towards the concrete bunker blocks of the Shadwell housing estates. By the time he reached the Tower of London, it was clear from the enormous tailback ahead of him that the way ahead was closed. He had no choice but to head south of the river over Tower Bridge and then cut through a maze of one-way streets towards the eastern approach to the M40. He glanced at the clock on the dashboard. It was already 3.50 pm and he was not yet through central London. Breathing heavily, he told himself to stay calm and tuned the radio to Classics FM, but just as the opening of Beethoven's Piano Concerto No.5 with its thrum-thrum theme filtered through the speakers, he found himself wedged the wrong way down a one-way road and had to reverse before an oncoming lorry. Finally, he saw Lambeth Bridge up ahead. Swinging the car through the oncoming traffic, he crossed the river with the spires of Parliament and the huge span of the River Thames to the right with St Paul's at its core.

It was now 4.15 pm. Even though the air conditioning was set at 19 degrees and there was a fresh wind outside, beads of perspiration stood out on his forehead. The traffic began to ease, allowing him to concentrate on something that had been haunting him ever since he picked up Daniel's note. Was he travelling alone? Had he waited until Nicholas left this morning and then gone to pick up his luggage at someone else's place? Had the whole of the last few days been nothing but a way of achieving closure? As Nicholas finally maneuvered the car through the blocked arteries of Earl's Court and onto the raised A4, he had a vision of *two* people at the departure gate, two people with adjoining seats, two people that had planned the whole trip together as soon as they had first met.

The Mondeo trembled as he swung round the Hogarth roundabout and accelerated towards the M4. Beyond the signs for Chiswick House and Kew Gardens he could see the dreamlike descent of a large 747-000 over the flat fields, and in the far distance the anvil shape of radar on a tower building. He clenched his jaw and gunned the car towards Terminal Three. It was almost five o'clock by the time he had found a place in Long Term parking. His hands were trembling as he fiddled with the ticket, locked the car again and with his bag over his shoulder hurried off towards Departures.

Carefully avoiding the patrolling police, he negotiated the thousands of passengers wheeling their cabin luggage amid the crowds of wellwishers dressed in their coloured *saris* and bright *jellaba*s, their silk turbans and muslin veils, and looked ahead of him to see if he could glimpse Daniel. But in the crazy melee in front of Immigration, he could hardly make out who was departing and who was saying goodbye. Several times he had to move aside as a loaded luggage cart or the extended family of a South Asian passenger ploughed towards him. He was just wondering whether to try Starbucks when he caught sight of a padded green jacket he recognised.

He looked again. If it wasn't him it was someone very like him. He must have left it to the very last moment to go through. 'Daniel!' he shouted and raised his hand. 'Daniel!' He tried to push his way towards the departure funnel, but he couldn't get past the crowds. By the time he reached the barrier, the figure in the green jacket had gone. He shouted again, more forlornly this time, but there was no reply from beyond the barrier.

'Shit,' he hissed to himself. He took out his phone and dialed his number, but there was no tone. Even if Daniel had switched it on before now, he would have turned it off for the security scan. Telling himself not to panic, Nicholas hurried to the elevator and punched the button several times. Nothing happened. He punched it again and again until, very slowly, the doors closed. Once on the ground floor, he headed for the Cathay Pacific reservations and ticketing counter.

He was lucky. The shock-haired man ahead of him was just finishing his credit card payment. A ticketing agent with tightly drawn back blonde hair and a delicate peach fuzz on her cheeks asked him how she could be of help. He explained that he wanted a ticket to Hong Kong in Economy on the next flight. The young blonde gave him a radiant smile. 'It's almost boarding time, sir. I'm afraid the flight is full. We can put you on the later one.'

Nicholas swallowed. 'Thank you, but I would like to get on this one if possible. Is there no room on Business Class? My wife's in Hong Kong and is just giving birth. I need to get there fast.'

The ticketress's smile broadened until it seemed to fill the entire Departures Hall. 'In that case, we'll put you on Business Standby. I can issue the ticket for the next flight.' She quoted him the price, took his credit card, punched in some information on the computer and picked up the phone at her side. 'The ticket cannot be cancelled once it is issued,' she warned and began filling in his credit card details. Nicholas looked at his watch: 5.38 pm. He knew he had to be at the gate by 6 o'clock to have any chance of getting on the flight. Seizing the ticket from the slightly bemused ticketress, he hurried over to the check-in desks and went straight to the Business Class counter.

The young male ground staff in his tight waistcoat seemed rather more harassed than his ticketing colleague. He efficiently checked in Nicholas, stickered his bag and shunted it onto the moving steel carousel.

'Is that all?' he asked with an ironic flick of his eyes towards the luggage.

'Yes,' said Nicholas. 'A short trip,' replied the young man while continuing to stare at his computer screen.

Nicholas wondered what he could see there: *Frequent Flyer. Cheats on lover in 54A.* Nicholas picked up his standby ticket and thanked the young man, who jumped out of his seat, vaulted the weighing machine and took him by the arm to a flight assistant with a walkie-talkie in her hand. 'Fifteen minutes,' he said to his colleague.

The assistant's ample breasts rose and fell as she led him at a rapid pace through Fast Track, where to his relief his passport was given the most cursory check, and then waited for him on the either side of the security scan. There was a slight mix-up with his mobile phone, which he had to pass back through the gate to put in a box for the scanning machine along with the keys to his apartment. Finally, he was through security and they were heading at a jogging pace through the Departures Hall.

'We're coming. Passenger at Gate 12,' said the woman into her walkie-talkie, followed by some sort of coded talk that was indecipherable in the distorted crackle of the radio.

'Thank you,' blurted out Nicholas in her wake. She looked behind her to see if he was keeping up, but said absolutely nothing. For a second Nicholas thought back to the smiling ticketress and wished it were she who had accompanied him. He wondered how she would have reacted if he had told her the real story. Perhaps her friendliness would have turned to anger and she would have said that he deserved everything that he got, that if her boyfriend had treated her like that he would have had the boot. On the other hand, she might have calmly explained that Daniel had issues of his own.

Nicholas's whole body was sweating now and still they were not in sight of Gate 46. Almost every one of the moving walkways was out of order, which meant that large stretches of the corridor were no-go areas of Korean or Japanese or Chinese tourist groups, many of them wheeling their hand luggage with funereal slowness behind them. 'Excuse me!' said his guide in clipped English as the ranks of travellers reluctantly parted. Their diffident expressions remained unchanged as he almost collided head-on with an electric buggy carrying two elderly passengers, its lights slowly flashing. Finally, the flight assistant guided him to a huge satellite with passenger bridges like the spokes of a giant wheel.

At first he thought she was going to lead him to a long queue of passengers having their passports checked, shuffling onwards like a beaten and bedraggled army, their eyes fixed to the floor. But then he realised she was heading for another gate. Gate 46 he saw as they came up closer, and here the line of passengers had disappeared. The green boarding light was no longer flashing and the ground staff was packing up their printouts and stickers. However, one of them was talking into a walkie-talkie, to which his guide urgently responded as they approached the desk. He could see the captain and his deputy in the darkened cockpit crouched over their controls, hands and arms reaching up to flick switches and check data.

'Please wait,' said his guide as she took his Standby pass to the ground staff. There was a long but rather desultory conversation, punctuated by shrugs of the shoulder and calls on the phone and walkie-talkie, while his well-padded protector reluctantly argued his case. Nicholas tried as hard as he might to catch the eyes of the supervisor, but he seemed to look everywhere else but at him as they continued their discussion. Finally, his guide turned back with a shake of the head and came over. 'Very sorry. The door just opened for a late Standby in Business. Economy is full. We've asked the chief purser and they're seeing if there's anything else.'

Nicholas stood in the middle of a cluster of abandoned baggage trolleys feeling totally lost and abandoned. He could see the slowly moving steel glowworms inching forward in gradual motion across the darkened tarmac, creating their own dance of destiny between the symmetrical footlights that warned and guided them. And he had an odd sense of alienation, as if he were observing but not participating in the life and aspirations so brilliantly on display inside the plane's windows. He looked at the Business Class ticket in his hand, with its comforting blue fringe of acceptance, and he knew why he had missed the flight. It was there on the ticket in his hand, in the empty box where a seat number should be, in the words 'Standby' printed at its head. He had been on standby for most of his life, and at the very moment when he was to achieve a seat on the upper deck, he was too late.

Suddenly he had an idea. He was still carrying his mobile in his jacket pocket.

He took it out and turned it on. The screen came to life with a burst of music. He opened Messages and typed in a short text: *I'm waiting at the gate to get on board. Taking the next flight. Love u, C.* There was just a chance that Daniel would keep his mobile on while the airplane pushed back.

His guide was signaling something to him. He moved away from the baggage trolleys, his heart beginning to race, and towards the gate. But then he saw that she was crossing her arms in a gesture of no-go. 'Sorry, next flight!' she shouted. He stopped dead in his tracks and tried his best to put on a brave face in front of the ground staff, who were now donning their jackets and looking at him for the first time with open skepticism.

He retreated from their stares just as the snub nose of the Boeing 747 began to move backwards from the stand. It receded with agonising slowness at first, as if mocking him, and then began to pick up a little speed as its sleek fuselage slipped backwards and turned at a 90-degree angle to the satellite.

He found himself at the window, staring into the darkness lit by several other tubes of light, and he lifted his right hand in the faintest attempt at a wave. For a moment he could see no response in all the windows he scanned, but then towards the back he imagined the flicker of a hand, perhaps a face pressing close to the Perspex, a square face with short spiked hair silhouetted by the cabin glow. And as the plane turned on its own axis, he felt his phone vibrate and he looked down to see the message: *U r crazy. I'll wait for you at the airport. Love u always. D.*